MADOC

Jenn LeBlanc

THE Sadist AND THE Stolen PRINCESS

MADOC : ATONEMENT

Dedication

TO THE PAIN

my thanks :

RHONDA MERWARTH :
EDITING

PRODUCTION :

KATI RODRIGUEZ :
ASSISTANT OF ALL THE THINGS

SHELLY DAS :
PRODUCTION

KIMBERLY DISTEL :
MAKE UP / HAIR

SHANNON MARIE :
SPECIAL EFFECTS MAKEUP

DANIEL HERNANDEZ :
ASSISTANT TO SHELLY DAS

BETH CRNKOVICH :
ASSISTANT TO SHANNON

PENRY :
SPECIAL GUEST

JOHNNY AND ADAM :
YOU KNOW WHAT YOU DID

credits:

GEORGE MADOC JAMES DANFORTH
Tyler Johnson

WILLOW JAMESON JONES
Holly Lynch

CALDER
Steven Dehler

LULU
Shelly Das

ROYAL GUARD
Daniel Hernandez

a note about the illustrations:

*These illustrations are meant to be
a work unto themselves.*

They aren't meant to depict the scenes with perfect accuracy in setting, costuming or design. They're meant to accompany the text and evoke the emotions of the scenes in the same way the words do.

More of a companion than a direct visual translation.

Certainly you will notice discrepancies between the scene and details in the images, but that's the nature of creation, some things don't work visually when they do work with words.

Thank you for understanding and I hope you enjoy this illustrated edition of Madoc.

Hugs n' smooches,

Jenn

PROLOGUE

August 1885

Madoc stared at the letters patent and regretted every single thing he'd done since the day he died. In truth, he quite regretted most of the decisions he'd made prior to that point as well. He crumpled the missive and threw it in the fire. The vellum flared before curling in on itself, turning black as tendrils of red highlighted the edges then dimmed completely. There was nothing left of it but the red waxed seal of Her Imperial Majesty dripping into the ashes.

That was it then. He knew the letters would garner him first-class accommodations on any of Queen Victoria's ships traveling to England, but he didn't care. He'd pay for something in the service quarters where he could travel in obscurity. Where he'd be free to use the people he wanted then toss them aside without drawing notice.

He finished burning the paperwork from his desk. The men who'd brought him here were dead or in prison, and he was never going to return to India, so he had no use for it. He'd leave the haveli to the serving family who'd been taking care of it, and him. All that was left to do now was hire a horse and guide, and pack what he'd need for the long journey across India and the ocean, by steamship.

This was what he'd wanted all along, was it not? To return to England triumphant and reclaim the title that had been his so briefly, that should have been his the moment his father and elder brother had died, the title that should be his now. Somehow, it no longer seemed a lofty goal. It was somewhat short of triumphant due to the circumstances he'd brought upon himself and his family.

He walked out to the center courtyard and down the steps that led to the cellar where he'd kept Calder. Where he himself had been kept until he'd agreed to do what was asked of him—things he hadn't done, abhorrent things he refused to do.

The manacles still lay on the floor, the chain pulled from the wall where Calder had managed to yank it free—something he'd not been able to do under similar circumstance. But perhaps he'd loosened it for him in some measure. Or it could well be that Calder was just a stronger man. He was absolutely a better man. Mads had been impressed with Calder. He'd been stronger than Madoc had thought he would be, but Madoc apparently had a talent for underestimating people.

Mads crouched and lifted one of the shackles, running his hands over the rough iron, feeling the interior of the metal that had scraped his, and his cousin's, wrists raw. His cousin—he would have to face Calder once he was back in London. He would have to face all of his cousins now that he was officially The Warrick. Worse yet, he would have to face his brother. The man who'd held the title so briefly in his stead. The man he'd injured so gravely as to ruin his entire life. Madoc still had issues understanding what it was that had made his father so angry as to send Grayson away, but the blood on his sword, the act of causing his injury, the triumphant sensation of power and completion...that had been very real and the only thing Mads had considered since.

Madoc hadn't communicated with any of his family since Calder and Quinn had left India. He didn't exactly expect them to reach out to him. Part of him had been hopeful they'd leave him here to languish, forget he existed. But he knew his request to remain hidden until he chose to return had been ignored when the letters patent from the Queen had arrived. There wasn't anything to be done about that now, however, so tomorrow... tomorrow *perhaps* he would go home.

Home. He rolled it around in his mind for a moment, but it still didn't feel anything like somewhere he wanted to be. Perhaps that was what home meant for others, but for him...home had never been a place he wished to be.

Three days later

Banging echoed throughout haveli before sunrise, certainly surprising all the inhabitants as it woke him. Considering the possibilities, Madoc knew he should have been expecting this. He rose and looked over the balcony to the dry courtyard below, the summer night wearing thin against the heat of the rising morning. His man shuffled across the centre courtyard to the main door to answer it. It was quiet for a moment, then Madoc heard shouting. His man's sleeping jacket swept the floor when he was pushed aside and several uniformed British soldiers entered the courtyard, their boots kicking up dust as they walked.

Two of the soldiers looked up at him and he leaned on the bannister. The smaller of the soldiers wore blindingly polished boots, his uniform covered in shiny brass buttons. Mads could hear more men shouting from out in front of the haveli as his man attempted to argue with the men at the door.

Boots-and-buttons opened his mouth announcing to the haveli-at-large, "By order of Her Imperial Majesty, you are to return to London." Then he raised his face to look at Madoc as though he knew him. He didn't. If he had any idea of who Mads was, he would do no such thing.

Madoc gave a single nod. "I'm aware. I received the letters, and I intend to leave today. As you can see, my things are packed," he said, sweeping his hand towards the stack of cases in front of the guards.

Boots-and-buttons faltered, but his bigger, broader, compatriot continued.

"We are to escort you," the soldier said as he pushed past the other.

"I've no need of escort."

"We will carry out Her Imperial Majesty's orders regardless your wishes. You'll make ready to depart within the hour."

Madoc stood and brushed dust from his palms as he watched the two men. "As commanded," he said. "you may load my trunks."

The bigger man pointed to the stacked trunks and cases, waving men forward to begin loading them. Madoc's man walked into the courtyard and looked up to him, but Mads waved him off. There was no point in him getting injured over the inevitable.

Madoc went back to his room and cleaned up in the cool water next to his bedstead then changed his clothes. He dressed for travel, which was to say he wore a traditional Indian caftan and loose-fitting trousers. He slid his feet into the boots by his door, wrapped his head and face in several lengths of linen to keep the sand out, then he turned, flung his feet over the edge of the window that led to the street and jumped, disappearing into the waking crowd.

ONE

February 1886

adoc's knee hit the floor hard enough for the crack to resonate throughout his body, as the sound did throughout the hall. Since his hands were shackled at his back, his left shoulder hit next, followed by his forehead.

"Do get to your feet so We are not forced to look at this ugliness," Her Imperial Majesty Queen Victoria commanded. Madoc assumed she referred to his face.

"Your Majesty," he said quietly. He used his forehead for leverage to push himself up, then his shoulder for balance. He wiped the blood from his chin on his shoulder as he managed to get one leg up, then the other. He stood tall, turning his left to face her, as he'd trained himself to do, as he'd become quite familiar with the reactions of people who met his scars first.

"Better. We are not accustomed to Our dukes being presented in such a manner at court. None have come before Us quite so bloody... or quite so shackled."

"I imagine there may have been a few."

"Not who also drew breath."

The silence that followed the gathered indrawn breath of the crowd spoke volumes. It had been quite a bit of time since he'd been presented at court, and never quite like this. "Apologies, Ma'am. I had no other options presented me."

"Well, you did believe running was preferable to returning to London and taking your place as ordered. We cannot begin to tell you how put off Warrick was when We told him he would need to retain the responsibilities *absens haeres non erit* for a time."

"I can only imagine how difficult it was for him to—again—take up the title he'd already stolen." He spit the words out and immediately ducked his chin in apology.

"Danforth, you are well aware that as We believed you *dead*, Warrick was called to serve the crown as necessary. What followed with the title was entirely your doing."

"He's not the Warrick," Madoc ground out between his teeth as the muscles across the ridge of his shoulders tensed. He hated hearing the title that belonged to him by birthright in reference to someone who was, in fact, not him.

"He is at the moment," the Queen said cavalierly. "You wouldn't be aware of the necessary change in title, as you yourself were, once again, *unreachable* for a time."

"Is that how we refer to death now? Unreachable?"

"Would you prefer to be unreachable now?" she asked, and the stillness that followed sent his hackles to rise.

"No, Ma'am."

"You were unreachable," she said, "for a time." It was delivered with a finality that warned him to shut his mouth and brook no argument.

"I was, Ma'am," Madoc said as he looked up to her, then around the room at the crowd of faces. His cousins and brother were here somewhere—they had to be. Perhaps even his wife. They would not have missed this dressing down, certainly. There weren't as many people in attendance as he'd thought there might be though—at least there was that. Yet he was certain those who were at Court today were a well-curated group. Her Imperial Majesty didn't need uncontrolled gawking at the expense of The Crown. He waited in the silence until she seemed appeased with his chagrin, and the atmosphere around him changed minutely.

"Danforth, We've no time for this. Our granddaughter arrived from Prussia, and We're expected at tea to announce her marriage."

"After this?" He felt like an afterthought, or chore, as she changed demeanor and prepared to shuffle him off.

"Of course. Life carries on as it always has and as it will in the future—with or without you. If you think yourself indispensable, remember We weathered your first death just fine. There is no shortage of fine men looking for title in Our United Kingdom. Now, you are to take the title and uphold the family, *as is your duty,* to The Crown. How that comes to pass is entirely up to you, though another alliance with a strong family would do much to rectify your position in society after your past indiscretions."

"You mean a marriage."

"As I said."

"You'd terrorize one of your precious virgins for the future of The Empire?"

"What, exactly, do you think they're for?" she asked, and Madoc shifted. He knew she wasn't as cold as she was letting on at the moment, which told him just how angry she was and he would do well to back off and allow her to say whatever she wished—if only to be done with this.

"That's the sole option, is it?"

"There are always options in life, Danforth. You may refuse the title *malo mori quam foedari,* at which point your brother will again ascend as before, a third time—that may be a record—" she considered offhandedly before continuing, "—and you will be prosecuted as the commoner you will be for your actions against Our British peers."

"Commoner," he said. The threat was quite clear. Take the title and make amends, or face prison, more likely death, for his crimes against Calder. "Three times a duke does seem a bit excessive. There seems no choice at all."

"There is always a choice," she said, capturing his gaze. "Perhaps *you* made your choice too soon."

"I assisted with—"

"Believe me when I say this, what you've done to bring those men to Our attention has already been taken into consideration. It is, in fact, why you are *standing* before me now." The woman before him now was more Queen than he'd ever seen her. Strong, sure, and staid. She'd spoken; there was nothing more to be discussed. His heart stuttered as though his blood had refused it at her command.

She lifted one finger.

The master at arms struck the floor with his baton.

That was it then.

The crowd gave the appropriate respect when she stood. He bent cautiously and gave a leg as best he could in his bindings as she approached. The soldiers at his shoulders remained vigilant.

"As you wish," he said.

"Don't run from Us again, Warrick." She let the *k* in his title bite his ear before continuing. "No good will come of it for you."

"Ma'am."

She twitched a finger, and a guard came forward, tossing his travel pack to his feet. Her black skirts swept an arc over his leg then disappeared from his view. He straightened. A soldier took his arms and released the shackles. He winced at the pain that shot through his shoulders when he brought his hands in front of him and rubbed his wrists, flexing his fingers to restore the blood. He listened for a moment to the voices around him but dared not pick any from the crowd. He turned to the exit before lifting his gaze.

A shuffle at the door centered around a young woman in ivory. She stood out from the crowd by virtue of the colour. He couldn't make out her face beneath a mesh veil that wrapped her from the top hat on her head to her upper lip. Her mouth parted as she looked at him, standing there in tatters, not even a shadow of his former glory. He glanced away. The granddaughter of a queen had no use of a man like him. A group of men moved past her, and his attention homed in on them. These men he'd once known quite well. Six of them with brown hair, two with blond. It was one of the blonds they protected with their very presence whom Madoc was most familiar with now. He would require atonement of the highest order.

Calder.

He watched as one of those heads glanced back and he looked on the face so like his own—before it had been ruined—and he remembered. There was one other man who perhaps required a

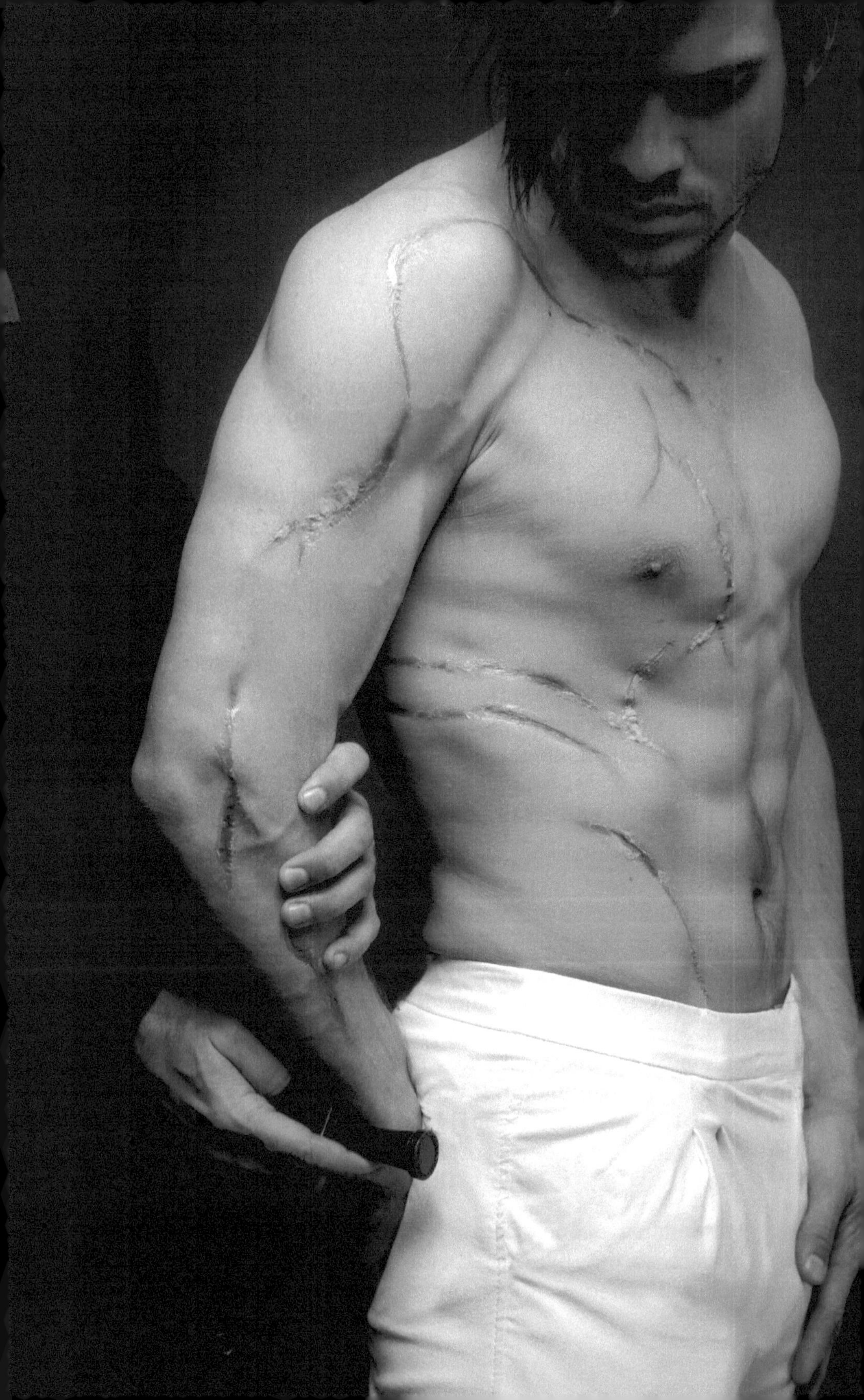

great deal of atonement. He hadn't laid eyes on Grayson in years. Quite the reunion this had become... The expression on his brother's face was stoic enough as to be frightening. Gray put his hand on Calder's shoulder and turned to follow the others. The message was clear, and Mads knew that reconciliation of any sort would come at a great cost to them all.

Mads dug a shirt and coat from his travel case and managed to dress in the carriage on the way to Warrick House. He looked disastrous but at least he was clothed. While he stood staring at the front door, wondering if he should knock, it swung wide. A man in grey opened and held the door, waiting.

"Your Grace."

Mads gave his left side to the man as best he could, but by virtue of the hinges on the door he had to pass him with his ruined side. He walked into the foyer he remembered so well and turned full to meet the man as he wished.

He nodded. "Your Grace, I'm Mr. Bolton. I'm here to see to the transfer and make you familiar with the entailments as they stand. Warrick—" he cleared his throat, "—the previous Warrick—managed the title well." Mads made no effort to respond, simply watched the man as a bead of sweat percolated from his temple and slid down to his jaw. Bolton cleared his throat again. "If you continue the management of the holdings in the same manner, the estate should be fully solvent in no time, possibly even profitable."

That pinch of annoyance shot across his shoulders. "He ruined the title, only to restore it?"

"No, Sir, he came to an insolvent title," Bolton said, a bit affronted by the assumption. Madoc stared at the man, wondering just how much he didn't know about his father. "Your things were brought here in your absence. I believe they were kept in the salon, so as to be out of the way. I can take you around the house, then we can arrange for a time when I'm able to return to show you the bookkeeping."

"There's no need. This is my property; I know my way through it. If everything's in the study as it has always been, I'll manage. Where's the staff?"

"There is no staff, Your Grace. Warrick—your brother—pensioned them off when he came to the title. Those he hired have been placed at his other properties. Warrick House has been closed since your expected return. He used the study to maintain the entailments as necessary."

"There's no one maintaining this property?"

"No, at the time he didn't consider it necessary."

"What about my mother?" Madoc asked.

"She and your sister are at the country estate held by War—your brother—Danforth," he stuttered this time.

Madoc looked away, seeing the fine dusting of filth that had settled on the furniture in the hall, the cloud on the windows. "Our family home didn't require attention?"

"Since Danforth pensioned the majority of the staff when he first arrived until he could repair the books, much of the house was already closed and had yet to be restored. The living areas were all very well taken care of until he was told he was no longer to hold the title. I believe he was attempting to be respectful. The previously kept areas should require naught but a good cleaning."

Madoc narrowed his eyes on the man, attempting to suss out any bits that might be lies, but he held steady, so Mads nodded as he considered his next move. Did he need somewhere to stay the night? Did he even have the money to spend the night somewhere? His purse, which had been in his travel case, had disappeared before the case had been returned. He'd abandoned many of his possessions in

India on the assumption that he was coming back to a flush title. He should have known better.

"Your Grace," Bolton said, "if there won't be anything else, I'll be on my way. I've left my contact information on the desk in the study. The house is on the exchange, as is my office. Any pertinent numbers are also on the desk, and you're welcome to ring with any concerns."

"That's fine then."

Mr. Bolton nodded and walked out, closing the door behind him, and leaving Madoc standing in the waning light of the afternoon.

"I suppose that's the welcome I deserve," he muttered.

He dropped the one bag he had to the floor—a cloud of dust swirled around his ankles. He went to the front closet to flip the main electrical switch. The lights in the foyer flickered a bit then buzzed their way to a mediocre brightness. Dust motes floated in what sun had managed its way through the windows. Looking up to the web-covered chandelier, Madoc understood why Bolton hadn't turned the power on.

He left it on for now so he wouldn't break his neck wandering the house after dark. He walked to the main staircase and went up to the family suites. Opening door after door, he realized this house had been well lived in while he'd been gone. Something in his gut twisted at the thought. It wasn't the same feeling he got when he'd lived in this house with his family. It was a warmth observed.

Though the bedrooms were closed up for holding, the furniture covered and rugs rolled, he could see they'd been redecorated. The rooms were more welcoming than he remembered them ever being. There were small touches a woman would bring to a home she loved. His woman had done this. His Cecilia. He twitched his shoulder to release the sudden knots of tension.

A certain pain speared his chest at the realization, and he closed the last bedroom door behind himself carefully so as not to damage anything or disturb the dust that surrounded him waiting to fall. The woman who'd loved this home had been promised to him. She was to be his, but she belonged to someone else now. His brother. She was the one thing contracted and held by the title that would not be restored to him, that much was certain. The pain of it bloomed, and he pushed a knuckle into his sternum to remind himself that he was awake, a trick he'd learned as a captive. Whenever they thought he'd died, someone would grind a sharp knuckle against his breastbone to shock his system, and thus whenever he thought he might be dreaming, he would do the same, the pain reminding him he was yet alive.

He felt the flush of his anger and loosened his cravat to attempt to lessen the heat. Controlling his temper was something he'd worked on. Not by choice, though; it had been more by necessity, as the men who'd ultimately captured him to bring him back to London had made the consequences of such anger quite unpleasant for him. But he missed it—his anger. He missed it because it had become his most constant companion over the years. In that respect, the soldiers who ultimately captured and returned him to London had done him a favour in reminding him of his control. Because the pain he wanted... wasn't his own.

Madoc wasn't sure whether he liked to cause pain because of the anger, or if the anger caused him to like to cause pain. They went hand in hand for him at this point, so avoiding all of it was to the benefit of those around him. Yet...he did remember a time before the pain. But like a distant mirage it was equally untouchable.

Madoc walked through the house to the far wing. The Duke's wing. He opened the door to the duchesses' rooms and took a step inside. It was as beautiful as he remembered, soft like a woman, peaceful. Foreign. As he'd grown up, this room had been the only one in the house that had taught him what that warmth meant. His mother had been warm in here, in her private quarters, away from his father. Somehow now, though, it felt cold, different from the other rooms where time had been spent to make them welcoming.

When he walked through the adjoining bathroom to his father's room, he realized why. Madoc's wife had lived in *here* with his brother and not in the duchesses' room. In this room he could see the warmth, the touches. They'd lived in this master suite together. He could see the use—that the rug was new but had wear patterns where they walked often. This room was more recently abandoned, but he could tell they'd lived here together for some time, and it was then that he knew how much his wife truly meant to his brother. *His* wife. *His* brother.

His temper rose again. Again he attempted to stifle it. This time when he walked out of the room, he slammed the door and heard the crack of the wood as the dust rained down on his shoulders. He coughed through it as he brushed at his shoulders and chest and wondered just how long the house had been uninhabited—a year? He ran his hands through his hair and shook his head. The outside soot of winter in London certainly didn't help the air of abandonment.

Madoc went back downstairs to the foyer and followed the wall to the study, opening the door. It was plain this room had been well used and tended. It stood clean and warm, so he knew what Bolton had said was true. This room, at least, had continued to be used consistently. He could stay here, sleep on the settee before the fire. But even here he saw evidence of a man and wife in love. It was an unbearable feeling—like the soft touches of a lover against his skin— and it made him uncomfortable.

He needed to inspect the books to see how much money he had so he could destroy what his brother had created and rebuild it to his liking, but there was no possible way to get anything done tonight, so he intended to track down the birch mistress his father had always visited. If nothing else, he needed to see her to find some relief. He needed her to take the edge off this very new, very specific anger he now held towards his brother
because of his wife.

TWO

April 2018

illow pushed her reading glasses to her forehead and rubbed the bridge of her nose, closing her eyes and breathing slowly. She was perfectly exhausted, the deadline for her research trip loomed, and she had yet to find the name of the woman she'd been looking for.

She went to the reference desk and asked for the next bound volume of news sheets, then hauled it back to her table in the grand foyer of the library. She set it down and let it fall open to the center of the book, landing in the winter of 1886. She flipped to the back of the month—where the ads were placed—and skimmed the text, looking for one that would lead to the name or address of the birch mistress she'd been hunting. She needed this one last little clue to justify the research she'd been doing into the Victorian underground.

Her finger ran down the set type, her archival glove hovering cautiously to keep from damaging the old paper and ink as she searched. Her breath stilled when she found the number string she'd been told to look for.

The Iron Duke

7. 2. 4. . 89. . 31

There it was in black and white—her next clue. Well, grey and yellow. She sat down and stared at it. *The Iron Duke.* She took the volume back up to the desk.

"Alfie, I found this reference..." she pointed to the advert on the back of the news sheet. "I'm wondering if there's any info on this location in the same late Victorian time period?"

"Willow, you know I need an approximate date."

"1885 to 1890?"

Alfie looked over the top of his glasses and typed a search string into the computer then pushed his glasses back up his nose and tilted the screen as he scratched his chin.

"What? What is it?" Willow leaned across the desk, attempting to see what he was looking at that had made his eyes go wide and sparkly.

"Give me a minute," he said and wandered off.

Willow leaned further, trying to see the screen.

"Ma'am," the deep voice came from behind her, "I'll have to ask you to leave if—"

"Here it is," Alfie said as he sat back at his desk, paying no attention to what was happening. "This is a collection of papers recently discovered in what we believe to be an old brothel near Grosvenor Square. Not a brothel, actually, more of a specialized house that catered to very rich men who loved very depraved things."

"Depraved?" she whispered, and her heartbeat kicked in her chest.

"Sorry, wrong term. Not depraved, but not status quo prossies either, you know? BDSM, and such. A Birch House." Willow reached for the box, but Alfie swept it out of her reach. "This hasn't yet been cataloged. You cannot touch it. You know the rules."

"Alfie, this is exactly what I've been searching for. Can I... Can you... Would you mind assisting me?"

Alfie looked at the clock behind his desk, then back at her. "We only have fifteen minutes until closing."

"There's nobody else here right now..."

"Can't we do this tomorrow?"

She bounced on her toes, giving him the most watery, pleading eyes she possibly could.

"Oh, blast it all. Listen, Will, no touching. I mean it. I'll open the box so you can see what's in here, but no touching. Understand?"

She nodded, hands pressed together in promise at her breastbone. Alfie sighed and set the clamshell box back on the desk then stood and pulled on a pair of archival cotton gloves before opening the lid. Willow covered her mouth to stifle a screech of excitement. She could hardly contain herself. Alfie's eyebrows pinched together as he looked at the paper on top. Willow leaned in.

"That's the news sheet I just brought..." she started. "No, wait it's a different day but—"

"Yeah the dates are two weeks apart, but that's a pretty crazy coincidence," he said. "What's this say?" He pointed to writing in the upper right corner, the legibility of which was in question. "I can't make it out."

"May I?"

He pointed at her hands in warning and turned the case to give her a better view.

"It looks like...'trust the process—' That's impossible." She straightened and felt the blood drain from her face.

"What is it?"

"I think it's my name...well, not *my* name, of course. It's just another insane coincidence."

"That's insanity," he said and turned the box back again. "Can't be." Willow pulled out her phone and took a picture of the corner as he looked at it. "Hey," he warned.

"Just to blow it up, get a better look," she rushed to say. He grunted and flipped the lid back in place, then put the box beyond her reach. "Thank you for letting me see. Can I work with an archivist tomorrow?"

"I'll put you on the schedule. Just check in in the morning."

"Thank you, Alfie."

She carried the original volume of news sheets back to where she'd been working all week. She took a picture of the advertisement then looked through the rest to see if there were any other clues she could've overlooked. She didn't think there'd be anything else, but she took pictures of the entire news sheet with her iPhone just in case.

She closed the massive book and made another note in her notebook, highlighting the volume where she'd found the news sheet before returning it to the reference desk. She thanked Alfie and left the Maughan walking out to the cool dark of the London streets. She was no longer tired. The rush of finding what she'd been looking for was exhilarating. In general, researching in London was a lonely existence. But she never felt alone in the silence of a library bustling with bodies—data kept her company, and now that she had new data, she intended to saturate herself in the possibilities. All those glorious possibilities...they were her peace.

She pulled out her phone and looked at the images she'd taken, reading all the ads. *The Iron Duke.* It had to be a pub. She Googled it. The pub was still there, or some semblance of it anyway. The name at least, and it was incredibly close to where she was staying.

She opened her maps and set it for the hotel then added a stop at the pub. She started walking down Chancery Lane to High Holborn. She made her way to Marlborough, then Maddox, where she slowed. She looked up at the old street sign, and a shiver ran her shoulders. She took a picture of the sign, posting it to Instagram before moving on.

As Maddox gave way to Grosvenor and she crossed the square to Audley, she started hearing the sound of typical Friday night bar revelry. She pushed through the entry to The Iron Duke and soaked in the chaos.

She'd never been much of a partier. Being such an introvert crowded spaces always gave her anxiety, unless she had a very specific focus that allowed her mind to forget that she should be nervous. Tonight, that was the numbers in the news sheet.

The back of the bar was overtaken by a large stage, a bedazzled drag queen giving life to an old Donna Summer anthem from the 70s with all her soul. She was mesmerized for a moment by the spectacle of it all. The crowd flung crumpled paper at the queen, and still she performed. It took Willow a minute to realize that the crumpled paper was money. The drag queen left them lying scattered around her feet, ignoring the money as she performed her heart out.

Wow, there was so much here that her little researcher brain wanted to dig into and tear apart. The modern craft of drag, channeling a 70s diva, the costuming, the crowd... It was a lot. She made a mental note to start a notebook about drag culture and the like.

She leaned against the worn bar top, nodding when the bartender pointed at the single tap. She wasn't exactly a fan of beer, she bought it out of respect for the proprietor. The bartender brought her a pint and smiled, his grin sweet and genuine. He was young, maybe twenty-five or so with a thick crop of ginger curls sprouting from his crown.

"Good evening," she yelled over the melee, and he nodded. "You worked here long?"

"I'm gay," he yelled back.

Willow straightened awkwardly on her bar stool and smiled. "Oh... Sorry, I'm not... I'm not hitting on you. She leaned closer so he could hear better. "I'm so sorry, I'm a historian. I'm not hitting on you."

"History Monday thru Thursday. Drag Friday to Sunday," he said with a grin.

"Yeah. Okay. Thank you!" She tipped the glass to him and turned back to the show. There was a pause, then the queen introduced another queen named Essie Ex. Willow giggled and wished she were that clever. She leaned back against the bar again, watching the banter between the queens and enjoying herself for a moment.

She was just starting to relax—perhaps it was the bitter swill, or perhaps it was simply the super-happy environment—when she saw something at the edge of the spotlight on the back wall. She stood, abandoning her pint on the bar as she pushed through the crowd toward the edge of the stage. All of her attention was on that spot on the wall behind the stage, which looked to be the actual wall of the pub.

She apologized to patrons and squeezed herself through the crush until she was right against the stage, where she leaned over, oblivious to what was happening around her. She reached across the stage toward the carving of nine cats on the wall. Even the sound of the bar faded as she inspected it, the queens' voices falling to the background. She stood, staring at the carving until the spotlight moved, and an eight-inch, spiked, red-sequined platform heel came down right in front of her.

"Anita Tequila is coming for you, sweetie," said Essie Ex.

She looked up, and that was when she realized two things rather quickly. One, that the bar hadn't just hushed because she'd tuned it out, it had hushed in real life, and two, she was the reason. "Shit. Shitshitshit." She trailed her gaze up the long bedazzled leg to the tight corseted body, and finally, the perfectly painted face. "Fuck. I am sooooo sorry." She turned apologetically toward the crowd that had her hemmed in at the front of the stage.

"Sweetie," Anita Tequila said, "the show is up here, not on the wall."

"Yes, ma'am, it—" she started, but a large, dramatic gasp from Anita stopped her, and Essie guffawed, almost doubling over.

"Ma'am," she screamed, pointing at Anita. "She said 'ma'am,' and you aren't the Queen of England, so that just means you're an old queen."

Anita turned her attention from Willow to Essie. "Biiiitch! Excuse please, who you callin' old? You came up with Divine."

"Divine is a treasure!"

Willow slid along the stage until the spotlight was no longer near her then tried to duck back into the crowd, but it was one thing to slide forward with the rapids and another to fight your way against them. She looked along the back wall and saw a door that probably led to the kitchen. She pushed toward it. "Please, oh please," she mumbled, wanting to get out of here before her anxiety got the better of her. She'd been having a good night, and she could come back during history hours—like the barkeep had said.

She got to the door and as she brought her hands up to the brass plate she looked back at the stage, hoping she'd been completely forgotten. The door swung at her, catching her cheek and forehead. It knocked her back and as she fell, she saw the horrified face of the ginger keep shouting through the small window. "Bollocks!"

Her butt hit the floor. The door swung wide again and she dodged it, only to smack her face on the leg of a barstool.

He came through the door. "No, oh blast, no..." he said, but it sounded like it was in a bottle. In the middle of the ocean. She shook her head.

Bending toward her, he reached to help her, his hands coming to her upper arms but...they didn't feel solid; they felt like they'd touched her another day and she only now felt the ghost of him. She almost cried out, out of fear, but then she was falling again, even the ghost gone. And even though she knew, logically, that the floor was at her back, she pinwheeled through darkness until there was nothing but a single deep voice.

"Fuck's sake," it said. And she reached for that voice with every bit of her consciousness.

February 1886

Mads knocked seven times, paused, knocked twice again, paused, then knocked another four times and waited. A massive man with shoulders nearly as broad as the doorway opened it and stood blocking his entry.

"Thirty-seven," the man said.

Madoc waited.

"Nine," the man said, and Madoc kept quiet. "Eighty-nine," the man grunted finally.

"Thirty-one," Madoc replied, and the man swung aside like a second door. He walked down the long hallway that would go towards the front of the house and waited for the front parlour door to be opened. When it was, he walked through without looking back. Everything about this entry to the house was meant to ruffle him, to give them cause to send him away. He knew better than to fall prey to that so he would suffer their tests of patience.

He sat on a long, low chaise, his legs sprawled before him, his elbow on the arm. He remembered this place well. It hadn't changed all that much since he'd last been here with his father, preparing for his first taste of a woman. He closed his eyes and leaned his head against the curling back of the chaise. His father had decided, not long after Grayson had been sent away, that it was time for his son to learn about women.

Of course, to his father that meant prostitutes and birch houses, not respectable, marriageable, societal women. "You marry for the title. You fuck for the pleasure. You never fuck your wife. Wives and pleasure don't mix. Don't ever make that mistake," he'd said. Mads hadn't known what to think at the time. But the moment a hand beyond his own had touched his cock, he'd known there was an entire world he needed to explore.

He'd been reticent watching his father torture the prostitute who'd pretended to love what he was doing to her.

The door opened, and he lifted his head, prepared for anything. A woman dressed entirely in a vibrant green entered and sat opposite him, drawing her legs up beneath her voluminous skirts. "Give or receive?" she asked as she drew on a long cigar.

"Give," he said quietly. He leaned forward on his knees, kept his head down, his scars turned away.

"Pity," she said to him. "I'd hoped you'd take after Daddy, particularly as your brother has yet to discover me. Regardless, we don't know each other, so you won't be allowed tonight. Tonight you must accept what's given so you understand the seriousness with which I say this. With permission given, you may hurt the people in this house, but you bring harm to any of them, and I will destroy you. Is that acceptable?"

"There's no chance—"

"No. You must receive in order to give. There are rules—follow them or leave. Do you accept these terms?"

"If I must."

"Let me explain one other thing. Until I'm comfortable with your submission, you'll not be allowed to master anyone beneath this roof, and there's not a single house that will allow it if I turn you away. So you submit, and you learn, or you'll never get what it is you want in my London."

Madoc's heart raced at the thought of pain, but he nodded, acceding to her wishes. She knocked on the wall behind her head, and a tall woman came through the door opposite the entry. She was dressed so scantily that he was hard-pressed to refer to it as something more than fabric. Her long red hair tumbled down to her waist like the slowest of rapids. She made him nervous with a single look, which was in itself a novel feeling. Perhaps this was a bad idea. She inspected him tip to toe then twitched her head and turned.

He followed.

The room she took him to was dark. It was lit well enough and nothing was black, exactly, but the colours were all so deep that left on their own, they could have easily been mistaken for it. He ran a finger over one of the deep-red dressers, over the midnight-green counterpane on the bed, across the top of a blue-black chair. It was a black rainbow, an oil slick in water, and he drowned in it.

"Do you understand what's going to happen to you?" she asked.

"In theory," he responded. He knew it would involve pain; what else was there to know?

"Have you ever submitted to a birch mistress?"

"Never."

"Have you ever submitted to anyone?"

He studied her for a moment while he decided how he wanted to answer. He shook his head.

"I'll find out what that pause was in reference to soon enough. Until then, introducing men to pain is one of my greatest loves. You'll never be the same again. You'll wish you'd done so sooner." Her face was blank, and it pained him to not know what she was thinking, whether it be joy at the thought of bringing him to his knees, or arousal from beating him into submission. For him, expression was everything, and looking at her, with no expression to soak in, he realized she knew this above all and had already begun to attempt to dominate him. He decided to put her in her place.

"Doubtful," he said finally and turned the scarred side of his face towards her, then asked a simple question. "Just how much do you think you can hurt me?"

She smiled and he flinched, knowing she'd won the battle anyway. "More than even you can possibly imagine. More than you can take."

He should leave. He should cut his losses and walk out of here. But he *needed*... "How will you know how much I can take?"

"You'll tell me—whether you want to or not," she said, then she stood tall and narrowed her eyes. She smoothed one finger down his jaw, avoiding any of his scars, and he flinched at the softness of it. She grinned and pointed at the floor. "On your knees."

Madoc stormed back into the parlour. "I've taken everything she has to give me. Now let me have what I want," he yelled at the woman in green. He'd spent over an hour with her birch mistress and had blood caked on the backs of his thighs to prove it.

The woman looked up at him and twirled her finger in the air, asking him to turn around. He did. He stood there, his trousers sliding low on his hips and naught else, waiting for her judgment.

His birch mistress walked in and smiled, running a gentle hand over his shoulder. He shrugged her off.

"No. You may not yet give in this house. Not until you learn to take," she said.

Madoc turned back to the Green Mistress. "What do you mean by this?"

"I mean you don't yet respect the pain. You're here merely to endure what you must in order to get what you want, but that isn't how pain works. Pain rules us all, but you still believe yourself to be its master, and no man who believes himself master will wield that sort of power in my house. As a giver, you are not in control. I need you to understand exactly what that means. You merely endured the last hour as a means to an end. You learned nothing. But take heart, you may return in a week and try again once you've healed enough."

His already tensed muscles notched into painful knots that threatened to double him over. "You won't change your mind?"

"Once decided, my mind is very rarely changed. But if I do, you'll know. I believe you've learned that there is no subtlety to me."

Mads dressed and left the Birch House about as angry as he'd arrived. He walked back to the pub up the block. He went straight to the back after ordering a pint of ale, finding a table in a dark corner. He sat, carefully, leaning forward on the table instead of back into the chair. He looked over the men, the whores, the barkeep. Watching everyone.

A small cloaked figure entered the pub, picking her way through tables, chairs, and patrons. He wasn't sure what she thought she was doing, but it was obvious by her carriage that she didn't belong here. He could tell by how carefully she walked and how tightly she held her cloak that she wasn't at all familiar with a place like this.

She walked to the wall at the back, examining it before she ran her hand over the carving he'd only recently become familiar with. Had the birch mistress changed her mind? Was this a gift? *Once decided, my mind is very rarely changed. But if I do, you'll know.*

He stood and turned, hiding the woman in the shadow of his form before speaking.

"What is it you search for?" he asked and felt her body shudder and freeze in place.

"I don't know," she whispered, and everything in him tightened. She had an accent he couldn't place, but the voice and speech of someone in the peerage, just as he'd thought.

"Would you like me to help you find out?"

"I—I—" Her breath came in heavy, uncontrolled pants. "Please," she whispered.

"Please what?" He took her arm through her cloak and pulled her against his body, half expecting her to scream; instead, she melted into him until he couldn't tell where his body ended and hers began. His breath stuttered from his lungs.

"My grandmother will be quite unhappy if you harm me," she whispered, he could feel her body shake beneath the layers of fabric like the one dead leaf in a clutch of living.

"Who is your grandmother?"

"Someone you well know," she said, the vibration of her voice sending pangs of want to his gut.

He spun her around like a top. She looked up to the ceiling, and the light caught her eyes, wild and wide and searching as he trapped her against the back wall with his body. Her face flushed red and her hand came up to hold his arm. He could taste her fear, but there was something missing. This wasn't what he wanted. She couldn't be who he thought she was. He needed to calm her and return her to her people before she ran across the wrong sort.

He was the wrong sort.

"Please," she said with one hand pressed to her breast. Her fingers clutched the edge of her corset through the fabric of her shirtwaist and she closed her eyes. He watched as she faltered and struggled to breathe against the feminine confinements.

He took her other arm in hand and held her when she slipped, his hands seemingly the only things holding her upright as her breathing became erratic, then her head tipped to the side. Her mouth went slack, her eyes stayed closed, and her face was suddenly peaceful as

though the tension had simply drained away.

He let the truth of it sink in. He'd just scared the wits out of this girl to the point that she passed out. No way was she some sort of professional. If he was discovered, it wouldn't bode well for his newfound freedoms, such as they were.

He wasn't sure what to do. He certainly didn't want to call attention to his menacing of this small innocent in the back of a pub, so he wrapped one arm around her and held on to her to keep her from hitting the floor. She stirred against him, her brow creased in concern as she bit her lip and one hand wrapped around his lapel and held on.

He shifted her in his arms, and the full weight of her settled into his belly, releasing whatever trepidation he'd held. She leaned her weight into his chest, and the movement between them felt like the beginning of a thunderstorm, when the sky was full of electricity ready to strike.

"Fuck's sake," he mumbled. He looked around, but nobody was paying a bit of attention to him. He lifted her, sweeping her into his arms. She was so small. Her body weighed nothing by comparison. He looked around the pub again, then moved towards the back entry and stole out into the cold dark of the alley.

He gave her a gentle shake to attempt to rouse her, but she was still. "Fuck all," he bit out. He went around the corner to the line of carriages waiting and asked each of the drivers if she belonged to them. Part of him, a large part, hoped every time the answer would be no, and when none acknowledged her he felt something akin to relief. He crossed the street and yelled at a hack, which pulled up to the curb. He got in, bringing her with him and giving the man directions through the window after he closed the door.

When they arrived at Warrick House, he paid the man and carried her to the front door. Only then did he realize he'd no idea what to do with her. The house was filthy. The single room worth occupying was the study.

He managed to get in the house without dropping her, pushing the door shut with his boot before walking to the study in the dark. He laid her out on the settee, then went back to lock up. His hand rested on the bolt and he let his forehead hit the heavy wood of the door as he closed his eyes. What was he doing with this girl in his house? He wasn't going to lie to himself and say he'd brought her home out of the goodness of his heart because the pub was a dangerous place.

He'd brought her home because he'd felt like he had to. Somehow he'd known she was necessary to his life. He'd had no regard at the moment for what she wanted or needed, who she was, why she'd been there, anything. God he'd essentially just kidnapped a woman. What was he doing?

If his family found out…if the Queen found out…

"What have I done?" he asked, but nobody heard him.

He returned to the study, pacing behind the settee. The only light coming in was from the moonlight cheating through a split in the heavy drapes. There was a telephone on the desk; he could call the exchange and have them send the police. Tell them he'd happened upon her in the park and had brought her here out of fear for her safety. It wasn't so far from the truth.

He looked down to the pile of woman and fabric then snaked one hand behind her, finding a seam in her dress and tearing it, giving him room to squeeze the front of her dress, shifting the panels of her corset until a few of the hooks released at the top. She shifted into a breath, and a jolt of electricity so sharp it flashed in the darkened room and shocked his hands, surprised him. He let go. Certainly it was nothing but the buildup of static he'd been feeling between them released, but something shifted in his gut. It was something profoundly true and precious, like a woman opening her thighs for him. He jolted upright and took several steps away from her. She wasn't going anywhere.

THREE

Willow heard a scraping noise, drapes on a rod, and she took a swift breath as her eyes popped open. The darkness around her was so complete she couldn't even see her hand in front of her face. She blinked as she sat up on the cushioned surface and felt around her. She was on a sofa of some sort, the seat narrow and the back stiff and curved like a cradle of hard velvet against her. She slid her feet to the floor and put her hand on her chest, her breathing so constricted it felt like a vise around her every time she tried to take a deep breath.

She pulled at her collar, the fabric stiff and slick, not at all like the soft T-shirts she wore to bed at night. She ran her hand down her chest. Her breasts were compressed behind the stiff line of what she knew to be a partially opened steel-boned corset...something she'd never worn in her life. Her heart raced and her breathing quickened even as she attempted to keep it shallow, because she knew she had to or she would pass out—again? Is that what happened? Where was she? She must be dreaming.

Right? Dreaming. This has to be a dream; it can't be happening. How the fuck would I have gotten laced into a corset without my knowledge?

She tried to track back to where she'd last been. She remembered the Maughan, she remembered walking to the pub, remembered finding the cats in the wood, a glitter ball and a stiletto? Impossible. But what then? She closed her eyes, not that it made a bit of difference. She searched around her chest and back, looking for the zipper or whatever kept the dress closed, because she needed to get the corset off before she passed out again. It was so tight. Too tight. She couldn't breathe. As she slid her fingers into the laces at the back of her dress, he spoke.

"Tell me who you are, and I may return you to whom you belong." The deep voice came out of the darkness to her right, snaking around her and seeping into her very consciousness like a heavy cloud that calmed her breathing and heart. It twined with her nerves, tangled in her senses.

She put her hand to her chest and her heart rate slowed until she no longer felt the urgency to be out of the corset. Strangers made Willow anxious, so this feeling was like nothing she'd ever experienced. She had the fleeting thought that she could simply no longer care where she was and thus never leave. That thought terrified her enough that her heart rate picked back up.

"Fuck's sake," she whispered, remembering the voice from the inn.

"Pardon?" His voice was deep and inquisitive but it was only the blush at the top of his voice; she could tell there was much more to it and she wanted to reach for it like it was a tangible thing, grab it, hold onto it, breathe of it.

"Who are you?" she asked.

"I— I'm inconsequential."

"Nobody is inconsequential." Her knees pressed together as though in answer; there was definitely a consequence to knowing this man.

"I am," he replied. She suffered a long pause and tried to discern where he was. "People can't know that you came to be in my possession. It wouldn't look good, considering my past." His voice continued like a drug, calming her system again without conscious permission.

"Considering your past... And how, exactly, did I come to be in your possession?"

"You fainted at the Iron Duke. I couldn't find anyone who knew who you were so I brought you here to recover. Which you have, and now you must leave."

"At the drag show?" she asked, but it sounded ridiculous for some reason. "Are you one of the queens?"

"I am not... the Queen." She had the strangest feeling that *his* queen was not one of the queens she was thinking of. "She sounds nothing like me."

"Never mind. Okay, Alright, well. I'm staying at Grosvenor House on Park Lane."

"Grosvenor House. You're staying with the Duke of Westminster? Are you a relation?" He sounded quite tense all of a sudden, and she wanted to calm him.

"No, I don't know the Duke of Westminster. How would I know any dukes? I'm a researcher. Isn't he a godfather to Prince George? I'm staying at the hotel. Grosvenor House. It's a Marriott. Does that help? Can you call me a cab?"

"Miss, Grosvenor House is held by The Duke of Westminster. He's not godfather to any Prince George to my knowledge, though if another has been born in these last few years, I suppose..." He paused and she waited, unable to speak for want of his voice. She listened and heard a sound like fingers scraping the skin beneath the scruff of a beard as he thought. "I can arrange for a hack, and ask. I admit I've been away from London for some time. It's possible there's a new hotel, though I can't imagine Westminster would appreciate a hotel being named for his home."

She heard him stand, then a streak of midnight—the momentary shimmer of a slightly less darkened world—came into the room, not far enough that she could see her surroundings, but enough that she could at least see her own hands. She looked down at her clothes— not her clothes. "Can I ask you a question?"

"You may ask."

His words seeped into her nerves and she laughed as she understood the undercurrent of what he said. "Whose clothes are these? What happened after you took me from the pub?"

"Those are the clothes you were wearing when I found you. They are yours."

"They're not. I've never worn a corset in my life." She was dreaming then. That would explain how drawn she was to whomever this was.

"What kind of woman are you then? Are you a servant? Housemaid? Your clothes speak to the upper class. Peerage even."

"I don't... I'm a researcher. I wear normal clothes. Jeans, T-shirts, skirts, shirts. I'm not a maid, but I think most women who work as maids also wear normal clothes. And the last time I checked, nobody in the peerage in London still wears corsets on a daily basis—if at all—so this is ridiculous."

Her answer was met with a silence that buffeted her bones. He could be right next to her and she would have no idea. Her hands started to shake. After a moment she saw the shift of shadows in front of her and she knew he was kneeling at her feet, or she was deluding herself out of fear making the shadows dance in the dark. She took a deep breath; her nostrils filled with wool and sweat, copper and cinnamon.

His hand came up to her knee, and a shock passed between them, the flash bright enough that she saw the strength in his hand before the dim. He inhaled so swiftly she felt a sharp tug in her gut that seemed to pull from her very backbone until she swayed toward him.

"What's happening?" she asked.

"Static."

"That didn't feel like static electricity."

"No." His voice was hollow.

"I don't know what's happening."

"Nor I," he replied. "But I tend to think perhaps this is some sort of trap on the part of my cousins to have me locked up again."

"What? Why? Locked up? Are you...are you dangerous?" Was she insane? Like any man who was actually dangerous was going to own up to that fact.

"Yes," he said quietly.

"I—" She didn't know what to say to his boldness but she felt her fight, flight, or freeze response decide upon freeze as her muscles turned to what felt like stone. Her back stiffened, and her fingers curled into the skirt covering her knees. He took another sudden breath as though in reaction, but he was as blind as she was—wasn't he?

"It bothers me how innocent you sound," he said, and she knew he was getting closer to her by how soft and loud his voice was.

"It bothers me—" She had to stop and take a few breaths, force her muscles to relax, before she could continue. "It bothers me that I'm sitting in the dark of a stranger's house and he's accusing me of something. I have no idea what..." She closed her eyes and breathed of him, his heavy male scent sending sparks through her as much as the static had. "I want to run but I fear if I stood you would catch me." She bit her tongue. Why would she goad him like that? He moved infinitely closer and his proximity slid her fear from her head to her pelvis like a blocked funnel released. The feeling was confusing, strange, frightening but not—she concentrated—it was not unwanted. She had no idea what this was, but his presence soothed as much as it threatened, and the combination was enough to wake her ever-sleeping arousal, and that fact did, ultimately, bother her.

This man was a stranger. She should be frightened, *solely* frightened. She should not be turned on for any reason. That would be...that would not be right.

"You do not want to run from me. I know this house like my own hand and I..." he took a deep breath that sounded suspiciously like he was smelling her before his voice dropped to a menace of a whisper. "I would enjoy the chase. You can't hide from me, and more likely, you would hurt yourself. I would not be pleased should you hurt yourself. I recommend against it." His breath washed over her, his words stealing the air from her lungs like a syphon, like...an incubus building her want only to feed off it later.

"You recommend against hurting myself or against displeasing you?"

"Either one," he replied.

She squeaked and felt the cushion beneath her tighten as though he'd pushed into it on both sides of her, or grabbed it, or something, then the pressure was gone.

"Please," she said and she felt a slight breeze as he leaned back on his knees as though when he moved, he pulled the air with him. Her body followed until she forced herself to stay.

"You sound—" He paused and she waited, but he didn't seem to be interested in finishing the sentence.

"I sound...?" she prodded.

"You...sound different from the girl who was looking at the wall in the pub. You sound like a woman."

"I am a woman. Why..." She stopped and took a deep breath; she felt as though she were on a rollercoaster and every time it came back to the loading dock, the safety harness cinched tighter and the car took off once again. She wasn't sure she'd ever been so frightened in all her life. Why was he saying these things? They were so... ominous, so threatening and yet...she didn't feel the sort of danger she thought she should. She felt this odd comfort, which scared her more than any of his actions, because this was the sort of feeling she was familiar with, just never with a stranger. "I feel I need to tell you again that you're frightening me."

"I'm aware."

"And you don't mind it?"

"I will not tell you how it makes me feel."

"I have a feeling I already know. Sir," she added. She wasn't sure what had made her call him that, perhaps all her recent research. She could almost feel his head cock to the side, his eyes narrow in the dark, and that was when her body fully tipped from fear to arousal.

"That's not... You shouldn't call me that."

"No? What should I call you?" She asked and her nipples tightened against the inside of her corset. She closed her eyes even though it didn't exactly change what was unfolding.

"If you know what's good for you, you won't find a need to call me anything."

His words slid down her spine and rested low in her back, sending tiny pulses through her hips that settled in her center, hummed through her sex. Made her wet. She waited, willing her body to stop reacting to him, terrified of what would happen next. He was either going to show her what fear was, or he was going to release her and she would know the fear of never knowing. She wasn't sure which frightened her more.

"Are you going to hurt me?" she asked, but he remained silent. Instead of being frightened, she had the sudden feeling she was perfectly safe with him, no matter what. Never in her life had she felt such a connection to someone. Never in her life had she wanted to be so terrified. Never in her life had she wanted something like this so much. Not with her former boyfriend. *Not ever* with *any* of her boyfriends. She felt a trust with this stranger that she couldn't reconcile or quantify. She was lost, she was found; whatever happened next would tell her what the rest of her life would look like.

She took a deep breath, sending the calm from her center out through all her veins and nerves to the farthest reaches of her skin. A tingle of serenity came over her, settled on her. She let her body go soft and pliant for him. She let herself trust, as she hadn't ever trusted anyone.

She allowed herself to be given up to her fate.

Madoc wasn't entirely sure what had just happened, but the electricity that coursed his skin seemed to steady into a slow buzz, seeping into his flesh and sending signals that told him to be calm. He felt this small thread wend its way through his system and reach for her in an unnerving and unstoppable manner. He needed her. He wanted to frighten her, to give her pain. He knew she wanted it from him; there was this feeling in the pit of his stomach that she was made for him.

At the same time he knew that wasn't something he could do. She was a stranger, innocent. Somehow he was aware that this woman wasn't sent for him. However they'd come to be together, wasn't by the design of the birch mistress. He'd no idea who she was, why she was here, why she'd come into the inn or how the fuck she'd ended up in his house.

Part of him didn't care.

What was he thinking? This was insane. Beyond the pale. Absolutely impossible. He needed to get a hack, figure out where she was staying and send her there. But what he wanted was so much more than that. He wanted to continue to feel her fear; he knew he would thrive on it. He knew it would feed him for months. Just this small amount of fear was going to carry him for quite a while. But he didn't want to give her up just yet, he couldn't, and the noose that had slung 'round his heart tightened.

He absolutely couldn't touch her. He knew if he touched her, he wouldn't allow her to leave his house. If she was going to stay, she had to make the decision knowing full well what it meant.

He sat back on his heels and stared at the space where he knew she was, soaked in her fear, her release—he could smell it on her. Her heartbeat was so strong and steady it heated her skin and made her scent powerful to him. He inhaled, leaning towards her, and heard the small sound of her acknowledgement. He wanted to bury his face in her lap and breathe. It pushed him forward.

"You're frightened," he said.

"I've told you as much," she replied, her sweet voice thick like honey with something more than simple fear.

"You're much more than merely frightened." He leaned in slowly, and though her breathing acknowledged him, she didn't flinch. He placed his hands on either side of her hips then pushed his face towards her lap as he inhaled her arousal, moved up her body until he was breathing the pulse of her neck. All without so much as a touch. His cods grew heavy against his thigh, his cock thickening. He pulled one hand back to feel the thickness, give his cock some room.

"I am," she said *sotto voce.*

Madoc had never met a woman like this. He'd never met a willing participant in fear. In pain. He'd met many whose fear or pain were entirely valid, fear and pain of the garden variety you could say, and men and women whose fear and pain were given in exchange for money or favours. But this was different, and it fed a part of him he'd yet to feel. This was what he'd gone to the birch mistress for, but hadn't received.

"You shouldn't be here," he said and sat back, to make even more room in his trousers. He didn't even know who she was. Why she was here. What she was doing in the pub. Whether or not he could trust her. "Who are you?"

"My name is Willow."

"Willow," he repeated. Birch rods were made from willow. "So you were sent to me," he said simply. She must have been, for him to use. The pain he'd endured had given him this gift. Maggie had sent her into The Iron Duke for him to use, to sate his need. She *had* changed her mind. His cock lengthened further and he had to shift to give it more room, adjusting himself again. "How long are you mine?" he asked, but she didn't answer. He could feel the fear coming off her in waves, almost a tangible thing he could grasp, hold, keep for his use later. "How long?"

"I don't..." Her breath came in little puffs against his chin as he leaned towards her. "This corset," she said.

"I can help you with that, but I need to know how long you're mine," he said again.

"For as long as you have need," she whispered, and he grabbed her. He slid his hands around her waist and up her back where he found the separation in the fabric and yanked, listening as the stitching popped and he ripped through to her waist. He took a knife from his boot and slipped it into the laces of her corset until he had leverage to slice through them. The sounds she made as he handled her were fuel to his fire. Her first full breath against his neck carried the sound of relief, and he almost wished he'd left her bound. He kept that information for later.

He wrapped a hand around her neck, felt the muscles shift as she swallowed against his palm, then he squeezed ever so slightly until her hands came up to his forearm, her fingers digging in to his skin. "Don't tell me to stop," he said. He didn't know what he would do if she told him to stop because in this moment, he didn't think he could. It would take everything in him to do so.

"I won't," she whispered.

"Don't tell me to stop," he repeated, with a little shake.

"Not yet."

His other hand went between his knees to her feet. He took one ankle, lifted her leg and placed it on the outside of his thigh, then repeated with the other. He sat there, tracing the bones of her ankles as he considered. He tried to find his way through the chant of *don't make me stop* that was marching through his subconscious as if that would make it so. His thumb ran the edge of her jaw before releasing her neck.

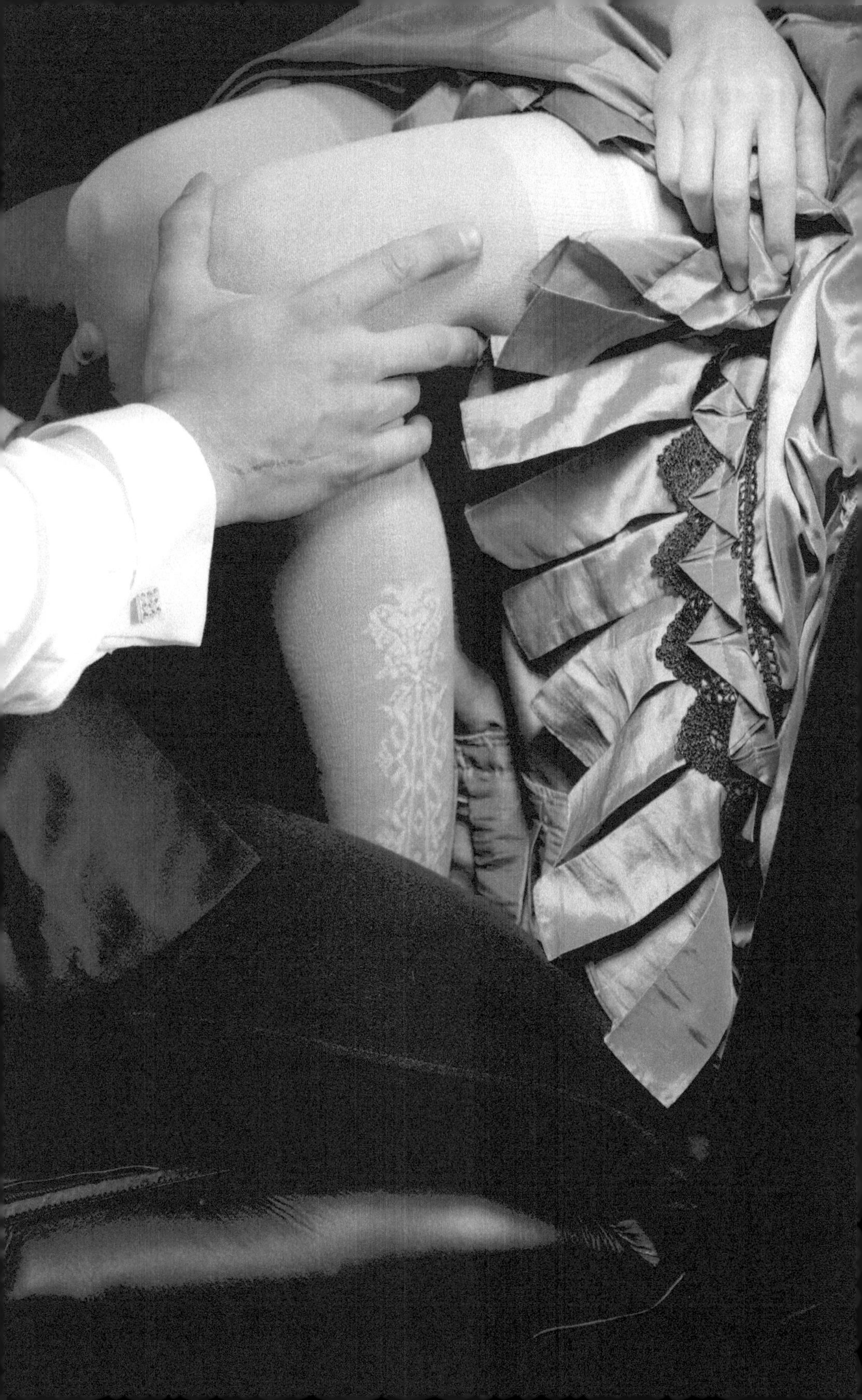

He cupped her calves, his thumbs running up and down the bones of her shins. Her breathing matched his movements, and pretty soon he felt as though he were in a trance. He slid higher, his fingers smoothing to the back of her knees as his thumbs made circles over her kneecaps. He heard the rustle of her skirts, then felt the fabric drawing up her legs, off his arms, then his hands, until all that was left was the sound as she dragged the skirts up her thighs. He froze. His breath caught. He shook his head—he shouldn't. But he *wanted*.

He leaned forward until his forehead met the edge of the skirt fabric and he inhaled again, and this time without the bulk of the fabric between them, he savoured the sweet scent of her. Lavender from soap and a heaviness that was all blessedly her. He knew she was wet, so wet he would slide and never stop. He wanted to touch her.

As he leaned back, his hands smoothed to the tops of her thighs resting there as he breathed, considered. He stared forward where he should be able to see her face, if it simply weren't so dark in here. He willed her to allow whatever came next. He was too frightened to ask permission.

He reached down with one hand and unbuttoned his trousers to release his cock, stroking himself until it gave liquid, gathered on his thumb. He lifted his hand and pressed his thumb to her lips. He felt her draw a quick breath around it, but she turned away just as quickly and his other hand tightened on her neck as he leaned towards her.

"Please," she said. "Please use a condom."

"Are you afraid my mettle will do you harm?" he asked.

"It's all I ask. Just use a condom," she said, and he nodded against her cheek. It was enough of an intrusion in the fantasy to burst the bubble. Her breath steadied and her muscles started shifting as though she were preparing to fight him, and not in the way he liked. His own arousal lessened, and he released her. He stood and walked to his desk, buttoning his trousers on the way.

"Don't move," he said. He pulled his heavy greatcoat from the back of the chair next to his desk and rifled through it, finding the packet of condoms. He turned, his fingers playing with the packet. He watched as she shifted on the sofa, just the smallest hint of movement in the dark. "Willow," he whispered, and her name on his lips felt like a blessing. "You should go."

FOUR

"Where?"

"Grosvenor House. Or Hotel, wherever it is you're staying. But you cannot stay here."

"My clothes," was all she managed to say. She'd no idea what to do. She didn't want to go anywhere and what's more, she didn't really know where she was to begin with. Though she must still be in London and she'd be able to get a cab to the hotel rather easily.

"Your cape should cover you enough to get back to your hotel."

"And my things?"

"You had nothing, just the cape you wore. You had no reticule nor anything else in your hands."

"I don't know where I am. I don't understand how I got here, I don't know where my things are, and my clothes are not my own. None of this makes sense."

"I understand what you're saying, but if you get back to where you came from, get your bearings, you'll be fine."

She nodded even though she didn't believe a word of it and she didn't think he believed it either. It felt like she'd swallowed a rock that grew heavier by the moment. "At least tell me your name?" The request was met with silence as he considered.

"Wait here," was all he said as he walked from the room, closing the door behind him. She shifted on the sofa, trying to put herself together some. After what seemed forever he returned, opening the door so she could see beyond the room. He was nowhere in sight. The light cutting inside was enough to tell that this was a study. It was well designed and belonged to someone with money. She walked to the door and looked around the large foyer, which looked very little used, to find a man standing at the front door. Somehow she knew this man was not the same one who'd been with her in the darkness, and she shied.

"Ma'am, I've been requested to return you to Grosvenor House," he said, and she knew this man's wavering voice absolutely did not belong to one who'd brought her here. So where was he? She looked over her shoulder as she nodded and crossed the foyer, trying to catch a glimpse of her host, but he was nowhere to be found. Her stomach dropped to her toes, an emptiness opening up low in her belly.

The man held the door for her, and she examined him as she walked through the entry. His trousers had a fall front, his jacket a high collar and close-shaped stitching. He wore tall boots and old gloves; old-fashioned.

She slowed as she approached, looking down at her own clothing. The long cape was an expensive heavy velvet with intricate embroidery along every edge. Her shoes were a delicate fabric,

heavily embroidered. She walked out the red front door to a stoop, which went down several steps to a cobblestone street where a horse-drawn carriage waited. Every step she took felt like it was in the wrong direction.

"What? No," she said.

"Ma'am, he's already paid my fee. You've nothing to be concerned with. I'll take you straightaway. It's naught but a few streets over."

She looked out over the park and saw the gas lamps that lit the street. Her head spun. She took a step back inside the house, shaking her head the entire way. "Where am I?"

"Ma'am, this is Hanover Square," he said with obvious discomfort. "Warrick House. The duke himself bid me take you to Grosvenor House."

"The duke..." She looked back into the dimly lit house, wondering where he'd disappeared to. "Warrick?"

"Ma'am, we should be off."

"I don't belong here. I don't understand what's happening. I can't..." She spun away from the entry, her cape sweeping around her ankles and sending motes of dust flurrying through the foyer. "Warrick?" she begged from the entry. "Please." But there was no answer. She stared into the deep corners of the foyer past the grand staircase, the upper reaches of the house shrouded in dark. Then she looked back to the driver. "I've got to be dreaming," she said mostly to herself, but his eyes narrowed on her.

"Ma'am?"

She nodded and looked back to the street, to the carriage, to the cobblestones and the wrought iron fences. "Alright," she said. "Alright." She walked down the steps to the carriage and it all felt like a dream then, as if she watched herself doing these things, like she was watching herself living a BBC production. She was somehow leaving herself behind in the house. The rock in her belly grew heavier the farther away she got; it attempted to slow her but it also grounded her—that rock, it calmed her, but not enough that her head stopped feeling like a balloon above her body. The footman gave her his hand and helped her up the steps on the carriage. Then the world passed in the shadows of the night and the rock twisted in her gut, telling her she was making the biggest mistake of her life.

When the carriage came to a final stop, she looked out the door to a building that resembled the hotel she was checked into, but it was not the one where she was staying. The driver came to open the door but she held on to it, refusing to let go.

"Take me back," she whispered. "Take me back to the duke."

"Ma'am, I was told to bring you here," he replied, and she could see the fear in his eyes.

She refused to step down, looked him square in the eyes. "Take me back now, or I'll fight you every step of the way," she said, and then she took his lapels in her hands and went limp.

Madoc lay on the settee, his frame twisted so his feet could rest on the footstool he'd moved to the end so he could fit himself. It was a horribly uncomfortable arrangement. Tomorrow he would hire someone to clean out the important rooms in the house so he could sleep in a bed. He knew it was ridiculous to not simply go upstairs and toss aside the dusty covers on one of the beds and sleep there, but he couldn't bring himself to sleep in a room that seemed to hold so many joyful memories that didn't belong to him. He would have all the furnishings packed up and sent to Grayson, wherever he was. He wasn't sure why they'd been left behind. An entailment included the building proper, not the general fodder of its current occupants.

He threw his arm over his eyes and tried to slow his breath and his mind, but her face assaulted him from the depth of his memory. Her sweet, innocent face. He'd watched her as she'd walked through the foyer, and he'd seen her as she'd gotten into the carriage and looked back up at his house. Her wide-set, large, blue eyes, her small nose, her full lower lip. Her top lip was smaller, but sharp, like two peaks. Fear had smelled so beautiful on her.

His cock grew heavy as he thought about it. How her breathing had slowed but stilted. How her heart had pushed the blood through her veins, the scent of her arousal... He smoothed one hand down the hard ridge of his cock through his trousers and concentrated on her mouth, that sweet bow of a mouth, how she would drop it open and inhale a breath to steady herself as her fear intensified. How

she would lick her lip, then bite the tip of her tongue as though she tried to stifle whatever was to come out. He unbuttoned his trousers and reached for his cock, then froze when he heard thumping echo throughout the entry.

Suffice it to say, Madoc wasn't expecting to hear the door after they'd left. He expected that the house would remain perfectly quiet until...well, for quite a long time, since he wasn't expecting visitors of any kind any time soon. He stood from the settee, adjusting himself as he walked through the foyer, wondering who was banging on his house so late at night.

He swung the door wide to find the driver he'd sent the woman away with. He stood there breathless, carrying her over his shoulder. He snapped his hand back from where the door knocker had been.

"What the bloody hell is this?"

"Your Grace, she demanded I bring her back. I argued, but she refused to leave the carriage. Then she grabbed me and had a fit—I didn't know what else to do. So I brought her back."

Madoc took her into his arms. "Hold your tongue."

"Yes, Your Grace, of course." the man replied then he turned, closing the door as he left.

Madoc shifted towards the front window that let in a bit of the light from the streetlamp outside and stared down through the limited light in the foyer. He'd not imagined her incomparable beauty. Petite and lovely and fragile and all the things that frightened him most about her, because she brought out this odd emotion in him, the need to protect her, juxtaposed with his need to terrify. Perhaps that wasn't quite correct. The two needs were much more mutually dependent than that. He simply wasn't sure how. That was why he'd sent her away to begin with. He didn't trust himself with her. But here she was again...in his arms and under his complete control, and at the moment the part of him that wanted to protect her outshone the other by far. Just the weight of her body held him steady in a way he was completely unfamiliar with.

He carried her to the study and managed to get her out of her cape before laying her back on the settee where she'd been only a short while ago.

What the hell was he supposed to do with her? He left the door to the study wide and swept the curtains open behind his desk so he could see her somewhat better. So that when she awoke, she might not be quite so frightened as before. He knelt next to her, running his finger down her cheek. Her skin so smooth and soft, so very different from his calloused, hard hands. He pulled his hand away, wiping it down the fabric of his trousers as though he could soften the skin to be not quite so abrasive. It wouldn't work, of course, yet he tried.

She turned her head and nuzzled into his arm, her hands curling beneath her chin as she settled into sleep. He obviously couldn't return her to Westminster tonight, so he should allow her sleep. He ran his hand down her jaw again. Tried to feel her with the softer skin on the back of his fingers, between his knuckles. He adjusted himself on the floor, and she seemed to follow the bit of his arm that was next to her, so he shifted as best he could without moving it. Such an odd reaction to someone who'd quite literally and willingly scared the wits out of her.

He wondered at that, at what it meant. He whispered, "Are you awake?" But she didn't respond. She seemed so...comforted by his presence. Such an odd and disarming feeling, to be of comfort to another. He racked his brain, trying to think of a single instance in which he'd experienced this, but came up empty. Empty...that was as good a descriptor as any for what he'd felt all his life, before she'd stumbled into his arms. That his body felt somehow fuller at this moment was such an odd sensation, that his blood felt heavier as though it flowed with more meaning than before...

He closed his eyes and rested his head on his own hand, his hair grazing her side, the heat of her seeping through his scalp, dripping through him like honey, warming and opening him up in ways he never knew existed—ways he anted to run from. His skin tingled, not uncomfortably, and he almost felt weightless. He allowed himself to experience all of this whereas before he might have shaken it off, like the pins and needles of a hand falling asleep. But this was in no way discomfiting. It was the opposite—and that was the problem. He could not allow himself to be so unguarded in this new life of his. He decided to allow this, momentarily, but tomorrow she would have to take leave of him and he must revet his walls to prevent anyone else coming this close.

FIVE

Willow rubbed the sand from her eyes and rolled to her back, stretching until her feet met with the end of...whatever she was sleeping on. It certainly wasn't the hotel bed. She took a deep breath, and the exhausted salt scent of him reminded her of what had happened the night before, the memories flooding like the crest of tide. She'd pretended to pass out so the driver would have to return her to him then she'd feigned sleep, but the comfort of being so close to him, and being so exhausted from all of it... she'd truly fallen asleep.

She opened her eyes, allowing them to adjust to the new light that filled the room. The shadow of him moved away from her and she reached out, smoothing the warmth of the fabric next to her where she knew he'd been all night. She closed her eyes again for a moment, shifting her arm to the warm spaces, absorbing the heat and breathing deeply of the scent that had reminded her of him. It was musky, like he needed a good blowing out in the fresh air. There was something else though, some sort of spice under the rest of it, and she wanted to get to that, to figure out what it was exactly, and where it came from. She'd turned her face into the cushion as if to breathe nothing but the scent of him when he finally spoke.

"I'll see you to Westminster, and that will be the end of this," he said, and her heart seemed to stall in her chest until she pulled her fist to her chest and rubbed it back to life.

"I don't want to go. I don't know Westminster."

"You cannot stay here."

"I understand you don't want me here, but I don't belong there. I realize I don't belong here either, but I honestly don't think I belong anywhere at the moment. I'm not sure what's happening to me but..." She sat up and looked around. Perhaps last night had been a dream? Or parts of last night? She closed her eyes for a moment, remembering how frightened he'd made her, and how much that had soothed a part of her soul. Her body reacted to the memories before she could shake them off, and she pressed her knees together.

"What do you mean?"

"I mean...they took me to Grosvenor House. That isn't the Grosvenor House where I was staying. I'm not sure how to explain this to you, but I don't think this is the London I'm familiar with."

"It isn't quite the London I'm familiar with either. I've been gone too long to know this London. Much has changed. But if you were at Grosvenor House yesterday, it will be the same today. If you're a guest of Westminster, you're a guest of Westminster. That much is simple."

"But I'm not a guest of Westminster. The Grosvenor House I know is a hotel. It's run by Marriott. It's...it isn't a property held by a man or a title. It's a business."

"Grosvenor House has never been and will never be a hotel. That is patently ridiculous."

"I apologize; however, what I'm telling you is what I know." She stood so she could look at him. She was met with the strong line of his back in his rolled shirtsleeves and vest and realized she had yet to see his face. She'd never quite realized how incredibly sexy a man in a shirt and vest could be but here was this man, and she wanted to run her hands all over him. If only he'd allow for it. A scar slid down the side of his neck past his collar, and she wondered how far it went. It wasn't a friendly scar; it had been a deep and painful wound, undoubtedly, because what she could see of it looked perfectly terrible. She wanted to know them—to know his scars may be to know him as well.

He turned from the window and caught her gaze, his eyes wide as they adjusted to the dim inside the study, and she realized he'd turned to his left with purpose because there were no visible scars on this side of his face. This side was perfect, and beautiful, and he stole her breath. His hair was disheveled, falling across his forehead in places, sticking up in others. She could tell even from this angle that his nose wasn't quite straight. His eye was a light color, maybe silver or grey, but with the lack of color in the room surrounding them she wasn't sure. His gaze travelled her figure, head to toe, taking her in, and she felt every single move like a caress to the point that she closed her eyes to stop the feel of his hands on her body. She stayed that way until his shadow covered her. He was close. Her heart raced and she had to inhale to catch her breath when it was knocked from her without so much as a touch.

"Please," she said.

"Please what?" His voice was within touching distance. The words floated across the crest of her cheek then rested on her shoulders like a warm blanket and that particular sinking feeling returned, that extreme calm she couldn't seem to control.

"Let me stay with you until I figure out what's going on. I don't know why, I don't know how, I just... I feel like I need to be here right now. I'm afraid to leave. I—" The rough skin of his finger across her lips quieted her instantly. She inhaled around his finger, and he pulled back just as quickly.

"You don't belong here," he said, and she felt her fear release in a tremble that suffused her body. He took a breath. "But," he continued, the word drawing some thread from her, slowly, like the wisp of a promise unmade. "I will allow it, for the time being. The greater issue being there is no place for you here." The last of those words were forceful enough that she shied from him.

She opened her eyes, and he immediately withdrew, walking back to the desk, keeping his face turned away. "The house is huge. I'm certain I can find a small space within these walls and be no trouble to you whatsoever."

"That isn't exactly what I meant. Beyond that you put both of us in danger with your very presence in my house, the only room in this house worth occupying is the one we're in. The rest of the house looks much like the foyer. It's a dusty, unclean mess."

"I can clean. I can help clean the house, if that's what you need. I can be your maid. That's what you need right now, isn't it? Someone to bring the house back to working condition?"

"I do, but I intend to hire a proper staff once I look through the books and determine what condition the title is in."

"You...don't know?" she asked as she tried to catch his gaze, get him to look at her full on so she could see him.

"I do not. Do you think I lived in this study for some extended time? I returned to this house just yesterday, not long before I met you. As I said, this London is not the London I'm familiar with."

"Oh..." That explained the mess, she supposed, and also provided for an opening. "Well, until you determine the status of the title, I'll be your maid...in exchange for a room. You'll need a room as well? I can clean the master first." She could see the muscles of his shoulders tense at the words and realized there was much more going on here than a simple return home from abroad. "Or I can clean whatever room you would like to occupy, then another of your choosing for myself."

"So be it. Just stay out of my way, and if anyone comes to the house you must hide. Nobody can know you're here. It would cause issues with my family, certainly, particularly if you belong to someone in the peerage like Westminster. I shudder to imagine what would happen should someone discover you here when you shouldn't be."

"Yes, sir." She was a bit absent-minded as she thought about what he was saying. That she was owned by a man, there was no question in his voice; it simply was. She was a woman and thus was owned by a man.

"You will address me as Your Grace, as all the servants of my household will do," he replied.

"Yes, Your Grace." She fell silent, unsure of how to ask for what she needed.

"What is it?" he asked after what felt an eternity of unbearable silence. When he turned away from her, she thought maybe she'd be able to ask for what she needed.

"I need to know where cleaning supplies might be kept, and I need to know which bedrooms to clean first. And what you'd like cleaned after that—I'm assuming the kitchen. Then I promise to leave you be," she said.

"The sooner, the better." He was clearly frustrated, walking past her through the door. "Coming?" His voice boomed through the empty foyer.

She went.

He walked across the foyer, dust motes dancing behind his back like children teasing a bully on the playground. He went through a door on the far wall, at the back of the foyer, and she followed him down a hall, then down a flight of stairs and finally to a large kitchen. There was a second, separate access to the outside via a set of stairs.

This room wasn't quite so dusty, for whatever reason, but it smelled terrible, as most unused kitchens tended to do. He opened a door that led into a pantry. Behind that was a second closet. She leaned past him to see that this was where buckets, mops, and other cleaning tools had probably always been kept. He waited until she nodded, then he turned and brushed past her, not pausing for her to keep up. Apparently she was dismissed.

"My lord," she said quickly, and the stillness that fell upon the room told her he'd stopped somewhere beyond her sight, but within hearing. "I need clothing. I also...still need to know which rooms to begin with."

"This way," he replied.

She emerged from the pantry and followed him across the kitchen to yet another set of stairs that went up the back of the house. She tried not to watch the muscles of his ass and thighs work against the taut fabric of his pants. The stairs switched back and forth, with closed doors at each landing, until they emerged in a darkened hallway, two stories up. She followed him down the hall to the right as he opened door after door, pausing momentarily then moving on. He finally opened a room at the end of the hall and nodded. "This will be mine. I'll have furniture delivered this afternoon and moved into the room. Have it ready within the hour, and when you hear them arrive, hide."

She nodded. "And for myself?" she asked quietly.

"Any room you can find on the floors above us. No other rooms on this floor need to be cleaned. There should be clothing stored on the upper floors. You may have whatever you can find there. If there is nothing, leave a note in the study. Do you require anything else? I'll be gone for the day at least. I'll have food sent for the pantry, and I'll leave the access door unlocked for them. Lock it once you know they've come and gone. And remember, if you're in the pantry when they arrive—"

"Hide," she finished, and he nodded. He left her standing in the hall. She watched as he walked determinedly for the main staircase, which was just beyond the door in the wall they'd come through. A servants' passage. It would come in handy whenever someone came to the house. There had been other staircases in the wall; the one she'd been on continued up, presumably to the third floor, where she would be staying. But since he was leaving, she would take the main stairs. She saw no reason she couldn't use them as long as nobody was around to know she did. He'd left footprints in the stairs like steps in the snow. She wondered if she'd ever see Colorado again.

She walked to the door at the end of the hallway to find a large bedroom with a closet and attached bathroom. It was completely barren as though it, and whomever had lived in the room, had been stricken from memory and use. It only needed a good sweeping, the cobwebs pulled from the walls, ceiling, and windows.

She turned and went back down to the basement. Tossing her cape over the counter, she lifted her skirt and untied the petticoats, and let them drop to the floor. She grabbed one and tore the lowest ruffle from the bottom. She listened for a moment to be sure she was alone, then she removed her top and the corset beneath it, adding them to the pile on the floor. She used the ruffle to create a sort of wrap shirt, tying the ends at her waist. The skirt she had on was heavy, so she let it drop to the floor as well, then put the petticoat back on. It would have to do since she didn't have underwear of any kind on. She tried to keep that from bothering her but every time she paused, it nagged at the back of her mind, just like the rest of this—whatever this situation was—did. Particularly when she paused to think about the night before, when he'd spread her legs and breathed of her.

She shuddered and closed her eyes, steadying herself before she tripped while standing still. She pulled some fabric forward between her knees and tied it to the front for makeshift pants.

She needed to do whatever it took to stay here. With this man. In this house. That was the one thing she knew for certain, so that was what she concentrated on as she filled a metal bucket and set out to clean.

Madoc shut the front door as softly as he was able, which wasn't quite as gently as he would have liked. He stared at his hand on the door handle for a moment before turning to the street and flagging down a cab. The Hansom pulled up, and he got in. "I require the day. I'll compensate double for your patience."

"Your time, milord," the driver said. "Where to?"

"I need furniture, and it needs to be delivered today, nothing elaborate."

"There's an estate sale over near Regent's. Should be nicer furniture. An Earl's private possessions, milord."

"Fine then. Go there."

"Yes, milord," he said, and they were off.

That afternoon, after arranging the last of the deliveries he needed to survive for a while, he got back in the cab. He almost headed back to his house, but then he decided on one more stop. "Iron Duke on Grosvenor," he said, and the driver pulled into the street.

When they arrived, he paid the man and sent him away. Then he stared at the entry, wondering if he was safe visiting this inn so early in the day. Probably not. He walked around to the rear of the establishment and went through the service door. He walked through the dim backrooms and emerged slowly into the tap room, sweeping his gaze through the room before going to the wall where he'd found the woman the night before. Willow. His jaw clenched when he remembered her name and he swore he'd keep it from his mind until such a time as it would no longer affect him.

He stared at the carving, wondering what he'd thought he could glean from returning here. He ran a thumb over the cats just as she'd done, feeling the sharpness of the wood. The splintering of the recent marks. She'd been so appallingly timid when he'd first spoken to her. He thought he'd scared the life from her. It seemed he had. When she'd awoken, she'd been entirely different, still frightened but... somehow not at all the same person. She'd even smelled different to him, as if that were even possible.

He dropped his hand and clenched his fist. He wasn't going to learn anything here. Perhaps the mistress would know who this woman was. He certainly couldn't approach Westminster.

"Why hullo, milord, 'tis been some time since ye've been here," a small, feminine voice said from behind him. He froze.

"You've mistaken me for someone else," he said over his left shoulder.

"Come now, Milord, just because ye've gone and married doesna mean ye've cause te be rude."

"I'm not married. As I said, you've got the wrong man. Leave me be."

She didn't do as he asked; she leaned one shoulder on the wall on his left and smiled up at him before he could turn away from her. He knew the moment she realized her error by the fear in her eyes. "I beg pardon Milord," She said and scurried away,

Madoc went straight for the rear of the pub once again, ducking out the back before anyone else took note of him. He bought a news sheet from the boy at the corner and turned to the back, looking for the new password. He found it and walked towards the Birch House. He knocked, was allowed entry, and followed the hall to the same parlor. Today it was lit much better, the windows at the front of the house open to the waning sun as though this was naught but a residence off of Grosvenor Park. But... it was most definitely not merely a residence off of Grosvenor.

The same woman, this time dressed head to toe in a vibrant red, entered the parlour and bade him sit again. "It's much too soon. You must heal before you're allowed to give. You were informed of the rules last night."

"I understand. My return today is for information. Did you send someone to me?"

"What do you mean?"

He watched her expression to gauge whether she spoke in earnest. "I found a woman at The Iron Duke last night. She was looking for you. I'm wondering if you're missing someone, as she won't tell me who she is."

"I'm missing no one."

"Well she was looking for you. She found your brand on the wall then proceeded to faint. I took her...to protect her. She is at my house, but she cannot stay there and she will not tell me to whom she belongs."

"Perhaps she was to be a client? Perhaps she'd been referred and had yet to make her way here."

"Perhaps. She seemed to have... an awareness," he said.

"Awareness?"

"She wanted to be hurt and she wanted me to do it."

"And did you?"

"I did not. She refused to tell me who she was, and it became apparent you'd not sent her to me."

"I'm impressed," Maggie said with a honeyed smile, and he was finished. While this woman was adept at playing these games of power, he'd entirely too much to deal with at the moment and wished for simple, straightforward answers, not allusions to her perceived power over him.

He stood. "If you learn anything, I will return."

"And if I learn something before you return?"

"If you know how to contact me, you may send word—with discretion," he said, then he turned and left the way he came. He'd sent the Hansom on its way, so he walked the few blocks back to his house, but when he arrived he couldn't bring himself to enter. He walked around to the mews and through to the rear gardens. Even these had not been tended. It was as though his brother had simply up and left, evacuating the property and leaving it to waste. He supposed he couldn't blame him for that.

He fought his way through the grey and brown weeds and dead growth to a bench at the back of the house that looked up to the ballroom. It was one of the most beautiful rooms in the house...at least that was how he remembered it. The main chandelier had been damaged, and there were bars mounted on the walls in odd places. It no longer looked like a room for a celebration.

He rested his elbows on his knees as he twisted his fingers together. He didn't want to be here, and he didn't want to do this. He wondered if Grayson had felt the same when he'd been forced to ascend to the title. Calder had said as much. Calder had said Gray had no interest in the title. He'd said he was grooming his heir to take the title so he wouldn't have to retain it. What kind of man returned to claim a title he didn't want? Madoc knew exactly what kind of man, but it wasn't the sort of person he remembered his brother to be. His younger brother had never been a man Madoc would consider to be honorable. Then again, the last time he'd seen Gray, he wasn't yet a man. Perhaps he'd been wrong about more than he knew.

At one time, Madoc had wanted the title. Very much. Now he wasn't so sure. How was it that a man who'd raised his sons with a thirst for power now had two sons who wanted nothing but to walk away?

Had the Queen required it of Gray? Of course she had. He wondered now if she'd known Gray had intended to abdicate once his heir was trained up. Madoc also wondered why he wouldn't simply let the title pass to his own son once he was old enough. Why couldn't he wait? Why wouldn't he? Wouldn't his own heirs be disappointed that he'd foregone the title? It was their blood right. Even if they abdicated, ruling was still in their veins.

He had too many questions and no answers. He could write to his brother. Open the lines of communication. He'd been told he would need to mend those relationships. He was certain they would not take the first step to that.

Perhaps these simple questions were the beginning he needed to open that door. He looked up as the sun burned its last breath into the twilight then disappeared behind the trees. A light at the back of the house caught his attention; he hadn't realized until now that the lights were on at all. They burned on the upper floor, a soft curtain blowing through the window.

She'd been told to choose a room on the upper floors there and it looked like she'd done so. He wished he didn't know which room she'd chosen. The breeze sucked the curtain back in then seemed to travel through the house until it blew another soft curtain out of another window on the family floor. He knew which room those curtains belonged to. He'd asked her not to clean the master suites and he wasn't at all happy to learn she'd been in them.

SIX

Never in her life had she been this exhausted. She thought certainly she could manage a bit of cleaning, but this body of hers wasn't cooperating; it wasn't as strong as she thought she was, didn't have the stamina she thought she'd had. She could scarcely clean the cobwebs from the ceiling of one room without feeling the pains of work deep in her arms and shoulders. She didn't at all feel like herself, but that was patently ridiculous, wasn't it? She wanted to lie on the floor and nap, or pack up her skirt and take off.

A dozen times already she'd prepared to leave, to abandon this idea of hers. But more than a dozen times the memory of him had seeped through her exhaustion and pushed her forward. She'd cleaned his rooms first then explored the house, looking for a space of her own. She'd chosen a room on the upper floor as he'd instructed. She'd managed to clean most of the kitchen before her arms had given up on her. She wanted a bath but refused to use the tub in his rooms.

The master suites though...if his rooms had a bathtub, they certainly did. Her curiosity had definitely gotten the best of her so she'd searched them out. She found them in the long hall at the opposite side of the house from his rooms—the rooms he'd told her to avoid, of course. The master suite was beautifully appointed. She could see the care and detail that had gone into decorating it and could tell the people who'd lived here had enjoyed the space. His parents, she assumed, and if he were Duke now, that meant they were dead. Or at least his father was. Was that it? Was he grieving the loss of family?

She wandered the suites, searched the wardrobe for clothing. She found a silk bathrobe and long chemise wrapped in paper and ribbon hidden at the very back of a drawer in the tallboy. She took it. There was no chance she was going to wear it with fifteen layers of grime on her though. She laid it on the bed, a light cloud of dust making her sneeze. While she'd worked, she'd considered all of her options and had decided there were two alternate possibilities at this point. She was in a coma and dreaming, or time travel existed—and time travel certainly didn't exist. Sheldon had proved that on *The Big Bang Theory.*

The reasons for her conclusions rested solely on the quality of the house and furnishings that surrounded her. These pieces were museum-worthy. Furthermore, they hadn't been created by current machining techniques. The workmanship on the furniture in this room pointed to the early 16th century, while the condition of the furniture said Victorian. She assumed late Victorian, since there were marble-topped tables throughout the house with dark grey to black marble on them. Which meant Victoria was in mourning. She'd found the white marble tops in the attics of the house, stacked as if they'd come to use again someday.

Willow knew better though. Victoria remained in grief until her death and she dragged the whole of England with her, her sorrow so complete. Unless the marble tops here were for the family. Well, no, because they were covered in dust; these tops had been placed before whatever had happened, happened.

There was no other option. She was in a coma and this was a dream. She wondered who was sitting at the edge of bed she slept in. Would her parents come all the way from Colorado to be with their only daughter? Did they even know she'd been hurt? Did they even care? She already knew the answer to that question and it was unequivocally no.

She stood from the bed and attempted to brush the dust off, but her clothing was entirely too filthy. She gave up and went toward the door she assumed would be the bathroom. She moved through the room with the massive clawfoot tub and tiled floor to the door beyond, hoping to find linens to make up the bed that had been delivered and placed in his room.

What she found in the room beyond the bath stilled her breath. She held on to the edge of the doorway to steady herself on overtired feet and sore muscles. Then she reached out and ran her hand along one of the chrome tubes. The shower was a giant circle of metal with shower heads lining the pipes, pointed toward the center. It was called a ribcage shower because it resembled exactly that, and for her it was a dream come true.

She slipped from her shoes, leaving them in the bathroom, then turned the knobs on the shower, smiling as the pipes groaned and water sputtered through the tubes, a rush of rust-colored water shooting out toward the center before rinsing clear. So decadent. He would never need to know she'd found this and used it, right? If he did...what true harm could come of her? Not to mention this, all of this, was a coma-induced dream. Or nightmare. Probably dream. But nightmare seemed to fit better, considering how her day had gone. Who the fuck dreamed about cleaning house?

A masochist.

She brushed the thought aside and stripped out of her tattered pieces of cotton, leaving her misshapen cleaning rags next to the shower before stepping between the streams. She wouldn't have cared if the water was cold, but when it was warm, she nearly melted to the floor. She couldn't remember feeling so much relief and pleasure in all her life. The day's grime washed away, and she bowed her head to allow the water to stream through her hair. She was surrounded by jets of warmth. Why had these gone out of fashion? They did use quite a bit of water.

She needed to stop thinking and enjoy this.

She flung her head back and ran her hands through her hair, smoothing it down her back as she wondered how long she'd have under the jets before it ran cold or he showed up. At the very least, she was going to run out of warm water. There was no way around that. "This is magic," she said to herself, and the sound of her voice made her smile. The small tiled room had the perfect acoustics for singing in the shower.

She belted out the one song she knew she could sing without warmup or hesitation. "Just a small-town girl..." She shook her hair behind her to loosen any tangles as she danced and sang and tried to enjoy the moment to the best of her ability. She opened her eyes and reached for the bar of soap she'd remembered seeing in the little tray attached to one of the chrome bars. It was rough, felt like melted salt, and smelled like lavender. She smoothed it across her skin, and through her hair as well. She'd nothing else to use so this would suffice. The lavender bloomed in the steam around her, and she relaxed more than she had in years. She reached out and held on to the bars as the water washed the soap away with her worries and the lyrics singing her tension away.

As she ran her hands over her body to rinse, her voice faltered. This body didn't feel like the one she remembered. It felt softer and rounder, except for her waist, which was pinched more than it should be, as though she wore a corset every day. She wasn't lean by any means, but she wasn't this, and it felt foreign to her. She decided to shake it off and sing louder to force her worries away. "Don't stop—"

"I wasn't aware I'd said you could use these rooms."

Willow stopped singing. She flung one hand out to the nearest pipe and froze, soap running down past her eyes. She willed the voice to have come from her head. She used every bit of energy she had to wish him away, but she felt his presence like a weight against the steam, pushing at her from behind. She stood in this room naked, no way of defending herself, no way to hide, soaked to the bone and surrounded by this ribcage shower like an animal in a cage for an audience to poke sticks at, and she couldn't even open her eyes for the soap streaming down her face.

Goosebumps traveled her skin though the water was still perfectly warm and there wasn't a breeze in the room. Her nipples tightened to sharp points of sensation, drawing her breasts up with them. A streak of fear ran down her spine and settled in her pelvis, warming her belly and pulling her knees together.

"I've no doubt...you heard me." He was a master of the dramatic pause. The steam played tricks with the sound because it came at her from every direction, pushing against her body and making her sway. She couldn't let go of the bars and risk slipping to the floor so she didn't. She held on tighter. She heard a splash of water and wondered what it had been. It had come from beyond the actual cage, but the entire room was tiled and that meant the entire room would get wet when the water was on.

He was behind her. She knew he was. He was standing just on the other side of the bars she leaned on. The steam moved; touching her skin, caressing her.

"Not that I mind entirely, finding you in this manner." His words surrounded her again and pinged her clitoris, warming her mons and flooding her vulva with the warmth of blood. Her pelvis tipped to give access and she lied to herself that it wasn't what she'd intended. She made a noise that she simply couldn't have controlled even if she'd tried. She wasn't sure she could replicate it either, should he ask. "Tell me no," he said. She didn't know what the question was, but she remained silent nonetheless.

The water from the floor sloshed as he moved closer. A finger ran down her side, from just under her shoulder blade to her waist, and her skin tightened from the sensation. His hands slid around her waist and pulled her back against the bars. Her head fell forward. Her grip loosened.

"No," he said. "Hold on and don't let go." The words were spoken at her neck, his lips moving against her nape before his tongue licked from the line of her hair to just between her shoulder

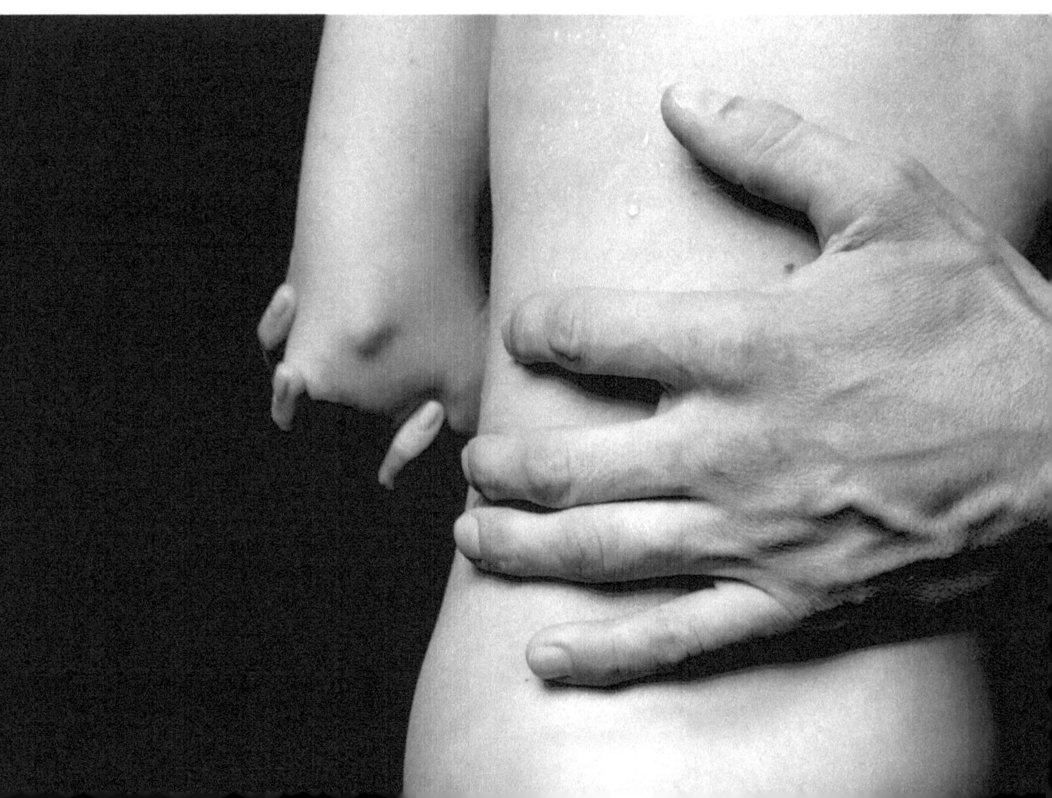

blades. He kissed and then sucked the water from her skin, and the pressure bloomed from his mouth with tendrils of arousal searching for purchase.

"I don't even know your name," she said.

"Is that a requirement for you?"

"I... I..." She couldn't find any words to finish the sentence.

"You don't need to know my name for this," he decided for her, and she whimpered.

She wanted this, but she was too frightened at the moment, and not in the way in which she preferred, and that fact loosened her voice. "Stop," she whispered.

His hands released slowly, like he was making sure she had her footing. The steam surrounded her as he stepped away, a swirl of cooler air mixing with it. The water began to chill. She opened her eyes to an empty room. "I'm sorry."

She cut the water off then walked to the entry, taking the towel from the bar where he'd placed it. She ran the towel down her face, breathing for a minute before drying the rest of her body. She wrapped the towel around herself then picked her clothes up off the floor. She rubbed soap across the pieces as fast as she could then swung them through the puddles in the center of the floor where the drain was slow. She wrung the water out and hung them across the bars of the shower. They were all she had at the moment besides the soft silk nightgown she'd found. She may need them again. Or not. She could wake up...

Please don't wake up, not yet.

She shook her head; the fight inside her own soul was enough to keep her occupied without any help from this man. She knew he was waiting in the next room in the same way she knew that how far her hair was hanging down her back today was farther than it had yesterday by several inches. She took a deep breath and stepped through the bathroom to the bedroom.

He leaned against the large post of the canopy bed, the canopy bed that was now stripped to the clean sheet beneath the blanket. The silk nightgown and robe were tossed to the floor as unnecessary in a very clear request.

He was still dressed but for a jacket. He wore a cravat, waistcoat, and pants. His arms were bare to the elbow, his sleeves rolled up, crossed at his chest. The fabric of his shirt strained over his biceps. He watched her, hiding the face she already knew was there.

"I apologize," she said.

"I heard you."

"I..." She stopped. "I need more than... I can't. I'm sorry I came in here. I'm sorry. I won't do it again." She wasn't sure she was brave enough to say the other things she wanted to say, even if this was a dream. Her body shook head to toe and she didn't know if it was from the dissipation of the heat of her shower or the proximity of this man. He waited patiently until she decided to speak, unnerving her. "I want you to touch me. I want..." She choked. Swallowed several times against the lump in her throat. She held her neck with her hand and closed her eyes.

"What is it you want?" he asked from much closer than she thought him to be.

"I'm afraid."

"I like it when you're afraid."

"I'm aware. I'm also aware that for some reason...so do I."

"Then what is the issue?"

"I don't understand these feelings and I don't know you. I have to know I can trust you."

"You can trust me."

"You don't even know what I'm asking of you."

"I think I do. I think you like the fear. I think you feel fear the same way some people feel arousal. I think you feed off it and you like to come off because of it. That's what I think."

Come off. God it sounded so decadent it sent a signal through her veins telling her body that *YES, that was exactly what she wanted.* She wasn't sure how to respond to that. He was absolutely correct, but still...she didn't know him, and she didn't know how much she could trust him...except she had this idea that she could and perhaps that was what frightened her the most. She wasn't sure she could trust someone like this. The last person she'd trusted with her life had let her down—that was all she really knew of trust. "I can't."

"You can't what?"

"I can't do this. I want to. You're right, I do. I want...something. You can tell—I can't hide it. I want it. But I can't. I don't know you and I need to protect myself. This isn't right. I don't understand why I feel like this with you."

"Neither do I, but I know I've never felt this with someone else."

"You can't—" she stopped and closed her eyes, trying to steady the heavy beat of her heart, "—you can't tell me you've never done something like this. You know exactly what you're doing when you frighten me."

"Yes I do and I have, but not like... People who are paid for their fear react differently than you."

"Oh."

"What do you need to know of me to allow me this?"

Oh God, he truly wanted this of her, and she really wanted to give it. What did she need in order to allow this man to terrify her in all the best of ways? She considered the request for a moment before she realized she already knew just what she needed. Trust in return.

She opened her eyes and looked up into his. "Where did the scar come from?" She reached toward him.

He turned and left.

Madoc knew he could have had exactly what he wanted if he'd only opened his mouth and answered her question. She'd almost broken down into submission, he'd almost had her. All he needed to do was prove he could be trusted. She was gloriously smart. But she asked the wrong damned question. The one question he would not answer. How could she have known that would be the breaking point for him? Somehow she knew that to talk of his scars was akin to gaining his trust.

He walked down the hall all the way to the other end of the house and into his new bedroom, shutting the door behind himself. He knew she wouldn't follow. He'd see her again soon enough. He knew she wouldn't leave; she had nowhere to go—but it was more than that. She *wanted* this as much as he did. She wanted to trust him. He simply wanted her.

He pulled his shirt off and tossed it in the corner, then stepped out of his shoes and trousers, leaving them pooled in the middle of the floor. As inviting as the shower in the master had looked, he wasn't about to use it. He would make do with the old tub and hand spray in his own bathroom. He stepped into the tub and sat down, his knees pushed up to his chest. He hadn't realized he'd grown quite so much since he'd been here last. He stretched his legs out, letting them dangle from the end of the tub.

He turned the water on and sprayed himself wet, then lathered with the soap from the ledge and rinsed. He shut it off and stood, toweled off, and went back to the bedroom.

The estate sale had proved a boon; he'd found more than enough furniture for his own rooms, and some for hers. Though he wasn't sure where they'd put them—he'd told them to find a room that was empty and make use of it. He planned to have the furnishings moved once he knew what room she'd chosen. It was all ridiculous, really. She was going to leave him long before she would have need of a furnished bedroom. But something about the set had spoken to him and he hadn't wanted to leave it behind.

The Earl's title had fallen to someone who didn't know how to manage land, and he had to sell off quite a bit of property in order to pay most of the debt against the entailments. Madoc didn't know him. He didn't care. He'd bought what he needed at a good price then had hired the maid and kitchen staff who'd been released from the household.

The new household would move to his house once the auction was complete, by the end of next week. He had until then to figure out this woman.

He shut the light off in his rooms.

A week seemed plenty of time to get what he wanted from the woman in his attics and be rid of her. The woman in his attics who didn't follow his directions. The woman in his attics who wanted him to touch her, wanted him to frighten her. His cock rose in approval and he stroked the length of it as he walked to the bed and crawled up to the headboard. He knelt there in the dark, remembering the smell of her fear. Remembering how she'd reacted to him the night before. And he stroked. He skimmed his hand the length of his cock and cupped his bollocks, one hand on the headboard and the other attempting to please his aching flesh.

He tried. But it wasn't going to happen.

He kicked aside the counterpane and slid between the sheets, staring out the window into the night wondering what she thought of him now. What would it matter if he told her about the scars? She wasn't anyone. She was of no consequence. It wasn't exactly a secret anyway, was it? Everyone in London must know about him at this point, so what difference did it make if one more woman knew? But something about her told him that sharing that story, sharing his scars with her, was more than just telling stories in the dark. It meant more than gaining her trust. She was different. He didn't just want to tell her what happened; he wanted her to understand him.

His want of her was so heavy it almost felt like snakes writhing beneath the surface of his skin. He should probably avoid her, figure out where she belonged and take her back and be done with it before he managed to get himself into trouble. Or he could tell her what had happened, get what he wanted from her, and then be done with her.

He closed his eyes, and the stars from that night flooded his memory. It was all he could see really, the stars so bright out in the country without the heavy thick of the coal smoke weighting down the air throughout the city.

He could see the black shapes against the stars—the people who'd tried to kill him.

The screams of his father, the heat of fire that burned his eyelids until he could no longer shut out what he saw—his father and brother writhing in unavoidable agony.

His face was ruined by then, but he wasn't feeling anything. He lay there in the weeds listening to his father and brother burn. Then he heard the men talking. They found him in the ditch across the road and dragged him back up next to the smoldering carriage where the smell of his family burning...

They started talking to him as though he knew them, and the realization dawned that he wasn't the brother they were looking for. They discussed his ruined face, decided it didn't matter. The

other men were supposed to pay for one of the brothers; it shouldn't matter which they delivered.

He heard a shot ring out and thought for sure it was for him, but it wasn't. One of the highwaymen fell. They stripped Madoc's clothes, his jewelry. They put them on the dead man and tossed him into the fire with his father and brother, and Madoc didn't care. He was beyond caring.

His father had been a terrible man. His brother hadn't been all that much better, and he didn't know the dead man, the one standing in for him, the one who'd been part of this conspiracy. Madoc's only concern at that point was what came next for him, but even that hadn't been of that much interest. All he knew at the moment was a pain so complete that he couldn't move, though the entirety of his body wanted to move, to attempt to get away from it. It was the worst kind of need.

The rest of that night passed in a blur of shadows and light. He remembered pieces of the journey that had seemed to take forever. He realized later why that was. The men who met them were the ones who realized he was going to be a problem because he wasn't the brother they wanted. They'd wanted the other one. His brother had been the mastermind, it seemed, and now he was dead.

That was when everything had gone from terrible to horrific.

Madoc rolled to his back and stared at the heavy folds of fabric that made up his canopy. The red was deep enough to remind him of the Birch House, but it wasn't the same as theirs; this red was red even in the dark. He felt a breeze sweep beneath the door to his room and pulled the comforter back over his body. He was hot-blooded, rarely sleeping with covers, but he'd lived in India long enough that this sort of bitter cold had become foreign to him.

There was so much he needed to do. Reconcile with his family in a manner acceptable to his Queen. Restore the title and determine what to do with it. Find a way to live under the scrutiny of the *ton*. Get Willow underneath him.

He'd been back in London for two days and already he was in more trouble than he knew what to do with, and the longer he ignored it the more trouble he would find himself in because he knew, somehow he knew, that this woman was much more important than she was letting on. He'd no business being in her company, much less watching her shower, forcing her to clean his house, and terrorizing her for pleasure.

He closed his eyes and thought about that first night in the dark. His other senses heightened for lack of sight. The feminine scent of her. The wavering fear in her voice. The heavy arousal in her heartbeat. He allowed himself to drift on the thoughts of her.

SEVEN

Willow had taken a sheet and torn it in half to make herself a sort of sleeping garment because the silk...she couldn't bring herself to put it on. She'd left it on the floor where he'd tossed it.

She crawled into the small bed she'd managed to haul into the room she'd chosen. She'd found soft linens in a closet that hadn't been too dusty and it felt really good to snuggle beneath them. Now she just wanted sleep. She closed all the windows, stilling the massive georgette curtains that had danced all day, sucking the dust out of the house. She curled up under the pile of blankets she'd put on the bed and tried to warm herself. The day itself hadn't been too cold, but the chill was starting to settle in now that the dark was coming. The pure stillness sent her brain working.

She'd known he wouldn't tell her about the scar. She could see in the way he moved that he was too cocky for it. That he believed the scar had ruined his face and changed how he interacted with the world. She knew the scar had taken the life he was familiar with and turned it upside down into something he loathed, and he'd yet to recover from that.

She watched the frost bloom on one of the windows and she hid under the covers, thankful that her hair, at least, was almost dry. She breathed slow and heavy, letting the warm air from her lungs fill the small fabric cavern around her. She was still cold. She rubbed her arms, then rubbed her hands together. Perhaps she should have figured out how to heat this place before now. It was just that she'd worked so hard today, she really hadn't been cold at all and the day had been mild and, like, she was used to having a damned thermostat. Beyond that, how was she to know she could freeze to death in her dreams?

She heard the steps on the staircase complaining and knew he was coming. For once he wasn't tempering his steps to keep her from hearing him, she knew he stepped with the intention of her knowing because he was walking rather heavier than necessary. This wasn't the game she wanted. This was something else. He came down the hall and into her room without a word. She heard him fiddling around, heard the clang of metal, wood thunking against it. He was building her a fire, and she nearly cried from relief.

She heard him pushing the grate on the fireplace and waited until it was quiet again. She peeked out from the blankets to see a fire burning bright, the heat already seeping into the bedding around her. Then it was the cool of the air as the blankets lifted, the weight of him behind her, the small bed shifting under his large frame, and her body rolling toward him as he stretched against her.

"I'll not allow you to freeze to death," he said.

"The fire seems to be working well enough," she replied, but he didn't bother to acknowledge that she'd spoken, only scooted closer and curled his frame around hers. She'd never felt a body with so much heat. "With you here, I certainly won't need the fire. I might even need to crack a window. Are you aware of how hot you are?"

"It's been mentioned. Quiet yourself. I'm exhausted."

She snuggled into his frame, half expecting to meet a hard penis at her back, but she didn't. He was soft and pliable, at least as soft and pliable as any moss-covered stone, inasmuch as such a tall, hard person could be. She felt comforted in the lee of his form and soon her eyes were too heavy to consider the fire anymore and she drifted off to sleep hoping she wouldn't wake up at home, before she woke up here again, with him.

The warmth of this woman... He was aware his body was a furnace. He knew his regular body temperature seemed higher than most, surely higher than most of the women he'd met. Even in the dead of winter he was hard-pressed to want to cover himself with blankets or quilts. A sheet was sometimes more than he could manage and even that would often end up a trial, wrapped around his legs and trapping him, giving him nightmares.

He closed his eyes and breathed deep, the lavender of the soap she'd used in the shower infusing the air he took into his lungs. She smelled like a summer garden; she should have butterflies buzzing 'round her head. Birds singing on her shoulder. Small animals stealing morsels of food from her fingers. Madoc took another deep breath. He needed rest. Tomorrow he had to tackle the management of the entailments, figure out where the title stood and what he would need to do going forward.

He also needed to figure out how to make amends with his family. He supposed it would be easiest to start with his mother and sister, as they'd actually had something of a relationship before he'd "died." He imagined they knew what he'd done since then though. He imagined the whole family would wait until he spoke first with Calder, and then with Grayson. Or should he approach Grayson first? His grievances towards Grayson were older than that with Calder. Perhaps simpler as well.

He swept the thoughts from his head and concentrated on his breathing. He needed sleep. Doubtless it would be more difficult since he was here with this woman in his arms. What had he been thinking? He shifted, and she pushed her hips back, the roundness of her arse nudging into the cradle of his thighs, warming the warmest of his flesh. His grip around her tightened, and he heard her suck in a breath.

"I apologise," he whispered and lessened his grip.

"Did you have a nightmare?"

A nightmare? He did in fact have one, but it was a waking nightmare, nothing that haunted his actual dreams. "I would need sleep in order to have a nightmare."

"You aren't sleeping?"

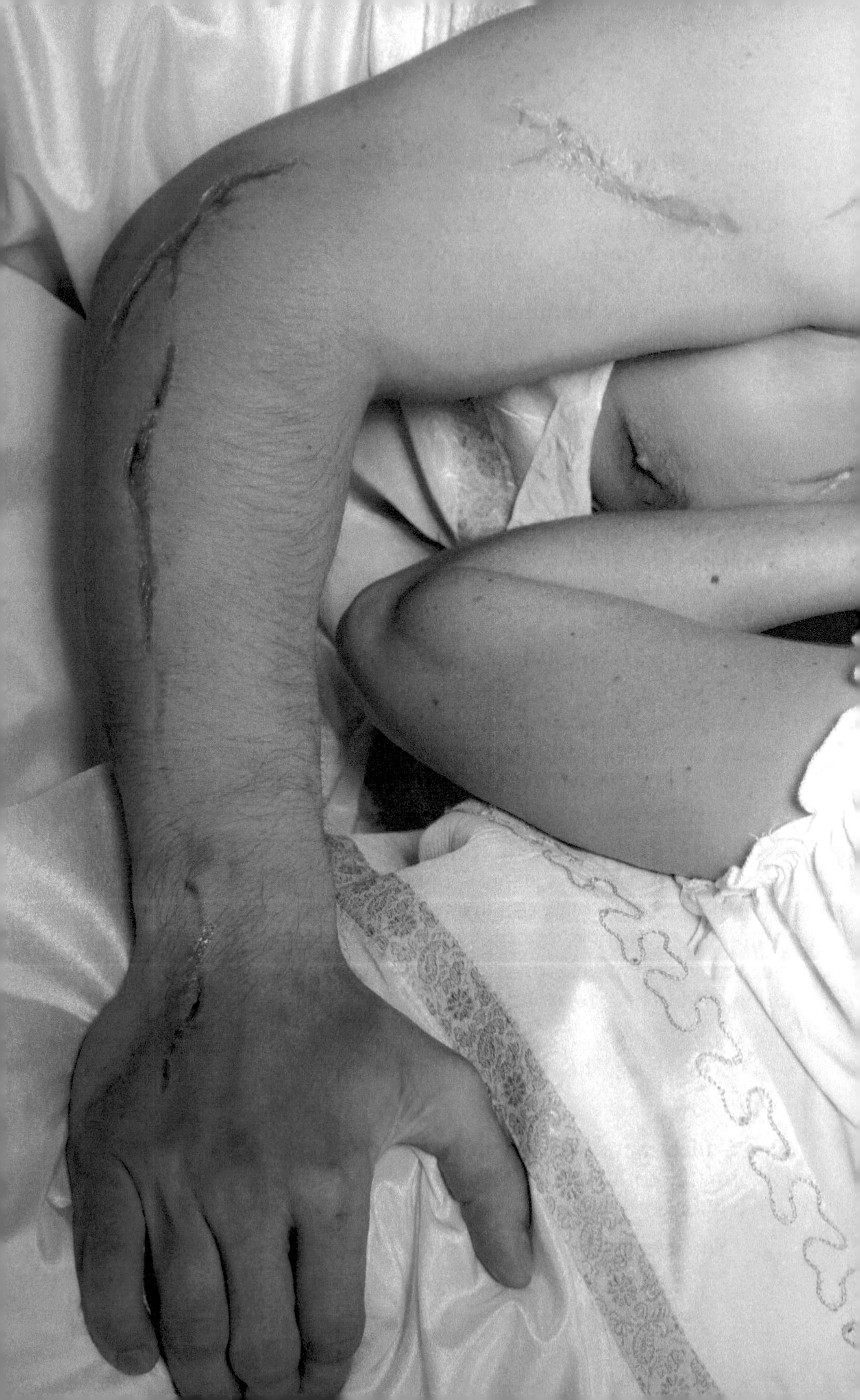

"I'm attempting to. I've simply too much to consider at the moment."

He felt her wiggle loose of his hold then flip over, tossing her hair behind her and pulling her legs up until her shins rested against his thighs, her arms tucked in front of her, her hands curled beneath her chin. She was perfect, the light from the moon casting a soft glow through the room, illuminating her face.

"Tell me," she said.

"Tell you...what?"

"What's on your mind? Besides the stranger in your house, I mean."

He almost smiled but quashed the impulse. "My family... Families are a difficult thing."

"Oh yeah, I hear ya. My parents basically disowned me because they didn't approve of...me, I guess."

"My entire family disowned me, but the Queen of England has deemed we are to behave as a family again, and therefore I am left to repair the damage done."

"What happened between you?"

He shook his head, and she reached up with one hand, running a cool finger down the longest length of the scar on his face. He'd forgotten she would be able to see it since he was lying on his left side. It showed great patience that he didn't stop her. Patience enough to be awarded a medal really. At least he thought so.

"Did it start with this, or did it end with this?" she asked. God, but she knew how to ask questions.

"A bit of both. My issue with my brother culminated with this. For the rest of my family, it had only just begun, really—though they'd no idea of it."

"Sounds like quite the story."

"Not the sort told at bedtime, however." Her lower lip pushed out into a pout, and his gut instinct was to tell her whatever she wanted to know until she drew it back into place. Instead he reached towards her and pushed her lip until they both met evenly once again.

"I feel so strangely drawn to you," she said. He waited to see if she said anything else because he was more the type to collect information than to give it away. "Do you...feel it? It almost feels like there's a physical...something between us. That if I tugged, you would fall."

"Tug all you want; you won't bring me down."

"Oh, is that a dare?"

"A dare? No, merely fact. A little thing like you, bring me to my knees? Hardly. Now close your eyes. Sleep. I can feel the exhaustion in your muscles. You worked hard today. You need rest."

"I have more to do tomorrow."

"Or you could rest tomorrow if you're over tired."

"Are you calling me weak?"

"Not at all, but I saw your dress. You aren't a servant." He ran a hand down her arm, "You're a showpiece, not a worker. You were put on this earth to be served—not to serve—with the explicit purpose of becoming a wife."

"Is that what this is? Are you trying to take me down a peg?" She tried to say it nonchalantly, but failed. He heard the stifled concern in her voice, or perhaps it was disappointment.

"Absolutely not. As you know, I wanted nothing more than to return you from whence you came."

"I mean that little to you, do I?"

"How could you ask me that? It's been a very intense sort of relationship. I should mean very little to you as well."

"You should, but somehow you don't, and I've no explanation for that. It's this...this..." She put her fist to her chest then tightened it against her breastbone, and he did feel some small tug, like a thread around his heart was pulled. Probably because she'd said he should feel it. "I just... I don't know. I'm so tired."

He reached up and closed her eyes. Sweeping her eyelids down and holding them closed gently, as she fought—like a butterfly fights a leaf—until she stilled, her breath evening out.

He watched her for a time, running his hand up and down her back, listening to her breath come and go, the little puffs of air hitting his chin. Then somehow, like magic perhaps, he drifted off to sleep as well.

He sat up in the bed and looked around, trying to figure out what had awoken him. Eventually he realized his panic was because *she* was gone. They'd fallen asleep together but he was alone in the bed now. He tilted his head to listen and heard sound from the water closet in the hall. Her footsteps were small and rapid as she returned and nearly jumped on top of him trying to get back into the bed. The whole of her body shivered. He pulled her into his arms and held on to her until the convulsions softened and she melted against his chest, and just as easily he fell asleep again.

The first thing he realized when he awoke next was that he'd slept the entirety of the night. It wasn't even dawn, but full daylight, when he flung his feet out of bed and sat up. He knew without looking that she wasn't in the room, or even on the same floor. He wasn't sure how he knew this, and it crossed his mind that perhaps this was what she was talking about, this thread that if tugged would bring her to him.

He closed his eyes and concentrated on her, felt the air shift, but shook his head when he realized how ludicrously he was behaving.

"Good morning," she said.

He opened his eyes to find her standing before him with a tray. The scent of meat and coffee wafted towards him. "Good morning." He scooted over on the bed and bade her sit down. She put the tray next to him, then sat on the other side of it and handed him a clean white napkin. On the tray were pancakes covered in butter and syrup, sausages, a glass of orange juice, and a cup of coffee. "This smells delicious. But we should probably take it downstairs, not eat in your bed. I wouldn't want to attract rodents."

"Rodents?" she screeched.

"Yes, hardly a surprise. Every house in London has them, particularly on the highest and lowest floors." She tucked her feet beneath her...what was she wearing? He reached out and slid his hand along the edge of the sleeve. "What is this?"

"It was a sheet. I have no clothing. I found..." Her voice faded and he knew what she was referring to. The night dress and robe he'd tossed to the floor in his brother's room.

He nodded. "I'll rectify that for you today then."

"So you're keeping me?"

"Keeping you?" The way she said it should have bothered him but it didn't. He wanted to keep her, and he could tell she wanted to be kept. "I wouldn't exactly say that. I won't purchase anything but the most basic necessities for your comfort, nothing that would call attention once you return to where you belong."

"Oh." She handed him a fork and a knife and waved at the pancakes.

"You're not eating?"

"No, I ate while I was cooking, I couldn't help it."

He nodded and pulled the tray to his lap and ate everything she'd made. Only when he was done did he realize he'd done so rather too quickly to be seemly.

"It was good then?"

"It was, thank you."

"Good. The one glass of orange juice used half the oranges you had delivered though. I hope that's okay. I just really felt like drinking some OJ."

"Whatever you feel is the best way to use what I have in the pantry."

"Thank you. There are things I'm not entirely familiar with, so..."

"Don't trouble yourself—I've hired a kitchen staff. They'll start at the end of next week. They can deal with whatever you choose not to."

"So...what happens next?"

He searched her face, skimmed his gaze over the whole of her before coming back to her eyes, which were trained on him. "I simply do not know."

EIGHT

Willow watched as he hailed a carriage and was gone, leaving her there on her own once again, she assumed for the day. She wasn't sure what she should do. He'd told her she needed to rest, to recuperate from all the work she'd done the previous day, but lazing about seemed to go against everything she'd ever been.

What she wanted to do was to get out of the house, maybe go for a walk. She pulled the skirt and top he'd cut from her and slid it on, letting the nightgown she'd made fall to the floor.

She took another piece from the bottom of her petticoat and wrapped it around her middle to keep the top closed. It wasn't something she should be seen in, but it would do to get some fresh air. She slipped her shoes on and went down the stairs to the back of the house.

It was obvious that the room at the back had been a ballroom at one time. Now it was a bit of a mess and looked like it had been retrofitted to be a combat training center. There were barres on one wall, mats lying around the room, and areas taped off where there was quite a lot of scuffing and gouging on what had once been beautifully intricate inlaid floors. They may be sparring squares perhaps, but they seemed so out of place in a room that had been built for formal parties.

She pushed the handle on one of the French doors, and it opened easily. Checking to be sure it wouldn't lock behind her, she slipped out into the overgrown gardens and wandered.

She could see what the landscaper had done here, the remnants of a lawn and path, hedgerows and rose beds, bushes and flowers. All it needed was someone with a green thumb to love it. She wasn't sure she was that someone. She felt she had more of a black thumb than green, but boredom really was the devil's underpants, and if she pulled this house into shape, boredom just might resurrect this yard someday.

She walked toward the back, where stables lined the mews on the other side of the garden wall. She inspected the gate in the massive wall to the stables, then followed an overgrown walkway toward the far corner, where she found an old glass greenhouse hidden behind large, established oaks. The frame seemed rather sturdy, made of metal with glass panes, some broken. It looked like it hadn't been used for much more than storage for a long time. Whoever had done the most recent landscaping in the back yard hadn't bothered to extend the work to this farthest corner. She could feel the warmth the green house created even in its ramshackle state.

The door scraped against the stones of the path, complaining as she yanked it until it opened wide enough for her to rethink going inside. She yanked it one more time, and a pane of glass fell from the ceiling, crashing to the floor somewhere at the other end of the glass house. This might be a horrible idea. She shook the door to be sure nothing else was going to fall then stepped inside.

There were tables and trays of dead plants along the walls, and even here there was a winding rock path that led to the center of the greenhouse, where she found a big old tree atop a mound of earth that broke through the paving stones. It was large but barren, certainly hoping for spring to come soon. Considering it had thrived in a glass house here in England, she thought it was some sort of citrus tree. She knew they had an obsession with orangeries—fresh citrus fruits like oranges so foreign in such harsh natural conditions. Being from Colorado, she'd no experience with growing citrus either. Melons, peaches and apricots, apples, and other fruit trees absolutely, but Colorado, much like the U.K., couldn't support wild citrus, and growing them indoors was a practice...well, much like this. It wasn't for the uninitiated gardener for certain.

She smoothed one hand up the trunk of the tree that stretched toward the filthy broken glass ceiling in its abandoned home. She wondered at that—if the glass had required hand cleaning to scrape the London filth away. Sunlight sprinkled through the holes in the ceiling, strange rainbows like mist around her. She hoped the tree would survive winter and perhaps come to life again in the spring, but she wasn't very hopeful in that regard. She wanted to restore the glass house for it, give it a reason to live.

"What do you think you're doing?" The booming voice shook the panes of glass around her, and she heard another plate slip its mooring and fall to the floor somewhere beyond the tree. She turned to find him staring, horrified, from the entry. The shock on his face curled her stomach.

"I—wanted to get out of the house. I thought it would be okay to explore a little out here, where nobody would see me."

"And nobody would know if you'd been sliced to bits by falling glass either."

"It seemed stable enough until you started yelling," she said, and as if to punctuate her statement, another piece of glass, though smaller, tumbled to the floor at her left. She glanced around, only then noticing how much of the glass was shifting in the frames, little shards sprinkling down in a rain of crystals every few minutes, making those rainbows she'd thought were mist. "Perhaps I should have thought this through." Her pulse raced.

"Perhaps you should have," he said. "This orangery was abandoned years ago because it was much too dangerous and the repairs needed entirely too expansive." He looked around the entrance, then lifted a heavy oiled canvas tarp from under a pile of debris. "Don't move." He shook the tarp out, fighting with old creases as he stalked toward her. She almost told him to stop, that she would come out, that there was no point in him being in danger as well, but she couldn't force the words from her lips. Perhaps she wanted to be rescued.

Or perhaps...she wanted him to feel the thunder of her heartbeat. As another pane of glass fell, this time closer to her. She felt her body awaken and realized it wasn't the rescue from him she craved. She wanted to feed him her fear. She wanted him to come to her, to earn her fright.

She reached behind her to steady herself with the trunk of the tree, since her legs were starting to feel more like jelly than muscle. She closed her eyes and waited, not wanting to see if something happened to him. She heard a metallic groan, then another shower of glass behind her. "I'm sorry," she whispered.

His shoes crunched as he stepped, destroying fallen shards of glass beneath his feet as he picked his way through the detritus toward her. She leaned back, centering her spine against the tree, her hands holding it at either side behind her hips. She allowed herself to feel the fear, for him...for herself...for whatever came next.

The cool air of the orangery shifted, her skirt ruffling in a slight breeze that swirled around her legs and seemed to spear its way up her skirt, impossibly. She took a deep breath, then released it slowly. Again. She repeated it until her head felt looser on her neck, the tension from her fear giving way to something else. Something she'd never understood...until she'd met him.

A breath. A release. Control of something uncontrollable.

His hand came up and hovered at her neck as if to draw the pulse from her. Then his fingers swept the length of her neck from her collar bone to her ear, finally resting on her pulse, a mere ghost of a touch. She let her head fall to the side to give him access. She wasn't sure what had compelled her, just that when she was frightened, and

he was part of it, there was something beyond the fear, something more exhilarating, something that engaged the whole of her—body and soul.

His rough jaw scraped the skin of her neck, sending chills throughout her body, his breath warming her just behind her ear transforming those chills to goosebumps.

"I'm sorry," she said again.

"Don't apologise." His voice was like the growl of an engine waking her senses. He licked the side of her throat, ran his tongue up the edge of her ear, his warm breath filling the shell of her ear with calm. She slipped against the tree and his other hand came to the base of her ribcage, supporting her, pushing her back, holding her in place. The hardness of the tree pinched her spine.

The thread that connected them twisted, her heart thumped between her ribs, and she inhaled until her chest brushed his, her nipples scraping the inside of her dress as he pressed harder. The bark bit between her shoulder blades and she flinched, a pained sound escaping before she realized it was her. His hips pushed into her, the evidence of his arousal cradled at the valley of her hip.

Colors painted the backs of her eyelids, stunning rainbows in electric hues blending and separating only to come together again in an explosion of sensation that slipped through her system, lighting her nerves on fire in a delicious dance. Her skin cried out, wanting more skin—less clothing. She wanted him against her, she wanted to feel his skin—and the intruder that was their clothing was a constraint too cruel to bear.

Her breathing stilted as his deepened, his breath so slow it felt like a warm breeze against her chilled skin, and she had no idea how he could seem so very in control of himself when she was so out of control in this moment.

She lifted one hand and skimmed a finger up the fine fabric of his deep blue coat, then wrapped her fingers around the edge of his waistcoat, holding and pushing. Her other hand searched beneath his coat and waistcoat to the small of his back, sliding into that sharp valley carved of muscle and bone, the shifting of his hips against her changing the topography, his spine steady as his pelvis pulsed. She searched his chest for a way in, a way past his clothing, a way for any part of her—no matter how small—to be in contact with any part of him that nobody else had access to.

She heard the warning screech of glass shifting like nails on a chalkboard and she tensed, her hand fisting the fabric that kept him from her, pulling him closer, her heart pumping blood, her lungs stilling. When the glass shifted again, the following silence was deafening. Both of them froze in place. The long muscles of his neck stretched against her cheek and she knew he raised his face to the sky to find the offending glass, and the fear she felt for him was so tangible it shattered whatever had been brewing between them.

She tilted her face and licked the soft underside of his jaw. He moved, and her eyes opened on his gaze—intent on her until the quiet was broken by the sound of that pane slicing through foliage and shattering just behind her. She screamed and clawed at him. "Please." And he was there, his mouth taking the plea from her and into himself. She needed that definitive, specific pressure at her core like she needed the touch of his skin. She tried to slide her hand between their hips but he took it and held it above her head against the tree as he forced his other hand between them, pushing hard through the fabric to her mons, where he ground the heel of his hand until she shattered against him like the glass that fell as he watched.

Stunned.

Her eyes closed and she waited for mortification to cover her like a shroud. She tried to decipher the look that had been on his face, realizing it was something like wonderment. She stilled, calmed. No longer in fear of embarrassment, she felt a certain pride bloom in her in what it seemed she'd gifted him. She leaned her forehead against his massive chest as she tried to catch her breath. She still wanted to hold the smallest piece of his skin to her palm, so she yanked at the tail of his shirt, sliding her hand beneath the fabric so she could cup the upper curve of his hip. It wasn't enough, so her fingers slipped beneath the waist of his pants, filling her palm, and she had nothing left for the world but breath.

When she opened her eyes, he was pulling the giant piece of canvas over the both of them and bidding her to hold it. "Take this. Hold it as high above us as you're able." Then he lifted her in his arms. She wrapped one arm around his back and pulled until the canvas was over his head, making sure to leave a small opening where he could see. "Just hold on until we're out of here."

He started moving, glass crunching beneath his feet as he stumbled, fighting to keep them both upright since he couldn't pick his way carefully across the floor. He tripped on something, and she grabbed onto him, hoping the fall wouldn't hurt too much, but he caught them both and righted himself, kicking away whatever was in front of them.

"Calm yourself," he said. "I need to be able to see at least."

She looked up at him in the dark of the canvas shroud and without any warning, reached up to him with her mouth. "Thank you," she said against the soft underside of his chin; she loved this small, soft, undamaged piece of him. He growled. At least, that was the best description she could come up with in her mind for when she would remember this moment in the future. He tucked his chin, bringing his mouth to hers.

"I cannot see," he whispered against her lips, and she loosened her grip around his head, letting the light come through like it had before. He shifted her in his arms, then moved forward. When they got to the entrance, he shouldered the door open wider, the groaning of metal and crashing of glass behind him louder than it had been before. He took two steps, and she dropped the tarp, watching as more glass fell and shattered on the floor.

"It's a beautiful building," she said, and his gaze swept to hers, his eyebrows drew together, distorting his cheek as the scar pulled.

"It's ruined."

"That doesn't make it any less beautiful. The tree at the center strives to live regardless the damage that surrounds it. It's just waiting for someone to love it enough to care for it, bring it back to life." She ran a finger across that eyebrow and down the scar. He blinked when she came to the crease of his eye, and when she reached his mouth, it dropped open on a breath and she ran her thumb across his lower lip. "You've such soft lips," she said, and his eyebrows crinkled.

"And do you have extensive experience in the feel of a man's flesh?" His voice was wary, this giant of a man who seemed to fear nothing.

She felt a line of energy run from her tongue to the back of her throat and down her spine to settle in her pelvis. "Does that matter to you?"

"No, actually, as long as that experience stops with me."

"I haven't much. My experience in men's flesh is rather limited. It isn't nonexistent, but there hasn't been—"

"I'm not sure I should know this," he said as he closed his eyes and loosened his grip on her. She wrapped her arms around his neck, letting her legs slide down the front of him until they touched the ground to steady her.

"I'm sure you have extensive experience in the flesh of women, do you not? Perhaps in men's flesh as well."

"Women, yes," he said. "Men..." He paused, and she tensed—why, she wasn't quite sure. "Perhaps not as much and not in the way you may believe."

She was surprised by that admission from him. As much as he seemed to want to keep from her, it was an incredibly intimate detail to share. She wasn't sure how she should respond—though she knew she needed to. "And what way is that?"

He shrugged, a simple lift of his shoulder, a small crinkle of his chin. "You are perfectly aware that I like to experience pain in a way that isn't quite in keeping with convention."

"I'm aware."

"Then you can imagine that I can experience the pleasure of someone's pain without more traditional intimacies." He watched her closely, his gaze intent, focused and unnerving. She realized that he was no longer holding back—he didn't turn his scars from her, he looked straight into her gaze and allowed her to look upon him in return.

"I am currently imagining all sorts of things," she said.

"Involving me?"

"Every single one of them," she replied and saw his mouth twitch and realized that it was actually a smile. But the way the scar passed down his cheek and across his mouth, the muscles worked in reverse, making him scowl a bit instead. She cupped his cheek, running a thumb over the small piece of his skin that wasn't damaged on that side. "Can you feel this?"

"I can feel your thumb. I cannot feel most of your hand. Though when you run your cold little fingers down my scar, for some reason, I can feel them like tiny shooting stars through my system that emanate from your fingertips."

Willow lost her breath and it seemed a full minute until it returned. "Do you still intend to be rid of me?" she whispered.

"My intention…in this moment is to never be rid of you. But I may not have much of a choice in that." He reached up and took her wrists, pulling her away from him. "You are missing from somewhere. I cannot keep you from your family."

"Is this it then? Is this how it happens? Is this how I wake from this dream? You push me away back into the world? That's kind of how I imagined it would happen. But never in my life have I wanted to be Sleeping Beauty left to rot, because the dream is so much better than the reality and I don't want to let go." She slid her hands against his lapels then curled her fingers around the edges and held on as though by steadying her hold on him, she would be able to steady her voice and the rest of her as well. "Why are you so desperate to be rid of me?" Her voice wavered regardless.

"I told you, I cannot afford a scandal, and you taste like nothing but."

"I taste of scandal?"

"You taste of much more than that."

"And you still don't want me?"

"My want of you is irrelevant when you belong to someone else."

"Someone who must not care much for me if they haven't come looking." There was nobody to look for her here regardless though, right? He was convinced she belonged to someone though, and she tried her best to see his point of view. She wished he understood hers.

"That may be somewhat true, but I don't imagine anyone would come to this house looking for someone like you." He lifted the fabric of her skirt, sliding it between his fingers as if to judge the cost of it. Then he released her and when he stepped back, she felt her world tip to the edge and knew whatever she said next could send it crashing down, or save her.

Willow took a steadying breath. "I want you…to frighten me," she said, and his gaze narrowed on her. She held it, pleaded as best she could, silently.

"More?" he asked, and the word was more breath and confusion than sound.

"Yes."

"Why?"

"You know why."

He paused, as though searching for something in her countenance that might explain to him why she was asking this, but even she didn't know. "I can't do that," he said finally. "It's a risk too heady, which makes it entirely too dangerous."

"We risk nothing. You said yourself you're perfectly capable of feeling the pleasure of pain without intimacies. I assume that means you can get off without fucking, and I assume you're male...so I'm aware of how that's accomplished." His head tilted at her words, and she feared she'd gone too far.

"And you?"

"I think we're both aware of how my body works at this point."

"But if you know it's coming, it won't work."

"If I know?"

"This is a delicate balance, between fear and pain. Fear has to be true, it has to be real. Physical pain is so simple by comparison."

The thought of physical pain sent her heart fluttering again. She wasn't sure she could ever allow for something like that again, but she missed the want of it. The actual thought of it. Because she'd refused to allow for something like that again, until just now. Until him.

So perhaps she would trust him regardless.

Mads watched as her eyes dilated and her mouth dropped open on a breath, her breathing heavier, her body shifting to a remembrance he wasn't privy to. "Tell me." He wanted to hear it; he wanted to take it in and drink the memory of her pain.

"He...liked to mix the fear with the pain. He liked to frighten me with it." Madoc shook his head, knowing full well the purpose of fear from pain. "He would flog me," she whispered and her body seemed to fold into itself, away from him. She drew her hands up under her chin, her shoulders curled in and her chin ducked, hiding her face from him. He didn't want this from her. He took her chin in his hands and coaxed her face up to his.

"Whatever he did, if this is the memory of it, it was wrong. I want the memories of anything you do with me to be empowering. I don't want anything I do with you to elicit this sort of response, and that's why we cannot do this. I do not have control of what it is you want from me."

"You seemed to control yourself in the orangery just fine."

"That was...exceptional but I much prefer to experience the fear of others, not my own."

"What do you know of all this?"

"All what?"

"Pain...and arousal," she whispered, and he swore the scent of her bloomed around him like a rose.

"I've experience. I've seen how a professional should react. I know what they should do. This is not it."

"I'm no professional."

"That makes all the difference." A tear streaked her cheek, and he wiped it away without hesitation. "You deserve better than whoever made you feel less than."

"So do you," she said and reached up and covered his hands with hers. He wondered what she meant by that until she shifted, cupped his ruined cheek in her cold palm. He felt the words then like they were written on his flesh. He allowed himself to lean into her. Why did this woman open him up so easily? How did she manage to get the truth from him like this?

The quality of light shifted and a chill suffused the air, and she shuddered. Whatever moment they'd had passed just as easily as the time had. He turned to the house and took her hand, pulling her along behind him. They entered through the kitchens, and he released her at the threshold then took a kettle and put it over the fire, stoking the embers in the grate so he could warm tea.

It was difficult for him to remember that she was so much less than he was and required so much more care. She was fragile by comparison. And where had she come from? She walked into the room and slid onto one of the stools in the corner, watching him remove his great coat and coat. Rolling his sleeves.

"I can make three things. Soup is one. Speak up now if you object," he said. He heard no objections, so he cut a glance to be sure she was paying attention, then placed vegetables on the the cutting board. The tea kettle whistled, and he pulled the serving pot from the cupboard. After sprinkling various spices and cubes of sugar in the bottom of the pot from the spice cabinets he filled it with the water and set it aside. He poured the rest of the water into a pot and started dumping vegetables into the pot, adding some of the spices he'd used for the tea. He put the kettle back over the fire and went to the ice box and brought out a large hunk of meat. He tossed that into the large cast iron pot and placed the lid on it and hung it over the fire across from the kettle. Then there was nothing left for him to do. He watched the pot and the kettle for a bit then brushed his hands off and turned. "It's going to be a while before the stew is ready to eat. Hours, actually. Tomorrow."

"Why did you—"

"I needed something to do." He walked over to the kettle and breathed the steam that rolled from the lid when he lifted it. Heaven. He took two teacups from the cupboard, grabbed the ewer of fresh cream from the icebox, and poured a heathy portion in each cup then swirled the tea in the pot and added it to the cream. The strong scent of the tea reached her, and she smiled.

"Is that chai?" she asked as she walked up and took one of the cups.

He nodded. "It's the second thing I know how to make."

"And the third?" she asked, looking up at him over the cup as she blew across the lip.

He shook his head. He wasn't sharing that yet, if ever. He dragged the stools over to the large butcher block and bade her sit across from him. "I don't know how we'll go about it, but we do need to figure out where you belong."

"I've been thinking about that."

"And?"

"I'm afraid to say what I think because I don't want this to end." She dodged his gaze.

"What do you mean by that?"

"I just... I'm starting to believe the impossible, and if I know anything about the Victorian era, my opinions will get me chained to a wall in Bedlam."

NINE

e watched her from across the butcher block, the keen awareness of his inspection sliding along her nerves and bringing them to heel.

"You believe I would have you committed for your opinions?"

"I believe that society as it is does not allow for opinionated women."

"It does when their opinions are acceptable or—"

She looked up at him. "Or?"

"Or...they are cherished. A family has complete control of the women therein. A woman would not be sent away if her family decided she was of no danger, no harm to herself or to them. However—"

"However?"

"However," he continued, putting his teacup down on the wood surface with a loud clink. "I'm certain if you believe telling me your theory will bring this to an end, that—for now anyway—you should keep it to yourself."

She let out a breath and looked away. She was desperate to talk to him but was equally frightened by what that discussion could bring. In the movies, when there was a coma dream, the moment it became real was the moment they woke up. She definitely wasn't ready for that, not that she had any actual control. It niggled a bit, at the back of her mind, that this didn't feel at all like a dream, but she once again discounted it as impossible.

"You aren't going to ask me why?"

She inspected him. She assumed he'd meant he had no issue in sending her away if he thought her insane. She let out a hard breath and put her teacup down next to his. "Why then?"

"We are not family. I have no power to protect you. I don't know if I ever will, and unless or until I do—"

She cut him off. "I will keep my opinions to myself." So, he believed whatever she was to say would be wholly unreasonable. Well, it was..

He nodded. She looked away again as a defined sting bloomed behind her eyes at the realization of how alone she was here. She had nobody to talk to, and he'd just removed himself from the trusted column, putting himself firmly in the not-to-be trusted column. She shook her head because it was better this way. Telling him what she was thinking would make it much too real. If she were here—like, really truly here in Victorian England—then...well. She was in more danger than she could even attempt to conceive. When he'd said they needed to figure out to whom she belonged, it hadn't been a figure of speech. As a woman, she quite literally belonged to a man. Somewhere. If she started spouting stories of the 21st century she'd be locked up in Bedlam regardless his attraction to her because she was not his property. He was correct.

So she needed to stay in hiding until they figured out what that meant, what was going on, before she could figure out what to do. The one thing she was certain of, more than anything, was that she needed to be near him. That feeling hadn't lessened in the last day. If anything, it only grew stronger the more she was with him.

She spun the empty teacup on the butcher block, and he refilled it. She held it in her hands, letting the heat suffuse her skin and warm her. He stood and lit a few candles. "Why not turn the power on?" she asked.

"I... Well the last time I was in this kitchen, it didn't have electricity. I suppose that's a habit I'll need to become familiar with."

She nodded. "How long were you gone?" she asked and then watched as he considered her.

"Long enough."

"I'm finding it difficult to balance the want to know you with the want to keep you at arms' length."

"To protect yourself?"

"No," she said quietly.

"To what end?"

She took a deep breath then stilled herself, bringing her hands to her lap. "For the purpose of *Our Game.*"

"Our game?"

"You know what I mean.'

"Do I?"

"Yes," she said. "You do. You know exactly what I'm referring to when I say *Our Game.*"

"I suppose I do, though I don't view it as something quite so trivial. Do you?"

"Trivial? Not at all. But what would you have me call it?"

"Sex."

She laughed, and the stiff cloak of reality lifted a bit until she saw his rather serious gaze. "Well...that's rather blunt and non-specific," she said as she stared into the cup again.

"Is it?" His head tilted and his eyebrows came together as he held her gaze, and she wondered if he was attempting to get her to say certain things, or if he truly wanted to know what she meant.

"Yes. Sex can be a whole host of things, but should definitely include some P in V action."

"P in V?"

"Penis in vagina," she whispered, staring at her hands twisting her makeshift dress. "I wouldn't hesitate to say we've not done that quite yet." She only said it aloud to goad him, and goad him it did.

"Not quite. Though you have come off..." He paused and when she realized he was waiting for her, she looked up. "Against my hand," he finished, and the shape of his mouth as he said those words were cast into her memory. "Is that not specific enough for you?"

She swallowed, reached for her teacup to clear her throat, but her hands were shaking such that she decided not to test it. "Yes," she whispered. "I did, and yes it is." A shiver traveled from between her shoulder blades to her tailbone, spreading against her hipbones and anchoring her in the chair. She felt her spine settle into her hips as though to tell her she wasn't about to go anywhere.

"That wasn't sex?" he asked, refusing to release her gaze.

"I don't know what that was."

"Why do you have this need to give everything a name?"

"I like to know exactly what I'm agreeing to. I like to know exactly what's going to happen to me," she said.

"That seems contrary to your reaction to me."

"Not necessarily."

"Then by that reasoning, calling it a game is not nearly enough of a definition."

She closed her eyes and took a deep, anchoring breath because she knew exactly where he was going next, and while she wanted him to do this it was just so...different from anything she'd ever experienced. And yet, wasn't this what she'd been asking for? "No."

"No what?" he asked.

Her eyes popped open. "Why are you doing this?"

"Doing what?"

"Forcing me to speak like this."

"Is that not exactly what you've asked of me?"

"I suppose one could take it that way."

"Then tell me, is it enough?"

She paused, counted to five as she closed her eyes once again before responding. "No, it isn't enough of a definition."

"Then let's define it, shall we?"

She nodded.

"You need to look at me if we are to discuss this."

She opened her eyes, training them somewhere above his chin but below his mouth. It seemed a very safe place to keep her gaze.

"What is it you wish for me to do?" he asked.

"I want...I want you to frighten me."

"How do you want me to frighten you?"

"I don't know."

"I need to know."

"How can I know what I want if I've never—" She stopped and swallowed.

"I find it difficult to believe you've never been frightened, as I have direct evidence to the opposite." He paused.

"Well, yes. Obviously I've been frightened. I've only just... But I've never related the fear to sex. That's not something I've ever... Until you—I just don't know—"

"You don't know what?"

"How to do any of this." She could scarcely hear herself; she feared he hadn't heard her at all until she hazarded a glance up, only to see his eyes go dark with want, searching her own gaze and holding it with his.

"Any. Of. What?" He bit the words out, insisting she give voice to what she meant.

"This...you know, relationships and sex and stuff." Keeping her eyes on him was proving difficult.

"Relationships and sex and stuff," he said, and it sounded absurd coming from him, sending a tiny spear through her heart at the very idea of the normalcy of it. "Is that what we're doing here?"

"Maybe?"

"No," he said, but there was barely any breath behind it, forcing her to look up to his mouth once again to be sure he even spoke.

"No what?"

"No, it isn't. We're talking specifically about sex and fear. That is what we are defining right now."

"I've never... I'm not... Well, I wasn't popular in school. I mean—I was more interested by history and research and really insanely nerdy things. I never had a boyfriend and—"

His finger against her lips stopped her rambling. "Boy...friend?" he said and the word from his mouth was so patently ridiculous that she bit her lip to keep the laughter from bursting from her in a sudden and inappropriate manner.

She'd had boyfriends who had attempted to turn her on, get her wet. It had never happened, and she'd stopped them every time.

She'd thought perhaps it was about pain. She'd thought it was about being restrained. You know, a healthy, run-of-the-mill, BDSM relationship. As if.

She'd started to believe she was somehow broken. That this myth of wetness was beyond her. She thought she would never discover what it was that would make her body respond with a partner, and now, in the span of two days, she'd been almost constantly wet.

Here he was offering up everything she'd ever wanted, if only she could manage to get past her internalized humiliation and answer his damned questions. Fuck, even the questions were making her horny. The way he was demanding things of her. Refusing to let her off the hook. The way he was searching her face right now as she thought about all of this.

She took a deep breath and composed herself then opened her mouth, but before she could say anything, his finger slid against her tongue, then his thumb was under her chin and he held her like that. He tasted of cinnamon and cardamom and salt. He pulled slowly until they were nose to nose leaning across the table.

"Have you ever had sex?" he asked and she took a breath, prepared to launch into her explanation once again, but he gave her one shake and she stopped, swallowing around his finger. "Are you chaste?" She closed her eyes, trying to still her heart rate because she was terrified of scaring him off and her want of him...she wanted so very much. "Have you ever had...a penis in your vagina?"

She shook her head before she lost her nerve.

"Fuck," he said, He released her then stood and turned his back on her. She watched him run his hands through his hair before balancing them on his hips. He was going to refuse her because she still had the small matter of a hymen. A minor bit of membrane, nothing more. She hadn't given it much thought; she'd had better things to do with her time and—to be perfectly honest—until she'd met this man, until she'd been in his darkened parlor, she hadn't been turned on enough to wonder what it would be like to be rid of it.

"It's not that important," she said.

"It is when I need to know what you like. What you want. What you're willing to allow. It makes it difficult to frighten you if I don't know what your ultimate needs are. There is a delicate balance between the two. If you don't have any idea of either, then—"

"Oh, but I do have an idea, I mean, I'm not chaste and ignorant. I'm merely without experience. And I want to learn what I want... with you."

He turned. "Perhaps we should start with the basics then," he said quietly.

"Basics?"

"Yes, basically a little *P in V action,* as you so eloquently put it."

"Please never say that again."

"Why? You aren't interested?"

"I am, but I find that you saying that is about as far from what I want to feel as I can possibly get." He paused and considered her; she felt like she walked a tightrope.

"Fucking, Willow. We're talking about fucking. I want to fuck you. Do you want me to?"

She wished she could answer but her mouth had gone dry. She nodded.

His face fell and he looked to the floor. "You don't want me for this."

"But I do."

"A woman's first experience with sex can be painful. You should want someone to be delicate."

"I should, should I? I don't. I want *you* and I want it like *this*."

He closed his eyes then opened them slowly, demanding her full attention. He stood and came around the block. He moved slow, like a cat, taking her arms in his hands, pulling her up against his body. Her breath left her in a sudden rush, her heart racing faster than she ever remembered; chills cascaded down her spine and made her head spin. She closed her eyes and let her head fall back, baring the full length of her neck to his breath. "Is this what you want?" he asked, and she felt the heat of his breath on the edge of her jaw as he spoke.

"Yes," she said. "Oh God...yes."

"Are you going to allow me to do what I wish?"

"Yes," she replied.

"Do you have any other requirements that need mention before I take you to my room...to fuck?"

She couldn't answer though she knew she needed to. He gave her one hard shake. "Condoms," she said.

"I have them." He shook her again.

"Intercourse?" she asked.

"Yes."

"Nothing else."

"I'm going to find you. I'm going to frighten you. I'm going to put myself inside you in the manner we've discussed. It will not be gentle. I will not be tender. Is that what you want?"

She choked when she tried to swallow from the very want of him.

"You must answer me," he said.

"Yes," she said. "Please God, yes."

"Go to my room. Take your clothes off and wait for me. Do not shut the door."

He let go of her, and she backed away from him, afraid to take her eyes from him now.

"And Willow," he said, catching her gaze and not releasing her. "There will be pain. That cannot be helped." The words were hard. Harsh. They hit her like the percussion from a thunderbolt. The blacks of his eyes expanded, choking out any color held there.

There will be pain. She turned and ran without a backward glance.

When she got to his room, she stopped and did her best to catch her breath. She just couldn't seem to get it under control and then she realized she shouldn't be trying. So she allowed it to race. She looked around, finding the room had been set up perfectly. A massive four-poster stood directly across from the entry bedecked in cream-colored velvet and red satin curtains. It didn't feel like something he would have chosen at all.

The linens on the bed were equally bright and cheerful and not at all like him. She wondered if he'd even seen it yet. Of course he had. He hadn't slept in it though. Last night he'd gone up to her room and joined her, so this bed had yet to be used. She heard the distant creak of wood and turned to the door, her breath catching in her throat. She swallowed and her hands went to her waist, untying and unwrapping the fabric that held her clothes to her. She let it all fall to the floor then pushed her shoes off. She wondered if he'd known that was all it would take for her to be naked.

She stared down the hallway but saw nothing. She kicked her dress and shoes to the edge of the room out of the way and turned to the bed. She walked over and ran her hand along the coverings, around the post at the foot of the bed and up the side to the pillows. She stood there and stared at it, how beautiful and inviting it seemed. She wondered if she should crawl between the sheets. She glanced back to the hall but still saw nothing. She was getting bored already. Her heart was calming. Didn't he understand?

She turned toward the large wardrobe on the adjacent wall and walked over, the slight groaning of the floor boards beneath her feet muffled by the heavy rug that had been brought with the furnishings. She ran a hand down the front then opened it. Several black suit coats hung in the wardrobe. She ran a hand along the shoulders' edge. Several black waistcoats hung next to them, the solid wood of the hangers poking out through the arm holes. A clutch of soft, snow-white shirts came next, followed by several pair of black and grey pants. Simple. Understated. These clothes were absolutely his choice. On the inside of the door hung the long strips of cream silk he would use around his neck. Cravats—not in the Victorian favor but definitely in hers.

She opened the drawer below the hung clothes and was stunned by some of the most beautiful, vibrant silks she'd ever seen. As she reached out to run a hand over them, the lights went out with an audible thunk. With the flick of one large switch, the house fell silent, and dark, around her. He'd cut the breaker. She'd heard the metal-electric sound of it. Her heart raced and she realized as it thumped against her ribcage that catching her slightly off-guard had done the work of a thousand fears.

There will be pain. She turned toward the windows and stumbled a couple of feet, but her depth perception was off. The curtains in here, it seemed, were quite adept at cutting out the light.

She heard the quiet groan of wood and swung toward the door—or did she? She couldn't tell. She reached out into the dark and froze. He was here.

She knew it was him. She knew it was... But maybe it wasn't. She shifted again toward what she thought was the entry to his bedroom, her hands flung wide in an arc around her, hoping to find something to hold on to. They did. She felt his hand slide around her wrist and close like an iron shackle. But it didn't feel like him. It didn't smell like him. Until she caught it. The heavy wool scent of his coat was gone, as was the wax polish of his shoes, but she caught scent of the starch of his cottons, and that spice...that spice...

She reached with her other hand—if she could feel the scar, she would know—but he caught that one as well and squeezed it a little too hard, as though he knew what she was about.

There will be pain. She screamed as her knees buckled. He moved his hands to her hips before she hit the floor and picked her up, tossing her to the bed behind her. She flipped over and grabbed at the covers, trying to get away, but a large hand wrapped around her ankle and pulled. He bent her over the edge of the bed, her legs kicked open. She heard him take a deep breath—not in the way you would if you needed air. He was breathing of her, and she was humiliated. The shift of air on her exposed mons cooled her skin and her heart raced, pushing blood through her system. She felt wetness dribble down her inner thigh.

He groaned on another inhale, then his hand was there, his thumb at the crease between her buttocks, touching her where he shouldn't, his other fingers sliding through her wet flesh until he found the proper entrance to her body. He pushed, and she felt that specific twinge of resistance. The whole of her body shook and fought against him and the sudden burn.

His words echoed in her mind again—*There will be pain. That cannot be helped*—and she remembered the look in his eyes with a suddenness that sent a chill through her. She then understood what he'd said fully; it wasn't a warning per se, but that this time, with or without her specific permission, he would savour her pain along with the fear. Her heart thumped between her lungs and her breath stalled momentarily.

He stopped. Leaned into her. Took another breath. Buttons scraped along her back and she knew he was still fully dressed, save the coat. She concentrated, wanting to know what this looked like. She was completely naked, and he... Shirtsleeves, rolled up—she could tell by the soft hair of his forearms, sending shivers through her skin. Trousers, she could feel the wool of them against the backs of her thighs. No shoes; she'd felt nothing but skin when he'd kicked her feet apart. The buttons... He still wore the waistcoat because this fabric was heavier and scratchier than the soft fabric of his shirts.

He kicked her legs farther apart until she strained on her toes to keep from sliding off the side of the bed. Her hands scrabbled against the soft sheets for purchase. One of his hands came down to the small of her back, pushing her into the mattress as his legs spread hers and his cock slid between her buttocks. He took one of her hands and pulled it behind her back, then down, wrapping her fingers around his length.

He slid her hand around his cock, and she knew it was so she would know he wore a condom. It felt different than what she was familiar with—the snug latex that clung taut to a hard shaft—this was softer, smoother, loose in the way the skin was on the back of your hand. He didn't release her though; he held her hand tighter between them, her fingers tangled with his as his cock probed between their bodies, between the folds of her vulva. He grunted as the tip of his cock met the give of her body and in one not-quite-smooth stroke, he flattened her hand on his belly, her fingers framing his root, and he pushed himself into her.

She expected more resistance, but other than a moment—at which she tensed and he pushed harder—there wasn't much. Yet she did cry out, for her, for him, because it was a moment she needed to mark and to release, and a scream was her only option. She was immeasurably glad of it, however, when she was rewarded with an ethereal exhale of pleasure from him. A breath of hot air along her spine that cooled at her nape. A tightness in his hands as he held her hips steady. A stillness that marked the moment as valuable to the both of them.

She guessed the lack of resistance was because she'd never been so wet in her life. Not with porn, not with fantasies, not in reality. As he paused there, his breath puffing against the sweat on her skin, she savored the feel of his cock in ways she'd never even considered: the slight sting of the stretch at her entrance, the heaviness of him filling her, the tip of his cock nudging the entrance to her womb deep within, the warmth of his balls against her mons below that. She flexed her fingers against the skin that protected his testicles, savored the feel of them as they drew up to his body. He pulled her hand away, withdrew his cock, then pushed back into her with a burn until she thought he would come straight through. She closed her eyes. She fisted the fabric beneath her. She savored what was left of the twinge from her virginity and she gave away any wish she'd had of ever leaving this place.

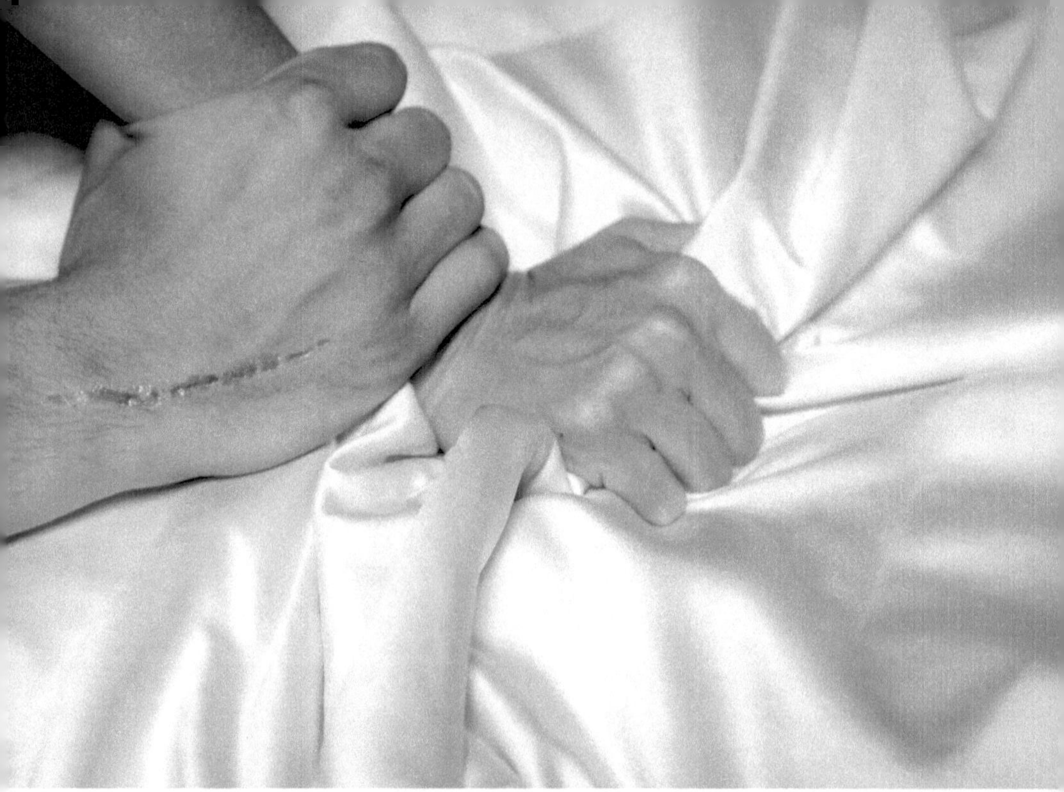

Madoc froze cock-deep in the stranger he'd kidnapped and terrorized in his home a mere two days after being threatened by his Queen to behave. What in the bloody hell was he doing? He closed his eyes and concentrated. Her fear had been so perfect. He hadn't been sure it would work, her knowing he was coming—him knowing she was ready for him. But it had, better than he'd imagined, and it had been so beautiful. The smell of her arousal proved how much she wanted the same as he did, just from a different...approach.

She wiggled beneath him, and he tightened his hand on her wrist until he heard her breathing change. Then he released that hand and let her pull it to herself. He pushed his hands into her hips, holding her steady for his cock, allowing the rest of her body to flail a bit. All he needed from her was her pelvis and what lay inside it. The rest of her body would be fun to peruse, but right now his mind was filled with the softness inside, the heat of her blood coursing, the way her body hugged his cock so snug from having never been used in such a manner.

He never wanted to learn who she belonged to. This entire thing was a mistake; he knew it, she knew it, yet here they were. He withdrew a fraction, and she shifted under him, her body attempting to hold on to his like it belonged there.

He leaned over her as he pulled back, taking her ear between his teeth and sending a hiss of breath across her cheek. "What do you want?"

A small cry escaped her lips, then a small sob, and his already hard cock pulsed with more blood, demanding release.

"What do you want from me?" he yelled as he pushed back into her.

She cried out.

"Tell me to stop."

"No," she replied.

"Oh, now you have a voice."

"I always have a voice," she said between whimpers.

"Am I hurting you?" he asked in a sudden crisis of conscience—and it was a crisis because his conscience simply didn't care.

"Yes," she said, "and I want more."

He leaned back and pushed one hand through her hair, fisting the strands and pushing her into the bed as he held her hip with the other and pushed, and pushed, and pushed.

"More," she whimpered.

He pulled back as far as he could without leaving her body then pushed back in and picked up the rhythm until the only sound in the room was the slap of his balls against her pussy, his grunts against the air and her breath against the soft tick of the mattress.

His whole being buzzed like the new electricity that coursed this house. Mostly unproven, somewhat unsure, decidedly dangerous. In his life he'd never experienced a pleasure such as this. No one had given this to him, allowed this of him in such a selfless manner, invited his need and accepted his truth. It was a heady experience. How could he possibly give it up? His eyes burned deep in his skull and he closed them against it. Concentrated on the feel of this woman, the wet, the heat, the fear, as his pulse raced and focused as though his heart had slipped its mooring and traveled quite remarkably lower in his belly until it caught, unable to continue further until it shot the very life of him through his body quite uncontrollably, exploding against her womb.

He came off so hard he saw spots, the whole of his body tensing before he collapsed across her back, still moving inside her with the unrestrained jerks of his muscles, the heat of his seed flooding what space there was inside the condom.

She whimpered, and he tightened his hand in her hair, a warning. "You'll come off when I allow it," he said.

"Yes..." she said, hesitating.

"Madoc," he said. "You'll call me Madoc."

"Yes, Madoc."

He slid one hand beneath them, wrapping his other arm around her neck without withdrawing his cock. He gave her two long, languid strokes, angling his hips to push himself steady against the front wall of her pussy. "Now," he said and pushed his fingers to her clitoris. Her body shook and convulsed around him, her arms reaching for leverage against anything, finding his forearm and digging her nails there, which sent a shock so fierce he came off again. He yelled and doubled over, pushing her into the bedding then up onto the bed as he followed, unable to get himself deep enough, shocked to his core that it was even possible. When it passed, he collapsed on top of her fully, savoured the feel of her aftershocks on his flesh, the squeeze followed by the rapid butterfly-like spasms that held him in place. Madness.

He couldn't stay.

He withdrew from her body and his room, leaving her there.

He paused in the hallway water closet, disposing of the condom and relieving himself before putting his clothes to rights. Then he walked down to the front entry and threw the switch that would turn the electricity to the house back on. He walked across the entry to his study. He sat in front of the banked fire, his hand soothing his sated penis as he let his head fall back against the settee. What had he done? Exactly what he'd wanted to do since the moment he'd met her. What she'd wanted him to do to her. His lust was slaked in a way he hadn't ever felt before. His soul was quiet.

All he'd done was make the both of them happy, and tomorrow—tomorrow he would do what his Queen wanted of him. He would face the world and he would find his brother. And Willow? God. Willow. He had no idea what he was to do with her.

TEN

Willow lay partly off, but mostly on this massive bed of his, letting the weight of her body pull her off the side of it, sliding until one foot, and then the other, touched the floor. She kept her eyes closed against the darkness that surrounded her like a suffocating fog. She pushed her belly into the softness of the covers, trying to calm her racing heart and lungs. The lights switched back on before she'd even caught her breath, breaking the peaceful reverie. She pushed up from the mattress and stumbled, immediately turning to sit, since her legs were too wobbly to stand.

She slipped a hand between her legs, testing her vagina with one finger and wincing at the burn from the slide. It isn't necessary to tear a virgin open— unless you're a sadist. She pulled her finger back and pushed her whole hand against her flesh to sooth it. She'd never experienced anything like this in her whole life. She wondered if this was how it would always need to be with him, if this was how *she* would always want it—or need it. She wondered if now that he'd sated himself if he'd be done with her. Take her somewhere and leave her. Be rid of her, her smart mouth, and the hassle of her presence in his life.

She didn't think so. If he felt anything like she did, there was a lot more the two of them needed to do together. This wasn't over by a long shot. She closed her eyes against the sting and pulled her hand from between her wet thighs and leaned back on her hands.

This is just the beginning. It has to be. There was a piece of her that had taken that thread of a connection and bound it, making it stronger, not weaker. He had to have felt it as well, so why had he left her? Maybe he needed time to comprehend what had happened between them? She did. She definitely needed a moment, because what had happened was way more than what she'd expected.

She looked around the empty room, walked to the wardrobe, and reached for one of his shirts. She saw a streak of blood on her hand. She turned back to see the blood on the sheet, the partial hand print where she'd rested. If he were an ancient Viking, he would take this sheet and hang it from the window so the world would know that she belonged to him. Or was that the Scots? Whatever it was, all this blood was likely to do was anger him for ruining his new sheets.

She walked to the bathroom and stood in the bathtub, rinsing herself in the cold water, not waiting for it to warm for her. She dried herself with a towel that she left on the floor. She glanced at the bloodstains as she passed the bed but decided she wasn't wholly responsible for them, so she wasn't going to do anything about them. This was his bed. His space. If he'd made any effort toward making her comfortable in here, she might have felt the need to clean or tidy. He hadn't, and so she didn't. This was his space; he'd invited her here for a specific purpose and that being done, he quite clearly wished her to leave—and so she would. It didn't feel malicious, leaving a mess. It felt more...a thank you. He might actually appreciate the sight of her blood.

She turned back and pulled out one of his shirts, sliding it over her head. She pushed the shirts over, making a gap between the hangers at a waistcoat, and ran her fingers down the buttons. A shiver reminded her of the same buttons pressed along her spine. An aftershock, or a booster shock, from her recent orgasm traveled from the center of her chest straight to her clitoris, rushing it with blood and forcing a grunt that she failed to stifle as she bent forward, trying to relieve the pressure she felt from simply standing with her legs together. The awareness of her pulse was so strong there it was as though her own heart had relocated for a moment.

Once she gathered what was left of her composure, she turned and walked quietly and carefully from his room, her hand on the wall to steady herself the whole way back to her own. She took his shirt off, draping it over the back of a chair, before crawling into bed naked as the day.

She'd thought she would drift off easily, considering how exhausted she was, but she found herself staring out the shrouded windows to the dim light outside. She didn't want to sleep. She wanted to live these moments for as long as she could for fear of losing them altogether.

She heard the gentle creak of the stairs as she drifted. The warmth of his arm wrapped around her waist, his big hand spread out to hold her ribcage below her breast. He pulled her back against his frame. He was still fully dressed. She steadied her breath further, letting herself sink into a twilight sleep, soak in what it felt like to be in his arms. He probably had no idea she was awake. He tucked his face against her, the tip of his nose grazing her earlobe, his lips sending warm air across her shoulder, the strange warmth of a tear dropping to the sensitive skin behind her ear and sliding down her nape. It was the last thing she felt before her dreams took over.

When she woke, he was gone.

Willow dressed in his shirt and her drawers then wandered the house looking for him, knowing she wouldn't find him. When she came to his bedroom, the door was wide. It felt like an invitation so she stepped inside. The bed had been made, and she walked over to it running a hand up the edge. She'd felt perfectly welcome entering this room, but entering his bed—which was so closely made—was something entirely different. Nevertheless, she pulled back the blankets against the keen prick of invasion. The sheet had been changed—*he* had changed the sheet. She glanced around the room to see it looked exactly as it had before their...tryst. She opened the wardrobe and, save a single empty hanger in the row of shirts, everything was in perfect order. She ran her hand down the front of the shirt she wore, a certain possession taking hold of her senses. Surely he'd seen it the night before or this morning. He was observant enough that she knew he would have noticed it, and left it for her. As she remade the bed she wondered where the laundry went. What clothes he wore.

She spent the day cleaning random areas and rearranging the house to what she felt would be more useable and comfortable. When she wasn't working, she wandered the study looking for books to read. The majority of them were treatises and instruction manuals on various subjects, but with little else to do, she managed to make them interesting.

Upon his return, he professed how busy he was and disappeared inside the study, the door solidly closed. The unspoken command obvious. She spent the afternoon in the parlour across the hall, reading through the papers she'd collected. When the light began to soften, she heard a door creak, but no footsteps, no closure. So she put aside the reading and stepped into the entry. Across the foyer she could see the study door, still closed, but up the wall from where she stood she saw the servants' door to the kitchen stairs open. She followed.

He hadn't entirely abandoned her to herself; the stew he'd made the day before had been warmed and a bowl prepared and left covered on the butcher block for her. It was a strange feeling—being alone, but not alone. That she knew he was at home, somewhere, comforted her; that she knew he didn't want to speak with her discomfited just as much. She needed to know he was okay. More than that, she needed him to know she was.

After eating supper, she walked up all those stairs, taking the main cases as opposed to the servants walks. She had no idea where he was. It seemed all the doors to the house had been closed to her, relaying exactly where she was meant to be. The fire in her room had already been tended, probably while she'd been distracted by the stew in the kitchens. He was skulking around the house like a spirit, but she hadn't tried to cross any of the lines he'd set for her, so why was he doing this? Could he not stand the sight of her? Was he angry about the bedsheets? The towel? The shirt? Everything? Nothing? Was he disappointed? *Oh, God.*

She shook the concerns from her mind and undressed, laying her clothing across the chair, then crawling between the sheets. Even with the fire banked early, she was cold without him. She stared at the curtains until, like a ghost, he swept into her room, checked the fire, and joined her on the small bed. He did not allow her chatter. When she opened her mouth to speak, he shook his head slowly, his breath skating across the width of her shoulders as he did so. He was silently insistent about her going to sleep straight away. So she attempted as he wished, but hoped for more regardless.

The following day was much the same as the one before, and it troubled her that she fell into the pattern of it without much complaint. She'd always been rather compliant, particularly with dominant men. It had been an uneasy existence at times. She tended to defer to dominant personalities whether she wanted to or not, regardless if it was deserved.

It rankled at times, the whole of her psyche revolting against this visceral need to bow.

But with him it all felt so different. She wanted to bow to him, she wanted to force him to make her bow, and she also wanted to bring him to his knees and she knew, somehow, that she could.

It was odd, this small life she found herself in, and it wasn't until the next evening she realized she hadn't given much more thought to where she was and why she was here. Beyond her want to understand him, and her reactions to him, she hadn't given anything much thought.

That bothered her. She should have been trying to figure it out. The only reason she began to think of it now was because she'd run across a news article about changes to the systems of Bedlam, reminding her that should she open her mouth, she would end up there—whether this was a dream or real life. *Real life*—preposterous.

She didn't belong here in this Victorian existence. She'd managed to suss out that it was 1886 from one of the news sheets he'd left lying around in his study, and of course that they were in London. She'd actually reached for her phone when she'd seen it to compare the dates, but her phone, as with the rest of her life, was not here with her.

So beyond what she'd read in that news sheet, she'd no idea. 1886, though, was the year she'd been researching—trying to track down the birch mistress. London was the city she'd been researching. So if she was in a coma somewhere, then it stood to reason why she was in this place, in this time.

What showed true lack of reasoning was why she was with him. What purpose did he hold in this dream life? Was he the embodiment of every question she'd ever had when it came to sex and fear? He seemed created to answer those questions. Yet he was an anomaly; he hadn't existed anywhere beyond this dream even though she would swear she'd somehow felt his presence the whole of her life. He was as familiar as he was a stranger to her.

She would walk past his study and know he was in there. She would walk past the study and know when he *wasn't* in there. She knew when he was coming, when he left. The moment she felt him leaving, she would run to the window to look out. Without fail, he'd look up to her, as though he'd known she were there as well. But he wouldn't stop. He carried on—ascending the steps to the cab and with a whistle and a twitch of the reign, they'd be gone. Perhaps she was losing her mind. Perhaps this was more psychotic break than coma.

Whatever the reality was, she hoped this behavior wasn't a harbinger of things to come. Perhaps he was just as concerned about what they'd done as she was. Any decent human being would be, wouldn't they? He'd frightened her with cause. He'd come after her with the explicit purpose of terrorizing her and taking her virginity so she would then be able to...what, tell him what she wanted in bed? The problem was that since that night, there was only one thing she wanted in bed—him.

Madoc stared across the park towards his house. He'd nowhere to go but he couldn't stay here and at the same time he refused to be far from her. He wasn't getting anything done by sitting in the park, and yet he couldn't force himself to move from the spot. When he woke in the study, it was a constant battle to concentrate, to keep his distance. When he left the house, the need to return to her was a soul-deep tension.

He was entirely lost. He'd no idea what he should do next. He wanted to speak with his family and yet he didn't, because they would put an end to the woman in his house if they discovered her. Part of him, a very old—very young part of him, wanted to be friends with his brother and cousins again, but that part of him had been driven out so purposefully he wasn't sure he even remembered it faithfully. Certainly none of them were the same people now. The people they were before it all had gone wrong. He certainly wasn't, except...that he was, or he wished to be—to a certain extent. He wanted the family he remembered.

He didn't know how to do what it was he needed to do. Not with her, not with them, and not with himself. So here he sat in the middle of the small park in front of his manor. Doing none of what was required of him.

"I can't say I'm surprised to find you here." The voice came from just at the edge of his periphery, and Madoc stilled, the only sign of life his breath gently thickening the air in front of him. He would know his voice anywhere by its similarity to his own. Madoc ran one hand down his face, rubbing the bridge of his nose before turning to look at his brother who approached, quite intentionally, he was sure, from his right. Grayson would be met with the most prominent feature on his face, the scarring. Madoc waved at the bench in invitation, but Gray shook his head. "I'm passing through. I've no intention to— I've somewhere to be."

"Of course," Madoc replied; he heard the frustration in his brother's voice. Knew his brother didn't want to be here any more than he did. "I won't keep you."

"No, as you do not command me. Regardless your title, you won't keep me. That's something you should—" Madoc waved him off, uninterested in his posturing, and Gray fell silent, in direct contradiction of what he'd only just said. Probably out of habit, certainly not out of respect. Madoc smiled halfheartedly at the thought but didn't point out the fact to Gray. He wanted to be done with this conversation; he wasn't prepared for it at the moment. He wanted to think about Willow, and nothing else.

"Gray..." He considered his words for a moment. Should he grovel now? Should he hit his knees? Should he beg and plead for forgiveness? Should he attempt an explanation? Should he do what he wanted to and stand up and push back? "I wish for you to know that I don't expect to command you, or anyone."

"You...will not address me as a familiar. We are not familiars, you and I."

Madoc nodded. "Apologies, Lord—"

"Danforth is sufficient."

"Danforth." Madoc swallowed past the lump in his throat and attempted to continue, having been solidly reminded of his place in his brother's life. "We are not the same people we were. While I'm required to be here, forced to be, really—"

"You could face your crimes at court."

"Yes, that would certainly be the alternative. Thank you for the reminder." He was losing his patience. He looked up to his brother to ask him for silence. "As I was saying, regardless the position, I understand my true place in this family is not at all *in* this family. Please believe me when I say I understand that, particularly where you and Calder are concerned. I will not press the point beyond the request of my Queen."

"Better now?"

"Not at all. You're assuming my purpose."

"Am I? Did I misread the shackles?"

Madoc laughed stiffly. It was humorous. He had a point. "You heard the directives. You know what it is I'm tasked with."

"Calder," Gray said, and it wasn't at all a question but more of a warning to tread lightly.

"Yes. Calder. And you. What passed between you and I was caused and effected by our father, but what passed between Calder and I was very much of my own doing."

"He was but a stand-in. For me."

"This is true. Absolutely. But what I did with Calder—*to Calder*—was because of who he is, not because it was what I wished to do to you. If you had shown up, let's just say the same things would not have happened. You may not understand that without a great deal of consideration, but know that it is true, and for that I am painfully aware of the debt I owe him." Madoc considered for a moment. His intention in inviting Grayson to India had been to orchestrate his return. If he were being honest with himself, there'd been more to it than that. But Calder's arrival in his stead—

"Do you mean to blame *me* for what happened to him?"

"No! No—not at all. I only mean to say...I only mean that...the same wouldn't have happened to you."

"That may be, but even so, it doesn't change what you did *actually* do. That you—" Gray stopped when Madoc met his gaze head on, but Grayson turned his gaze away as though to chastise himself for saying something he shouldn't. "That is not a discussion between us. What is a discussion between us is what your intent was were I the one to find you."

"I never got that far," Madoc said.

"And you never will. But your intent is what counts at this point, and as the Queen is intent on us keeping her abreast of your... rehabilitation, it's necessary for you to make moves towards amends or some semblance thereof. But... I've no time for you today."

"You came to me."

"I did, pure curiosity."

"Should I call—"

"Absolutely not," Gray said, and Madoc was silent by the force of the pronouncement. "You are to go *nowhere near* my home and *my* wife. Not ever." Gray took a step towards him as his voice menaced quietly, his body shifting to threaten, and Madoc stood to face him out of sheer self-preservation.

"My wife," Madoc replied quietly before he could stop himself, and Grayson grabbed his lapels and brought him close. The anger emanating from his brother hit him in waves of heat like a slap to the face. He held his hands up between them. *His wife.* Cecilia had somehow slipped his mind. He shoved his brother away.

"She has never been, and never will be *your* anything. First and foremost, understand that. Whatever machinations you intend, she will have no part of. You'll find yourself dead before I allow it."

Madoc had never seen his brother so...determined. Powerful. Grandiloquent. "Threatening a member of Her Imperial Majesty's most cherished peerage, Danforth? Have you learned nothing from holding my title?"

"I've learned more than you could possibly know," he said then released Madoc's lapels with a shove that sent him reeling backwards before he caught himself against the bench.

Madoc forced the anger down into the pit of his stomach as he righted his clothing and straightened his countenance. A glance of light off a window caught his gaze and his memory was flooded with a blackness that held the memories of a more recent night with a different woman. He looked to his home. Knew she was looking out over the park. Possibly seeing him squaring off here against someone... How did this look to her? But for his own scarred countenance, the two of them had often been mistaken for the other.

Madoc held his hands up again, allowing his muscles to relax, his posture wilting, "Apologies for my…" He shook his head. He couldn't even force the thought to speech. He could still feel the anger of the loss of Cecilia like a living thing squirming against his belly and he tried to release it, but it wasn't something he was yet prepared to deal with. They'd known each other in every way but one. Her blood should have been his. He needed to know how their relationship had translated to his brother. He wanted to know how much she'd shared of them. How much of their privacy was now public. What did Grayson know of the kind of man he was? Was Gray a good husband to her?

Mads wasn't going to be allowed to deal with that now, though, if ever. And he certainly wasn't to be allowed to speak with Cecilia, and absolutely not in public. He knew he was the one who needed to beg for amends from his brother and cousin, possibly his former betrothed, but at the same time, he'd been wronged as well. He was not at fault for the actions that had sent their whole world into the spiral that had ended with him being tossed to the stones in front of the Queen. The men at fault for that were either dead or being held for judgment. Madoc was the only one, the lucky one, who had done any wrong and been set free. Why was that?

"Warrick," Gray said to him suddenly; it was the first time he'd heard the title spoken to him and it set him aback. "You have much to account for."

"I do," Mads replied, and Gray turned and walked away without another word. Madoc watched until Gray disappeared down a side street. He supposed that at this point there were no other words to suffice. He'd been chastised and threatened and accepted, of a fashion anyway. What more was there to do but return home? He sat down on the bench, leaning his head back and closing his eyes.

"The resemblance is not as strong as I expected, but it is truly striking."

Fuck-all. Another voice Madoc would know anywhere, though it seemed different somehow.

"If I hadn't seen it for myself, I never would have believed it."

Her voice was heavier, world-weary perhaps, more knowledgeable. He couldn't bring himself to look at her. He leaned forward resting his elbows on his knees. Gave thanks that Gray had left the way he had so she'd approached from his left. Blessedly. His forehead fell to his steepled fingers. Perhaps she was an apparition. The only way to find out for sure was to open his eyes and look. He didn't. He left her hanging, and she waited there complacently. He could feel her righteous indignation, her judgment, her pure hatred of him like a heavy soup, the scent of which wafted to him on the breeze.

She wasn't going away.

"Ceci," he said quietly, "you're going to get me killed."

Cecilia shrugged; he heard it in the shift of fabric. He knew it in the way he remembered her. A good shrug was the replacement for a whole host of comments that were beneath her notice. He opened his eyes to find her skirts just skimming the toe of his left shoe. The purple satin pleated in a low ruffle that ran the border of the skirt, which was certainly gathered at the back for a profound and perfectly gathered bustle. She stood tall with her hands held perfectly just below her waist, the ring—the duchesses ring glinting in the sun. Cecilia had always been meticulous—there would not be a single hair out of place. The wind dared not stir her for fear of retribution. She was born and bred to hold her title—how did she feel about losing it?

She'd been his perfect match. Unbidden, the face of Willow flared through his thoughts like an apparition, reminding him of what waited back at his house. The longer he did nothing about Cecilia, the more precarious his afternoon became. He stood again and turned to her.

"Listen," he started, but when he looked into her eyes, all thoughts fled as if he'd never considered what to say to begin with. "Who...?" He took a step forward, and her gaze narrowed. She was exactly as he remembered, so perfect—perfectly poised, perfectly beautiful—but there was something about her...those eyes, the hold of her chin, the pure hatred and defiance that emanated from her. Perhaps that was it; her disdain was directed at him. "Cecilia?" He reached for her. And then he remembered, *The resemblance is striking. If I hadn't seen it for myself, I would have never believed it.* Why would she say that? What was happening? He pulled his hand back a fist.

"Lady Danforth," she corrected, and her voice poured through him like whiskey, stinging all of his fresh open wounds.

"My Lady," he said quietly. "I...beg pardon for my— Are you truly— You know me." He pressed a hand to his chest. "You've known me to resemble my brother for all our life. Why would you comment—"

She twitched, and he noted her realization that she'd made an error somehow. "That's a speculation borne of insanity, Your Grace. You aren't attempting to soothe your wounded pride with the belief that I am anyone but who I say?"

He dropped his hands to his sides, exhausted. "No, My Lady, of course. It's my error," he said, but he couldn't stop inspecting her. He knew this body, easily; his hands had covered it in various ways. She'd allowed for a great deal of exploration, but that was where his acknowledgement ended. She didn't seem the same person at all. "I beg pardon," he said and found he meant it. He didn't know this woman. It must be a function of his absence.

She nodded, and something passed through him then, like a harness releasing its grip. He'd no interest in this woman at all, not anymore. He looked towards his home, considered the woman who waited there. How different she was from this woman. How different Cecilia was from back then as well. Cecilia had been more of a companion; they'd explored certain things...would she have allowed what Willow had? Never. He didn't need even a moment's contemplation to come to the realization. Though he'd tested her, tried her, attempted to get her to understand this need of his, she'd never conceded to any understanding of him. Her fear was much too formal—borne more of necessity and learned servitude than of need.

"Why have you come to me?" he asked.

"I wish to know your intentions."

He shook his head, placing his hands on his hips as he considered her. She was stunningly beautiful, that was an absolute, but she was no longer his. "All of my intentions?" he asked, a hand to his chest as though to pledge nothing but the truth.

She shrugged, and he laughed, just a short burst of recognition.

"I intend to do as the Queen has asked of me. Beyond that...I have no intentions."

Her eyes narrowed on him, then her arm shot out and she took hold of his neck as she slid her other hand into his coat under his arm and pressed. He tried to stop her, but a dizziness came over him, his vision swirling, his limbs useless. "Stay away from my family," she said.

He tried to nod, but any movement from him sent a searing pain through his arms to his fingertips. He looked into her eyes and attempted something akin to compliance. She released him and stepped beyond his reach. His hand went to his neck, feeling the three points where her fingers had seemed to reach past his throat to his very spine. "You're deadly."

"Quite," she replied. "You may deal with polite society in London, but believe me when I say I am no such thing. I will come for you if you hurt anyone in my family and I will have no qualms with ending you."

"Christ."

Her head tilted to one side as she inspected him, her face expressionless in its porcelain beauty. God, she was beauty personified just as he remembered, but still she was not *his* Cecilia.

"I have no ill intent towards *your* family. I only wish to follow Her Imperial Majesty's orders to the letter and live as quietly as possible in service to the Crown. My only available option."

"I hope this is true. If you need..." She paused, pulling back from whatever it was she nearly said. "Apologies— your similarity to my husband is clouding my judgment," she said, and he saw the cracks by which everyone in his family could be reached. She knew nothing of him in reality. She only knew stories. He didn't understand why.

"I will not use you against my brother, yet I *am* required to repair my relationships as best I can. I will not speak with you behind his back after today. I will not pursue any sort of relationship with you, as that in itself would destroy what trust I may be able to build with my brother. Now you need to leave."

She nodded, and something in her eyes told him she approved. Her eyebrow went up. "In that case, I'll see that you receive appropriate invitations to begin your..." she waved a hand in the air, "what do we call it? Your readmission to society?"

He felt the pull of his scar against a frown. He'd prefer to stay hidden. This forceful reintroduction to society, to family? Not something he had any interest in, yet here it was. "Thank you. I will look for them. I imagine I would not receive a single invitation without your intervention and therefore...if I am invited, you may expect my attendance. Much as I have an aversion to showing my face in society."

"Concerned someone will come looking for revenge?" she asked and he grimaced—he shouldn't have said anything, because his discomfort was more personal than that. Revenge was easy. "The scar." He winced at her words. "The Dowager Duchess of Greensborough has seen fit to hold a masquerade. That might be good for your first foray in public, I imagine."

He considered it. That could either work in his favour or be disastrous, but he figured any appearance in society could end up that way. He took a deep breath. "I will attend if she sees fit to invite me."

She nodded, cast a glance around the park then gave him one more stern look. "Don't even think about following me." Her words and tone were odd and reminded him of something he couldn't quite put a finger on.

He held his hands up and moved back to the bench, once again taking a seat. He watched as she walked from the park, quick yet controlled. She went to a carriage, and the footman opened the door and she disappeared inside. Mads leaned forward, taking a closer look at the carriage which...seemed to have emblems blacked out on the doors. He shook his head and closed his eyes. Well. That explained why the stables in the mews were barren.

ELEVEN

illow didn't have any idea who the woman was but she could see, once she approached the carriage near the front of the house, just how beautiful she was. Beautiful and cold or perhaps just determined. And yet there was something so familiar about her. She wanted to stick her face out the window and yell. Or wave. She had a compulsion to get the woman's attention and talk to her; it was unlike anything she'd felt before except...with Madoc. She managed to resist though. She knew Madoc would not be happy about something like that. The woman looked up to the window, and in her haste to get out of view, Willow tripped, falling back to the floor and taking a curtain panel down with her.

"Noooooooooo," she said quietly, the fabric settling over her head as it pooled around her. She was going to be in so much trouble if he found out. She untangled herself and crawled to the window to look down, doing her best not to stir the remaining curtain. The woman was already in the carriage, the conveyance tipping as the driver mounted the box. The curtains on the door were swept aside by a single gloved hand, and Willow ducked beneath the window sill. She waited until she heard the skid of the carriage wheels on the cobblestones, the metallic clank of the horse's tackle as it rumbled down the street. She lifted one more time to see where Madoc was through all of this, but he was gone.

She rolled to her back and just lay there on the floor, hoping he wasn't on his way here.

Part of her wished she'd been seen by that woman. That she'd been discovered. It was probably because she felt so alone, that she had no friends, that she simply yearned for someone to speak with, a friend. Why she thought that woman would make a good friend, she'd no idea.

She started to move and her hand brushed against the manuscript she'd been reading before getting distracted by the shenanigans in the park. She lifted it. The manuscript was a study of the LaBouchere amendment, which had been passed in 1885, attached to a bill for the protection of women and children. It had been in a stack of papers and treatises on his desk. Good to know politicians hadn't changed much over time. Laws were a fascinating and integral part of all of that research because everything was connected. So as long as she was here, she might as well continue her research. This treatment included all the arguments from parliament as well as the final vote and the swift repercussions, though there weren't many listed. It was crazy to think that a law like this one hadn't changed all that much over the decades.

Centuries. Because she was in Victorian England. Or a coma. Or she'd suffered some sort of psychotic break and she was already in Bedlam or whatever the modern equivalent was. She closed her eyes and threw her arm over her face, her nose snug in the crook of her elbow. At some point she was certain she was going to break...again. Or for the first time. This was all so...impossible. Madoc had told her flat-out not to trust him. But she needed very much to have someone to talk to. It just was all a perfect impossibility.

"I brought the settee up here so you wouldn't have to laze about on this floor," he said with little masking of his disdain. She'd grown up hiding in orchards to avoid chores; a bit of dirt had never upset her.

She sat up but as embarrassed as she was, she couldn't turn toward him. She pulled her knees up beneath her chin, wrapping her arms around them. He came over and faced her, leaning his hips against the windowsill, his arms crossed over his chest, stealing the breath from her. He'd once again removed his coat. His relaxed nonchalant demeanor was more proper than she'd ever been in the whole of her life. She supposed that was a remainder of his high birth. The son of a duke after all. An *actual* duke, for pity sake.

"You saw her?" he asked.

"I did." She wasn't sure the safety of this admission, considering she was supposed to be staying out of sight. "She's beautiful," she replied finally.

"Yes. She is that." He looked to the floor, adjusting his stance.

"Who is she to you?"

"She..." he started, and his gaze went out the window over his shoulder to where they'd spoken together next to that park bench. "She was to be my Duchess." The admission was quiet.

"Oh. But...not now?" she asked, and he shook his head.

"No, not now. Now she's wed to my brother."

"Oh that's..." She wasn't sure what that was, but gauging from his response, some part of him was disappointed in that. She tamped down the jealousy that burbled in her gut. "I'm sorry."

"Don't apologise. There's nothing you could have done, nothing you did. It simply wasn't meant to be," he said then his gaze caught hers and as hard as she tried to shy away, she couldn't. His eyes narrowed on her as he considered her, and she felt exposed, like she'd been laid out naked. For him. She wasn't of course. She was as clothed as she could be for a person with no wardrobe to speak of.

She curled in on herself, attempting to make her presence as small as possible, because that look made her feel like jumping all over him and she had the distinct feeling that wasn't a good idea. He shook his head then released her from his gaze. "She may not be mine, but she is family, and I have amends to make with my family. She's to arrange for an invitation and perhaps from there..." He shrugged. Something she hadn't seen him do. Madoc used words with the precision of a razor. It seemed beneath him to use an action as simple as that to convey words.

"You still love her?" she asked and immediately wished she could take it back. This jealousy wasn't hers, just like this life wasn't hers. There was no reason for it. She ducked her face behind her legs, avoiding the look she knew he was giving her. She saw the shadow of him and heard the creak of his leather boots, the slide of fabric, before she felt his hand coax her head up to look at him. He was crouched in front of her, examining her. "I shouldn't have... I have no right. I don't know why I—"

"It's not an apology, but it serves the same purpose, so you'll stop." He took a deep breath as he considered her. "You've no cause to be jealous," he said finally, then he pulled his hand back but his gaze refused to allow her to look away. "Whether because our relationship doesn't warrant it or because there's naught to be jealous of." He stayed there, his elbows on his knees as he once again inspected her. "I'm no longer entirely sure I ever loved her. What we had was a contract and a...friendship or companionship borne of that contract. Nothing more than that. I thought there was more but I must have been mistaken." He stood and walked past her. "There are only a couple of days left before the staff moves into the house. We need to... I don't know. You can't be here."

"I know. But I have nowhere to go." She felt so inconsequential.

"You don't know anything?"

"Nothing you're willing to discuss," she snapped, and his stillness washed over the room, settling even the dust motes in sun.

"Perhaps…perhaps it's time for us to have that conversation."

She shivered. She wasn't sure if his change of heart was because he was willing to be sure of her safety or because he was tired of a stranger in his home. She didn't know what to tell him but she knew she needed to figure it out pretty quick.

"I'm going to warm the stew. When you're ready to talk, come to the kitchen." He turned and left. His footsteps became faint in the hallway, and fainter still as he descended the stairs, leaving her alone in this room. It felt rather like a tower at the moment, and she Rapunzel in need of a good hair piece. And a chef. She was becoming tired of his stew.

As the stew warmed, the fat melted back into the heavy thickness of it and he stirred, mesmerized by the swirls. The chai was steeped but would soon cool, and he had yet to hear a sound from above stairs.

He continued to stir. He needed to keep her safe—whatever that meant. Not knowing to whom she belonged was the biggest problem, and thus he would need to know everything she could tell him in order to discover what it was he needed in order to protect her. He needed information. He could do nothing without it, and if he knew everything, he would find a way to protect her.

He still wasn't sure he should know the things he needed to know. She'd made it sound like it would put her sanity to question, which was perilous for her, but only for as long as he'd no responsibility for her.

"Hi."

He turned at the small word, wondering at the fact that she'd snuck in here without making him aware. He couldn't let his defences down so easily. It wouldn't do either of them any good. She perched on one of the stools at the butcher block, her elbows on the surface, her hands twisted together, hiding most of her face.

"Hello." He ladled a bowl of stew and handed it to her then made one for himself and poured the tea. Then he sat across from her. "Tell me who you are."

"Everything?"

"Let's just start with who you are and where you come from. Let's concentrate on the facts of your life to start, and then we'll fill in as needed." He figured that would be a safe enough place to start.

"Okay." She stirred the liquid in the bowl, then took a sip. It was a bit hot so she sucked a little air in and put the spoon down. "My name is Willow Jameson Jones. I'm originally from a very small town in Colorado, the United States. I currently...or, um—" She stopped, shook her head, closed her eyes and attempted to catch her breath. "I thought I wanted to be a doctor. I thought I wanted to study the treatment of chronic pain. But I realized at some point that my obsession with pain wasn't outwardly focused or quite so technical. It was more psychological than medical. I moved to Los Angeles to attend FIDM after seeing an exhibition about clothing that was designed to kill, designed to protect, designed for beauty— but killed by accident.... This is too much information, isn't it?" she asked, he shook his head and urged her to continue.

"Please, tell me more."

"I studied the history of design. After I graduated, I moved to New York City with my degree and the hope that I would find a position in the Metropolitan Museum of Art, where I would have access to the world's most incredible archives. Eventually I was lucky enough to land an internship. I've worked there for about five years and finally got the chance to assist on curating a show about the Victorian underground. That brought me to London to research an infamous birch mistress. I'd found evidence of the mistress in several articles at the Maughan from 1886 that referenced The Iron Duke, but they were closing. I took pictures with my phone and decided to walk back to my hotel on Grosvenor. I stopped at The Iron Duke—" She paused, and he realized it was his fault.

He remembered the night he'd brought her here like it was engraved in his mind. Every single moment of it. He ran a hand down his face to clear whatever expression had stopped her, then he nodded for her to continue once again. "It was a drag show—um—men dressed as women lip-syncing to popular music. I saw the carving on the wall. The next thing I remember, I was here. With you." She paused, and he watched as her breathing stilted, though she did her best to control it. "In the dark." The words were almost inaudible as they reached out to caress his senses. She had to know what she was doing, but he needed to get her back to the point of all this.

"I've heard of Los Angeles and New York City. I'm not familiar with the museum you're referring to, but The Iron Duke is familiar to me, obviously. Those pieces are simple. But researching a birch mistress for an exhibit about the Victorian Underground...that... brings me pause." It wasn't possible that she was searching for the same Mistress Maggie he knew, though it seemed so. It had taken months for his connections to track her down before he'd returned, but they had found her. "You didn't mention family."

"They don't deserve mention. We had a final falling out."

"Over?"

"Politics. My life simply doesn't fit with their paradigm."

"What else?

"I was born on June fourteenth, 1991. I was researching the museum on June sixth, 2018. From what I understand from a news sheet I found in your study, it's 1886. These are the facts as I understand them. My entire life in one paragraph...or two," she said with a sad smile.

It took a moment for him to register that he was staring, that his heart was racing, but his breathing wasn't keeping time. The noise that roused him was the clatter of his spoon to the table—he realized on some level—but he could neither prevent it nor anything else that happened as he watched her. He leaned back, steadying himself with both hands on the block. "It's not possible."

"I understand. I do. And I've been wrestling with the idea that perhaps I've died, or I'm in a coma, or I'm insane and I've been committed or...believe me, I've considered everything. If you have any ideas..."

"I'll consider everything you've said. I have too many ideas to list but—"

"But you hesitate to share them because you also think I'm mad. *We're all mad here*," she said with a small laugh before going on. "What I'm telling you is impossible. I understand that. I also understand that it's asking a lot for you to trust me. But I need you to understand how alone and terrified I am. Consider that if what I've told you is true...just consider..." Her shoulders fell and she seemed to shrink away from him. He could feel the fear come off her, but it wasn't quite the flavour he appreciated. This fear brought out his protectiveness, demanded he believe everything she said and it went against everything he knew to be true except for a single fact. She was here, and she was his. Somehow in his deepest soul he knew she already belonged to him.

"You can trust me," he said, and her gaze flew to his, so hopeful it made something in his chest ache. "Eat. You need strength."

She nodded, pushing the stew around in the bowl. "You have people coming soon, maids and such. What happens then?"

"You'll take a position in my household," he said then considered. "Something that will allow for you to be in contact with me often and won't draw concerns. Household manager would require you to be in charge of the others, so that won't do. Perhaps a cousin of indeterminate origin. That should suffice for now." He nodded. It would work, perhaps. Everyone had cousins, and nobody would argue with him. Except perhaps his own cousins, but they weren't even speaking with him, much less challenging anything he said. "You'll move to the family suites."

"I like my room upstairs," she complained but then she glanced up and whatever she saw in his countenance had her concede. "Tell me where to go. Most of the rooms are still uninhabitable save yours and the master's quarters."

"Then take his rooms."

"They're yours you know. You're the master, the Duke."

"I do know, but those rooms will not be mine."

"Won't your household comment on my being there?"

"Not if they wish to remain in the household. You liked the shower, now it's yours."

He watched her stifle the smile that brought to her unbidden and in return stifled the bloom of warmth through his chest. He turned to the hearth to refill his bowl. "Tomorrow will bring a chef. Let them know the food you prefer."

"The stew was good, just maybe not every day," she said quietly, and it warmed him.

He sat back on the stool across from her. "So let's assume, for the sake of argument, that you have come to me by some trick of time. What happens next?"

"I don't know. A week ago, I would have believed this impossible. I don't know how to feel about it today. Every time I wake up in your home, I'm struck by the thought that I'm exactly where I'm supposed to be. But that is so incongruent with the whole of my life." Not to mention reason and sanity.

"You believe you belong here?" he asked then watched her, carefully taking note of her every move, shift and physical tell.

"I feel as though I do. I can't explain it beyond that. In all my life I've never felt like I belonged anywhere. I've never been at ease. But I came to be here, and you... I don't know how to tell you how this feels to me," she said and lifted a hand to her chest. "I feel a connection to you specifically." She tightened her hand into a fist, pushed her knuckles into her chest as she closed her eyes and seemed to fight whatever it was she held on to, but as she pushed, he felt a responding tug in his own chest. "Though I did wish to be discovered by that woman, which in itself was an odd and unwelcome feeling because I do not want to be taken from here. It's you—" her gaze caught his, "—I feel a particular connection to. Impossibly."

He looked away, not wanting her to see anything in his countenance that might give away the thought that he knew exactly what she spoke of, because he did. He felt it as well. This intangible pull to her, this...rope that bound him, took the air from his lungs whenever he walked away, and gave it back when he was returned to her.

Insanity. He finished his stew and rinsed the dish in the great sink then reached for hers. She was watching him so closely a chill rushed his spine. He turned away but could still feel her gaze and was thoroughly unnerved by it.

"You feel it too," she said, her voice suffused with hope.

He dropped the bowl to the sink, the pottery clattering. He did feel it. And he couldn't steady himself enough to lie to her.

He needed to put a stop to this somehow.

TWELVE

He stood there, his back to her. His hands pressed to the edge of the sink, the tension a visible thing in the ripple of muscle across his back as he stiffened, held on. Dropped his head forward. "I may not understand any of what's happening, but I do understand I need to keep you safe. As irrational and out of...the realm of reason it is, it is one thing I know to be true. I feel it, to my very core, to the depth of my soul. So trust in that if nothing else. For whatever reason, I am charged with your protection and keeping, and I will do so to the utmost of my ability." His voice was rough like the sound of those carriage wheels on the rough cobbles of the street, tension barely bound by iron strapping attempting to shudder loose.

"I believe you. I trust you," she said quietly.

"So be it then. I have work to complete in my office. You...have the house." He left the kitchen, and her, without looking back.

She wasn't sure what she was supposed to do next. Was she to move her meager things to the master's quarters now? Should she stay in the upper rooms until tomorrow? She had so many questions and knew she wouldn't be getting answers, at least not tonight. Tomorrow the staff would arrive, and she still didn't have clothing. She supposed she did need to move to the family rooms. She cleaned up what was left from dinner and walked upstairs to her room. She didn't particularly want to leave it. She wasn't exactly keen on staying in a room he'd a specific aversion to. One she didn't understand. Because if he hated those rooms, he may not come find her in them. And that would hurt.

She gathered the fabric and torn clothing, realizing she had nothing here. Nothing but what she'd brought with her, which was quite literally the clothing on her back. She gathered it regardless and walked from the room.

When she entered the massive suite, it looked the same as it had the first day she'd found it but was now, somehow so much more grand. Poignant. The room spread out before her, the size and decoration only now overwhelming to her as she looked around. It was a beautiful room, and she was an intruder to whatever had been shared here. It was like the ghost of a relationship lived between these walls. People she'd never, and most likely would never, know.

Perhaps that was what she shared with Madoc. He didn't want to have anything to do with this room either, his reasoning surely a bit more involved than hers, but she felt it regardless, this feeling of intrusion. She didn't belong anywhere in this house except with him, and she was most definitely an intruder in here.

She dropped her things on the cushioned bench at the foot of the bed and turned to the hallway, moving quicker when she heard the unmistakable sweep of his heavy door at the end of the opposite hall. She bolted. She knew if he closed the door she would lose all nerve.

"Madoc!"

The door stopped, but he didn't come from behind it.

"I'm—" It bothered him when she apologized, so she stopped herself. "I need things. You expect me to be a cousin, but I have nothing, no traveling clothes...no clothes to speak of. I'm not sure how to manage any sort of ruse or...how do I explain this to your staff?"

She heard him shift, but he still didn't come from behind the door. After a moment he spoke. "I will obtain clothing for you tomorrow. They have ready-to-wear items at Harrod's. I'll arrange for a seamstress to come to the house. Tomorrow I will inform the staff upon arrival that you have been ill and wish to be left alone."

"Okay," she said, twisting her hands together so she didn't pry the door wider. She waited, but he said nothing more. Then the door began to close once again.

"Madoc." She said it quietly this time, and the door stopped but did not reverse course. Again. "I'm afraid of the room, I don't...I don't feel welcome there."

"It's nothing but a room."

"If that's true, then why don't you use it?"

The door closed, leaving her alone in the darkening hall. She sniffed, let out a breath, then turned and walked back to the room he'd given to her. By the time she'd reached it, it was dark. The fire was not lit, and she feared he would not come. She walked over to the massive fireplace and decided burning down the house was a bad

idea for a guest. He was already annoyed by her presence enough as it was. She removed his shirt and her drawers and carried them to the bathroom. She washed them both by hand then hung them on a towel rod to drip dry before entering the shower room. She realized this room was lit entirely by exterior lights, which was probably a good thing considering the amount of water involved, but it made it difficult to use at night. She turned back to the bathtub and ran water for a bath. It would feel good, to soak in a tub of hot water. Perhaps if she relaxed enough, sleeping would be less trouble for her.

She placed the plug and let the tub fill. She pulled oils from a shelf and smelled each one pouring some into the water as the heat rose and filled the room with a heavy curtain of steam. She breathed deeply of the scent of it, lavender and calendula, both soothing her as she tested the water and stepped into the tub. She leaned back, then slid down as far as she could, closing her eyes and doing her best to quiet her thoughts.

She was more at ease thinking of him than anything else. She avoided thoughts of family, of home, of where she was, of where she should be, of what could be happening. Her heart rate quickened in her breast and placed a hand there, her other on her belly, breathing into her diaphragm to calm herself as she shifted her thoughts back to him. His broad, heavy shoulders, the smaller waist and curve of his lower back. The way his ass had felt against her palm when he'd pushed against her, how it would feel if he were pushing into her.

She swallowed and slid her hand lower in the water, teasing and soothing. If she came, she would be too exhausted to stay awake. It had always taken so much effort for her to orgasm that she didn't bother with it often. This time though...she thought of the darkness he brought to her. The fear he gave her. The gift she accepted so readily. She slid her hand across her mons, her fingers slipping into the folds of her vulva, skimming over her clitoris, and she nearly came at first glance. Her body jerked, water sloshing over the edge of the tub.

Fuck. Her mouth dropped open on a breath as her lungs started pumping oxygen to compensate for the amount of blood rushing her system, then she touched herself again. She slid her other hand from her now-racing heart to one of her breasts. She let her head fall to the rolled edged of the tub, her feet pushing to the opposite edge to anchor her, her toes curled against the metal.

"Madoc." As she came, she couldn't help but to beg, "Please, Madoc."

He wasn't hard enough to fuck her. That was the single thought he had while he stood at the entry to the bathroom and watched her pleasure herself. Her eyes closed tight, her breathing stilted and catching. And when she'd said his name, he'd almost thought she knew he was here, that she was calling to him. Wanted him to come to her in the bath, to touch her, to take her. But he couldn't even if she'd wanted him to. Not yet. He would need more from her first.

She slipped lower in the water, her body lax and sated from her orgasm, and he shifted purposefully against the door frame. As she straightened in the tub, her eyelashes fluttered, drops of water hitting her cheeks when her eyes opened. When her gaze met his, him standing there watching, she flushed more, the pink of her skin from her orgasm deepened to the red of humiliation and now, now he could fuck her if he wanted to. He adjusted himself and her eyes followed and just like that he knew she wanted him as well.

She slid back in the tub as far as she could, pressing herself against the higher back, her feet slipping on the porcelain surface, not finding enough purchase to hold her steady. She covered her eyes, whimpered. She wasn't afraid but she was something that held sway for him. He took one step toward her, then another.

She turned and curled in a ball. "No," she said quietly. He stopped.

"I'll light the fire, shall I?" he asked. She nodded but didn't move. He left her there and went into the main bedroom and did as he said he would. When he turned from his task, she was there. She had a heavy towel wrapped about her, her hair wet and dripping to the skin she'd already dried.

"I'm sorry," she said quietly, and he tensed. He knew she was aware of it when she shook her head and almost apologised again. She bit her lip as if to stop the string of apologies he knew she wanted to let out. He waited until she calmed.

"I assume you've healed?" he asked.

"Healed?"

"There was quite a lot of blood on my sheets. I assume now that you've healed."

She flushed red all over once again, then nodded.

"I didn't want to..." He waved a hand towards her but her eyes were still closed and he wasn't sure what to say. There had been enough blood to frighten him. She'd seemed well, had behaved well, but he hadn't wanted to cause her further pain—not without permission. And so he'd left her alone. "Get in bed," he said and she did, letting the towel slide to the floor beside the bed after covering herself with the bedclothes.

She opened her eyes then, and took him in head to toe and back again. He wore naught but his drawers, since he'd intended only to come in here and sleep behind her, as he had every night she'd been in his house. Her eyes widened, and he realized this was the first time she'd seen him—so much of him—and he rotated his body away

from her view, attempting to hide the parts of him that horrified. When he turned his head to look at her, her eyes were closed, but she wasn't sleeping and he knew...he knew she did it for him.

"Don't," he said then waited for her to open her eyes. He wasn't sure why her seeing these scars affected him so much, but it did. She watched him and he turned, the firelight making a horror of his body, but she bit her lip again and waited. She was compliant, and it did something powerful to him. He walked to the bed and pulled the blankets away as she held on to the single sheet and curled her body to cover herself. He shook his head, and she stopped. "Do you want me to leave?"

"No," she whispered.

"Do you want me to stop?"

"No."

"Do you...want me?"

"Yes."

"Will you let me look at you?"

"Yes." She straightened beneath the sheet, and he took it between his fingers, right at her hip, and pulled it down. Her skin reacted to the drift of fabric, as did her nipples when the sheet passed over them. They were dark, the same colour as the inside of her lips. The buds tightened beneath his gaze. He realized then that he hadn't ever seen her either. Not really.

He ran a hand down the curve of her shoulder to her elbow, then across to her waist and back up the edge of her ribs. He lifted it from her skin just at the edge of her areola, let his fingers hover there, absorbing the heat of her body. Her shoulders came off the bed, filling his hand with her breast as her head pushed back into the pillow, and she let out a small groan.

"Madoc," she said on an inhale, and he wished his body would respond to that, because the sound of his name on her arousal was something to behold. He watched as she licked then bit her lip. He moved his hand to her other breast, hovering there until her body replayed the same movement for him. As though he were a conductor, her body the orchestra, her arousal the symphony.

He needed to make her come off. Needed it. He closed his eyes and remembered what she'd looked like in the bath, how his name had soared on her climax. He put his hands on her ribcage, his thumbs framing her breasts, and he picked her up and turned her so her legs hung from the edge of the bed on either side of his hips. He pushed her back against the bed with one hand and dropped to his knees, shouldering her legs and putting his face in her pussy.

His senses filled with her. Her scent, her taste, her feel... She twisted on the bed at the shock of it all but didn't tell him to stop. She thrust her mons against his mouth and tangled her fingers in his hair and pulled him into her pussy with a heavy sigh, and he inhaled her like a man starved for breath.

She reached down and took one of his hands from her thigh and brought it to her nipple. He skimmed his thumb over the small bud, bringing it back to the stiff peak it had been before. She put her hand over his and squeezed his fingers as she pushed herself against his tongue. She wriggled, and pinched him again. He took her nipple between his thumb and finger and pinched it. She shook, and whimpered, then she took his fingers and spread them wide against her skin and showed him how far he could go.

He slowed his oral ministrations, gazing up the beautiful, soft curve of her belly, waiting until she looked down at him through the valley of her breasts. When she did, he tightened his fingers, making dents in her flesh. She nodded, he squeezed harder, her breath stilled and she nodded again. He let go, adjusted her breast in his hand and squeezed once more, knowing she could bruise from the strength of it. She screamed, pulling his face closer as she came off, her swollen flesh giving a wetness he couldn't deny.

He slipped one finger between her folds at his chin, savoured the sweet aftershocks of her orgasm, pushed into the softness above her pelvic bone and circled until she writhed against him one more time. Her breath broke on delicate sobs as she tried to sip the air, but her breathing was so heavy he didn't think she could scream even if she'd wanted to. Her heels pressed into his shoulder blades, her entire body tensed, trapping him there at the apex of her body for what felt like forever as a sweet, sharp burst of flavour slicked him and she convulsed on his tongue, pulsed around his finger, and pushed into his spine with her curled toes.

He pulled his hand back, running the blunt edge of his fingernails up and down the outside of her thigh as he licked and soothed her, waiting for her to be done with him. Eventually she was. Her legs fell away from his shoulders and her hands pushed his face from her body. He stood and picked her up, turning her on the bed, putting her head on the pillow and covering her with the sheet. Then he went to the bathing room and splashed water on his face, drinking, cooling himself off. Never had he experienced such…emotion. She was wickedly spent, and he was devastatingly ruined for all others. This wasn't normal…this wasn't just fucking; this wasn't what two people shared in the expense of an evening. This was so much more and he knew it. She had to know it too.

He put his whole head into the sink and rinsed his hair, the back of his neck, letting the cool water sooth his skin as it tightened the muscles and frustrated his scars. He pulled back, pressing a hand flat against his ruined face to soften it, then dried his face and neck, his hands, before he wet a clean towel and took it back to the bedroom for her. He cleaned her, cared for her, then crawled beneath the sheets behind her. He moved to get close to her, but she rolled towards him first, catching his waist and pulling herself into his side. He wrapped an arm around her, held her tight laying back on the soft bed. He didn't even mind that her cool fingers played along the valley of the scar at his waist.

THIRTEEN

As she'd fallen to sleep, she'd expected to wake alone again, so when the light came and she wasn't, she remained as still as possible.

"I know," he said quietly, the sound coming more through the wall of his chest than his mouth, "that you're awake."

She giggled then put her fingers to her mouth to stop. He pulled them away. Placed them back at his waist, next to the scar. Her breath caught. "Will you tell me about it?" she asked, tracing through the hills and valleys of it, stopping when his abdomen tensed against her, moving when he managed to relax again. But he didn't push her away, so she kept at it, learning the topography of his damaged skin.

There was one large rill that ran down from his neck, seemed to travel his collarbone, where she could tell the bone wasn't shaped quite how it should be. The scar came down from a large callous on that bone, split in a V as it came to his nipple. The outer line of the scar bent at his waist, tracing the line of his external oblique before meeting the other scarred line and disappearing below the waistband of his pants. The entirety of it had badly puckered, as though the repair had not been done well, or done too quickly. It was the triangular patch over his lower abdomen that she skated her thumb back and forth across until he stopped tensing at her touch. His skin there was soft and perfect somehow.

His hand came down over hers like a lead weight, and she knew her time was up.

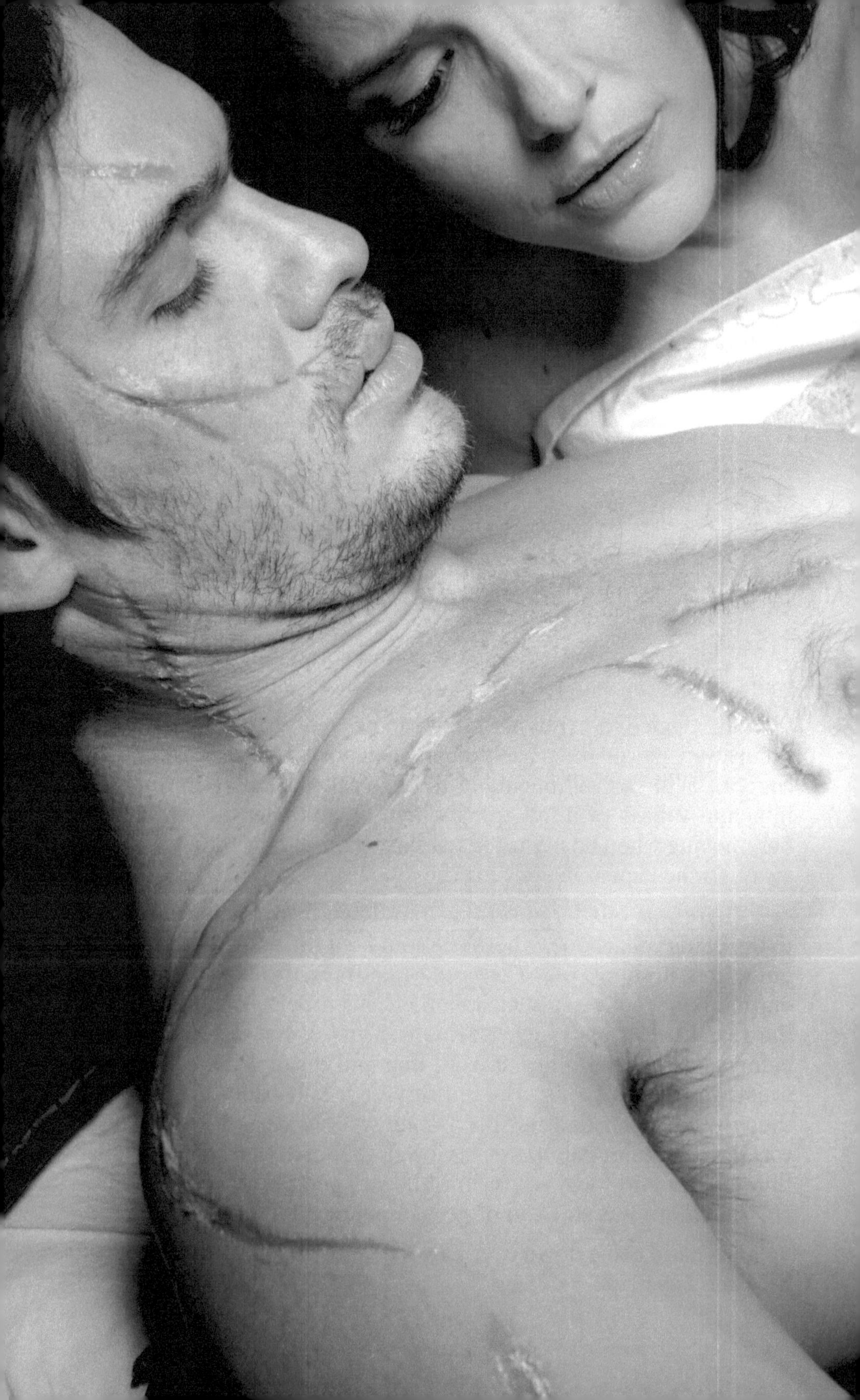

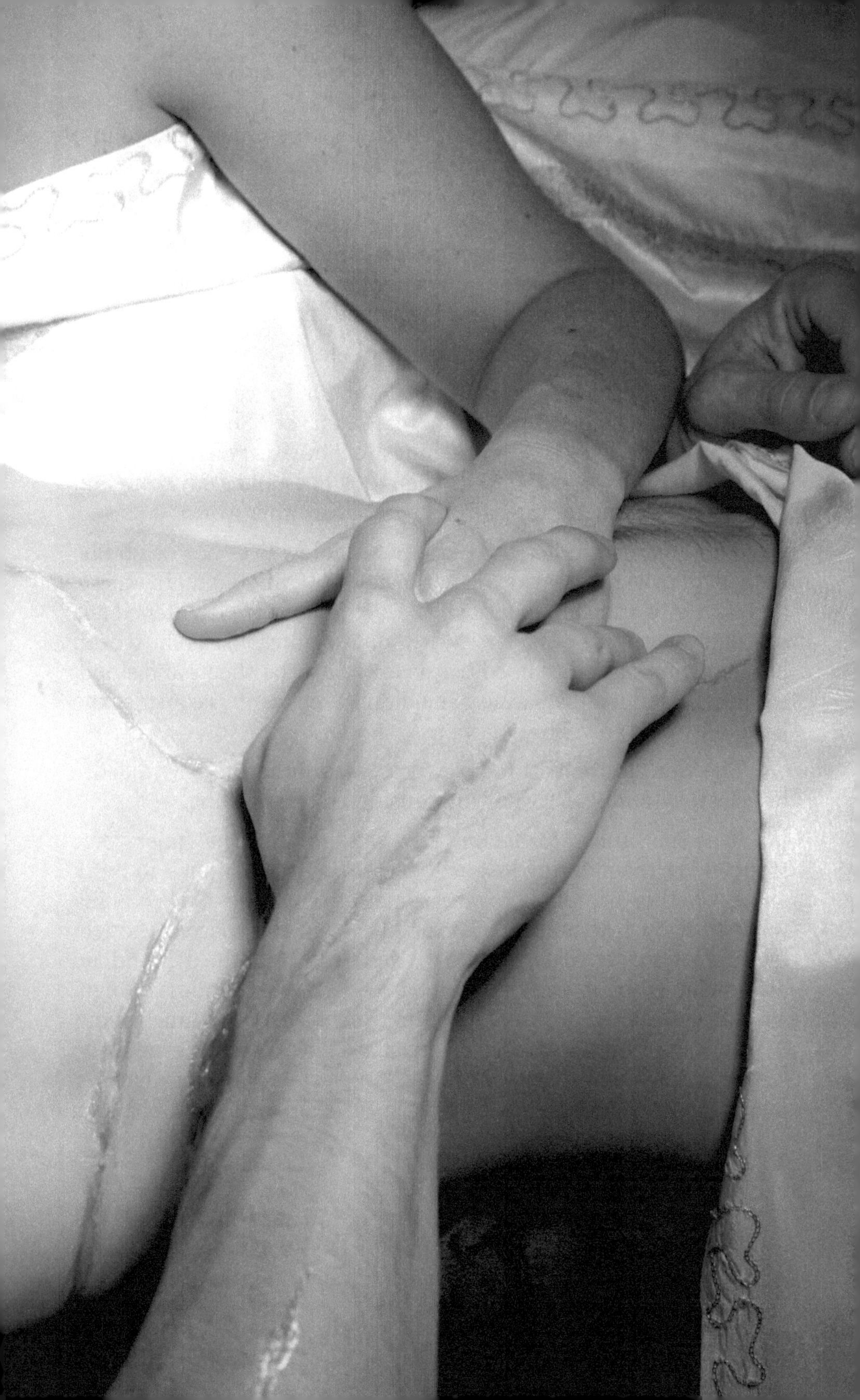

"I have to…" He didn't finish the sentence, so she snuggled into his side and closed her eyes, taking deep breaths and pulling the scent of him into her lungs. The cinnamon and spice, the sweat and skin. She let out a deep breath, and he rolled toward her, pushing her to her back. "I. Have. To get up. You are in need of clothing, and the household will arrive today. I cannot make excuses for your lack of attire for long. I should have done something much sooner, but—"

"But you were still trying to be rid of me."

His eyes closed for a moment and he nodded once, the expression on his face strangely pained from…regret, maybe? She ran her hand down his cheek, like she was brushing away the worry. He turned his face into her palm and kissed it. Then took her hand away from him and stood, walking for the hallway without another word.

Willow rolled to her belly and put a pillow over her head. She wished there were an easy explanation for all of this, but there wasn't, and the more attached to him she became, the more frightened she was that she would be taken away without warning, just as she'd been put here. She sniffed, rubbed her nose against the sheets and stood, wiping the sudden tears away. She didn't even want to consider the possibility of it now. She couldn't.

She went to the bathroom and dressed in her now wrinkled—but clean—clothing. Or what she considered her clothing.

Was she broken for feeling how she did? No. Her inner voice stopped her maundering just as it began. She wasn't going to think about whether or not there was something wrong with her being turned on by fear and pain. That had been unexpected though, because of the boyfriends who'd tried pain and she'd found no enjoyment from it with them whatsoever. With Madoc though, she'd never been so aroused in her life. She'd learned so much about herself wandering these large creepy halls. She supposed even if she were sent back, or woke up, or recovered, or the reverse of whatever means had brought her to this place to begin with, that she was already better for having experienced it.

She still didn't want to leave.

She walked down the main stair to the kitchens, finding he'd left a covered plate of eggs and potatoes for her on the butcher block. Along with a cup of sweetened coffee, a saucer on top to retain the heat. She was looking forward to fresh vegetables. She couldn't imagine how he survived on this. But then she imagined he didn't. He would have had a cook, of course. So why did he know as much as he did? He was a challenge to unravel, and her historian brain wanted to know more.

DeBretts.

If she could find a DeBretts, she could at least figure out his family lineage and then when she came across names, she would know why. She finished her breakfast and went up to his study. She wasn't sure how long she'd have before the staff started arriving. It almost sounded as though it were an entire family, not a group of unrelated people who worked together. That could prove interesting. Something else that could prove interesting was Madoc traipsing through the halls after dark to make his way to his unspecified cousin's room. Though marriage to cousins in the Victorian era wasn't anything anyone troubled themselves with. It wasn't until about 1960 that incest became an issue, because the blue Fugates in the United States physically showed the world what incest did to offspring.

Even so...the want to keep money and titles in the family far outweighed the fear of being born blue for many, and the gene that made people blue wasn't prevalent anywhere but in the Appalachian Mountains. It was much easier to ignore the Royal Haemophilia of Queen Victoria's line, as it was an invisible trait—until it wasn't.

She searched the bookshelves for DeBretts, finding a copy on a shelf with other reference books she decided to haul to her room as well. She walked out of the study and heard the sounds of people inside the house. Quiet discussion and shuffling. She stood still, trying to figure out where the people were. After a moment, she took off running, went up the stairs to the family suites and into her room, slamming the door behind her and sliding to the floor, dropping the books around her.

That was a bit too close.

She heard a knock at the door and froze.

"Miss, His Grace has let us know you're not well and to leave you be. I heard the door, and just thought I would introduce myself. If you have need of anything, anything at all, please pull the bell. I'll come straightaway. My name is Mrs. Crisp. I'm at your service."

Willow crawled as quietly as possible away from the door, getting into the bed then turning back to the door. "Thank you," she said, effecting the most sickly but loud enough voice that she could.

"Alright then, miss. I'll leave you be. Just...remember to pull the bell."

Willow nodded. She realized how ridiculous this all was and collapsed against the pillows. She was trapped in here until Madoc returned.

Walking through the brand-new building that had replaced the Harrod's he remembered became an exercise in patience. So much had happened since he'd last been in London. Things he'd expected to have remained the same were not. The original conglomeration of buildings that had been Harrod's had burned to the ground a few years prior, just before Christmas, and this new building was massive.

Avoiding the looks from shop helpers and misguided attentions from those attempting to push their wares at him was trying his composure. He'd seen men following him, attempting to be unassuming but sticking out rather like a sow in a stampede. He assumed he would be mentioned in the news sheets on the morrow, but there was naught he could do for that but kill the men and hide the bodies. Which he could not do, in truth. For various reasons, he managed to convince himself. He was scowling across a counter of women's accessories at one such man who was avoiding his gaze when a woman approached him.

"Might I assist you, My Lord?" she asked.

He turned to her, looked her over head to toe, decided that she was there for the purpose and agreed. "I need...things."

"Things, My Lord? I may need a little more specificity in order to complete your order," she said with a sweep of her hand over the counter.

"My cousin. She's visiting and there was... a fire. There was a fire at the Inn, and everything she had was lost. So I will need everything required for a woman."

"Oh, My Lord, I am terribly sorry about the misfortune. I would be more than happy to assist you, but mightn't she like to choose such personal items?"

"She is not yet well—because of the fire—and so I will need things for her before she is able to shop for such things. She needs... everything." He closed his eyes and pinched them between his thumb and forefinger. He was getting a headache. When he looked up, he heard her gasp and realized he'd turned his face enough that she could see his damage.

"I..." she started, then she stood tall, straightened herself and put her hands together. "Your Grace, I will do my utmost to assist you. I'm sure Mr. Herrod would be happy to extend credit to you, for your cousin, so you can purchase everything you have need of today."

He nodded. "Thank you." He waved his hand over the brushes and mirrors and other ladies accessories on the counter then looked up to her.

"Do you have an opinion as to style or cost?"

"Absolutely not gaudy, but not cheap. She's my cousin and should have things that suit her station," he replied, and she smiled then bustled about behind the counter, gathering silver brushes and combs and a mirror and showing him each selection for his nod of approval before setting it aside.

"Dresses? Under...things?" she said, and he nodded. "I don't suppose you have her measurements?"

He shook his head, then looked at the woman again, this time with a speculative eye. "She's shorter than you, by a few inches. She comes to about..." He brought his hand to his chest. "Here. And she..." He held his hands up, trying to assess the size of the woman's hips. She gave him a small nod and came around the counter to where he stood. After checking to see that no one, not even the men shadowing him, were paying much attention, he put his hands on her hips and waist, pulling them back as quick as he could. "Her hips and waist are perhaps a few inches more as well," he said, gathering his hands together behind his back when someone came around the corner and looked at them.

"And her bust?" she asked as she went to the counter and jotted notes on a sheet of paper with a lead pencil.

"Ah, also a bit larger," he said, and she nodded. A shot of crimson rose from the tall collar of her shirtwaist, bloomed across her jaw, and skimmed her cheeks. He looked away. "She will only have need for basics for the moment, until she is well. Then I will need a seamstress to come work with her."

"Sir, I can make recommendations for you in that regard as well. We do have several seamstresses on staff, or I can recommend a more fashionable dressmaker, if needed. For now, I will gather some dresses, undergarments, and...do you happen to know her shoe size?" she asked, turning back to him, her colour much restored. He shook his head. "Fine, I'll send a few sizes for her to try. You may send back the unused shoes, will that suit?"

"Yes, that seems the most logical. In fact, could you send a few sizes in the clothes as well, or—?"

"I believe the dresses will suffice, though I will include a few different corsets. I can come this week to fit them to her if it pleases you." She lifted a hand, and a meek child rushed from beyond the counter to her side. She listed off a host of things to the girl, who then started gathering skirts and shirtwaists and foundations, folding and wrapping each item with exquisitely printed paper and satin ribbon. "If that will be all, Your Grace, I'll have these packages to Warrick House this afternoon."

"Miss...?"

"Evaline," she answered.

"Miss Evaline, you have been most helpful. If you could perhaps do one more favour for me before I go?"

"Your Grace," she said with a nod.

"Might you be able to acquire a new traveling trunk for my cousin, pack all of these things inside, and have it then delivered?"

"Of course, Your Grace. That would not at all be a problem."

"Thank you. Warrick House in on the exchange. I assume Harrod's is as well?"

"Of course, Your Grace."

"Then you may call upon my household in the next few days to make arrangements for fittings."

"Of course, Your Grace."

"No, thank you, Miss Evaline." He turned from her, feeling much recovered from the initial shock of Harrod's, and left the building.

There were other things he needed, but they weren't attainable from Harrod's and he wasn't of a mind to manage it at the moment. He would also need the final bill from Harrod's in order to know where he stood with his accounts. There was so much more that needed to be done, and he didn't wish to do a bit of it. He'd hired his household, however, and he could hire an accountant should the books support one.

So his daily life should get easier. The less he had to do that would remind him where he was, the better.

He hailed a cab and was driven back to his home. Looking up at the large white façade with the shiny red door no longer made his muscles tense, but the reason for that wasn't something that was permanent by any means. As much as the thought pained him, he could not keep this woman. He had to find out to whom she belonged and he had to return her to him, because the two of them together would burn down both of their worlds.

FOURTEEN

illow sat in the bed waiting for the door to her room to open—it didn't. She'd watched him arrive, watched him stare up at the house, watched him disappear inside the front door. Then she'd waited. She didn't understand why he wasn't coming to see her. Except she did. He couldn't be seen in her rooms. It would be wholly inappropriate. Except it wouldn't be, as they were cousins and she was sick. It was reasonable for him to visit her. Wasn't it?

Damn. She just wanted to see him, for a moment, just put her hands on him to remember he was real and she was here and... something. She wasn't sure what.

A scratch came at the door, and she slid down in the bed, covering herself to her neck. "Come in," she said from the pillow.

The door opened wide, and the household manager held it as two men in livery brought a large trunk in the room. "The stage company has located your trunk," she said. "I can have someone unpack this for you once supper is underway. We are a small staff though, so it may be—"

"That's not necessary. I appreciate it, but I can manage. Please don't trouble yourself. I'll let my cousin know I prefer to take care of myself." She wanted to rip the top off the trunk and see what he'd bought for her. She was having a hard time being patient. The men finally located a bench tucked in the large closet and brought it to the end of the bed, placing the trunk upon it, then bowing to her and leaving.

"So be it," she said. "But please do ring if you need help, and don't overtire yourself. I would be happy to help a little later."

"I will. Thank you."

Mrs. Crisp left, pulling the door behind her, and Willow was up and out of the bed before the door had clicked closed.

She ran around the end of the bed, flipping the top of the trunk over to rest on the foot of the bed. The trunk itself was beautifully appointed leather lined with waxed canvas. It was filled with wrapped packages tied with ribbon. Wholly unnecessary, as she was going to tear through all of it in five seconds flat. She picked up the first of the packages though and could feel the fine weight of the paper, the heavy satin of the ribbon, and she realized she wasn't going to tear this apart. She would unwrap each piece and save the tissue and ribbons. They seemed to demand it of her.

She untied the first package to find a delicate silk chemise that was of such a fine fabric it was transparent. She set it aside and unwrapped the next, this one a corset of delicate green silk, heavily lined, with a steel busk. It was hand stitched, and the attention to detail even in this simple piece was astounding. She placed it next to the chemise on the bed and unwrapped more.

He'd purchased a complete wardrobe, skirts and blouses, silk stockings and drawers, several corsets and petticoats. It was lovely. At the bottom of the chest were several pair of shoes, which she assumed she was to try on and select those that fit since there were duplicates, and beyond the shoes were the most beautiful silver comb, brush and mirror. She looked in the mirror and had to stare in her eyes before she connected with herself. It was such an odd feeling after not seeing her reflection for so long.

Where were all the mirrors anyway? She poked and squished her face, which was hers, of course, but seemed somehow different. She put the mirror down and pulled out bath salts, towels, everything else she could possibly need. It was an immeasurable gift; that he thought so much about her care and keeping was overwhelming. She placed the salts on the small vanity and went back to the trunk, peering inside. There wasn't anything left, but she swept her hand around the corners nonetheless, as if he were hiding somewhere in there.

He wasn't.

She lifted the top of the trunk to close it though and realized there was another compartment, and this one held a beautiful hat and a travel bonnet, a warm, heavy cloak, and several pair of the softest leather gloves she'd ever had in her hands.

Everything she could possibly need. Save him.

She hung what was left from the bed in her closet then closed the trunk. And then she realized she had clothing and could be seen by the staff. She ran back to the closet to grab what she needed, then ran a bath so she could dress herself and find Madoc.

As she descended the main staircase, she heard voices from the study. She waited a moment, watching as a man left then proceeded past the foot of the stairs toward the kitchen without glancing up to her. He must be the butler, which meant five people she could count, so far.

Madoc had left the door ajar, so she slid into his study, waiting for him to notice her before approaching further. He was perched at the corner of his desk, rolled shirtsleeves and a vest once again. It seemed to be his preferred style. The single scar that traced his right forearm was more obvious in the afternoon light, where it spilled through the windows behind him.

He was reading a heavily embossed invitation. She took another step, since she felt a bit too intrusive as he hadn't noticed her yet, and when she did he looked up to her, placing the card and envelope on the desk behind him.

"Good afternoon," he said, then he smiled. It was odd, seeing him do so.

She nodded and couldn't help but to return that smile. "Good afternoon. I received the trunk and all the clothing, and I wanted to thank you for being so kind to me."

He waved her off. "It's the least I can do for a guest in my house." He stood and walked around the desk, and Willow took the opportunity to examine him further. She loved the way he moved, the way the fabric shifted and tightened across his back, his waist, his backside. He sat in the chair behind his desk then nodded at the chair opposite him. She went forward and sat down.

"Everything seems to fit well. I rewrapped the shoes to be sent back, as well as the corsets. I'm not sure what to do with them."

"Leave them wrapped in your room. I'll have Mrs. Crisp see to them. You've met her?"

"I have."

"Good. Mr. Crisp will serve as valet and butler, and Mrs. Crisp is household manager. If you need anything, ask her for it. Let her know what you'd like to eat and she will make the chef aware."

"Thank you."

He stood and when she started to leave, he waved her back. Then he went to the door to the study, looked out into the foyer, and closed the door, spinning the key in the lock. A chill ran her spine, and she turned back to the desk. She could feel him moving toward her in the shift of the air, the electricity at the back of her neck. Then his finger skimmed from the lowest exposed part of her spine up her neck to just below her nape. Her head fell forward as he moved against her skin, a silent request she seemed happy to accede to.

His fingers slid around the side of her neck, resting just below her ear, as his thumb continued to play with her nape. She closed her eyes and gave him leave to do as he would. He pushed her into a chair, then crouched at the edge of it, his hand coming down on her knee. "I've received an invitation for a ball."

"From your…sister-in-law?" she asked.

"The actual invitation is from the Dowager Duchess of Greensborough, via the hand of my brother's wife, yes."

She nodded, and he pulled his hand from her neck, rising to his full height then leaning his hips on the desk in front of her. "I think it would be advantageous if you were to accompany me," he said before he could change his mind.

Her gaze moved to find his, her expression one of fear and concern but also interest. "Why would you want that?"

"It's a masquerade ball. I think if we went to the ball, you might see someone you know. You might remember something or…" He considered her for a moment before continuing more truthfully.

"Perhaps we would learn who you are, which would tell me what I need to know to be able to protect you."

Her shoulders slumped and she looked past him towards the windows. "I see."

He crossed his arms over his chest, the fabric of his shirt pulling tight against his elbows. He straightened his arms and pushed the rolled cuffs up above the bend of his arms then crossed them again. "What is it you see?"

"You don't believe what I've told you."

"No, that's not exactly it. I believe..." He flushed and he rubbed one hand down his face then back up and down again to dissipate the heat before rubbing the sharp edge of his jaw with finger and thumb as he considered her. "It's not that I don't believe you. It's that you sounded unsure of yourself. The ton will be present. I believe we agreed from your dress that you are a member of the ton. I believe if you happen to know anyone, perhaps seeing them in person may open your memories. I believe that neither one of us knows why you're here and what brought you to me, but that we must find out, because I cannot protect you without that knowledge."

"Brought me to... you?" she said, and he pushed a hand to his forehead.

"You understand my meaning."

She nodded but didn't look convinced.

"There is one other matter. I...I would appreciate having an ally with me. You may be surprised to learn that you happen to be my only ally in all of England." He looked away because he didn't wish to see the censure he felt would be certain in her.

"I will do as you ask," she said. "But not because you think I'll recognize or remember. I'll do it because I know what it means to be alone."

He nodded but didn't look up to see her. Sympathy, commiseration, and the like weren't something he had any interest in, now or ever. "You'll need a dress. Someone will come this week to see to that need. Mrs. Crisp will let you know when she will arrive." He looked up when she didn't respond to find her wide-eyed and pale. "What is it?"

"I just… A ball in reality is much different from a ball in practice."

"It is."

"Am I expected to dance or… My experience with balls is movies, so my only point of reference is a grand fête with lots of punch and strange hors d'oeuvres. Waltzing. Promenading. Secret rendezvous…"

"No," he said before she could go further. She used the strangest language most of the time, and it clicked then— Cecilia. He suddenly needed to speak with her again. He shook off the thought for the moment and continued. "We have a simple purpose. To make an appearance, to allow you to see people who may be familiar to you, and to leave as expediently as possible." He didn't want to encourage any delusions of grandeur. This was no fairy tale; this was an important excursion with purpose.

"I see," she said quietly. "I was getting ahead of myself."

"You understand I shouldn't be seen with you. It's dangerous enough that I attend with you, but to put myself on display for the ton with an unknown woman would be ludicrous."

"Ludicrous. Of course."

"Please don't twist my meaning. You understand what it is I intend to say. Don't make me rethink this entire excursion. It took a great deal of consideration before I decided you should accompany me to begin with."

"I understand," she said, but it was quiet, and he knew it held a certain amount of disappointment. He wanted to smudge that disappointment from her forehead with his thumb and return the sparkle to her eye with the tip of his finger. But he couldn't. These were the facts. This was not an entertainment. This was important. "I understand," she repeated, "I do. I wouldn't want to put you in a precarious position because, quite obviously, that would put me in the same. I understand my place here. I will not be any trouble."

FIFTEEN

illow couldn't help but to be disappointed. Attending a ball in Victorian England would be the most incredible experience from a historical standpoint, from a research standpoint. The dresses, the dances, society. It perked her inner historian in ways she was sure she didn't comprehend just yet, and yet... she understood what he was saying, completely.

"I'll be fine. I'll behave myself, whatever you need from me."

"Willow, you do realize I have no idea what it is I need from you, do you not? You must understand that you and I...we may be on opposite sides of—whatever this is..." He paused, the tension full through his body. He pressed a hand flat to his abdomen, closed his eyes, and continued. "Out there, amongst the world, it's you and I right now."

"You and I," she said, taking the words as presented, letting them writhe together in her consciousness, like a cell splitting to create a new life. "So now what?"

"Now what?"

"Well. If this is what's coming...could we put it aside and just... be you and I until that happens? We've no control over that. But we can control where we are now and what we do until then. I have some clothes and I just... I don't know."

"The clothes are irrelevant. You cannot be seen with me in London. We cannot leave this house."

"Yes, it's just that we now have a definitive amount of time and we hardly know each other."

"It should remain that way. The less you know of me, the better." He stood and walked away.

"You're afraid I'll no longer like you if I get to know you."

"Actually, I know for a fact that you'd no longer like me should you come to know me."

"I understand how you could feel that way. Believe me."

"Fine, tell me something of yourself then—something you believe *I* would find abhorrent."

"Oh, um…" Willow thought for a long time about her life and the things she'd always thought of as being drawbacks to anyone who might want to pursue a relationship with her…it all faded when she related it to him. Because with him, none of it was a drawback, and what could have been a drawback was irrelevant.

"Nothing?"

"I hate lemons," she blurted out.

"Lemons?" His face scrunched as though the word itself carried the taste.

"Lemons. Everything about them. They're just so sour and bitter and...I don't understand the fascination."

"Lemons."

"I just...don't like them."

"Well, they're lemons," he said very matter-of-factly with a stiff nod.

"Are you making fun of me?"

"I would never. Well, I would, but not about this. Whatever that first lemon did to you must have been...terrible."

"You are making fun of me."

"Well, they're lemons." he said and lifted a shoulder in a distinctly uncharacteristically casual move. It was exactly the sort of thing she wanted from him, this unguarded bit of softness. The underbelly of the beast. "You put them in tea. You make candy with them. There are some rather delicious soups—"

"They're wholly unnecessary."

"Sailors would disagree."

"There are other citrus fruits that aren't so offensive."

"Sure, but what if you hate oranges?"

"Who would hate oranges? They're oranges!" she said, and the smile that broke across his face was lovely until he winced and pushed a thumb against the scar at his cheek and turned away from her, certainly aware that he'd dropped his guard a bit too far.

"Wait— it hurts when you smile?" She was appalled. How do you go through life in pain from simple acts of happiness? If an injury caused pain and you determinedly moved to avoid that pain... She stood and walked to him, putting her hands on his shoulders. His muscles tensed under her fingers, then began to relax. She smoothed her hands along the ridge of his shoulders, down his biceps, to his elbows. She pulled, and he drifted towards her, and she pressed herself along his back.

"I don't need your pity."

"Pity is the last thing I have for you. To survive what you have, to remain as strong as you do... I mean, I can't even pretend to know what it is you face, what it is you believe you've done that is so irredeemable—"

"It isn't a belief," he said and turned, towering over her, menacing. "It simply is. How could you understand? How could you have anything but pity for me when you know nothing of me? How could you profess to know what it is I feel, what it is I deserve, when what you know of me—the fact of it—is that I like to terrorize women?"

"That's not...at all what I know of you. That's not at all how I think of you, how I think of us—"

"There is no *us*, and the sooner you get that idea out of your head, the sooner you'll be able to move on." The *without me* was unsaid but hung on the drop of his lip—a tangible word left to hang between them while the *"You and I"* that had been slowly growing in her belly shrank against the denial of the *"Us."* "Perhaps that's what's holding you back to begin with," he continued. "The fact that you think there's something here, between us, beyond fucking and fear."

She lifted a hand and placed it on his chest. "Your protest is... How about you don't try to tell me what it is I know? How about you let me tell you what I believe?"

He tilted his head and held her gaze in defensive challenge.

She dropped her hands, twisting them together. "You've been nothing but a gentleman with me. Regardless what you believe. I don't know what you believe of...sadism, masochism. These words, I don't think they're even in use yet for you, but the fact is that when I'm from, they are. On top of that, they're common, meaning these aren't things only a few people are aware of. I studied the Victorian Underground because I wanted to know the origins of these words, the origins of the understanding of pain...as it relates to sex and arousal."

His gaze narrowed and his jaw relaxed, and she knew he was listening to her.

"You are not alone, though you may feel you are."

"Oh, I've never thought myself alone. Abhorrent, certainly, but alone? Never. My father liked to hurt people as well. He would hurt my brothers, myself, and laugh about it. My mother..." He shook his head. "I have never once thought I was the only man to ever feel this way. I learned from a man who lived these feelings to the highest order and attempted to teach all of us to follow in his footsteps."

"I have a feeling that how you feel about pain is a bit different from how he felt about it. Do you understand the difference between hurt and harm?"

"The words are the same."

"Not exactly. To hurt someone...it's more superficial, but to harm them, that's a more emotional and powerful sort of offense. I like...to be hurt, but in finding such, I shouldn't be harmed. Harm can be irreparable. Hurt can be healed."

"Semantics."

"Semantics are important when discussing pain. That's the first thing you need to understand."

"Why are you...why are you doing this?"

"Because you don't believe as I do. You don't think this is something that we can share. You think me a temporary thing, necessary for a time but not...not essential to survival. But I have come to believe you to be crucial to my existence, not just here...but anywhere."

"That's..." He twitched and walked around his desk to the windows of the study, staring out at the cold London afternoon.

"Madoc, I see beauty in the pain. This—what we have—is so rare, so exceptional. Do you know how many men I tried to share myself with before I found you?"

He looked over his shoulder to her. "You said there were none. You said—*and your blood said*—that *I* was the first." He punctuated the pronouncement with a tick in his jaw.

"You were the first man who made me feel safe enough, strong enough, sure enough, aroused enough, to want that. With you. But I'd tried before, Madoc. I've been beaten and burned. I've been whipped and cut and humiliated. But that's where it ended. Never have I been as connected, as aroused, as ready to accept your pain as I have since coming here...to you. I need you to understand two things. First, that this is something I want. This is something I need. This is a part of me. It isn't something I hate. This is who I am, and I am in love with the person I am when I'm with you."

He turned to look at her. "And second?"

"I don't want to live without you."

M

Mads thought about that for a moment, what it would mean to live without Willow after everything they'd done together. She may not yet know him, and perhaps that was what had him so frustrated, the fact that he believed that once she did know him, she would leave. And so he couldn't tell her. He couldn't shatter that look in her eyes that gave him leave to do whatever he wished to with her body, her mind.

God, this woman. Was what she said true? Was he made this way? Was he meant to be this counterpoint for her? Were they meant to balance each other so perfectly? It felt that way; whenever he touched her he felt steady, like the rest of his life was spent walking narrow, uneven boards.

"How do you explain away my father?"

"I cannot. He sounds like a terrible man. I don't know enough to judge him, and I'll never know him at all so perhaps I'll never be able to judge, but from what you've told me, Madoc, you're nothing like him. He may have well been a sadist, but you...you've never once done anything to bring harm to me.

"I've had to work to convince you that this is what I want, that you are who I want, that pain is how I want it. You've spent an inordinate amount of time making certain that I'm with you. If I were your victim, you would never have asked these things of me. You'd never have cared. God, Madoc, you make me a believer. You break me down only to build me up, and I am so much stronger for it, every time. I've never felt so strong. I've never..."

Her hands were shaking and she twisted them together then turned away from him. He wanted to go to her, to fix whatever was wrong. Was it true though? She had said no to him. She had stopped him. He had acceded to her wishes, but was that from respect or self-preservation? He'd seen what had ultimately happened to his father. He knew his father's associates had murdered him because he was beyond their control.

He pushed his palm against his side, the scars tight over his ribs. Angry as they pulled. "Look at me." He waited as she pressed her hands to her face, wiping tears away that should have been his.

"Willow."

"I'm—" He shook his head, and she stopped. "I'm frightened. I don't know what's coming. What I know is that you're working diligently to be rid of me, and what is to come of me then? It took centuries for me to find you the first time...what will it take next time if I lose you now?"

"You're not losing me."

"I am. The ball, you finding whoever owns me. You're obsessed with getting rid of me."

"Because you still fail to understand the position I'm in! You cannot be found here! My transgressions against my family, against the Crown—I was given a single chance for redemption and if they were to discover you, to learn what I've done with you? It matters not who you are. The only thing that matters are my actions towards you, and the Queen is not going to care if you consented to my behaviour. She will only care that I have not changed."

"I might understand better if you were to tell me—"

"I cannot!" he yelled and was immediately repentant because she took a step away from him. "I cannot," he repeated softly. "Please...if I tell you—you'll leave me faster than if someone were to discover you here. I cannot."

"You won't tell me because you fear losing me?"

He nodded, then closed his eyes on the knowledge that even telling her that much may lose her for him. He wished he knew how better to behave. To explain. To make her see. He wished he could simply bend her to his will, that she would stop arguing and understand, that she would accept what he told her. Why must she know?

Because she must.

He turned back to the windows once again.

Her skirts brushed his trouser leg, and he looked down. Her hands came up to his arms once again. Once again, he leaned back into her as she leaned forward against him.

"You are not the horrible person you believe yourself to be," she said. She didn't understand that she was wrong. He was that person. He had always been fairly good at objectivity and this one

thing he could see rather clearly based on the evidence he held in his memories. He was not a good person. He did not deserve her kindnesses, and he certainly didn't deserve the gift of her pain.

Perhaps he should just take what he could get from her, for once she did find out—and she would, rather sooner than later at this point—she would be gone. That was the objective truth of it.

He turned on her. "Do you consent?"

"Yes."

"Do you have any questions?"

"No."

"You should." She shook her head, and he took her throat in his hand and squeezed until she squirmed, her hands grasping at his wrist. She whimpered, her throat working against his palm. Then her hands went to his waistcoat, pulling him closer as she looked up into his eyes.

"More," she said.

He pushed his thumb to her pulse at the side of her neck until it seemed to slow and time stood still for him. He took one of her hands and pushed it to the fall of his trousers. She whimpered and he loosened his grip only to have her protest. She hit her knees and yanked at the fall, pushing him back against the window. "Willow," he said, but he sank to the sill, leaning back and letting the cold glass support him as she found his cock and swallowed. He lifted one foot and put it on the chair at the desk, pushing for leverage as he took her hair in a fist and she brought his other hand back to her neck. His head fell back to the glass as she moved on him, her mouth so wet and warm.

He looked down just as her cheeks hollowed out on his cock, the pressure almost too much, so he tightened his fist in her hair and she opened her mouth with an audible pop, her hand coming up to his with a complaint. Blood rushed him as she took him back between

her teeth, pulling his hips until she swallowed and choked around the broad head of his penis.

His hand around her neck tensed, and he felt the squeeze all the way to his cods the shock of it so strong he came off down her throat without another stroke. Her hands tightened on his hips, her fingers sliding into the waist of his trousers, holding fast as he came off, his semen flooding her throat as his boot slammed to the floor, his head hitting the wood frame of the window behind him.

God…fuck. He released her, and she sank back on her heels, but she didn't stop playing with his penis, licking and soothing until it became too much and he had to push her back.

"Christ, Willow."

"I want, Madoc. I want in ways I've never wanted before and if I have to prove to you that we belong together, then I will. In every single possible way."

Mads leaned there against the window with Willow on her knees between his legs, his sated penis resting on the crease of his thigh, her flushed face and red, swollen, defiant lips parted as though she wanted more, and he gave in to whatever it was she wanted for now. Because once she was gone…his life would never be the same.

They had one week.

SIXTEEN

This might be her favorite angle of him so far. Seeing the effect she had on his body, when she knew how difficult it was for him to be aroused—just like her—she felt a power she had nothing to relate to. She was like a superhero, this thing she could do to him that nobody else could.

Or perhaps they could; she didn't know. How could she? He refused to talk about his past with her other than to let her know he was a terrible person and she should be wary. Well, she was, but not of him.

Mads ran his hands down his thighs, as though to scrub the reminder of her off his hands, but then he took her face between his palms and leaned forward, bringing her to his, licking her mouth until she opened, then kissing her senseless.

The next she knew he was carrying her to her room upstairs. He tossed her to the bed, then removed her clothes without so much as releasing a button. She would have complained, considering she'd just gotten this dress, but fuck if she wasn't the horniest she'd ever been.

Naked on the bed, he spread her wide before him as he knelt between her legs, fully clothed. She smiled, and he tilted his head, narrowing his eyes, a look she was becoming so familiar with it sent her insides to curling. "Please," she begged.

"Please what?"

"Whatever you want." And she meant it.

"Anything?"

"God yes, anything, anything, whatever you want, Madoc. Just do it please, now." She felt like a snake trying to squirm free of its too-small skin; her nerves were alight with sensation and the only thing that would soothe them was his touch on her. He didn't touch her yet though. He stared at her longer, and she writhed, whimpered. God, he made her crazy.

He licked his thumb and pressed it to her clitoris, pushing it hard against her body as she shook and cried out, the pulse of blood between them so tiny but thunderous with every bit of her concentration on that single point.

His other fingers played in her folds, exploring her vulva, dipping into her vagina, then sliding against her other entrance. She froze, and he smiled. He pressed, patiently, watching her every reaction. She felt blood rush her face in embarrassment. She hadn't considered...but that small bit of flesh and muscle seemed to have a million nerves she hadn't known existed and as he circled the opening, his thumb pulsing over her clitoris, she couldn't control the way her body lit up. Nerves seemed to fire everywhere, every one of them from a straight line between her legs.

His finger stopped then rested just at the center of the opening. She gazed back intently, her eyes wide and searching. She'd heard anal sex was painful. She'd also heard that for some it was an incomparable pleasure. She hadn't even managed to have vaginal sex before him, so she'd never considered this really. He pushed slow, gentle, his finger pressing but not entering. Just waiting, pulsing.

He leaned down and wrapped his mouth around one of her breasts, sucking her nipple deep into his mouth, then when she thought she could be no deeper in his mouth, his teeth came down on her flesh. She screamed, and his finger slid inside her, pushing up, pulsing, as more fingers slipped into her vagina, searching and prodding there, and then she could do nothing but unravel around him like her atoms couldn't handle everything she was feeling and decided to give up all at once, exploding into a million tiny stars buzzing beneath this hard, heavy, solid human who was still latched onto one of her breasts, anchoring her between her breast and her pussy as she simply fell to pieces.

He released her breast, and she tumbled back to the bed; she hadn't even realized he'd been holding her above it, his arm around her shoulders.

"I want my cock in you," he said and after a moment in which she assumed he'd removed some clothing and put on a condom, he was there, pushing against the entrance to her womb, his hand pressed hard onto her belly as though to feel the very slide of him inside her.

She wrapped her legs around his, tangled her arms in his loose clothing and held on as he thrust, grunting and sweating to their end. He slid against the softest part of her, up above her pelvic bone. Grinding and thrusting, they were animals. Nothing mattered but his cock and her cunt and their end and when she came, it was with a guttural sound the likes of which startled her to her core. He matched it taking her shoulders like she were a rag doll and pulling her into his hips, impaling her on himself to the point that if he weren't wearing that condom, she knew his seed would already be inside her womb looking for purchase.

There was heat. Fire. He knew because his skin was warm, unbearably warm. He needed to get away from it. It was much too warm. He reached forward to push the fire away, but that was ridiculous. Fire was an immovable thing; it did as it wished and if it wished to take you, it certainly would do so—and now his hands were on fire.

He pulled them back and opened his eyes, watching the flames licking at his fingers. There was nothing beyond but fire for as far as he could see. He tried to put it out as well—he beat it with both fists. But the fire dodged his attempts as a masterful defence. He attempted to run but his skin, his skin was sliding off, not from the fire but from something else. His body was open, and he could see his guts, his bones, his blood.

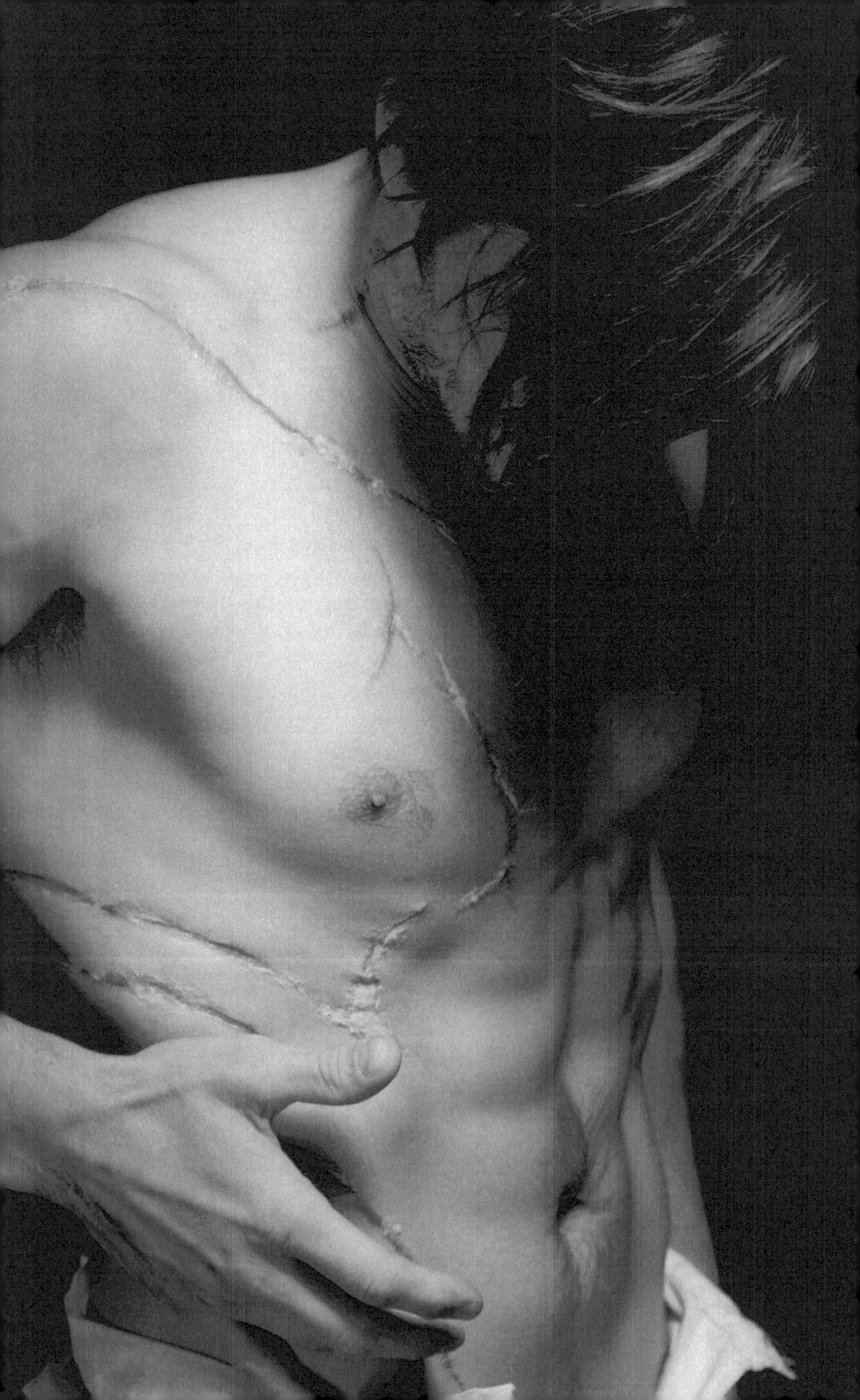

He looked down on his ruined body and wondered why he wasn't yet dead. *Atonement.* The word whispered in his head like an oath or a prayer. He screamed at the fire, "Was this punishment not enough?" Did he need to further his prostration before court? Did she require all of his blood?

His hand came to his belly, slipping against the sticky-wet, the smell of burning copper.

He bellowed.

Willow. He looked back up—she walked from the flames, cool in the storm of heat. She was a calm in his terror, and she reached for him. Pulled him close until his insides pressed against her, held in place and no longer in danger of spilling to the ground at his feet.

Her arms snaked around his torso, her skin the balm to the fire. Her lips soothed his burned flesh. Closing his eyes, demanding healing, demanding calm, demanding every bit of him belong to her, from his darkness to his fire.

He was hers. He would be hers until the day he died, and then he would pine for her until she joined him in the afterlife. There was no return; there was no second chance. There was Willow or there was death. He had a single choice to make, and make it he did.

She would be his forever.

He stilled, the flames cooled, and his heart steadied in his chest. He opened his eyes not on the apocalyptic landscape but on her...in his bed. Her arms wrapped about his waist, her head tucked to his chest. She'd been the one true thing. He let out a heavy breath, and she tilted her chin up to him, and smiled softly.

"You had a bad dream," she said.

"No, Willow, it wasn't bad at all." He ran a hand over her cheek and into her hair, turning her cheek to his chest and holding her there. He couldn't look into her eyes right now; he couldn't allow her to see the truth of his revelation in his. The sooner she was away from him, the better for them all. He would suffer the misery of losing her forever to allow for her to have a genuine life.

Her arms tightened around his waist, and he felt his insides shift, his muscles stretching against her arms. The comfort she brought him was overwhelming, and he wanted to stand and run from the room, the house, the country, this world, if only to stop the calm he was becoming too familiar with.

Chaos was his comfort. He could not become familiar with this sort of calm. It was fleeting, and would destroy him once it was gone.

SEVENTEEN

When the carriage pulled up to the front of Greensborough House, Madoc was nothing but a ball of tension and regret. Willow knew his entire family was supposed to be here, but she still didn't know what was between them. His family had gathered from across England to make an appearance as a strong family unit against the rumors that surrounded his return—whatever they were.

The carriage rolled to a halt, the door opened, and the step dropped for him to descend. He didn't move. Willow could hear the carriages that waited behind theirs, the rattle and shake of the tack on impatient horses held in place to allow the occupants to descend before the chattel were released to walk on. She reached out one small gloved hand to his knee and squeezed. He looked down. The creamy white of her gloved fingers were a strong contrast to the formal dark wool of his trousers. He pressed one gloved hand over hers, and she let the heat sink through the fabric and into her skin. He took that hand in his and stepped down from the carriage, leading her to the front entry.

"Perhaps I haven't truly considered what it is I'm doing. Perhaps this is not the best idea," he said, and she could feel his nervousness double over with every step they took. He placed her hand on his arm then waved the carriage to move ahead for the next group to arrive.

"Do you want to go home?" she asked.

"Home." He said the word and his eyebrows pinched in confusion as he took a full breath. "I cannot," he said, "go home." She knew he believed he had no choice in the matter, but there was something else in the way he said it. For today, he had to face his family. He had to, somehow, make amends. But he also had no idea how that would come to pass, only that it must. He turned to the entry and led her through. He removed his great coat, handing it off to the butler as she turned to allow a maid to take her cape. It was only then that he stopped, staring at her. His gaze swept her form up and then back down. She wore a peacock gown of deep blues and greens, the bodice fringed with feathers. Her mask matched the gown in its filigreed simplicity. He reached toward her and ran a hand along the edge, wincing. She wondered if he was thinking of the more permanent mask he wore every day, and a shiver traveled her spine.

He was simply impressive in his finery. Black cravat, black waistcoat, black trouser, black jacket, black mask with a silver crown and iridescent black feathers sprouting from the top edge. It was unlike anything she'd ever seen, but the strength of his jaw beneath it, the silver of the buttons, studs and cufflinks that played off the mask...he was goddamned stunning. Majestic. Incomparable. Straight out of a movie... She wished she could pay him proper respect for his presentation, but the gravity of the moment stole the want from her.

"Willow?" She turned and realized he'd sidled up next to her, whispering in her ear as she'd apparently lost her wits to a daydream here in the lobby. "Is everything all right?"

"Yes. Yeah, sorry, I just haven't seen you nearly so dressed before...this," she said and waved a hand at him. He caught it and put it on his elbow.

"Dressed? I'm always dressed."

"Yes... I only meant, well, formally," she said, and the realization of what he'd said sank in with remembrance of his buttons along her spine. *I'm always dressed.* She couldn't seem to swallow past the lump in her throat.

She may have been stunned, but he seemed somewhat stunned right back, not moving, simply staring around her, then at her, then back to the other guests milling in the grand entry. She wanted to turn him around and take him back to his house and lock themselves inside, forget the future and everyone in it—all she wanted was him and the body he'd completely covered up beneath all that fine fabric.

The crowd began to push them toward the staircase that led to the grand ballroom, and he pressed her hand against his arm before she could be pulled away. He held her there in a way she understood to mean she wasn't to let go, under any circumstance.

As they stood in the receiving line, he fidgeted, which was so out of character for him it pushed her concern. She tried to calm him, only to realize what the current problem was. Everyone was being announced at the door. He tried to move aside, but the way the entry funneled into the room prevented them from moving. If he turned and pulled her back through the crowd, it would create a scene. He took a card from his pocket and handed it to the man. The man reached his hand toward her and waited for a second card to announce her, but she simply stared at him. He turned away.

"The Duke of Warrick," he said. "And guest." The booming pronouncement silenced the ballroom, and rather defeated the purpose of the masquerade. Every head inside turned to the stairs leading to the dance floor like some sort of Victorian *Eyes Wide Shut* surrealist moment.

Madoc moved; she followed. As quickly as humanly possible, he made his way toward the gardens that bordered the ballroom, escorting her outside to the quiet of the abandoned balcony. Abandoned, because even with gas torches to light and heat the space, it was unavoidably February in London.

She shivered, and he turned to her.

"Fuck's sake," he said, then with difficulty he slid his jacket from his arms and put it over her shoulders, attempting to warm her, but she shivered regardless the thickness.

"Can we not go back inside?" she asked. He closed his eyes for a moment and looked around. "There." She pointed at lights coming through a tall French window near the edge of the house. She started walking toward the windows, pulling him along. She stopped just shy of it, peering through to see if the room was empty. There were a few men sprawled on a sofa in front of the fire, and she was immediately jealous.

He pushed the window open, wrapped one big arm around her waist and lifted her over the low sash, through the tall window, then plopped her down on the desk, proceeding to behave rather unseemly. She glanced over her shoulder to see the men stand, milling awkwardly for a moment, until Madoc looked up to them, "Get out."

The men shuffled off, closing the door behind them.

Madoc leaned back and examined her. His gaze paused at the feather border across her chest, his eyes going dark as though he'd only just noticed her. "God...Willow."

She leaned toward him, raising her mouth to his ear. "Whatever you want, Mads."

His muscles tensed beneath her fingers and his jaw ticked against her cheek. "Not here."

"You cleared the room for nothing?"

He twitched as though even his own body could not decide what it wanted. Or perhaps his body knew exactly what it wanted, but his mind was stopping him.

She looked in his eyes and saw the indecision.

"I want," he whispered. "So very badly do I want."

"What do you want?"

"To forget all of this. To lose myself in you and to never be found." His voice shook, and she realized the great effort with which he held himself away.

"Me too."

He stood tall and straightened her skirts, the disappointment in his own actions clear on his face as he turned away, and she slid from the desk. "We cannot," he said. "Not here, not now."

"I know. I mean, I don't actually know, because I've no idea what happened between you and your family. But I do understand this is all very difficult for you."

"No. You don't know. But perhaps you should."

Madoc walked deeper into the study toward the warmth of the fire. He stopped before it, then bent and stoked it, bringing it back to glory with some of the coal and paper that sat at the hearth. He crouched and let the heat of the fire burn into him, the warmth oddly more powerful wherever his scars lay, as though the flesh remembered and did not want to suffer again.

He swiped at his cheek and was surprised to bring his hand away damp, though he blamed his eye and the damage to his face, not something unholy like emotion. Willow came to stand next to him, one finger sweeping his hair behind his ear softly. The delicate touch more intimate than he could handle. She deserved more than him; no matter how he felt, no matter what he wanted, she deserved so much better than who and what he was. Not the sex, not the pain, not any of that...the rest of it. He wasn't the kind of man she deserved in her life.

But he knew she would never believe that, unless he told her just what kind of man he really was. He was determined the truth would terrify her. Rightly so. It shouldn't arouse him but somehow... He stood and turned to her, and this...how was this his first true look at her tonight? She stood tall and sure of herself, her shoulders back, baring her chest and neck as though she had nothing to fear in him. She turned, sweeping the train from her bustle behind her. The oil-spill black satin of her gown was shot through with iridescent green and blue threads the shape of teardrops. It was reminiscent of the oil-spill room at Birch House, and the remembrance of that night sent a spear of a shiver down his spine.

The dress swept from the very edge of her shoulders to meet at the center of her chest, allowing for more skin than he thought proper, or perhaps it was more skin than he wished to share with anyone else. He moved to pull her shawl up to her shoulders, only to discover there was no shawl with which to cover her. He would need to deal with the creamy expanse of her décolletage, the long, porcelain white of her neck, for the duration of the masquerade. In that moment it seemed a greater trial than dealing with his family.

He hadn't even given much attention to the mask she'd worn, made entirely of peacock feathers framing a filigreed metal. The feathers were intricately arranged, trimmed to fit her face perfectly, sweeping up her forehead and teasing the meticulously placed curls. The blue-violet of her eyes showed vividly from the mask, the light allowed in to highlight the color.

He reached up and removed his own mask, tossing it aside before untying hers and dropping it to the floor. He ran a hand down the smooth column of her neck, dipping his fingers past the feather edge of her dress to feel the beat of her heart fluttering there—she was aroused at just this touch, but he? He would need a bit more.

"Someone may come," she said nervously, perfectly, shudderingly, and he knew then he wouldn't stop at just a touch. If he told her the truth of what had happened, he'd lose her tonight, so he wanted the peace of her body one last time.

"Let them come," he said and she flushed in embarrassment the blood filling his cock.

He pulled at the edge, the fading marks on her breasts—from his hands, his mouth—just visible beyond his fingertips. He took her about the waist and drew her to his body, until there was no air between them. The decorative bodice of her gown caught at his waistcoat buttons, snagged on the studs of his shirt. He pushed his coat from her shoulders, leaving it unwanted on the floor as he stepped back to the settee and took her with him to his lap. She fought the layers of silk and satin until her bare upper thighs straddled his hips.

He looked down, his forehead against her chest, her breath unsteady, his matched, at the space between them. Mere inches felt like miles in this moment—the only true distance clothing and perception. He pushed her skirt up with one hand, his other on her leg where everything she wore led to the opening of her thighs and her naked quim at the apex of her body. He wanted to drown in her, to be lost forever in her lips, her mouth, her cunt; he wanted into her body in any and every way he could possibly be.

He unbuttoned the fall of his trousers, his hand stroking his cock.

"Wait," she said, and he looked up to catch her gaze, begging her to stop whatever this was, because it was going to keep him from doing what he needed to do—push her away. She released her hold on his shoulder, letting her reticule slide down her arm to dangle from her fingers, then flipped it open and reached inside, withdrawing a waxed paper packet with a condom inside. "A lady never attends prom without protection," she said as she slid it down his length.

"Who are you?" he whispered.

"Yours."

He wrapped one arm around her waist, the other between them, and in one swift, hard move, he pulled her tight against his hips, his cock slipping between her folds and into her body with little effort because she was so wet. For him, *Christ*, her body did this for him. She wanted him inside her—he belonged inside her. The feel of her was more than he'd ever realized. He kept his fingers there at her entrance, his skin against the most intimate of her skin. Where his cock couldn't touch her, he did. She was warm and so impossibly smooth and soft as his hips pushed up into her, lifting from the settee while his head fell back. He pushed his thumb to the apex of her quim and slid his own length against it as he thrust his cock into her.

She cried out, and he almost came from the sound of her alone. He reached for her, a hand across her mouth demanding silence, and her tongue slipped free tasting herself on his hand and fuck if that didn't turn his insides out. Blood pumped to his groin, her swelling flesh and his a tighter friction than moments before.

He pushed, balanced there with her perched on his cock, her neck long and wanting, her body tense and needing. He returned his thumb to the root of his cock between them and pushed his thumb and cock deeper and savored the guttural drawl of an inhale that came from her mouth then—

"More," she ground out as her hands fisted the fabric of his shirt and waistcoat. He needed to move. He brought his thumb back, sucking the wet from it himself this time. He wrapped his hand around her neck and brought her to him, taking her mouth and pushing her hips down, as he thrust into her as hard as he could. He would spill much too soon at this rate.

"Willow. Willow. I don't know how to—"

"Don't." she said against him. "I feel you trying to let go of me, Madoc. Don't. Please don't let go. Stay with me."

He couldn't get deep enough; he held on to her body and leaned forward. "I need..."

"Whatever you need," she replied.

He took her down to the floor, the light of the fire bathing her face and chest. He wanted her breasts so he pulled at the edge of the bodice, destroying the feathers in his way. Her breasts slipped free, presented to him like a feast. He took one in his hand and held it tight, as though to say, *these are mine and should not be kept from me.* He pushed harder and harder, pulling the fabric from between them, drinking her cries and drowning in the tiny shocks that jerked her body against him until he was tipping. His world spinning. He didn't know what was up or down, didn't know what was him or her; they were one writhing, messy jumble of bones and flesh and fabric quivering to release.

"Willow?" He was overcome. He had no idea what was to become of them. He couldn't fathom the loss of her, but it had to be done.

Her hands slid—one around his neck the other on his ass, her fingernails digging into his flesh to remind him of what she wanted. He sucked her breast into his mouth then bit into her skin through the layers of fabric, enough that her body convulsed once, then twice, then spread beneath him in shattered pieces as he also came off and tried to hold on. Her arms fell away, the muscles of her thighs vibrating against his hips when she tried to hold to him and failed. His own arm gave up his weight and he came down on her as carefully as he could. His weight seemed to sooth her. The tremors subsiding, her arms came back to life, her fingers playing with the edge of his twisted cravat, the waist of his trousers.

He closed his eyes and soaked it in. This moment, this feeling. He drew circles around the bite at her breast with one finger, lifted up and kissed her neck and attempted to set her back to rights. The edge of her bodice was destroyed, and he plucked at the broken feathers, dropping them to the floor, working to at least make her presentable.

"How will we ever face the ballroom now?" she said, and he pushed back to his knees and looked down at her absolutely destroyed countenance. Her legs splayed about him, fluid leaking from her vagina, soaking the fabric she lay on. He took the condom from his penis and tossed it into the fire, where it popped and shriveled, then turned back and looked upon her. She was incomparably beautiful. Everything about her called to him in a desperately wanting sort of way. A necessary way.

He didn't want to lose her. He didn't want to give her up. But they could not have a life together if she didn't truly know who he was. He had to tell her, and if she chose to leave him after that? He couldn't bear even the consideration. He could always restrain her, and the vision of her chained to a wall did strange things in his gut until he remembered the last person he'd chained to a wall. Calder. The thought shocked him back to the moment. His breath stilled and he stood and took a step back from her. Her legs came together and she covered herself as best she could.

"Have I offended you?" she whispered.

He started to shake his head but stopped, his chin canted to the side, his gaze holding hers. How could he tell her? How could he explain to her the things he'd done? He suddenly cared more for her opinion than any of his family. Bringing her here had been a mistake.

He returned to his knees, smoothed her skirts, helped her to sitting as he took inventory of the tears in her dress to see if there was any injury to her beneath it. Methodically he concentrated on making sure she hadn't been harmed as he'd hurt her. And that was when he understood—never would he ever wish to bring harm to this woman, but his very existence was hurtful to so many.

"I'm fine," she whispered and her hand came up and covered his scarred cheek, turning him to her. "I'm fine."

He nodded and stood, then picked her up and finished his inspection. There were marks on the backs of her legs where she'd lain on the cage of her bustle. He couldn't see the bite on her breast, but he hadn't broken her skin, so there was at least that, and they would check the rest later. He'd managed to mark every bit of skin she'd bared, save her face, but even her face was flushed well beyond convention. She had burns on her arms from the rug as well, but most of her had been covered in fabric. Then there was the avian massacre they'd left on the floor.

He put her on the settee then looked around the room, finding a tantalus next to the desk by the windows. He opened it and poured four fingers of whiskey. He downed two then handed her the glass and turned toward the fire.

"I'm more the man you think me to be than you know. That may sound... What I mean is that this— What we have between us is very particular to us. But it doesn't mean I haven't attempted to explore these feelings before. With other people. God, Willow... I am not a good man."

EIGHTEEN

Madoc looked into the fire and away from her. She sipped the whiskey, let it burn through her, strengthen her resolve. She wanted him to know that—whatever his past was—it didn't matter to her. It simply didn't. She knew this man. She no longer needed his story even if she wanted it, and it wouldn't scare her off regardless. She knew his true heart, his soul. The rest was secondary to that.

"Three years ago, my father had me murdered," he said. She'd not been prepared for that and her heart skipped. "He was running girls from India to England for various uses by men of a certain temptation. There was a group of them. He liked to call it a club... It was beyond reprehensible. I'd let him know that. I expected to be banished as he'd done to my brother Grayson after...well, I'll leave that story to him, should he wish to tell it. It doesn't as much apply to me."

He took a breath, and she lifted the glass. He took it from her and downed the rest of it then sat next to her, but away, not touching her. She crept one finger across the expanse and rested it against his knee, a delicate touch that was hopefully enough of a support for it to matter.

"He'd banished my youngest brother, but I was the heir. Our other brother was being trained up to the business as well. It became obvious to my father that I was not quite the same as he. I may have liked to cause pain in certain ways, but in fact he'd misread me completely. *He* simply liked to cause pain. I have a distinct purpose, and if the person I'm with isn't of the same purpose, I've no interest. That's what I learned from the fight with Grayson, the one that sent him away. Until that moment, I'd thought I was just like my father. It was that moment I realized I was not, but by then it was already too late to save Gray. I'd no control. We were still too young; there was nothing I could do... I..." He leaned forward and threw the glass to the fire, where it exploded in a cloud of glass and a burst of flame. He leaned forward on his knees. "Grayson has always been, and will probably always be, the best of us. But I digress." He took a steadying breath.

"Gray was gone. My father became bolder because the conscience of the house had been expunged. He sent my mother and sister to the country house. He started in with his plans in earnest. I'd no idea how to stop him, so I went along with it but undermined him at every opportunity. I lost important paperwork to the fire, I canceled orders for the houses he purchased. I fired the workmen on his projects. It went on for years before he caught on that it was me. He'd assumed it was someone on the outside, but since he shared everything with me, I always knew when he was up to something. Eventually though, he figured it out. He set me a trap. I fell into it easily, because it had become second nature for me to garner information and use it to undermine the works.

"His solution was to have me killed. It went awry though. I don't know how... My father, brother, and I were traveling to the country house. We were set upon by highwaymen. They set a trap for the carriage, but it was older and it didn't simply stop the carriage, it snapped the axle and tore the carriage apart. It was disastrous. I don't remember much other than being tossed clear of the conveyance, hearing the revelations that the only survivor was one they were supposed to kill. The decision to keep me and hand me over to the men who were in charge."

Madoc stood again, his hand rubbing down his side the scars reminding him of the pain from that night. "My father and brother were dead. They took my clothes, my jewelry, and put it on another dead man. They set it all on fire. Then they took me to India, away from London and any immediate reprisal should I be discovered. They held me captive. They healed me, only to torture me. None

of this had an effect on who I was, but I thought it did. I thought it was the precedent for who I was, because I forgot...I forgot so much that night. The person I was—the child I was— he was dead. They made sure I understood that. They intended to reseat me as Duke and take control of the entire operation, but what they didn't expect was for the Queen to find Grayson first and give him the title. It wrenched their plans a bit."

"But this isn't—" she started, but he turned and smiled. It was a knowing smile. He wasn't yet to the part of the story where he became the monster he believed himself to be. She watched as he stood to pace before the fire. The coal burned low, taking the warmth and the light with it. He knelt before it again, but there wasn't much coal left in the bucket, and no paper left to burn. He stoked it anyway, a few pieces flaring back to life, lighting his face.

"I was angry Gray had been welcomed home and nobody had bothered to come look for me. I thought it preposterous that they didn't know the body in my clothes wasn't mine. I was uncontrollably jealous, and it festered, bolstered by the men who'd held me. It took time, but I had them believing I was on their side, that they'd turned me and I would do anything for them; the problem was now Gray... Nobody would believe yet another accident killing a member of my family, followed by another miraculous return of an heir. It would have undoubtedly been investigated at that point. They'd thought to replace Gray with me quietly but...the scars, you know. They would need to explain them.

"I convinced them I could draw him to me in India, that he wouldn't be able to stay away if he knew I was alive. I told them we would switch—he didn't have to die; I wouldn't be resurrected, and we would simply exchange lives. I knew he would do it. I knew he didn't want to carry my father's title. He just didn't; this was his way out. It was perfect for all of us."

"But that's not what happened?"

"No it's not. And this is another part of the story I have no rights to, because once again I am not the victim in it. Calder came instead of Gray. What happened between Calder and I was unconscionable. I—" He closed his eyes, pinching the bridge of his nose between his fingers. The last burning ember began to wane. "I tortured my cousin. As I had been tortured, perhaps beyond. He was given to great suffering. At my hand. There is no defense of it."

As the ember flared one last time, he turned to look at Willow, his eyes red from exhaustion, pain, sadness. He took a final breath with the fire, and the room went dark.

Willow couldn't breathe. She wanted out of the corset, away from this house, back to his where she felt safe. She stood and tried to get room enough to fill her lungs. *Torture?* He had to be exaggerating. She heard him move, saw the shift of shadows as he stood. She stepped back to give him room to do what he needed, not wanting to trip him. "Please," she said. "Please take me home, Madoc."

"That is something I cannot do. Willow... you deserve better than me."

The door opened and a bar of light cut across the floor momentarily, then was gone with the click of the door, leaving her in darkness. She reached behind her for the settee to steady herself, then she picked up her skirts and followed him to the door. Once in the hall, she saw him slip around the far corner and ran to catch him.

"Madoc!"

He stopped. "I can't be here. I don't know what I was thinking. This was a mistake. I'm not prepared to defend my actions because there *is* no defense for my actions." He walked farther down the hall where perhaps he felt safer speaking to her. "Therein lies the problem; there is no defense for my actions and you should now

understand... Do not make excuses for me. What I have done—do not take this confession lightly, Willow. Because you were amenable does not mean that the others have been. I do not think I can uphold my promise to Her Majesty. My family will never embrace my apologies even were I to attempt some semblance of apology...if I were them I would never accept. This is..." He stopped and turned to her, the hall this far down empty of guests. His expression was harried, and he took her shoulders in his hands. "We can go to America. I will call you my wife and no one would be the wiser. We will disappear in America. They would never find us there, and we would be beyond the Queen's reach."

"Come now, Georgie," another voice cut in from farther down the hall. "Do you truly believe that your only option?"

His hands tightened on her, and Madoc froze. She watched every muscle in Madoc's face— his neck, his shoulder, his chest— systematically tense, freezing him in place. She looked past him to find a man coming from the shadows beyond them. He was dressed in the same formal black and white, a perfectly tailored, stunning gentleman. Exquisitely put together. He wore a simple black mask and a halo of gold. Though as he walked closer, she could see the halo was merely a trick of the wall sconces he walked beneath. His hair was a golden blond, and such a color that when struck by the light it glowed like a crown. His beauty stole her breath.

"Calder," Madoc said, and one of his arms came around her waist and brought her to his other side, placing her between his large body and the wall. Hiding her from the man.

"It's been so long, cousin, and how are you?" the man, Calder, said. Madoc crowded her against the wall behind him, and she grabbed his jacket, holding onto him to remind him she was there. "Aren't you going to introduce me to your...what is she? Your next victim?" he asked, and Willow knew she made a sound when she took a sudden breath. He spoke so nonchalantly—the words that came from his mouth were in direct contrast to the tone of his speech.

"No," Madoc said but the strength of his voice didn't support the answer.

"Well, then, shouldn't you introduce us? You're being terribly inappropriate. Has it been so very long since you've attended a ball?" he asked, and a ripple of tension went through Madoc. She tried to move to the side, but he blocked her again.

"She has no interest in you," he said easily.

"None? Perhaps she would have interest in what you did to me. Perhaps she would have interest in what you did to my family. To your own brother, Grayson. Perhaps she would have interest in just what sort of man she chooses to take to her bed."

Madoc moved then, her hands plucked from his waistcoat as he pushed his cousin across the hall and into the wall.

"My dear Georgie, have I touched a nerve?" he asked with a shallow laugh.

Willow could do nothing but watch. Madoc had him by the lapels up against the wall, was pushing his chest, his neck, making him struggle.

Willow walked over and took Madoc's arm. Pulling him away. "Let go, Madoc, let go. You cannot..." She tugged, and something in him seemed to shift, a realization of what he'd just done.

"No, Georgie," Calder said. "You cannot. Have you forgotten yourself so easily? What did the Queen say? That you were to make amends? This isn't quite how you go about that."

"Calder... I—" He shook his head, and Willow looked between the two of them.

"We should go," she said, not releasing his arm. "We should..."

"Run off to America?" Calder asked. "Perhaps you should. Perhaps you should leave the country and not look back. I'm not entirely sure that restitution is possible in this situation, George. With myself, or your brother. I'm not sure how you even managed an invitation—"

"Cecilia arranged it," he said, and Willow watched as Calder's eyes narrowed. She could see Madoc had lost whatever strength he'd had. "And you're correct, there is no true way for me to resolve what I've done. There is no way for me to make up for any of it. There isn't. I've done too much, endured too much. I should have been left to history. I should have been left to die."

"What?" She said it without thinking, and Calder turned his gaze on her.

"Who are you then?" he asked her. "Do you know who it is you accompany? All threats aside, you should know what it is he's capable of. You should know that your life could be in danger. Would you like to see the scars he gave to me?"

She nodded, and his gaze narrowed on her, his expression confused. "I mean, no, that's not at all what I meant. I just... You're Calder?"

"Oh, I see. So perhaps you do know a bit about who he is then? Well, if you know me so well, we might as well become friends." He looked her up and down his eyes resting on the broken feathers, at her chest, where they went wide with recognition. She knew he'd seen the marks. She attempted to pull the bodice of her dress higher, as he looked on. "Well, then. It seems we may already have much in common. By all means, lets share. You first."

"Calder!" The shout came from behind them and she turned, Madoc turning with her, once again putting himself between her and the new arrival.

"Quinn," Madoc said quietly.

"Calder," he said and lifted an arm, waving Calder to his side. He went. Then they stood there, two by two, inspecting each other. "Who is she?" Quinn asked with the jerk of his chin.

Calder shrugged and on him it was perfectly placed. He spoke with his body; he wasted no words on those that didn't deserve them, and apparently she was one.

She held on to Madoc's arm. "I'm sorry," she whispered. "I don't know what to do."

"Listen," Madoc said, attempting to shake her off. "I don't know who she is or why she's here, but she's not part of this. Leave her be. Take your anger out on me, do what you will—I deserve whatever it is you have to give, but she doesn't. She's innocent in this."

"You don't know who... She's rather attached to you for someone you don't know." Quinn said and his gaze traveled her from tip to train. "And seems to be well appointed for a nobody, if a bit *ruffled* for a ball."

"I mean she's nobody to me. I have cared for her since my return, but...she's naught to do with what happened between us and should have naught to do with me." Madoc turned his attention to Calder; she could feel the resignation, the fear, the worry come through him.

"So be it," Calder said. "I have no interest in harming those who have no issue with me. You, however...we need to have a discussion. Shall we start with you slamming me into the wall just here?" He turned a wrist, motioning to the wall next to him. "Or shall we begin with the dungeon you kept me chained in? Where you held me captive? Where you tortured me? You choose."

Torture... Willow's hold on Madoc softened and she took a step back from him before she realized she'd done so.

"Oh, I see she does have some sense," Calder said quietly.

"Listen, perhaps..." Madoc fidgeted. "Take her with you. Protect her. Listen to her. She is innocent in all this and she deserves to be cared for, protected. She...she's important. She knows nothing of who I am or what I've done. Please forget about me and help her."

Willow reached for him, but he gave her a warning glance and stepped away. "Madoc don't," she whispered, but he only shook his head, hardening his gaze.

Quinn turned his gaze back to her. His resemblance to Madoc was more pronounced, and she knew he was one of the cousins he spoke of. "What is your name?" he asked her.

"Willow," she replied. She reached for Madoc, but he pushed past his cousins, and without looking back toward her, he ran. They caught her between them, held her as she screamed after him. "Madoc no, please! Madoc, no! Madoc!"

But he didn't listen, and three steps more and he was gone. She sobbed and her knees gave, but the men, these two complete strangers, held on to her. They attempted to calm her. They tried to speak to her. She didn't listen. "Where has he gone? What will happen to me? Why did you do that? I need him. I need him, you don't understand?" she cried. "I need him. Please."

Quinn wrapped an arm around her waist and escorted her farther down the hall to an alcove with a small bench. It must have been where Calder had been before. He helped her sit, helped her arrange her bustle so she wasn't resting on the sharp edge of the cage. Little did he know she already had marks from that cage from this very night. She sobbed against the memory. She should have done something. She shouldn't have pressed him. Quinn crouched before her as he straightened her skirts delicately and ran his hand down her arms to sooth her as Calder paced behind him.

"What have you done?" She shook her head. "I have nothing, no one. He was the only thing... He was... You don't understand what you've done. I need him. Nobody else will understand..." She covered her face with her hands and sobbed.

"We should go. I'll have the carriage brought round."

Quinn squeezed Calder's shoulder and disappeared down the hallway, leaving her with him, the fallen angel who hated her.

"God help me, I don't know why he always leaves me in predicaments like this but it would be simply perfect if it would somehow stop," Calder said. He stopped pacing and crouched in front of her. "I understand you want Madoc but first we need to get you out of here as swiftly and quietly and safely as possible for that to happen. Since we have no idea who you are, it would be inconvenient for someone to recognize you now and lay claim. Do you understand? He's asked us to care for you. We may not be on good terms but helping you has naught to do with that." Willow felt as though her world was crashing in on her, the edges dimming. He shook her gently. "Listen to me. I'm going to help you. Regardless who you are, what you've done, what he's done, *I* am going to help you."

Willow nodded, resigned to whatever Fate had decided to toss at her next.

Calder reached for her, so she took his hand. "Your dress is a disaster." He picked at the broken feathers, straightened the seams, then attempted to put her hair back together where it fell from the pins. "I'm afraid there's nothing for it. We're going to have to get through the ballroom as quickly as possible."

He led her back to the study where she'd been with Mads. He picked the coat up from the floor and helped her into it, then handed her the peacock mask. He took her hand and turned for the door but she stopped, looking around the room for Madoc's mask.

"Please, his mask," she begged quietly. He gave her a concerned look then turned back to the room. He walked over to the settee and grabbed the pair of ribbons sticking out from under the settee, handing the mask to her. "Thank you."

As they entered the ballroom it seemed to still, like a slow-motion dream filled with shards of crystal waiting to slice a vein. Willow avoided those who watched as a path before them opened without cause. She ignored the temptation to gawk at all the people in the room and followed him. The crush parted before them then swallowed them up behind like rocks in a stream—except they were moving and the stream was not. He pulled her closer, putting her hand to his arm and holding her tight.

She realized, a little too late, that she'd forgotten to put her mask back on. She realized, a little too late, that this was what was causing the stir. Calder gave her a curious glance when women started to curtsey before her, men giving her a leg as she passed. She crowded into him, his grip on her arm tightening. She ducked her head and pushed the mask to her face. The curtseying slowed but didn't stop as the crowd had begun the whispers as soon as she'd been seen. So apparently she was someone.

When they reached the entry, Willow paused and looked back over the crowd, the path they'd made had filled with bodies as though it had never been, their attention to her just as fleeting.

Calder gave a gentle tug, and she looked up to him. "Who are you?"

She shook her head, shrugging. "I don't know."

Something like realization and terror swept across his features then and he turned and led her away with even more care and purpose.

It might have been the most difficult thing he'd ever done. It was absolutely the most painful moment of his life, and considering what he'd endured the night his father and brother had died—not to mention the months of recovery—that was saying something.

Twice he'd nearly stopped and turned back when she'd screamed his name, the pain of it like lacerations opening of their own volition. He hadn't stopped. And now he stood on the front steps waiting for a hack. He wasn't sure what he was to do, where he would go. He could return to his house for the night, but after that...there was nowhere safe for him, not in England, not in India, not in any of Britain's occupied territories, which included so much of Europe... he supposed America was his only option at this point. He would need to liquidate as much as he could, as fast as he could and leave this country and this life behind.

And God help him if the Queen ever found him.

A hack pulled up, and he opened the door and jumped inside before the footman could assist. He knocked on the roof of the carriage, and the driver turned back, opening the hatch. "Take me to the Iron Duke at Grosvenor," he said.

He made his way through the mews to the back entry of the house he wanted. Then he knocked. He screwed it up twice before he got the sequence correct because he was so distraught, but the man finally opened the door to him. Madoc walked through to the parlour but this time instead of sprawling on the chaise, he paced until she arrived.

"You're making me nervous. There is no chance I would allow you near one of my girls," she said.

"I don't want one. I don't want anything tonight but somewhere safe to rest. If I must pay a woman to share her room, then so be it, but she will not be touched by me."

The mistress nodded and tugged a cord. He already knew the statuesque redhead who came through the door and took his hand. The last time he'd been here, she'd torn him apart from neck to knee and he'd allowed it in the hopes that he would then be given leave to do the same to another. He hadn't been. Instead, he'd been turned away and had met Willow at The Iron Duke. The woman who'd changed his life. He'd never be able to repay the gifts she'd bestowed upon him, the lessons he'd learned. But she was lost to him forever now. He'd left her in the care of his cousins and there was no way he could retrieve her. It was the sanest thing he'd ever done.

He knew they would care for her. He knew above all else that his cousins were good men. Strong men. They cared for their family, for their own, and Willow; if they knew what he'd done to her, she would be taken in, given shelter, protected. They would see her as another victim and protect her.

He turned to the woman who sat in a soft blue chair, reading by lamplight. "Do you have quill and paper?"

She stood and retrieved what he asked for from a small drawer in her wardrobe then placed them on the small table next to her bed. "This will have to do. I usually write my letters in the parlour, but as you can imagine, it's much too occupied tonight."

He nodded. "No, this is sufficient, thank you."

He dipped the quill and placed it on the paper. He didn't know what to say; he wasn't sure who he needed to speak to. He watched as the pen leaked from the pressure. He blew on it, spreading the ink, letting it set. Then he began again.

Calder,

There is nothing I can do to make amends for what I've done. We are in full agreement on this fact. I would bend a knee and apologize if I thought you would accept it, but I don't expect you to. It is not for me to decide when and where you will allow my penitence. Know if that time ever comes, you have it.

What follows is the story of the Woman you must care for. She is a stranger to me. I know her only as Willow. I took her from The Iron Duke, terrified her into submission. Stole her for my own dark purpose. I kept her in my house. I terrorized her. I took her virginity. I caused her pain, willingly. I have stolen everything that was once innocent in her and replaced it with my own depravity.

Do not listen to her, she does not know me. If she argues with you show her this letter. Let her understand who I am. She deserves better. Though she is ruined, I would hope you are able to find her a place, a life, a husband to protect her. It is my single act of rationality that I place this woman in your keeping.

I will no longer be a worry to you and your family. I will break my covenant with The Queen and be gone from this country and this life. Tell Gray the title should have always been his. He was the one true Warrick. He was the only member of our family deserving. We all knew it, we always knew it, and it was why my father drove him away. He's always been a better man than all of us. I'm sure you of all people know that better than most.

Tell him I am sorry for all I've done. I'm sorry for the dishonesty. I wasn't the brother, the man, he needed to protect him when he was so young and vulnerable. Tell him I live at his mercy and will. Tell him he will never see me again unless he wishes it. Tell him I will wait for him at the Birch House. He will know where to look for me, and if he so chooses, he is to send word and I will return. I will face my Queen and my death with a clear conscience if it's what he chooses. It is the only thing left I am able to do.

If I do not hear from him in the next sennight, I will be gone forever. I will send my abdication to The Queen once I am far enough to be of no consequence.

Yours respectfully,

George Madoc James Danforth

He sealed the missive, smearing candle wax across the opening to prevent prying eyes as best he could. "Have this taken to Calder House. When you return, I'm yours to do as you will."

"I don't pity spank," she said then disappeared from the room.

Madoc considered that for a moment—that he wasn't even worth beating. He rolled to the bed and closed his eyes and wished for some sort of darkness—whether dreams or death—to take him and relieve his soul of this misery.

NINETEEN

illow sat in the carriage next to the angel, across from the other, who sat next to one of the most beautiful women she'd ever seen in her life. She had dark brown skin and her hair was smoothed back into a knot above her nape and sprinkled with delicate white flowers. She held a mask in her hands, and Willow held two, the last remnants of her night. Her fingers tangled in the satin ribbon that had held it to her face, released them, then tangled again. Her gaze darted from Calder, to Quinn, to her and then to her own hands and around again.

She felt a connection with this woman, similar to the connection she'd felt for Madoc's former betrothed. Less a connection and more of a...whisper of a memory she couldn't place. It was like something she knew but couldn't quite put a finger on. She knew she'd never met this woman and yet she was there, in her memories as though she belonged.

The woman was holding her gaze, and Willow realized she'd been staring so she broke the connection, looking away.

The carriage rolled on, the only sound the wheels on the rough streets, the tack of the horses, the snap of the driver's whip. The carriage lolled around a corner, forcing Willow to lean into the man next to her, the heat of him like a furnace against her arm. He looked down at the contact and she tried to scoot away but there wasn't anywhere to scoot to, so she pivoted as much as possible, pushing herself into the corner and trying to avoid him.

"Do you believe him?" Calder asked somberly, and Willow looked to Quinn, only to realize they were all looking at her.

"Me? Do I—"

"Yes, you. Do you believe him?"

She'd no idea what he meant by it. She'd believed everything Madoc had said to her— up until he'd abandoned her with these people. "Which part?"

"Do you believe he has relinquished you to our keeping?"

"I'm here, so it must be true, and yet...I don't. I don't believe he would do this to me. I can't believe it."

"Why is that?"

She shook her head. It had been difficult enough to trust a single stranger with no contact to the outside world. But to trust these three...even if he'd told her she should. Even if she did believe that much of what he'd said. She didn't want to. She didn't want to trust them; she wanted to go home—no, not home—back to him. That was home.

"He told you to trust us," he said quietly. His tenor had changed; he sounded almost sympathetic. He was definitely less abrasive and demanding, and she looked to him, his gaze on her, his expression open, and Willow knew she had no choice.

"There's this...there's this hole in my chest that only becomes wider the farther from him I get." She held his gaze, pushed a fist to her sternum as though to ease it inside between her lungs, to attempt to fill the gaping hole she knew was there. "I don't know how to survive this. I don't know anything about this world—I don't know anything about of any of you. I'm alone and now at your mercy. Until tonight, all I knew of you was that Mads was estranged and required to reconcile." His demeanor didn't shift; he didn't censure her. He waited, his silence asking for more. "I don't belong in your world," she said quietly, and there was a spark in his eyes that lit the smallest thread of hope in her.

"What did you say?" the woman asked quietly, and Willow turned her attention to find one of them shocked and the other terrified. She realized what she'd said and clapped one hand over her mouth as though to prevent herself from speaking further.

Calder shook his head.

"Oh, God. Nothing, I'm tired, rambling. I shouldn't have said anything. I just... Please take me to him. Leave me at his house. I cannot be without him. It's not possible. Please."

Her words seemed to fall on deaf ears; the woman's expression didn't shift at all as she inspected her. Then her hand went out to Quinn's knee. Squeezed. Willow watched as Quinn nodded. Calder tapped on the wall of the carriage with the silver ball at the tip of his cane. A hatch in the roof opened, and a face peered through.

"Take us to Roxleigh House," Calder said, and the hatch closed, the horses slowing then taking a corner, and another, heading in the opposite direction.

"Who is Roxleigh?" she asked.

"Our cousin. It must seem there to be a never-ending supply," Calder said, his eyes on her, his words lighter somehow. He was attempting to calm her. It was so odd to her that he could do so with a simple gaze and a few easy words.

"There are more of you?"

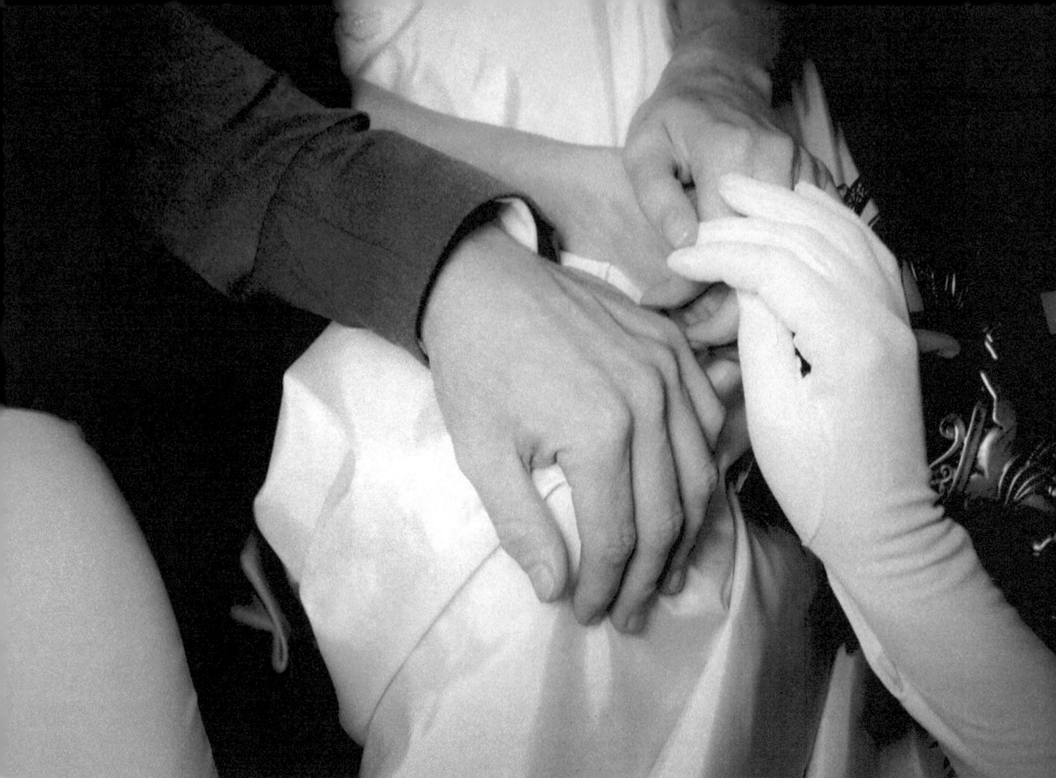

"Quite a few more," he answered. "It seems we are a constant stream of cousins...and their particular wives." He smiled, almost showman-like, and Willow tipped from calm into a strange discomfort.

"Particular...wives?" she asked.

"Yes—"

"Calder," Quinn warned. "Leave her be. We don't know. We can't know."

Calder turned his attention out the window, Quinn's followed—but the woman, she kept her gaze on Willow.

"My name is Willow," she said and steeled herself. She wasn't going to get through to these men with the one constantly stopping the other, but the woman...there was just something about her. "I don't belong here. I'm not from this... place." That felt vague enough while not being the least bit vague.

The woman nodded. "My name is Celeste. We *will* take care of you."

Willow's chest caught in a sudden sob, then she nearly doubled over from the power of it. She'd been holding herself together since they'd walked through the ballroom with all those eyes on her. She could finally breathe and her body demanded the air as much as it demanded the release of her tears. Celeste reached across the carriage and took her hand. Calder, without looking, put his gloved hand on her knee. Quinn pulled a handkerchief from his breast pocket and pushed it into her other hand.

After a moment, the carriage rolled to a halt. She heard the door open. The loss of warmth from the hands was accompanied by the carriage tipping as three people descended, then waited for her. She swiped at her eyes and her nose with the handkerchief Quinn had given her. A small white gloved hand reached into the carriage. She took it.

Madoc stared into the fire. He felt nothing. He cared for nothing. He wanted for nothing. He saw nothing but flame. He shut down every single thought he had that would shift to her, and thus he shut down every single thought. He didn't consider America, because he'd wanted to hide there with her. He didn't consider Warrick House, because it was where he'd lived with her. He didn't think upon the ball, because it had been where he'd abandoned her. There wasn't a single safe place for his mind to go, so he stared into the flames and thought of nothing but how good it would feel to burn. To finally be engulfed by the pain. To lose everything. To finally be free of this body, this mind, this world that hated him so very much.

"If you're to remain in my rooms beyond tonight, I'll need you to bathe. I may be a willing participant in many forms of torture, but the smell of you rotting in your own skin is not one of them. I'll have the bathing room cleared and prepared for you. I'll have someone retrieve you when it's ready. Bodily if necessary..." She waited impatiently. "Acknowledge me."

Mads nodded. Pieces of what she'd said filtered through his self-induced haze. The door opened, then shut again. Madoc started to drift into the flames once more, until someone touched his shoulder. He stood and turned on them in a single motion. She was tiny, no more than a child, perhaps ten years old. A crisp white mobcap and apron covered her black maid's dress. He stepped back, and she craned her neck up to him, her eyes growing wider as they went. When she spoke, it was so soft that Madoc had to lean in.

"Milord, the bath is ready," she said; he nodded. He'd been prepared to fight. But he'd also been prepared for a guard of some sort, or even the birch mistress to come for him—not this small child.

"Why are you here?" he asked.

She dipped her chin, her eyes sweeping the room as if to find the answer he wanted hiding in one of the corners. "To...let you know that there's a bath ready for you. In the bathing room. Down the hall. Milord." She lifted one tiny arm and pointed with a scarecrow-like finger toward the back of the house.

"No," he said, tempering the natural cadence of his voice to soothe her. "Why are you in this house?"

"Where else am I to be, milord?"

"What is your name?"

"They call me Alice, but I don't believe 'tis my name."

"Alice? Why don't you believe that?"

"Because they call all of us Alice, milord."

His head jerked as though his mind refused to process that statement. "How many of you are there?"

"Five or six, usually, milord. But we get too old and must leave or be trained."

"Trained." It wasn't a question; he knew exactly what she'd meant, but she went on, heedless his discomfort. He put his hands on his hips, his fingers digging into the flesh that bordered his hipbones.

"Yes, milord. If we're to stay, we must be trained how to take the whip or give it. 'Tis our only choice. Train or leave."

"And how soon will you make that choice?"

"Until last year I was to make that decision soon. But the new law means I have three more years to do so."

"You're thirteen?" he asked.

"That's what they say and so I am. But the new law, ye see, means I cannot be trained until I'm sixteen now. I have to wait. Put off the mistress something fierce, that did."

"Are you safe here until then?"

"I am, milord. Why wouldn't I be? Mistress takes care of us here. 'Tis warm, 'tis safe, there's food. If I were on the streets—"

"She took you from the street?"

"Aye, she did, milord."

"How long have you been here?"

"Long enough to know 'tis better than the streets."

"Had you chosen yet? Whether to train or to leave?"

"I had, milord, yes."

"And what was your choice?"

"To train, milord, of course."

Madoc stilled, allowing the knowledge of that to sink in. That this child could have been his partner in a few short months had circumstance been different. Would he have taken her? No, he would have refused, but others were not so particular as he was to have women as opposed to children. Others were quite the opposite, in fact. "Why did you choose training?" he asked, crouching down to her level.

"I never took to the cooking or sewing that we're learned here. I wouldna be able to find work as a cook or seamstress when I left. And—"

"And?"

She fiddled with her fingers, before looking back up to him. "Well, once we're trained, we get a name of our own."

"You could choose a name should you leave."

"Yes. Cook, or Seamstress."

Madoc looked away.

"Alice!" The yell from below stairs caught him off guard and made the girl run. He wanted to stop her. He wanted to save her. He wanted...something; he didn't know what. He was shamed, again, by who and what he was. That children were pulled from the streets to train into the women here for his enjoyment. He closed his eyes.

"Did Alice not tell you the bath is ready?" his mistress asked.

"She did. I have questions."

"I don't have answers. Not until you've cleaned yourself off."

His gaze narrowed as he considered her, but her tone brooked no argument and he was loath to argue. He gave a quick nod and followed her from the room.

The bathing room was filled with steam. What showed of the windows beneath the heavy velvet drapes was dripping with condensation, rills of water gathering and sliding to the sash. The room smelled of old wet that needed a good airing out. He supposed though, if this were the only bathing room for this entire floor there was no time to pause in its use.

His mistress followed him in the room and shut the door. He turned and looked at her. Tilted his head, narrowed his eyes.

"You don't wish me to stay? Most men—" He stopped her words with a twitch. "Yes, well. I'll leave you to it. But be warned that Mr. LaBouchere will be in need of a bath soon and he never knocks."

"LaBouchere?"

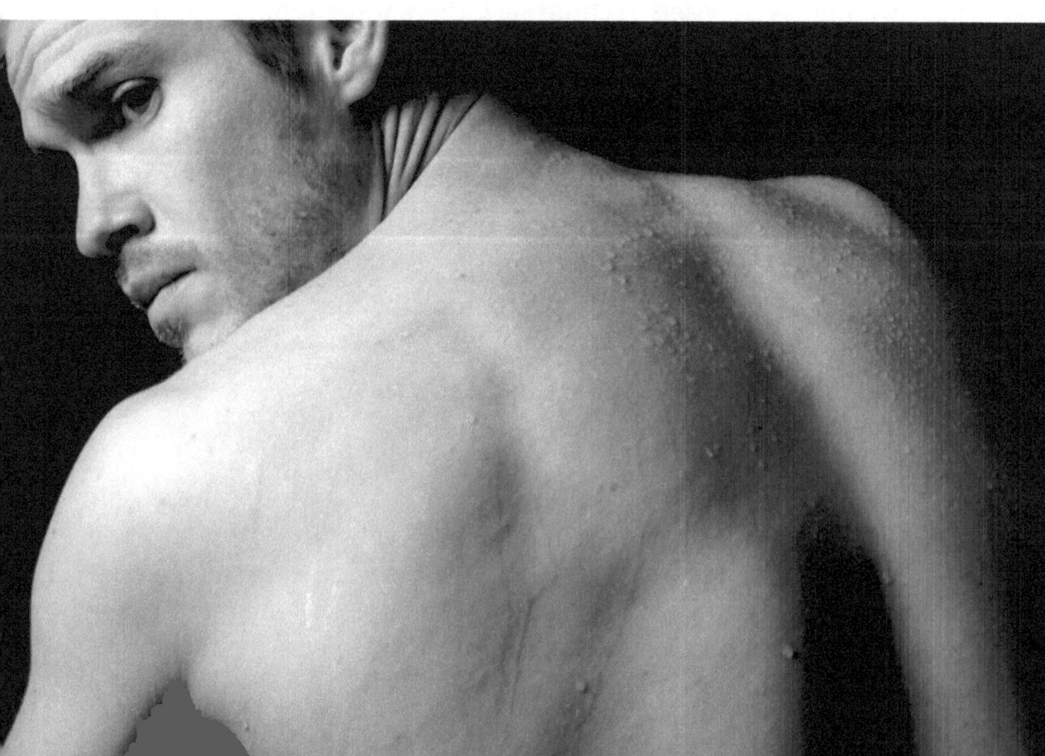

Her mouth tilted in an annoyed version of a grin. "His money is the same as the rest, perhaps more in abundance." She closed the door behind her, and with a metal click he was alone.

He stripped his clothes, tossing them into a pile on the floor to be gathered and cleaned...or burned. As he sank into the heat of the tub, he closed his eyes and saw the flames of the fire. The white-hot tongues licking his ruined flesh in a way he couldn't describe. Bathing felt like he was being flayed, the heat of the water reminding his skin what had very nearly ruined it. He managed his breathing, preventing his chest from filling too much, moving too much, stretching that bit of skin too much. Once his skin softened to the heat, he leaned back against the tub and sank down, his head resting at the curl on the back.

He stared into the steam that rose from the water and tried to make it the flames of the fire. Tried to lose himself to it as he had in the other room. But every shift of his muscles sent ripples across the surface, breaking his concentration and bringing her face to him. Her hands, so gentle and searching. Her expression, so open and wondering.

He reached for the bar of soap in the dish and washed himself, then scrubbed the soap through his hair before ducking beneath the water as best he could. When he surfaced, he forced a wave of water over the edge to splash the floor and the room felt smaller. Quieter. He looked to the corners but saw no one.

"Milord?" The voice came from behind him. Shaking and wary.

"Alice," he replied. He leaned forward on his knees, covering as much of himself as possible should she decide to come toward him. "Why are you in here?"

"I brought your towel and robe."

He nodded, turning his face toward her but still not seeing her. He did see the robe and towel on a wooden stand behind him. "And?"

"And...why did you ask me those questions? Were you truly interested in me?"

"Interested, yes. Not in the way a man has an interest in this house."

"Oh."

"Have you had interest from men in this house?"

"Yes, milord, though the rules are strict, you know."

He nodded again but that didn't make him feel better about the children quietly running the house as maids like mice, unseen unless they were seen. The problem was the tomcats hunting them. "What name will you give yourself?" he asked, wiping condensation from the brass of the faucet in front of him.

"Oh, no, milord, I'm not to choose. I'll be given a name."

"By who?" he asked and turned to look for her once again.

She stepped closer, to where he could just barely see her, the mobcap and apron floating in the dark of the room. "By whomever purchases me for training, of course."

He turned away. "Wouldn't you rather choose your own name?"

"I don't know. I'm not so good with words and names and the like. I think I would like someone to choose it for me."

Madoc pinched the bridge of his nose, closing his eyes tight against the simple knowledge she shared as though it wasn't even something to consider. His father had supplied girls like this. Though the houses he'd supplied hadn't followed the laws as strictly as this one seemed to do. But that group had been shut down. He'd assisted with that. It was perhaps the one good thing he'd done in all of his life. Though his intention had been that of bribery, not of noblesse. "You should go."

"But I—"

"There is no purpose for you in this room with me, that I'm aware of."

"But I—"

"Is your intent to create some purpose to which I'm unaware?"

"Yes, milord. I thought as you'd be interested in giving me a name."

Madoc dropped his head until his nose skimmed the water. His fists clenched in his hair. "No, you're a child. I have no interest in giving you a name, now or in future. You will need to find another patron."

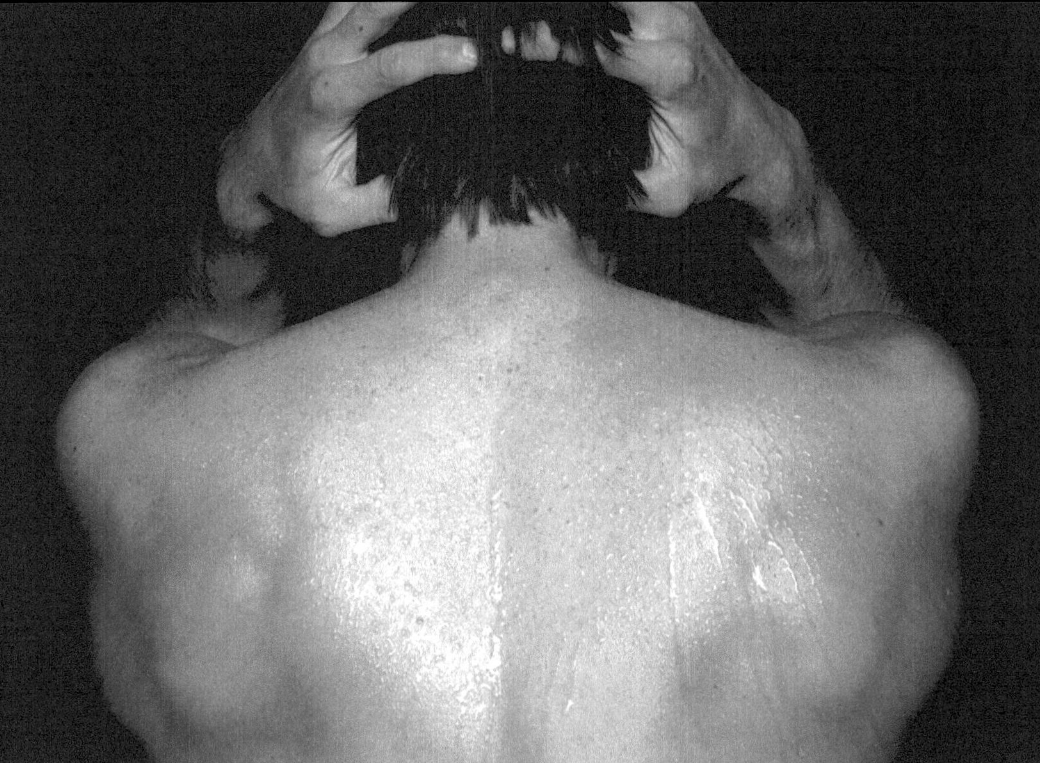

The door swung wide, and Madoc shifted attempting to cover himself further.

"Alice," the mistress said. "That's enough."

Alice curtseyed prettily, holding the edges of her apron as she dipped. Then she left. Madoc rested an elbow on the edge of the tub, turning his face away from the mistress. "Are you quite finished?" she asked.

"Yes. Quite. If you don't mind."

"I do in fact."

"Did you send her to me?"

"There are many ways to train the women who will work in this house," she said.

"She's a child," he protested but she only shrugged in response. "I'm not here for you to use."

"Aren't you?"

Madoc stood and gave her his back as he reached for the towel, sweeping it quickly over his body before pulling the robe from the rack. Before he could put it on, however, she'd come up behind him. Not allowing the room he needed to dress. "Do you mind?"

"I do, in fact," she replied. "You came to this house to use us once before. But now you take offense at the very thought that we have, under our protection, girls who will train to replace us. Girls who will grow up to be and do the things we do. Do you have the right to judge us?"

"If it's my coin, I have that right."

"Your coin didn't pay for your judgment. Alice is looking for a patron, as are they all. If she doesn't find one, she will be turned out regardless her training." Mistress took the robe from his hand and helped him into it, turning him and tying it loose at his waist. "It is either your place to comment or it is not. We know who you are, where you came from and what you want from us. Simply because you want it doesn't mean we are required to give."

"I already learned that lesson once. Or did you forget the trail of bloody footprints I left from your room the last I was here?"

"I remember. Do you?"

Of course he did. How was it that he was born to be so privileged and these women, these children, were born to be so disparaged? Treated as property, traded as commodity, discarded as useless. Madoc took a deep breath and thought of Willow once again. He'd discarded her in much the same manner; regardless of leaving her with someone he deemed safe, he'd been done with her and had set her aside like last night's leavings. If he'd thought to make himself feel worse, he'd been quite successful. Of all the people in this world he should be treating with the utmost kindness and respect, well, she was it.

The Queen had decreed Madoc was to make amends with his family and with the crown. How could he manage anything so noble when at his most basic he was anything but? He could save Alice— but no, that was patently ridiculous. There was no way for him to take Alice with him. He might be headed to prison. He couldn't even help himself.

He looked at his mistress for a moment, attempting to discern exactly what game she was playing with him. "I want Alice for myself. I want her kept. I want her protected. I do not want her trained, or learned in any of the manners of this house. If I'm her patron, I can do this?"

"Of course."

"Good. When I come back for her, I want her to have chosen her own name. I will send things to her. I expect her to... Can she read?"

The mistress shook her head.

"I want her taught. I will hire a teacher for her. Can this be done?"

"It can, though it would be disruptive to the household. What of the other Alices?"

"What of them?"

"Don't you think they'll be jealous of her lessons?"

"The teacher is for the house. Anyone who wishes can take the classes. Anyone who wishes to learn to read shall do so with her."

"Why?"

"Why not?"

"Do you think to alleviate her position? What of her coming of age? Will you return for her? And then what?"

"I know not. I only know that she'll not be like you."

"No? And what is so wrong with me? You think that if I had the choice, this life isn't what I would choose? Let me enlighten you. I had the same choice as Alice. I chose this life."

"At thirteen?"

"At ten."

"Choices like this cannot be made at ten."

"Some of us do not have the luxury of waiting to choose."

"It shouldn't be done."

"So you would prevent her making her own choices?"

"I would delay her making these choices. I would delay her... making *this* choice."

Mistress inspected him until he shifted as though throwing off a woolen sweater that chafed his bare skin. She nodded. "You can't save them all, you know?"

"I know. I can't save them all. I shouldn't attempt to save this one. But I will. If there are problems, if you cannot find me., find my brother. Tell him what I promised. He will see to it." With that, Madoc turned and walked away, brushing past a stout older man with a wide fluffed moustache. Then he ducked back into the mistress's room and closed the door behind him.

TWENTY

Willow hadn't expected to be treated as a guest. She wasn't exactly sure what she'd expected but it certainly wasn't to be put up in a beautiful room with the freedom to roam. The woman, Francine, had been so warm, welcoming. She'd embraced her and had led Willow to a guest room after Calder had spoken with her. She'd given her nightclothes to wear, shown her the library, given her a maid to see to her every need, apologized if the baby was too noisy, then left her to her own devices.

Willow supposed the maid could be considered a bit of a jailer, as she was ready at any moment to serve her and had been instructed to stay with her to keep her from becoming lost in the large manor house. But it didn't feel like jailer was her purpose. Calder and Quinn had departed with Celeste shortly after leaving her in the care of Francine. She'd been handed off and handed off and now was so exhausted from the night, all she really wanted was sleep to forget the ache.

Celeste had given her a warm hug, held her face in her hands and told her she would be back in the morning. That she was safe. That Francine could be trusted. This family...was so welcoming it was disconcerting. Perhaps because she'd never had a family so welcoming? Perhaps because she felt so alone in this world—save Madoc—that she strained for any connection? She had the feeling that his family was very accepting of everyone—save perhaps Madoc.

She bathed and dressed in a long nightgown then went to the library because she couldn't seem to sleep. She looked through volumes of books, more treatises like she'd found at Madoc's house, but also a lot more novels. She found an entire section of regency romance, though she supposed it wasn't actually considered that at this point in time. These books had spawned an entire genre, a multi-billion-dollar industry created by women for women. She'd researched the history of romance while working toward her degree, but the books weren't what had most interested her. It was the research that had gone into the books, the people, the clothing, the history. She loved Jane Austen more than Austen's words.

It was while researching those historical figures that she'd found the underground. The men and women who'd lived beyond the corsets and petticoats and pages. Finding them had felt like finding family—until she'd met Madoc. Until him, she'd been more of an interloper than a member.

She selected a first edition of *Pride and Prejudice* from the shelf. She'd never really liked it but God forbid she admitted that publicly. She had a hard time relating to Elizabeth and couldn't understand Darcy. Right now though, she felt a sort of kinship with the time. She sat on the little sofa in front of the fire and tucked her toes beneath her butt and started to read. By the time Jane was sick, Willow was exhausted, her eyelids too heavy to keep open and her legs too tired to carry her.

She took the throw from the back of the sofa and slid to her side, tucking in and watching the flames of the fire as she drifted off to sleep.

The hand over her mouth frightened her awake until she managed a deep breath for a scream but with it caught the scent of Madoc. Relief flooded her as his hand ran the length of her leg, quite determined in its course. She caught it with hers, stilled it. She shook his hand off her mouth. "Wait," she said, but his hand covered her mouth again, his forehead touching hers. She was completely disoriented. The fire had banked, the library dark. She closed her eyes and tried to remember how she'd ended up here—but his hands, pushing past her meager attempt to arrest them, were completely distracting to her. She felt the whimper in her throat, stifled by her lips, his hand pressed solidly to them. His reaction was immediate and swift, his body crushing hers into the seat of the couch she lay on.

She felt the hardness of his cock against the bones of her hip. His mouth replaced his hand and he bit her lip then pushed his tongue into her. She tasted a streak of copper on her tongue and said his name into him as thanks. "Madoc."

He bit her tongue, a reprimand as his mouth pushed harder against hers, sealing their lips and preventing her saying another word. His hands found her pussy and his fingers pinched, forcing a jerk from her hips as his heavy fingers slid between her folds and into her. She held onto his arms, unable to move or shift for the weight of him pinning her.

He stroked the slick wall of her vagina, pushing up into the perfect spot, then slipping away so rhythmically that she homed in on it. She concentrated on nothing but the pulse of that finger, the tip of it rougher than the rest.

Could he imprint himself on her most intimate flesh? She wanted him to.

"We should just speak with her, honestly," he said and it sounded perfectly clear, and not at all like him. But his mouth was still on hers and...she just couldn't seem to rectify it all. His hand stilled.

"We can't shock her," a woman said.

"Shock? Do you believe this woman would be shocked by anything at the moment? If she's like you—which I will concede for the time being, though how all these women keep falling from the sky yet astounds me—there isn't much that will shock her." The voice was low and gravelly, almost so much so that he was difficult to understand. One thing was certain though, it wasn't Madoc's voice at all, and that realization settled—the weight of him lifted from her completely. Willow could see then as her eyelashes fluttered against her cheeks that Madoc had been a dream. She shifted, realizing it was her own hands covering her mouth and pussy. Her own teeth biting her tongue. She blinked her eyes wide, staring at the fire and pushing back into the crease of the sofa she lay on as she listened to the conversation behind her and attempted to determine whether or not she was still dreaming.

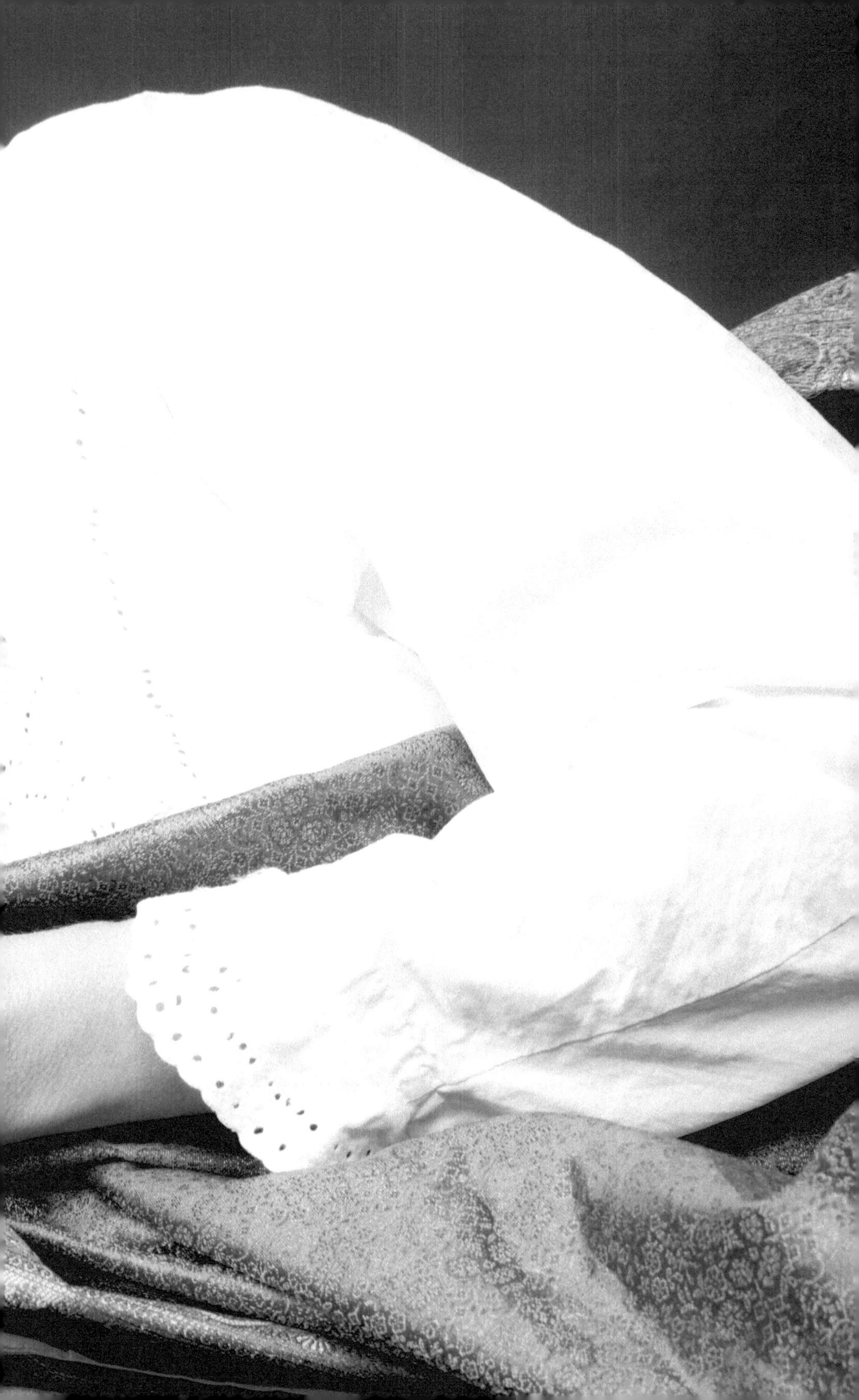

"It's true, but she seems so distraught. And the fact that she was put with Madoc...he's not at all a good person! How are we supposed to keep her from him? She can't be allowed to be with him. And then there's her grandmother—dealing with her will get interesting."

"Ah, see, my love, you are finally understanding the conundrum I was faced with when you were given to me."

Given? A chill rushed Willow's skin and she shifted on the sofa to try to hear better.

"Given to you?" Francine laughed, and the sound of it filled the room—dancing about through the shadows and making them stir.

The man responded with a growl deep in his throat. "Given to me." The voice was strong, sending goosebumps across her arms. It was muffled as well, too close to the other as though they embraced. Willow thought she should probably make herself known.

"Is that how you see it?" Francine asked.

"Of course it is. You were a gift. By what function I know not, but I know you were made for me as I was made for you. We were meant to be together. There is no keeping us apart. You've been in my life, you've been my wife, for nearly six years. Would you have it any other way?"

"Never," she replied. "But it doesn't mean I don't want to protect Willow from Madoc."

"Listen, my beautiful, meddling woman, you were worried about Grayson as well. Do you remember?"

"Of course I do, but that was different."

"How so?"

"You know how so—Stop. Stop, please let me concentrate. Oh..."

The room quieted, save the rustle of fabric and the heaviness of their breathing for a moment, and Willow considered crawling out of the room.

Francine cleared her throat. "This is serious. You know what Madoc's done. He's been censured. He could be hanged for what he did to Calder. This is...this is so much more serious than anything we've dealt with in the past. My concern for Lulu is very different from my concern for Willow."

The man grunted. She heard a few steps as they left the soft carpet and went to the windows bordering the room. "I agree. What I'm trying to get across to you at the moment is that there is naught that can be done about this tonight, and I am quite—"

"Quite?"

"Quite...sure that it will all keep until the morning when Calder and Quinn and Celeste return. I've sent a missive to Warrick—Grayson—so he should arrive on the morrow as well. Until then, we don't even know where Madoc is. Calder sent a note that he wasn't back at Warrick House. So please, my love, my heart, my soul, please—"

"Please?"

"Take me to bed." The words were gruff. Powerful. They tumbled from him and were immediately followed by a sharp breath and rustle of fabric. There was something familiar in his voice as though the origin of it came from the same place as Madoc...which she supposed it did. Beyond that it was the voice of a powerful man who was at the will of someone else. A tone she'd never heard from Madoc, supposed she never would. But the thought of it, that she would be that powerful in his life, that she would be someone who could command him, was definitely something she yearned for.

"You're so very demanding. Why is that?" Francine asked him.

He didn't answer for a moment, and Willow was afraid they wouldn't leave the study before getting it on. "Because I'm reminded of how lucky I am to have you. By whatever function, by the Fates or by God, I am lucky to have you and I wish to show you just how much I realize and understand that."

"But what about the Queen?"

"Let me deal with the Queen," he said in a voice that was so deep and guttural it bordered on terrifying.

"As you wish, my love. Yes, yes, my love," Francine replied.

Willow heard the steps again, a whoosh of fabric accompanied by a squeal then the quiet shush of a single pair of heavy shoes across the carpet. The door to the library opened, then closed once more.

Willow rolled over and put her face into the back of the sofa. She couldn't leave this house if the only place she knew of wasn't where she could find Madoc. He was the sole purpose she had right now and he was gone. She dragged his face from her memories. The way the scars twisted his expression, making him harder to read. The way they made him more beautiful, singular. She wanted to see all of him. She wanted to hold him. She wanted to fear him. She wanted to love him. She wanted him. She drifted off to sleep.

"Willow?"

She shifted against the cushion, her neck stiff from the position she'd slept in.

"Willow?"

She rubbed her eyes then blinked them open.

Celeste ran a hand down her arm from her shoulder. "Are you well?"

Willow nodded, trying to catch up with her memories. She'd met the woman last night after the ball in which Madoc had abandoned her to his cousins. Her breath hitched at the thought and she closed her eyes, then turned on the small sofa and sat up. Celeste sat next to her and patted her hands as she tangled them together in her lap. "I'm fine," she said.

"Oh...well, that says quite a lot then, doesn't it?" Celeste said.

Willow supposed it did. "I just want him. I want to go back to him. Why would he abandon me like this?"

"Perhaps he's frightened. Did you tell him the same things you told us?"

"Yes."

"He...perhaps he's overwhelmed?"

"No. That's not it. Maybe he's scared, I think... God I don't know what to think. I wish he would have talked to me first."

"That would have been ideal, though Madoc is currently in a position that makes having you in his house quite dangerous."

"For whom?"

"For both of you, actually." Celeste looked beyond her to the entry of the library.

"What is it?" Willow asked.

"I think we may know who you are."

"Who I am? I know who I am."

"Yes, of course, but the function of this...this..." Celeste spun her hand in a circle over her head.

"This...world?" Willow asked.

"No, the situation you're in. The same situation I'm in. The same situation several of us are in."

"Wait, are you talking about time travel?" Willow stopped moving, breathing, thinking for a moment even. As though someone had pushed a reset button and she had to come back to life. Her fingertips tingled and she shook them out.

"Of a fashion. Though I don't believe it's that sort of... It's not that simple."

"Time travel is...simple?"

"The idea of it is."

Willow nodded. "Okay," she said but heard the skepticism in her voice, and yet...what else was there? Clearly something had happened to her. "Sorry, I just..." She closed her eyes and let her muscles relax. Her whole body seemed to shrink into itself and she leaned against the back of the sofa.

"Celeste?" Francine called from the entry.

"Here," Celeste replied, and Willow listened as Francine walked across the room to sit next to them.

"Good morning. How long have you been in here?" Francine asked. Willow felt the heat rise under her skin as her heart skipped a beat. She closed her eyes and tried to pretend she didn't need to answer. "Last night, huh?" Willow nodded. Hoping that would be the end of it. She could hear the smile in her words and somehow she understood that this woman had the power to light up any room. She was pure joy personified, and Willow was...not at all that. She never had been. This woman was a cheerleader with a good genuine heart. It was disconcerting. Well, relatively speaking. She added it to the list.

"You said you knew who I was," Willow said, dropping all guard and pretenses.

"Yes, we believe you to be the granddaughter of the Queen of England."

Willow laughed. Like, bellowed. She didn't simply rustle the shadows in the corners; she scared the shadows from the building, scared the dust from beneath the furniture, frightened the flames back into the log.

Willow heard heavy steps running for the library and stood, turning to see who was coming, hoping one set of those heavy steps belonged to Madoc even as she knew they didn't. "Come on. That's got to be the most ridiculous thing I've ever—"

Calder came into the room, followed by Quinn and a third man who looked like a mix between Quinn and Madoc, but perhaps bigger and meaner somehow. Willow stilled.

"What's happened?" the man asked.

"What is— I mean, who…who is that?" Willow asked Celeste in as low a voice as she could manage. She reached out for comfort, and Celeste took her hand, standing next to her in a protective manner.

"You met Calder and Quinn, of course—and that," she said as she pointed, "is Roxleigh. Francine's husband."

Francine's smile beamed and she stood, turning to the men. "Hello my love," she said, and Calder and Quinn parted as though she'd struck an arrow and neither of them wished to be hit by it. Roxleigh's face transformed when he met her gaze, and Willow lost her breath.

"Wow," she said.

"Yeah," Celeste said. "But you do get used to it." Her voice sounded wistful, and Willow looked to her only to realize she was looking between Calder and Quinn with quite the same grin as Francine had when she looked upon Roxleigh. She watched Francine greet him, and as she took his hand and pulled him into the room a fourth man stepped inside, taking the breath from Willow like a punch to the gut. She tried to run. "Madoc!" she yelled, but Celeste's hand on hers tightened, and as Roxleigh moved aside she realized it wasn't Madoc, but a near perfect replica of his good side.

"It's her," the man said as he took her in. "That's Princess Dorothea."

"Um...what now?" she asked.

"It means," Calder said, "you belong to the Queen...who will be quite put out if you're not returned to her."

"Um..." Willow said again because she couldn't think of anything else to say at the moment. She wanted to know more about the man who looked like her Madoc. Instead of asking about him, she said, "I'm the granddaughter of the Queen. That makes me royalty, yeah?" Everyone turned to look at her then. She cleared her throat. "So that's a yes?"

The missive, when it came the next day, wasn't what Madoc had expected. He'd sent a note to Calder so he'd know how to find him, but this was from his brother and it invited him to Roxleigh House that afternoon. Which seemed such a ridiculous thing that Madoc actually laughed as he reread the paper—three times. The words didn't change. He sat on the mistress's bed and stared at the words until they bled into each other.

"Do you have a response?" she asked finally.

"What?"

"The boy is awaiting your response. It's a single word, I assume."

"Tell him no. Tell him to tell them I could not possibly."

The Mistress turned and left him in the room, closing the door behind her. What was he supposed to do? He'd told Gray where to find him but he hadn't meant for them to... He'd meant for Gray to come to him, to tell him what had been decided. He could not face the lot of them together. He couldn't face her with them. He knew he wouldn't survive the hatred that would be in her eyes now. It had been difficult enough to walk away from her at the masquerade, and there was one thing he knew above all else—if he saw her again, there was no chance he would be able to walk away from her.

The door swung open and Madoc put the paper on the bed, dropping his head to his hands. "You'll be done with me soon enough. I won't stay beyond the sennight as promised."

"I believe you."

Madoc stood. A rill of sweat beaded at his nape then broke loose and trickled the length of his spine. "Gray." He closed his eyes. "You're no errand boy."

"You refused the invitation. I'm here to convince you this is in your best interest."

He shook his head. "It's not. And it isn't in yours or Calder's—"

"That's where you're absolutely correct. Where you're concerned, there is nothing you can do that would be in Calder's best interest—save perhaps death."

"And is that what you've brought with you?"

"Death?" Gray asked.

Madoc nodded, a second bead of sweat trailing the first.

"No. We've much bigger problems than death, at the moment, though death does play into the problems quite well."

He figured it would. He'd assumed his family would refuse any chance at reconciliation. "Listen to me. I don't want to draw this out. I'm not deserving of the chance The Queen has given me and I'm enough of a man to admit I would prefer a swift and quiet end to being tossed in prison and eventually hanged. So if you don't mind—"

"You expect me to end you? You truly are a coward, which is not at all what I thought of you after all these years."

"No. I imagine not. But I'll not put Willow through this. I'll not drag it out before her. She deserves better than me and she deserves to know the truth and be done with it." Madoc was angry. He didn't want to dance with his cousins in these games; he wanted to be done with it all. He knew this was his end—there were no other choices for him. He turned on his brother. "I'm not the boy you grew up with," he yelled. "Nor am I the man who attempted to trap you. I won't be so ridiculous as to say I've seen the error of my ways... I always knew exactly what I was doing, right and wrong." He turned his back to him, not wanting to be able to read his expression any more. "There's no need for me to rethink anything or consider further. I knew what I was doing when I did it. I always did. I am as conscientious of that now as I was aware of it back then."

"Turn to me."

Madoc put the heel of his hand to his forehead and pushed. He wished he could visit an opium den to relieve the coming pain behind his eyes. The opium had been his saviour when he'd recovered enough from his injuries to leave the haveli. Once he'd convinced his father's men he was on their side and had been granted a modicum of freedom, he'd spent the majority of his time in dens forgetting who he was and what he'd done. And now...the cool silence of opium seemed a perfect escape from this life.

But there was no opium here. He turned. His brother was no more than five paces from him. The sharp polish of his shoes reflected the streak of light he'd allowed past the curtains and into the room. His trousers were fitted perfectly, the hem hitting just below his ankle and above the bridge of his shoe, the line so sharp it made Madoc wince. He closed his eyes.

"I want to see you. See what they did to you," he said.

Madoc looked down at the long shirt and drawers he'd worn to sleep in. "To what purpose?"

"Perhaps to find some sympathy in your injury."

"Then the answer is no. My injuries are not here for your sympathy. They're not a function of forgiveness if that's what you intend. If you're to attempt to forgive me, it's as a whole man, not a broken one. Not this one. It's as the one who injured you. You remember him?"

"I remember I trusted him."

Madoc looked up and caught his brother's gaze, held it. "That was your first mistake. You remember me? I remember me. I remember the day we sparred as though it were yesterday. I dreamt of that day nearly every night of my life until the accident. Then I dreamt of nothing but pain. But that day— I was made a man that day. I understood what it would take to get me off. Much as you did, no?"

"You—" Gray stopped, breaking their connection and looking away.

"Our father, Gray, liked pain, as do I. He liked to cause it. Liked to see it. He lived for it. So, too, do I. He raised me to understand the power of pain. The subjugation, the control, the absolute persuasion of it." The fact that he knew one distinct difference between what his father liked about pain and what he did was left unsaid.

Gray turned back, and Madoc refused to look away. "What did you want of me in Jodhpur? Why did you send for me?"

"I wanted you to know. I wanted...I wanted you to understand. I had hoped that perhaps we would—"

"Don't pretend to be someone you're not, Madoc. I've no interest in any stories of forgiveness from you, nor any lies between us. When Calder arrived in my place, you didn't treat him as family. You chained him to a wall and threatened him. Don't profess to different plans for me. I know everything that happened. Everything you said."

Madoc stopped. Closed his eyes. "He wasn't the one I wanted and was of no use to me. I wanted to know whether you were part of the group that put me where I was. I wanted to know if they were lying to me. I wanted to trade places if you were amenable. I wanted to know whether I could trust you," Madoc said quietly. "But he wasn't you, didn't have that knowledge. Therefore I had no use of him. At least...I thought not when he'd arrived, and I was so angry that he was there in your stead. That my prison would be extended further by the absence of you. I had the notion that I could learn something from him. I wanted to prove to myself that I was not the same as our father. Turns out, I was wrong."

"You're mad," Gray said.

"Perhaps I am. Consider who raised me. You think your life so tragic but consider where you ended up, and who you ended up being. Do you think you would have been this man who stands here now had you been raised by the same father I was?" Madoc paused and tried to calm himself, tried to relieve the pressure that built behind his eyes.

"No, but then I also believe I would have discovered my purpose whether or not he'd raised me. I believe we are destined for certain things and who we're born to or how we're raised only gives us a piece of who we are. The rest is left to us to fight or succumb to."

Madoc waited, expecting Gray to say something more. He didn't. "Do you believe I could have been a good man?" he asked and it was the most vulnerable he'd ever felt with anyone aside from Willow.

"I believe it depends entirely on you. It depends on who you were meant to be and if you've simply been on a detour...or if this hate was your path all along. Which do you think it is, Madoc? Who do you believe you are? There's a woman who insists—against all evidence and agreement to the contrary—that you're a good man. She insists you're thoughtful, caring, compassionate. This woman describes a man I've yet to meet."

Madoc slid down the wall next to the window until he hit the floor, his arms on his knees, his head back against the velvet baroque wall paper. "Willow."

"Yes. Willow."

"She doesn't deserve this. She doesn't deserve me. She deserves so much better, so much more."

"You keep insisting that."

"Because it's true," he yelled. "You shouldn't allow her to attach to me. She'll find someone eventually who can care for her the way she should be cared for."

"See, therein lies the problem, Mads, she refuses to give up on you. She refuses to the point she wants to destroy herself only to prove to you that she belongs to you."

"What do you mean?"

"Well," Gray said, and he walked around the bed, sitting at the edge in front of Madoc. He leaned over, his elbows on his knees, his face almost level with Mad's. "We know who she is and...it's not good. I must tell you, regardless what the rest of us dealt with in protecting our wives, you, sir, have chosen someone impossible for you to care for."

"I made no choices."

"That I understand more than you could possibly know."

"I don't understand."

"And I am loath to explain until I'm able to trust in you. For the time being, you're to take my words at face value."

"What do you mean?"

"I mean there is more happening than you simply finding a woman in a pub and kidnapping her then attempting to care for her. And that is all I'll say about it."

"Who is she?" he asked but Gray only looked at him. "Who is she?"

"Princess Dorothea Feodora Friederike Amalia Beatrice Alice Charlotte Auguste... Wait, no—Alice *Auguste* Charlotte Sophia Wilhelmine Victoria Viktoria Ulrike Elisabetta. Crowned princess of Prussia." Each name sent a thump of panic through Madoc's system.

"What...what are you saying?"

"Your woman, Madoc, is granddaughter to the Queen of England. How thrilled do you think Her Imperial Highness will be when she discovers you're meant to protect her granddaughter for the rest of her life?"

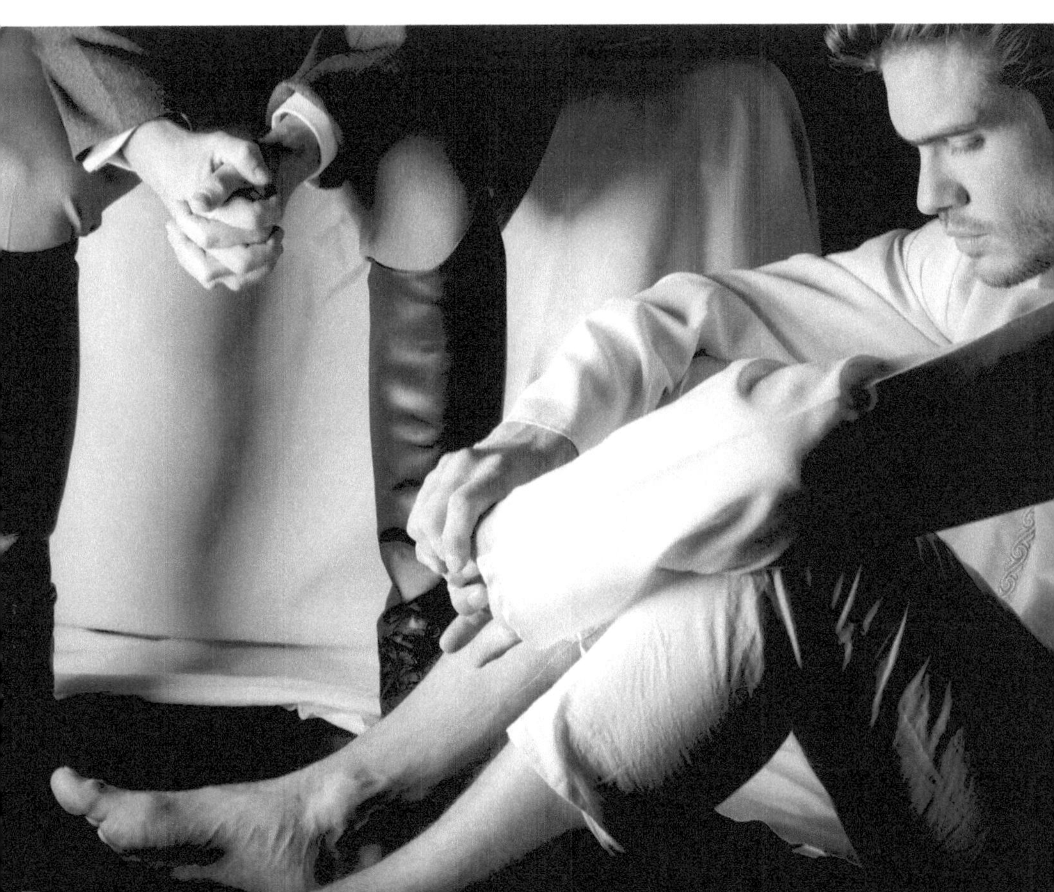

"That can't be... She should go back to The Queen, take her place—" Madoc pushed his knuckles into his breast plate as a pain so severe lanced through his heart then spread through his veins like poison at the very thought of sending her away. "Fuck-all."

"I think you're beginning to understand the bigger problem here. This isn't your choice to make and, sadly, your family are the only people who can help you."

TWENTY-ONE

illow woke from a nap with an ache in her chest so deep and wide she didn't understand how she managed. She pulled her knees up, rolling to her side like an infant, cradling the hollow space where her heart was suspended, beating slowly in the center. She could almost hear the echo of her want thrumming in her ears. Slowly, determinedly, lonely.

She stood and dressed, managing to tighten the corset enough so that it felt as though her heart were at least somewhat supported. It felt slightly more stable, vaguely grounded. She finished dressing on her own, having turned the maid away while she lazed in bed, then went down to breakfast. She found them all by the lyrical sound of their chatter, which she followed until it surrounded her. Lulu, Francine, and Lilly, Roxleigh and Perry.

These people who seemed to have enfolded her within their family seamlessly without a second thought. Something she'd never understood, because her own family had been...distant at best. A working function of having a place to live while growing up—but nothing more. This belonging somewhere was becoming too familiar, and she feared losing it above all else. Well, not quite. It gave her a sense of fullness that wasn't quite fulfilled because something major was still missing. Madoc.

She couldn't be without him.

She sat close to Lulu, Francine, and Lilly, eating small bits of food and listening to all the conversation around her. Luncheon ended, and the men stood to depart for whatever man-things they were off to do.

"Rox?" Francine asked.

"Yes?" he replied, and Willow was struck again by just how handsome he was, and just how full the light in his eyes was with his wife.

"Are you finished with the newsheets?"

He grunted his response and gathered them from where he and the other men had been sitting and handed them to her, kissing her again. It was such an odd thing, the two of them. Like magnets, their movements stilted as though moving away, one from the other, was truly difficult for them, but coming together was easy.

She knew how that felt. She closed her eyes against the remembrance.

"Thank you," Francine said then turned her smile on Willow and they all stood, Willow following.

The women went to the parlor that overlooked the gray square in front of the house. Francine, Lulu, and Lilly once again discussing meaningless things around her. She knew they did it for her sake, trying to keep her mind off whatever was happening, but the more they didn't discuss *it*, the more anxious she became. She didn't ask them to stop though, because it was still a comforting sort of chatter.

"Look at this one," Francine said, handing a news sheet to Lulu.

Lulu laughed. "Lord Everart needs to find a better way to get his rocks off before society grows weary of his shenanigans. I mean, this is his third public indecency, isn't it?"

"I don't see how they can continue to overlook his behavior," Francine replied.

"Privilege," Lulu said simply, and Francine grimaced.

Willow glanced at the back of the sheet in Lulu's hand and her heart stuttered in its lonely cave. "May I see that?" she asked, and Lulu passed it to her. Willow stared at the advertisement on the back in sheer disbelief before she managed to control her features for fear of questions she didn't quite want to answer.

The Ninth Cat
3. 2. 9. . 44. . 81

Oh. God. She smoothed the paper on her lap. This was the newsheet from the Maughan Library. She flipped to the front and read through all the stories, now able to recognize more of the names and places as she hadn't before.

"If you'll excuse me, I think I'm going back to my room for a bit," she said, trying to keep her voice steady as her heart thundered.

"If there's anything we can do, please, just let us know," Francine said, and Willow squeezed her hand and then Lulu's as she held the newssheet to her breast and walked from the room. She rushed across the foyer to the stairs. Once she got to her room, she laid the paper on the table next to the settee and paced the room, wondering what she should do next when someone knocked at the door. She opened it to find Lulu.

"I know you wanted to be alone but I feel like maybe it was that there were too many of us, so I just wanted to check to make sure you're okay. Believe me when I say I understand how difficult this transition is and how crazy this all seems at the moment, but I'm telling you I would not change anything in my life given the slightest opportunity," said Lulu, then she drew her over to the settee and took her hands. "I only want to say that I hope beyond all hope that you feel like this is where you belong, because it's where I belong and I want you to have that sense of belonging. I know that sounds odd and clunky but I wouldn't want to be anywhere else, not ever, not for any reason, and I hope if that's not quite how you feel that maybe you feel like it would be possible to feel that way someday soon."

"I understand what you're saying. And yes, I know I belong... but I don't belong *here*. I belong with Madoc. I don't— I can't be away from him for whatever reason. There's something inside me telling me that *right now* in this moment I cannot be away from him. There's something so urgent that I feel like crawling out of this skin that doesn't yet belong to me, as though I'm not yet a permanent fixture here and if I don't get to him I'll be gone, and what then?" Willow broke down crying. Something told her if she didn't get to him, she would never see him again.

"I'll help you."

Willow picked up the paper from the table in front of the settee. "I've seen this paper before. I saw it at the Maughan Library before... before everything happened. This newspaper has a clue to what I was searching for and it's the paper that led me to Madoc to begin with. I think I need to go there again. I need to go back to The Iron Duke."

"I can take you there. It's just across Grosvenor; the boys hang out there drinking beer. Ale, whatever."

"I need to go now. Can you help me? I'm nervous. I understand that people are looking for me—"

"Yeah, I'm going with you," Lulu said and when Willow opened her mouth to refuse, she stopped her. "Only to make sure you get where you need to be. I won't stop you from finding him. I'll do nothing that stops you. I will just go to be sure that you're safe. Is that acceptable?"

Willow thought a moment and decided it was probably a good idea. She was a complete stranger to the city—a complete stranger to this world and though she had an idea where she needed to go, she'd no idea how to manage should something happen. "Yes, I'd appreciate it if you came with me. But please don't tell anybody. Will they let us leave?"

"We're not prisoners, sweetie. I'll let them know we're going for a walk. I'll let them know that everything's fine and we just need some air. In February. In London." Lulu laughed. "Don't worry. Just meet me in the front foyer in about twenty minutes."

"Yes. Thank you. Thank you." Willow stood, holding the newssheet. She flipped to the section she'd seen at the Maughan with the name and the code. She tucked it in the pocket of her petticoats beneath her skirts then went to the wardrobe to find a warm cape so it would look like a reasonable thing to go for a walk. In February. In London.

Willow and Lulu walked silently, arm-in-arm, across the square. London was gray upon gray. The only color in the world came from the skirts they wore, blue and green, flashing from the opening of their cloaks as they walked. Lulu was adept at avoiding the deep slush puddles and navigating the park in front of Roxleigh House.

Willow was glad to have her along. With every step she took it felt like her heart pulled a little tighter to her breast.

When Lulu led her across the street, pointing toward a corner building Willow stopped, staring up at the façade that hadn't changed all that much over the centuries. The brass signage was a bit heavier. The years of polishing not yet wearing the expensive lettering down. The entry and windows were the original diamond-shaped, watered glass—not the storm-proof double-paned glass from the future inn. But the ironwork and the brick-and-wood façade was either the same or replicated—all she needed now was the low bass thump of the drag queen's music to take her straight back to that night. She closed her eyes, knew she was headed in the right direction, and swayed on her feet then walked toward the inn.

"You okay, Willow?" Lulu wrapped an arm around her shoulder, and she sank against her side.

"I was just here, one hundred thirty-some years from now."

"Now that's an experience I haven't yet had. That has to be bizarre."

"Where were you?" Willow asked.

"I was, well, I was in my dungeon back in Denver."

"Dungeon...as in BDSM?"

"Yeah." Lulu smiled.

"I...want to know more. I was researching the Victorian Underground." It was the first time she'd said that, knowing the person she was talking to would understand the meaning.

"Oh," Lulu said with a big grin. "We'll talk. I'll tell you all about it. Later. Promise."

"Okay. Okay, cool."

"You ready for this?"

"Fuck no," Willow replied. Lulu squeezed her, and Willow let out a deep breath. "Okay, now I'm ready," she said, and they walked for the doors.

Willow ran a hand down the bar, pushing the barstool in where she'd sat. Seeing the much-newer wood of the surface, the divot from bellies leaning against the bar not yet there. Then she turned to the back wall, walking straight for the marks she remembered from that night. There they were, nine sassy cats, the last one winking. They looked brand new. She ran a thumb over them and pricked her finger on a splinter. She used her fingernails to remove the splinter and sucked the bead of blood that followed.

Lulu touched it as well. "Nine cats, huh? I can guess what kind of establishment this is."

"Yeah, the Birch Mistress I was trying to find..."

"This is an address," Lulu cut in, pointing to the words beneath the carving.

"Mews," Willow said.

"Yep, at the back of this house." Lulu nodded. "Okay, let's go." She took her hand and pulled her along.

"I need to take you to Buckingham, Madoc. She's waiting."

"I'm not ready," he replied. How was he supposed to go there? He needed Willow like he needed breath. He supposed the sooner he went to the Queen, the sooner it would be over with.

"I can't put her off. You know the—" His words were cut off by yelling coming from below stairs, followed by thumping footsteps headed up to his room. "Well," Gray said, "I guess it's not up to me anymore."

"You told her where?"

"Do you suppose I would have to tell her where to find you?" he said and his annoyance was pure, and Mads knew that while Gray had probably told the Queen he was aware of his location, he hadn't actually reported that location.

"Which door?" The yell came from the end of the hallway, and Madoc's heart gave a stiff thump inside his ribcage at the recognition.

"Willow," he said and pushed past his brother opening the door. "Willow!" he ran. They met halfway, and she leaped into his arms, wrapping herself around him as best she could while she fought her skirts and held on tight. Something shifted; his heart thrummed rapidly. He wrapped his arms around her ever tighter. He would never let go again. "You shouldn't have come," he whispered against her neck. "I won't survive losing you again."

"Then don't do that ever again," she replied, and he held her tighter. Holding her against himself and turning back for the room as the Mistress shushed and calmed other visitors.

He went inside, kicked the door with his foot, only to have it stopped by someone behind him.

"Pardon," she said, and Mads turned to see Cecilia. His grip on Willow tightened as he considered why. "Ah, Gray, here you are." She beamed at him then pushed past Madoc and Willow and stepped into his brother's arms as Mads watched. He felt something like a key turning in a lock, the tumblers rolling together until they slipped into place. The key removed and tossed aside. This was how it was meant to be. His heart stilled, finally, and he could breathe.

He carried Willow to the bed and helped her to sitting, but she wouldn't release her grip on his shirt. "Don't," she said. "You can't... you can't leave me."

"I'm not going anywhere just yet. I promise you that, but I do have to get us some privacy. Trust me, I'll not leave. You'll not be taken. For the moment, we are together." She nodded, and he gently pried her hands open and placed them in her lap then turned to Gray. "You cannot... I cannot leave with you just yet. Please," he said, his gaze on the floor, his supplication to Grayson complete. His brother held all the cards, had all the control, carried his life in his pocket at this moment.

He heard Cecilia speak to his brother, and Gray grunted.

"Madoc...I cannot leave you here."

Mads nodded, resigned to the reality he'd created for himself. Gray had no cause to trust him, and he was going to have to accept that.

"You'll both come with us back to Roxleigh House. Tomorrow we will all go to Buckingham. Together. Get ready and meet us below stairs."

Grayson and Cecilia saw them to their guest room at Roxleigh House after a long, silent walk back across the square.

"If you are not here tomorrow..."

Madoc looked up into his brother's gaze, "I'll be here. I'll not meet your benevolence with malice."

"There's naught I can do but put my trust in you," he said then turned to Willow. "It's been a pleasure to meet you. I trust I'll see you tomorrow."

Willow remained silent, but when Cecilia walked to her and gave her a hug, she spoke. "Thank you for helping me, Lulu."

"If you need me, you know where to find me. Gray and I will be staying here for the night, as well." They hugged again, and Cecilia turned to him.

"Lulu?" he questioned. "You never were my Cecilia, were you?"

"No. *I* never was."

He allowed a single moment of sorrow for the woman he'd known. Then he nodded. "Thank you."

Her gaze narrowed on him, and she nodded once and turned away, taking Gray's hand and following him from the room.

Mads turned back to Willow, but he didn't move toward her. A bone-deep exhaustion borne from days of fitful sleep sank into his body. She yawned as if in answer.

He put a small chair up to the door to warn of intruders then walked around the bed, pushing the covers back and crawling in behind her. He removed her cape, loosened her dress, her corset. He wrapped his arms around her middle beneath the dress, skin to skin. She pushed her shoes off. He stretched out on the pillow, pulled her against his chest and covered them both. They slept.

TWENTY-TWO

When Willow woke, the room was quiet and full of late afternoon shadows. She felt calm, much calmer than she had that morning. She must have dreamed him again but it felt different; perhaps she was beyond the worst of the pain. She stood, staring out at the waning light from the window.

"You've managed quite the impression."

Willow turned, her hand clutched on the bedpost as she tried to hide behind it. She couldn't see him, but the calm in her being told her he was here. She wasn't going to jump up and find him though; she'd learned that lesson. She wanted to wait and find out what happened next. She closed her eyes. "Oh God, please," she said, and let her head fall forward to rest against the post above her hand.

"Both hands."

She did it. She wrapped her other hand around the post, and her breathing became heavy. She started to open her eyes, but he clicked his tongue and she stopped. She waited.

"How is this going to work between us?" he asked.

She shook her head.

"It is more and more impossible by the day. Do you understand that?"

She nodded. Whimpered. Wished. The length of her petticoats brushed against her toes but she knew it wasn't because *she* had moved, and her heart rate picked up.

"Willow." The voice came across her ear, the breath of it playing with her sensitive skin before sending sparks through her veins to her belly.

"Please," she said, and was immediately cold from the loss of him. "Please. Please," she said. Then she opened her eyes and pushed away from the bedpost. "Madoc, I'm losing my mind. If we have but a day left between us..." She turned to find him standing in the light of the window, his body in shadow. "I want you. I want this. But I am so frightened right now about what's to come of me. I'm not equipped to deal with this sort of thing. I'm not a strong woman. I'm not a leader, I'm a follower. I like taking orders and I like having my decisions made for me until I don't. But right now...I'm so lost. I need someone to do these things for me. You." She was exhausted. Mentally, physically, every atom of her being wanted a compression blanket.

"That's not true at all. You've been in control of this entire thing since the moment I met you. You think you're weak? That's ridiculous; you're anything but. If what you said is true—what they're saying is true, if what they've told me is true... Willow, you'd have to be the strongest person I know to be thrust through time to a place foreign to you and survive with the likes of me. Don't diminish who you are for my benefit, because I won't accept that for a moment. Do you understand me?"

"Yes."

"Good then, listen. Neither of us is welcome in this world. You've made my cousins love you, which..." He shook his head, "It's a touch awkward since I—well, I tried to kill one of them and took another as a prisoner. I think that speaks to my relationship with my cousins quite plainly, and my brother, of course, is an entirely separate matter." His voice was low; it sounded like she felt—tired. "If we're to survive this stay, here, I think we should attempt to do so together. You're all I have, Willow, and while I know you've probably made some friends in this family, as you should...you're all I have. Further, you're all that has consequence in my life. I need you. I am the one who cannot do this alone."

Oh God. "Look at me," she said.

His arms dropped to his sides and he shifted uncertainly. Then he took one step, and another, and looked at her.

"Is this all true? Is this real? Is this...is this my reality now?" She knew, even as she said it, that he didn't have the answer for that. The only person who could possibly have the answer for that was her. "I've been so lost, Madoc. I've been so lost without you," she said, then took two steps and wrapped her arms around his neck. "But when I'm with you, when I'm next to you...I'm found. I know where I belong. It's with you. The rest doesn't matter."

He lifted and as she'd done in the hall earlier, she wrapped her legs around his waist and held on as tight as she could. Refusing to let go. Because for the first time in days, she felt like she was home. She felt safe.

"Don't ever leave me like that again. I won't survive it." A certain calm came over her, washed through her veins like cool water clearing toxins and as she inhaled and it anchored her, her very breath wrapping around him, holding him to her. His fingers dug into the skin of her hips, pulling her tight against his sturdy frame. His muscles tightened like cooling steel, as though to hold her to him permanently.

"Never," he said and his voice was so rough, so deep and guttural it was almost unrecognizable. "You are mine. You were born for me. You will be taken from me only upon my death. I will fight for you from this moment forward. Forever."

And Willow felt every single one of her muscles release and melt into his as though they would become a single entity, nothing between them but the sweat of their skin. "Madoc."

He would never be rid of this woman. He would not relinquish her; he did not care the consequences of his actions—he would not allow her to be removed from him again. Not ever. Not by will or want or necessity. He would fight it all. He would fight everyone. Never in his life had he felt this emotion, this need, this base want. He wasn't sure he could release her, even as he knew he needed to. He was hard-pressed to even lessen his grip on her so he could look in her eyes.

"Willow, my Willow," he said. He tucked his chin and pushed his face against her hair behind her ear, simply breathing of her. He still couldn't figure out what it was she smelled of. Something sweet but wholesome—not tart or frivolous. He had no idea what it was.

As he allowed one hand to search her body, he discovered he could release his grip as she held on to him with such strength that his was unnecessary—and so he let go and she remained attached. His hands roamed her body possessively. He grabbed, he pinched, he pushed, he tested and when her breath quickened, his cock rose slow against the heat of her center. He took her head between his hands and coaxed her back so he could see her.

"Willow," he said. "You're mine." He licked her lower lip, kissed her eyelids, skimmed the bridge of her nose with the tip of his, placed a sweet kiss at the tip of her chin, and when her lips dropped open in a gasp, he took her mouth in a searing kiss that coursed his blood to the tips of his fingers and toes. He sucked her tongue into his mouth bit it then bit her lip, then swallowed her shock and cry. "Willow," he groaned against her and his own voice didn't sound familiar. Her legs tightened, her cunt rubbing the slow growing length of him.

"More," she said. "Please, more."

He slid one of his hands to the back of her head, gathering her hair in a tight fist. Pulling her back, he put his mouth on her neck, her pulse warming his lips before he sucked so hard he had to close his eyes as her hands fluttered on his shoulders.

"Yes," she begged. "More, please, more."

He slid his mouth down the length of her soft neck to the muscle that met her shoulder and he sank his teeth into her skin.

Her body thrashed against his, her hands taking his arms at his shoulders and pulling him into her. He stumbled, then moved toward the bed. Her hands dug between them, found the fall of his trousers, did not wait for patience. She yanked hard, and one side gave then her hands were on him and she cried, the wet of her tears sliding her cheeks and dropping to the soft bit of skin behind his ear then sliding down to trace his jaw. It sent a shudder through him that kept his muscles from moving properly. Another tear fell, flavoring the kiss he gave her.

He broke her hold on him, throwing her to the bed then crawling over her and pushing inside. Pushing and pushing. He took her hands and forced them over her head, holding her delicate wrists in one of his big hands as his other hand tore the front of her dress wide. He found the bite mark he'd given her the other night and his cock responded. He squeezed her other breast so hard he knew he'd marked her again, and the blood of his pride flushed his cock and he pushed more. Harder. Shoving her up the bed until her head met the heavy scrolled board at the wall and he reached up and held on to it, pushed her hands against it, and he fucked like he'd never fucked in his life.

Her fingers fluttered on his wrist and her body quickened around his cock and she came off with his hand covering her mouth to keep her from screaming his name.

He'd no idea how long she slept, but he couldn't take his eyes from her. He was exhausted. Bodily, mentally, thoroughly, in a bone-deep way he'd never experienced, not even when he'd been injured. Yet he refused to close his eyes. He wouldn't for fear that when he woke this time she'd be gone. Even blinking felt a chore and he found himself rubbing the dry from his eyes as they became sore.

He could not lose her again. He had no idea what would come of them. His sole concern was her.

The longer he had her and the Queen looked for her, the more trouble he was bound to be in. To kidnap a royal princess and not return her post haste—regardless if he'd no idea her identity in the beginning—the moment he'd discovered who she was, he should have taken her directly to the Queen. He hadn't. He didn't want to return her today either. He wanted as much time with her as possible, and the only way he knew that would happen was to hide.

Except...he didn't wish to bring his transgressions down on his family either. He would have to make it known that what he'd done was by his hand and none other. How he was to do that, he'd not a thought. Then there was his promise to Gray, one he'd managed to keep, one he now refused to break.

•

Madoc writhed in the flames that licked his body, sank into the heat of the singed earth. Hoped it would swallow him if only to extinguish the burn. He reached out to scrape the earth around him and caught fists of softness. He shook his head, blinked against the depth of his dream, saw Willow rising above him. Her hands on her own breasts as she straddled him.

"Willow," he said, a reverence to her body. Her hands came down to his chest, splayed across his naked skin. He shifted, trying to get the sheet between them, but she pushed it all away until it was just their naked bodies on the covered mattress.

"No," she said. "No. You'll stop hiding from me. If this is our last night together, if every moment we share is our last moment, you won't hide from me any longer." She reached past him to the heavy curtain that covered the window next to the bed and pulled until a cold slash of light came over the bed. "Why don't you understand?" she asked as she leaned into him. "Why don't you understand?" She traced the line of his scar from his cheek, down his neck, across his shoulder and down his abdomen where it faded at the softest of his skin, fighting him the whole way, pushing his hands away as he tried to stop her.

"What am I to understand, Willow?"

"These scars...they're so beautiful. Like rivers of life in your skin, they stretch the length of you, proving your strength and vulnerability." She leaned forward and licked the scar that ran his side, then sucked his nipple into her mouth.

"Willow...I don't understand."

"I heard your dream, Madoc. I heard the words, I heard you relive that night. You do it every time you sleep. You fight with death and you fight with life. You're caught in this purgatory of hatred..."

"Because I am. My life ended that night—"

"Did it?" she asked, and he looked into her eyes. She leaned forward, bringing her gaze closer to his, challenging him to say it again,

"No..." he said and released a breath that seemed had grown so much a part of his system that he hadn't known it was still there. The stale air released, he inhaled deeply of her, her life, her beauty, her impossible love of him. "No," he said again. "It had only just begun."

He flipped her on the bed, pinning her with his weight and his heavy angles as she writhed against him.

"Show me, Madoc. Show me what it means to be alive."

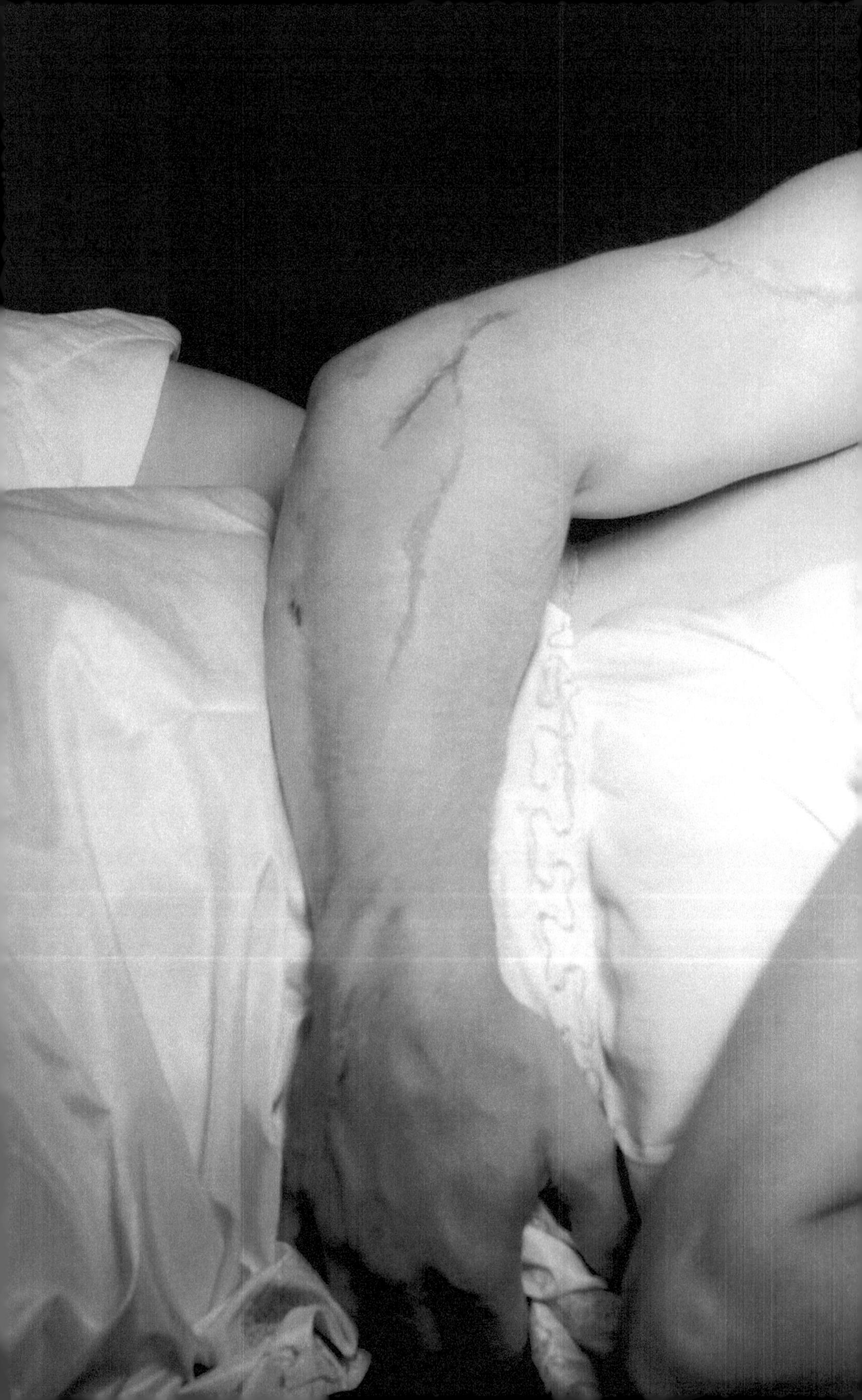

Dawn broke, bringing a different light with it, and someone scratched at the door. He lifted his head from the pillow, looking across her shoulder, making certain they were both sufficiently covered. "Come," he said quietly.

The door opened slowly and Grayson walked in. "You're here." He sounded surprised as his demeanor shifted from defensive to something softer. "I'm— Maybe you could come to the study so we can discuss—"

"I'm not leaving her. She's sleeping, and I don't expect her to wake soon."

Gray nodded and walked two steps closer. "It's time. We must tell the Queen; there's no way about that. We cannot keep this from The Crown. It's an impossibility."

"I'm aware, but...it must be me. I'll not allow something I've done to cause you more pain. I've done enough by my presence—my life. *I'll not allow* anything more to cause you or your family harm."

He nodded but looked away. "Let us help you with this. If after... you need to leave, then so be it. But for this, let us help. We will put the rest of it aside, for the sake of this woman."

"Are you certain you can do that? I cannot tolerate anything happening to her."

"I understand that feeling, and suffice to say that—at least that— you can trust."

"I realize I've been absent—"

"Death will do that to you."

"Yes, it will. You don't know where I've been, and I've no idea what's happened here. I imagine quite a lot since your return." Madoc shifted and stood, picking his drawers up off the floor and dressing as he moved around the bed and led Gray over to the chairs by the fireplace. He sat facing her so he could see if she woke. "What happens next?"

"Only the Queen can decide that."

"Will you take the title now?"

"No."

"Why? It seems the logical step."

"I never wanted it to begin with."

"I'm not sure I believe that."

"You believing it doesn't make it so."

Madoc considered him but still didn't necessarily believe it. He'd been so angry about the title; how was he now to believe that had all been a farce? The truth of it was that perhaps he didn't know why he'd been angry. *That* was difficult to admit. "I think perhaps I was aware that you didn't, but rejected the notion as preposterous. It was an excuse. I needed someone to be angry with and the man who'd tried to kill me, our father, was dead." Madoc watched Willow as she slept soundly in front of him. "I don't deserve your forgiveness. I failed you when I should have been a brother. Don't mistake me, I'm not asking your forgiveness and I've no expectations. But I do want you to know that *I know* I was wrong. You did nothing, Calder did nothing, Quinn did nothing. Everything that's happened, it was entirely on my head. I *am* sorry for the needless pain I've caused. I know there's no way to repair the damage." Madoc caught his brother's gaze. "I am humble before you and will do as you wish."

Gray stared at him for several long moments. He didn't move, didn't so much as twitch. "I find it interesting you've made such a change—" He stopped. "Interesting isn't the word and I'm not sure what is. In truth, there are probably no words for what has come between us. To say you suffered your crimes before they were committed is possibly going too far. The reality is...there is no finding our way through the maze that is the relationship we've had. The best we can do—now that we've come through, or now that we are returned to each other—is to move forward."

Gray stood, and Madoc followed him to the door. "I can only hope to gain your trust after it all. I understand that. Please know I will endeavor to do so with every action I take," Madoc said finally, and Gray nodded. He reached a hand out, and Gray took it after a long thoughtful pause and Madoc appreciated that pause and the consideration that went into it. It felt like a door long ago locked and barred was slowly coming open, the frozen lock slowly coming loose.

"The next thing to do would be to let the Queen know the location of her granddaughter," Gray said with a nod to Willow. "None of us could have known she was with you the entire time—"

"I didn't know either... Well, I didn't know it was her." Madoc turned to look at Willow sleeping so peacefully in the bed then turned back to Gray. "As I said, it should be me. I will go to her. I don't want to cause any further issue with you or the family. I will tell her it was entirely my doing, somehow. I don't know how—"

"Is this your brother? We didn't quite meet before," Willow said, and he turned to be sure she was modestly covered. Somehow she'd managed her way into a wrap of sheets, covering every bit of herself save her face from the tip of her nose up.

"This is my younger brother, Grayson Danforth."

"Someone mentioned the two of you looking similar, but I don't see it."

"We used to look alike," Madoc replied. "Not now though." He motioned to the scars.

"It's not the scars," she said. "Not at all."

Madoc nodded, his throat a bit tight. "Grayson and I...have long been estranged."

"So you're the man who cared for the title?" she asked, and his head cocked a bit as though the phrasing was curious to him.

"I am, yes," Gray said. "Welcome to our family." He dipped his chin to her but shifted his eyes to Madoc as he said it, and Madoc understood it was because he'd tensed and Gray was keeping track of the shift in his demeanor. Some things would take a while to heal. That much was certain. Madoc no longer wondered about the possessiveness Gray showed for Cecilia—Lulu. He understood how angry Gray had been when they'd met in the park. Madoc understood a lot about this now that he absolutely had not back then. It had been perhaps a week, but felt like a lifetime.

"I'm sorry about all the chaos," she said quietly, and Gray smiled, something Madoc didn't think he'd ever seen his brother do.

Gray looked away, hiding his reaction. "Never mind," he said simply. "I hope...well, I hope we come to know each other, though Lulu and I are headed back to the country in a couple of days. We hadn't planned on being in London quite so long as we've no residence here at the moment."

"You should take Warrick House. You'd already made it your home," Madoc said.

"Had we?"

"Yes, you had. That's not my home. It may well be entitled, but I'm not removing you. There is nothing there for me. I'll find another residence should we—should I remain in London."

Gray nodded. "Well, for now, let's leave it as it is. Who knows what comes next."

"Right," he said, because he may have no choice in the matter. "Fine then." They kept shifting as though they both had more to say but neither one knew what, and neither one was prepared to leave either. "Gray, I am—" Madoc put a hand to his chest; any words he managed to consider felt so terribly inept and inconsequential. He shook his head, closed his eyes and bowed his head.

"I know," Gray said, and he reached out and put one hand on Madoc's shoulder, and he felt the warmth of that touch all the way through his skin to his bones like he'd been branded. Then Gray turned and left, shutting the door behind him.

As quickly as it closed, Willow was there behind him, her hands on his arms, silently supporting him.

Her kiss against the back of his shoulder where his brother had just touched him brought him back. He turned and wrapped his arms around her. Holding her close before he had to give her back.

TWENTY-THREE

t had been strange to see them together, though it was easy to pick them apart, regardless of the scars on Madoc. She knew Madoc was the elder brother, as he held the title. That much was simple. But Grayson looked just as old if not older. He had wrinkles catching the edges of his eyes, but also a severe concern between his eyebrows that spoke to stress and not age. She understood then what the title had done to him. Or perhaps it was a bit more than the mere title.

Madoc released her, and she made her way across the bedroom to the bathroom. There was a tub on her left, which she started to fill, and shelves on her right—but no toilet. She walked past the tub and opened another door to find the toilet and a sink. She turned back to the shelves and perused the vials of oil and herbs. She picked out the lavender and vanilla and some other herb she didn't recognize but smelled wonderful. She poured small amounts of each in the water and shut the water off. She got in the tub, sinking to the bottom. She lay there, her feet tucked to give her body room to sink, and stared at the ceiling beyond the water, wondering if lavender was safe for the eyes. She blinked a couple of times, let out a breath then surfaced, pushing her hair back from her face.

"That's quite a talent," Madoc said. He was sitting on a small wooden chair he'd brought into the room, his elbows on his knees. "Willow," he said, and the way he said it sent a spear of dread through her heart.

"You're leaving me."

"It's...entirely possible that we will be separated. The fact is you must be returned to the Queen, and I must be the one to take you and to explain...I must tell her where you've been—what we've done. We cannot just abandon London for America. That isn't who I want to be...with you."

She felt cold, no matter the temperature of the water she was in, the steam still rising. Goose bumps broke out across her arms, and her heart stuttered. "I understand but...I don't understand."

"If there's any chance we are to be together, then she must know the truth of it. She'll not allow a member of her family to be disgraced in the public eye if there's something she can do about it. And she will choose the simplest solution as well, which...we can hope to be that you remain in my care."

"But what if..."

"You mustn't consider the options and neither must I. We would both go mad should we consider all the options, you know that. There are too many possibilities that would stop me from my duty, but it is my duty. I am the Duke of Warrick and I need to behave as such, as I was trained, as I was born to do. We must go to the Queen and hope she will be just and reasonable."

"I don't have the trust in Queen Victoria that you have, because what I know of her is as an outsider separated by history. I always had this nagging feeling that she was a romantic at heart, though she rarely acted as such for the public, particularly once Albert was gone. I just..." She looked up to find his gaze trained on her, his eyebrows drawn together. "What?"

"There is no situation in which you should speak with her. She'll think you mad."

"Well, she won't be the first of us, and it will give us something in common."

"This isn't trivial, Willow. This isn't something to be trivialized. You must understand, she may not charge you with an offense because you carry her blood, but she can insist you spend your life chaste as a nun. She can insist you be tied to a bed and your blood let to expunge the demons. She can insist you be stripped and inspected, and what then?" He came to his knees at the edge of the tub as he said it.

He reached into the water, pressing a palm to the bruise on her breast, until she winced and his irises flared. He skimmed his hand up to the bite on her shoulder, around the mark on her other nipple. His hands slid down her abdomen, through her folds, then he pushed against another bruise on her hip. Then he reached beyond her to the soap cake in the tray and traced her body from the bruise on her neck, to the bruises on her breasts, to the bruises on her hips, the bruises on her thighs. He washed them all gently, then washed the rest of her as well. It was all very distracting until he pulled his hand from the water and stood. He dried off and continued as though they sat in an office fully clothed, save his voice.

His voice was bare and raw, and she closed her eyes and felt the power of it. "She can insist on a whole host of things that you would not like to be party to. Please understand that above all else, simply being granddaughter of the Queen does not give you passage. You are one of many; you are not special in that regard. You are her property just as much as you would be any man's."

That did give her pause. Brought her right back to the nineteenth century and out of her happily-ever-after daydream. "Yes, I know. She was perhaps cruelest to those who loved and were devoted to her at times. I do understand that."

"You cannot speak to her."

"I heard you, and yet should she speak to me, I must answer, so what would you have me do?"

He turned back to her, his face drawn with concern. "I would have you tell her the truth of it. You went to the inn, you don't remember why. When you awoke, you were with me and you couldn't remember what had happened or who you were. The closer we stay to the truth, the easier it will be for both of us."

"When do we go?"

"This afternoon."

"So soon?"

"We must. If I'm seen to have kept you from those to whom you belong, it would be a greater offense than me having you to begin with. Knowledge is the key."

She nodded at him and sat forward, her arms wrapped around her knees as she drew them to her chest. "I'm frightened."

"As am I. But know this—if we are separated, I will find you. Somehow."

Willow rinsed and stood in the bath, and he helped her step out to the floor, then took the towel and dried her, inspecting all those marks he'd made and was so fond of as he went along, making quite sure she was dry. "Your dedication is remarkable," she said.

"I am your humble servant," he replied before seeming to think better of it. He played with a strand of her hair, then caught her gaze and held it for a moment. He went to his knees. "I am, now and forever, your humbled servant." He bowed his head. "Whatever needs you may have, know that I will see to them in whatever way I am able. Whether I am with or without you, my life is yours."

Willow reached out and ran her hand through his hair. Tucking strands behind his ear as he shifted then looked up at her. "Would you look at this?" she whispered. "A little thing like me has brought a man like you to your knees."

He made a valiant effort to suppress the smile.

It was obvious that he could not.

Impossible didn't do the situation justice.

He gazed up at her from his knees and never wanted to rise. She was everything.

She stood still, her head tilted to the right. Her arms stretched long against her sides. So incredibly beautiful. Her creamy, pale skin so perfect for his marks. Those from last night were still purple while the older bruises had faded to greens and yellows, making a rainbow of her flesh. He couldn't help but to trace them with the tips of his fingers, her skin pricking wherever his hands traveled. The whole of her was pinked from the heat of the tub—she was lovely beyond reason.

He wanted to paint more of his pain on her but he couldn't. There would already be questions should the Queen demand to inspect her granddaughter for some reason. He hoped to avoid that by professing to her from the outset that he'd ruined her—taken

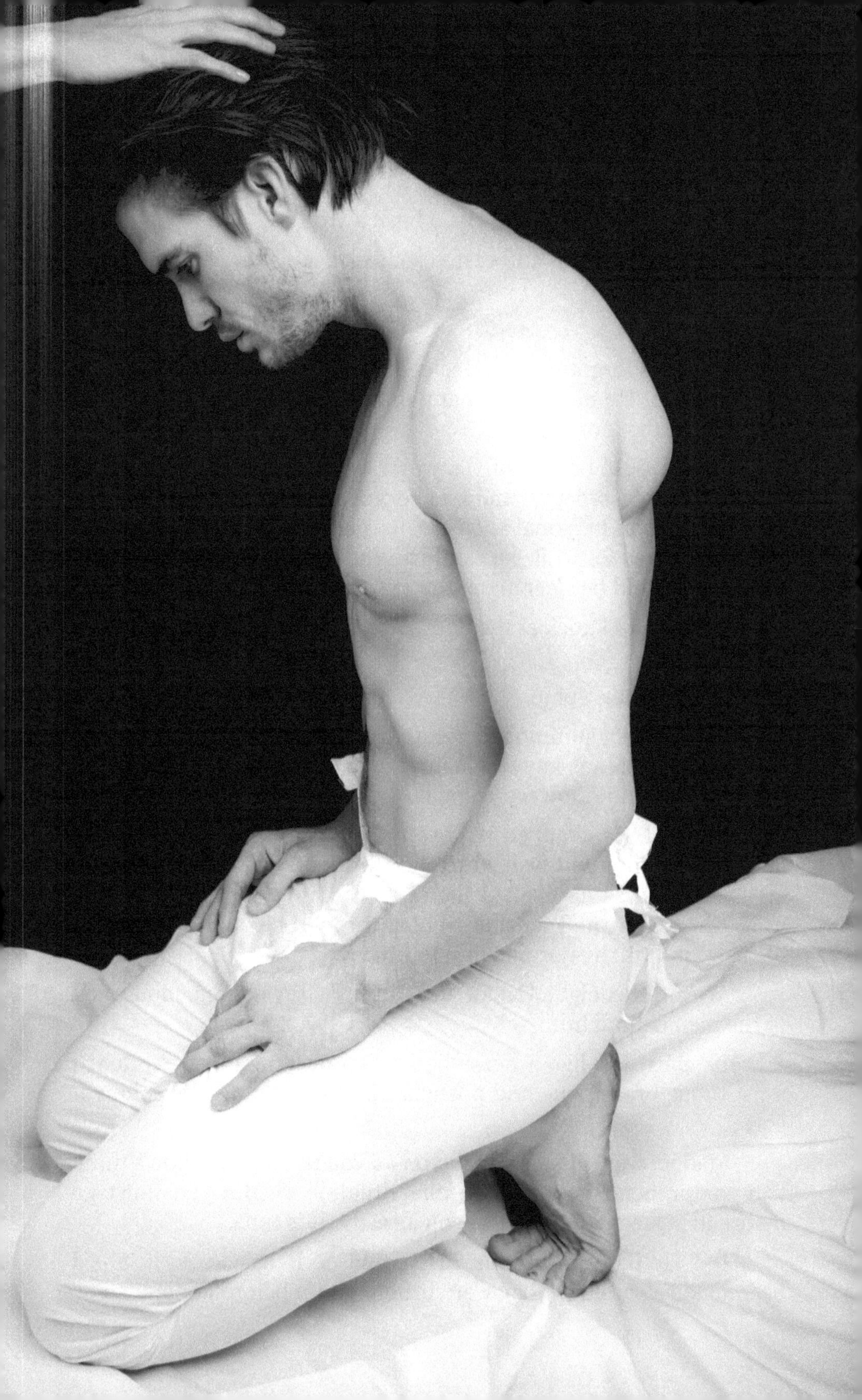

her maidenhead without permission. Though he hadn't known he needed that permission. At the time he'd well assumed her to be a woman of questionable morals. Not true; at the time of her ruination he had been fully aware that she'd been a virgin.

He closed his eyes and rested a cheek against her soft belly, his hands at her hips.

Alice.

He hadn't forgotten her. He needed to stop touching Willow. He needed sleep. He needed so many things that seemed well beyond his grasp at the moment.

Today would be one of the worst of his life, he'd no doubt of that. He'd professed guilt and had begged his Queen before, but not for something as personal and egregious as this. He could only hope Willow be cared for while he would be unable to do it as he was fairly certain he would be sleeping in the Tower tonight.

There was a knock at the door. "It's time to go," Gray said from the hallway.

A chill ran his spine.

"You've been summoned before the queen. We'll be with you," Gray said, and Mads knew he hadn't opened the door yet out of the fear that he and Willow were gone.

He stood. He wrapped Willow in the soft towel, then closed the door behind him and walked to the main entry to the guest suite. "We?" he said as he opened the door. Standing on the other side wasn't just Gray, and tension rippled through his body, settling in his back and thighs—urging him to run.

"Myself. Roxleigh...Calder and Quinn," Gray replied, motioning to the men behind him.

His chest felt like a horse had fallen on him and he clutched a fist to his breastbone and pushed. "This is it then. This is how it goes."

"Madoc, we will stand with you as you're judged. I don't think you comprehend how delicate the situation is. But you must go before the Queen. She expects you already. It is time."

"I—" He had no response. He could no longer avoid it. She'd been made aware that they were bringing him before her and so he had to go or suffer the consequence, which in this case was—at the least of it—banishment. Could be death. *There are always options in life, Danforth…* He nodded. "I'll make ready." He looked up at Gray, but he hadn't moved.

Gray turned and nodded to the others and they walked down the hall. "I'm not leaving, Madoc. I know how difficult this is for you, and I want to make sure you understand that *I* understand that fact. But what happened in India—the last time you were summoned directly and left to your own devices? That will not happen here."

Mads smiled; he couldn't help it. Then he turned and stripped.

"Must've hurt," Gray said from behind him, and Mads stilled; strangely he hadn't even given the scars a thought until his brother had spoken up.

He turned and allowed Gray to see the extent of it, his arms hanging loosely at his sides. "Very much so."

"But you're alive."

"I've noticed," Mads replied, looking down at his own ruined body.

"And now? Are you thankful for the evidence of your life? Carved there upon your skin to remind you that once upon a time you had been marked for death, but somehow…you survived? You cheated death."

"I hadn't considered it like that, to be honest."

"No?"

"No. I've always seen them as what should have been, not what could have been. What *is*."

"You've been living like a dead man instead of one who lives."

"I suppose I have," Mads said as he turned and pulled his trousers on. "Though I'm not sure you could blame me for living in such a manner as the Queen has yet to speak on it."

Gray nodded then turned to give Mads privacy. He finished dressing just as another knock sounded outside the door. He turned to see Lulu, Francine, and Celeste waiting patiently.

Lulu's fingers tangled with Gray's. She looked up to Madoc, something heavier than pity but still fairly unwelcome in her gaze. "We're here for Willow."

He nodded. "She's in the bath; he wouldn't leave us." Mads finished with a gesture at Gray, who returned the gaze, completely unapologetic.

"We will wait in the front entry," Gray said to Lulu. "Then we'll make our way to Buckingham, together."

She turned back to him and nodded then stepped aside so Gray and Madoc could walk out of the room, leaving Willow to the women.

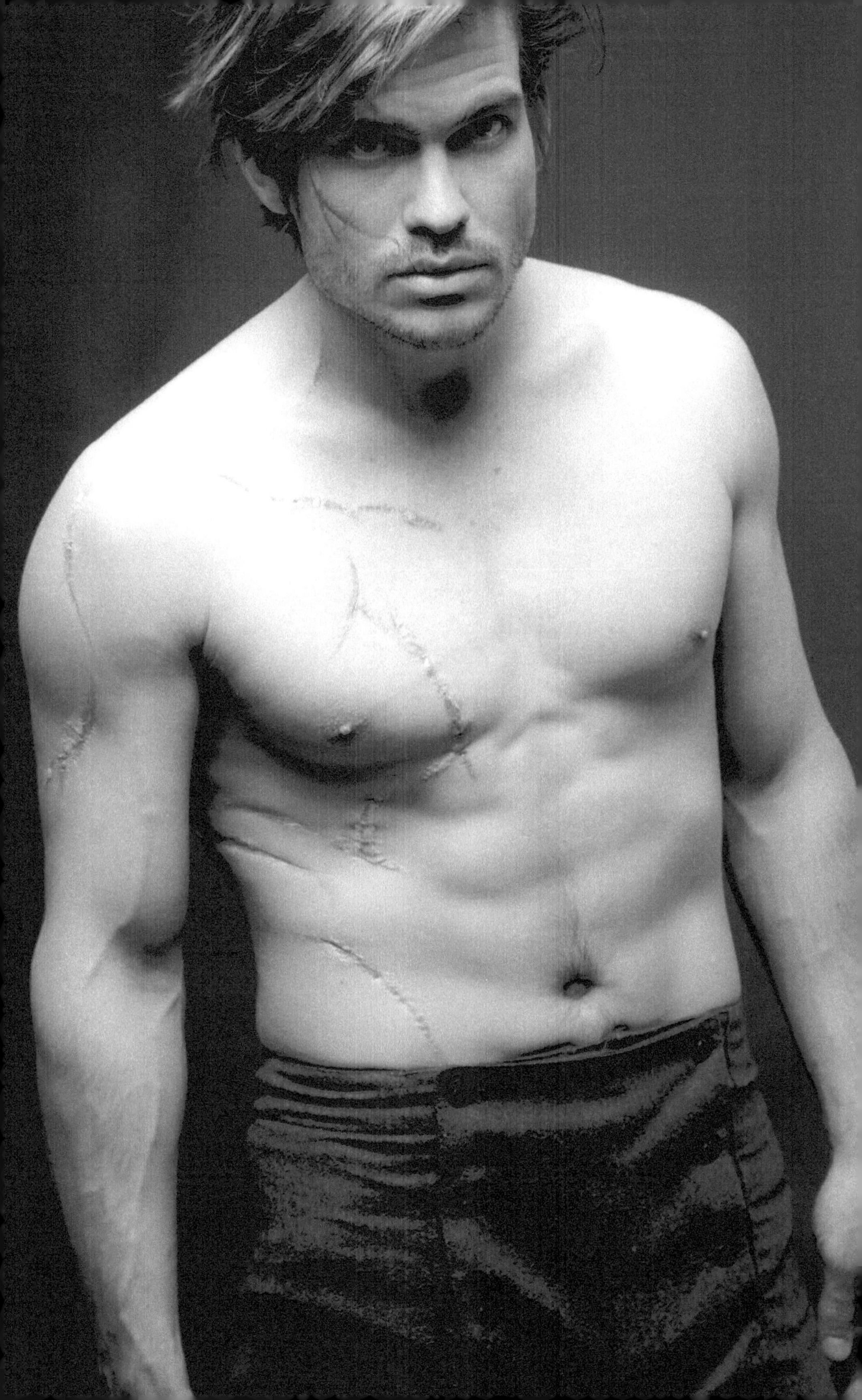

TWENTY-FOUR

uckingham Palace. Willow leaned her forehead against the bedpost while the strain of Buckingham Palace ran through her head. This was beyond anything she could have considered at the beginning of this...what is this? An adventure? She wasn't sure.

Buckingham Palace. *Oh God, what next?* But she knew what was next—the Queen. *Oh God, the Queen.* Her Imperial Highness Victoria Regina. How was this even possible?

She'd wanted to walk out of the bathroom, to comfort Madoc and perhaps ask questions, at least to stand by his side. She knew better though—at least that was what she told herself—the truth was that she'd been terrified.

Someone squeezed her hand and she turned to Celeste at her side, Lulu next to her. She'd completely forgotten they'd come for her, to help her dress, promising not to leave her side. She squeezed back, her grip weak because her muscles were vibrating so strongly at the moment.

"Fuck." She was going to Buckingham Palace.

"Exactly what I thought my first time," Lulu said, and Willow turned to her. "Well, it was the second day I was in this—" she waved a hand in the air, "—world, and it was my wedding day. So there's that."

"You were married your second day here?" Willow stopped and put a hand to her chest. The very idea of it was...as intense as it was comforting.

"Yes. Well, my first full day. Anyway, he was scheduled to be married, and the woman I replaced was the bride. I didn't see any reason to stop the whole thing, so..." She shrugged. "I may have been a bit delusional, I mean, it was pretty overwhelming."

"Do you ever consider where that woman went?"

"Every day. I can only hope it's worked out for her the same as it's all worked out for me." She squeezed Willow's hand.

"And it has worked out well since then? For you anyway?" she asked and was instantly surrounded in warmth—the women flanking her and rubbing her back and holding her hands and being so much more supportive and caring than anyone in her life had been up to this point.

"Yes," Lulu said. "Whatever the function is that brings us all here, it seems to be for the better. I can't even imagine my life before. I wouldn't return for anything. I know, in my heart, this is where I was meant to be, and I'm blessed by whatever brought me here. That isn't to say it was easy, at all. But it is where I belong."

Willow thought about that and knew how she felt. She closed her eyes, absorbing the strength and warmth that surrounded her. She knew in her bones that she belonged here and somehow everything would be alright. Somehow they were going to be okay. She would find him and they would figure this out. Queen or no queen.

"Are you ready to meet the Queen?" Lulu asked then, and Willow's knees went to jelly. Maybe she wasn't so convinced. She laughed to herself. "Trust me, I know how you feel. But we're here with you; you're not alone."

"Thank you. For everything, thank you," Willow said.

Lulu gave her a squeeze and waited for her to get her legs under her before they left the bedroom and headed to Buckingham.

They allowed Willow and Madoc to ride together on the way to the Palace. She imagined they thought it too much of a fight to attempt to separate them again once they'd been reunited in the foyer. She'd latched onto him and intended to never let him go.

They weren't alone in the carriage, however. Gray and Lulu rode with them, while the rest of the family, Calder, Celeste, Quinn, Roxleigh and Francine, rode in the second carriage. It felt like quite the procession.

She closed her eyes and leaned into him, breathing the air he breathed. Listening to the beat of his heart in his chest. Feeling the corresponding pulse where she had her fingers tucked at the edge of his gloves.

They pulled up in a small courtyard at the back of the Palace; it didn't look like anything she was familiar with. There were a lot of men in uniform there to greet them. Gray leaned forward. "We're with you," he said, and Madoc nodded.

"I wouldn't blame you, should this be a trap of some sort. Just take care of her. That's all I ask."

"I promise you, I will see to her if you are unable," he replied, and Willow looked up to catch his gaze. That almost had her in tears. The carriage door opened, and Gray stepped down, reaching back for Lulu. She could see the rest of the family standing together waiting for them. She took a deep breath, and Madoc kissed her temple, then stepped down from the carriage.

The moment he did he was restrained by two guards. He turned back to the carriage. "Be strong for me, Willow. I love you." Then he was dragged away.

Willow reached for him but had to fight with her skirts to step down from the carriage. Once she did she ran, but was caught by Calder. He and Lulu were saying something but she didn't hear it, fighting both of them as she tried to follow the men who had Madoc.

"No! You can't," she screamed, turned to Calder, "They can't. I can't do this without him. I simply can't."

"You must," Calder said, and she felt Lulu's arms and strength sneak around her waist, holding her steady as they were ushered toward the entry.

She did her best to keep herself together and be strong—as he'd asked. But watching him escorted off by armed men wasn't exactly her idea of a calming or reasonable occurrence. This was different from the last time he'd left though; she wasn't sure why it felt different—it didn't feel like their bond was tenuous, on the verge of shattering or dissipating or whatever it was that had given her such a panic that night at the masked ball. She breathed through the panic attempting to settle in her chest.

She watched them take him away, and she knew she would see him again.

They reached the entry and even as the men with her were sent to another room and Mads disappeared with the guards, she didn't panic. A strange and perfect calm came over her with the knowledge that she would see him again. *I will find you.* He'd said. She believed it.

Lulu squeezed her arm, and she followed them up the stairs and down a hallway to a parlour. It was covered in green and gold, the windows two stories high looking out at the waning sun. They walked to the seating near the windows, and Willow realized they were massive French doors. Closed because it was cold outside, but the light coming in was spectacular, considering they were in London. The room was warm, owing to two fireplaces at each end of the room that used most of that wall space. Balancing out the wall of glass, she supposed. She thought about the amount of coal pumping through just this house. Well, house would be a bit of an understatement. This was literally a palace and...well, it was literally *the* Palace.

She allowed the knowledge to wash over her once again, then took a deep breath and steeled herself. The doors opened again, and she heard the men enter and join them. She stayed at the window while Lulu and Celeste sat on the small satin sofa and Francine walked over to Roxleigh. A butler laid out a spread of finger sandwiches and tea.

"If Madoc goes to prison, will Gray take up the title again?" she asked when they all meandered closer to her.

"I've no idea. He's never wanted it and—"

"The thing that continues to surprise Us is the candor with which the women of the Trumbull households tend to speak when in mixed company."

Willow froze, Lulu and Celeste's backs going ramrod straight, their eyes wide before Lulu jerked and turned, pulling Celeste with her. They all curtseyed before Her Imperial Highness, Victoria Regina. Good Lord, but she was just like her pictures. It was bizarre. She looked each of them over then met Willow's gaze who, much slower than she should have, she was certain, cast hers to the ground.

"Your Highness," she whispered. "I beg your pardon."

Celeste and Lulu squeezed her hands.

"The thing We appreciate about it is that your husbands tend to keep you from making complete fools of yourselves when it matters, somehow. We suppose that will need to continue. For now, you may leave us." She twitched a hand in the direction of the men, and they bowed and left the parlour without another word. Willow thought for sure she should be upset but she wasn't. "For someone born a princess, this behavior isn't something We quite expected."

Oh God, she was someone else. She'd forgotten for a moment. She curtseyed again, this time staying down low, not knowing what the fuck she should even do. The Queen walked past them, taking a seat on a chaise.

"Don't loom," the Queen said, so they didn't. She waved a gloved hand at the tea set. "Make yourselves comfortable; there's no point letting all this go to waste."

Nobody moved. The Queen huffed. Then she shook her head. Willow was mortified. Francine started serving tea. Lulu placed a sandwich on a small plate and handed it to her. She stared at it.

"I have to be honest, Your Majesty," Lulu started. "You're perfectly aware of your effect on people; you must understand that effect is much more so under our particular circumstances."

"Should We choose to believe your circumstance."

"Of course, Ma'am. Of course. I understand that Warr—Gray—" She shook her head. "Apologies. Danforth. I understand Danforth explained everything to you?"

"Roxleigh attempted it years ago, but We told him to keep that sort of business to himself. We appreciate that since his return, Danforth has been nothing but loyal in all things. Truth be told, it wasn't something We'd expected from him. We should have, certainly, since he's served Us well for a decade. Though he was much more difficult when he was...in his previous position with the Crown."

Lulu nodded. "Understandable, I suppose."

"We...suppose," the Queen replied slowly.

"Your Majesty," Willow said.

"Once is enough. You may address Us as Ma'am," she said.

"Ma'am," Willow continued. "I'm so very lost. I appreciate all the support I've been given—"

"We support no one."

"Of course. I meant—" She waved a hand at Lulu, then tried a different idea. "I am lost. The only place I feel safe is with Madoc. He's been so careful and protective of me from the moment we met. I understand that isn't the man most of you know or believe in. But I would be remiss if I presented him as anything but the most thoughtful and considerate of men."

"He's a peer of Our realm. We expect nothing less of him."

"Of course. Yet I understand he hasn't always behaved in such a manner—"

"He was not always one of Our peers. His position now demands it of him, and that's something he understands implicitly."

"Your Maj—Ma'am..." Willow took a deep breath and put the tea cup on the small table with a clink, her hands shaking. This was it; she had one chance to speak up in his defense, to attempt to explain, and she wasn't going to squander it.

"Speak your mind," she said.

"I need him. I realize in this world I have no power, no rights, no...nothing, really. But I need him. And if there's any possible way you can see to return me to his care, I would be forever in your debt."

"You're already forever in Our debt by your simple existence. Do not forget that you exist at Our very pleasure. Anything We do above that would be considered a favor."

"I am so sorry, Na'am, of course. I just—" She tangled her hands in her lap. "I need him. I don't know what else I can tell you."

"Then I will tell you something. You are my grandchild, Princess Dorothea Feodora Friederike Amalia Beatrice Alice Charlotte August Sophia Wilhelmine Victoria Viktoria Ulrike Elisabetta, crowned princess of Prussia. You are part of the Crown. I expect certain things from you."

"Of course, ma'am. I'm just unsure I'm able to perform the things expected of one in my position, considering I don't even know what those things are. I will strive to please you but I must tell you I don't know how. Everything I know about this world was learned in hindsight or from Madoc. Without him... My greatest fear in this moment is losing him. My second greatest fear is disappointing you. Princess or no, I cannot behave as someone I'm not without the knowledge of what that entails."

"Well," she said and her eyes narrowed on Willow, who dropped her gaze to the ground. She twisted her hands in her skirts to try to stop them shaking. "As much as we don't appreciate whatever function it is that brings you to Us, We understand We must work within the confines of that function. My Dorothea spent years learning the proper etiquette and being prepared for a marriage to an heir of the Saxe-Coburg—"

"I can't—"

The Queen raised a hand, and Willow quieted instantly.

"You were brought here for a marriage by contract. You've been missing for entirely too long. You may be able to imagine what people have thought. It is unpleasant, to say the least. And now you've been returned to us, and We must return you to whom you belong, or to whom you are contracted to belong. As we speak, your groom is being calmed and prepared for your return."

"You sent the men away with purpose," Lulu said.

"Everything We do is with purpose," she replied.

Willow stood. "There is only one man I can marry."

"You will do as you're told. That is your lot in life. The sooner you accept that, the easier this life will be for you. Perhaps that is something this family needs to work on. Whyever you've been brought here does not change the fact that you are here, at Our pleasure, and must do as asked as peers of Our realm. You are contracted to marry. You will do so willingly within a sennight as soon as arrangements are made."

Willow's chest tightened and her vision swirled. She clutched at the corset edge beneath her shirtwaist, but she couldn't catch her breath.

His knee hit the floor with a crack and Mads grunted, once again pushing his shoulder against the floor and using his forehead for leverage.

"You stole my property."

"Unbeknownst to me, Your Imperial Highness."

"That has never been an acceptable excuse in this court."

"No, Ma'am."

"Warrick, you were given a specific directive to repair the damage done in your family. You failed."

"I have no excuse. I hadn't enough time for—"

"With nobody here to witness your shame, there's no need to mince words, Warrick. You were busy ruining my property."

Mads felt the complete shame of his life sink into his bones. He would have to accept whatever it was she had for him. "Ma'am. Willow..." He shook his head. "My family will protect her. They will take her into their homes and treat her as though she were one of them. She is one of them. She belongs in our family. She will be safe there and not shamed."

"She's not a member of your family, Warrick. She's a member of mine, and she was brought here for marriage. One you are ill-suited to provide in your current state, I daresay."

"I would provide for her, but I cannot give her what you require."

"You were to make reparations but what you've succeeded in doing, Warrick, is causing further damage to your house, as well as mine. How do you answer?"

"There is no defense," he answered quietly.

He watched as her chest heaved against a deep indrawn breath.

"Ma'am. I beg. I need her. She makes me a better man. I can be the man you need with her by my side. Don't take her from me. I am nothing without her."

"Therein lies the problem, you see? You cannot be The Warrick if you cannot stand on your own as The Warrick."

"I can. I can stand alone as The Warrick, but you've seen what I do without the temperance of that woman. What would you have me do? I am a better man for the presence of her. She gives you what I alone cannot. Is that not what you ultimately want?"

She didn't answer him; instead, she twitched her finger, and he was yanked up by the arms and taken away.

TWENTY-FIVE

illow had run out of books to read for the third time and was tired of asking permission and waiting for an escort to the library. She knew she should try to make the most of being in Buckingham Palace, but the Queen had been quite specific about her care. Willow wasn't to leave the Palace. She couldn't leave her room unless escorted, and then only for thirty minutes at a time.

The problem therein was it was practically a fifteen-minute walk through the winding passages and up and down stairs to get to the library, and she was expected to choose a single book each time. She wasn't even allowed to lounge in the library, as it was an inconvenience to her guards.

The knock at her door was unexpected but a welcome distraction. More than welcome. Willow walked to the door and opened it. It took thirty seconds to cross the room and turn the handle. Thirty seconds out of the rest of her boring day. If that was all she got from this, she was happy to have done it. She smiled as she pulled the door wide.

"Calder." Her breath caught as her smile fell and she stepped back from the entry, allowing him room to enter if he so desired.

"Willow." He moved past her carefully, inspecting her room as though he were interested, but it was patently obvious by his tense carriage that he was, in fact, not at all.

"Can I— What can I do for you?"

He paused at the windows, gazing out at the back courtyard of the Palace. One finger pushed aside the lace curtain that hung between the heavy brocade drapes and the glass. The light, muted as it was by the overcast weather, limned his face and caught his eyes. He stared into it as though he waited for someone to appear below.

Willow twisted her hands together and walked toward him. He didn't move. She didn't want to approach him, so she stopped at the foot of the bed, sitting on the wide bench there.

"My family," he said, "means everything to me. You may not understand what it is to be part of a family like ours, so I'll explain in the best way I know how. We are supportive. We are passionate. We are protective. We hold each other's well-being and happiness above all else. Madoc—" His jaw tensed and he took a breath, ruffling the lace when he exhaled. "Madoc has not been a member of this family for years. I do remember a time when he was simply another cousin, but that was short-lived once his father took him to heel." He let the drape shut, and the light dimmed as he turned to her. He gathered his hands at his back, standing tall, broadening his shoulders. His expression was of confusion, fear perhaps, and sadness, but it shifted quickly to determination. "He was dead to us, quite literally. I say all this because I don't know how much of the story you know." He caught her gaze then. Held it. "Or how much of what you've been told is true."

"He told me about the night he died. He told me...he told me about the things he'd done. He used broad strokes when discussing certain events, however."

"Ah, well, that could serve dual purpose. Might I ask, what did he discuss using said broad strokes?"

She swallowed, her throat suddenly dry. She knew exactly what he wanted to know. There was no point to avoiding it. "He said—" She tried to clear her throat to no avail and stood, breaking contact with him and pouring a glass of water from the pitcher on the sideboard. Then she turned back to him, gathering her strength. "He told me he tortured you. He said he would not go into detail, as it wasn't his story to tell."

"No?" His gaze faded, casting somewhere beyond her for a moment before drifting back. "Perhaps it isn't."

"He didn't want to speak on it, to give the impression that he was proud, that he relished his actions. He was very specific that he was a bad person and I should simply accept his statement as truth. He said that attempting to tell the story from his perspective of what happened, of what he did to you, would lessen what he'd done and take further rights from his victim. That the story belonged to the men he'd wronged, not to him."

Calder nodded and looked away but not before she saw something in his eyes soften. "I'm not sure how to reconcile this... The Queen has decided that we are to be as a family. But he is not part of that and hasn't been for quite some time."

"I believe he would like to be, if you would allow for it," she said carefully.

"If I would allow for it?"

"Yes, he... What he said to me was that he missed his family. He missed everything it meant to him, before it all happened. I believe he's repentant, that he understands what he did was wrong, and further, understanding that there's no possible way of taking it back, he wishes he could at the very least make amends, even just enough to be tolerated, perhaps someday even welcomed."

"But what he did—"

"Was beyond reprehensible. I understand that."

"How do you understand when you have no idea what it was he did?"

"I've done the best I could with deduction. You're hale and whole, and you appear healthy. You mentioned scars, however, and I can only imagine what those must look like, though they aren't so damaging as to affect your body mechanics. He said he tortured you; you've acknowledged that to be true. He didn't argue that you bear scars of his making. What he did was not consensual in any way. Putting all of these facts together leads me to believe that what he'd done was reprehensible."

"And how do you still care for him, knowing all of this?"

"The man I know would never do these things. Whatever state he was in, whatever position—"

"You understand that a thing once done can be done again? If you choose to believe it was the circumstance that brought this evil out of him, then you must understand that whatever that circumstance was then could happen again—and what then? Are you prepared to bear the brunt of his evil?"

"I believe men are capable of horrid things. I also believe men can change when they're willing and able to do so. I have faith in the human condition—probably naively so. That we're all salvageable. That we can learn and grow and better ourselves."

"That is perhaps a bit naive, in fact."

Willow nodded her agreement. "Do you mind?" she asked and motioned to the seating area. He shook his head, and she sat in one of the chairs by the fireplace. "I don't have an answer for any of this. I know that in my heart this man is part of my life, and I cannot live without him. I know that my judgment may be clouded because of that. But I simply can't— I can't live without him. I can't manage being here without him. None of this world makes sense except where he's concerned. If I'm not meant to be with him, then why am I here at all?"

Calder sat in the chair opposite her. "That's a good question. One the women have been working on. The whys of it all. They call themselves the Hardy Girls whenever they get into their research... You'll fit right in, you know. Regardless of what happens with Madoc, you're welcome in our family. We would never turn you away."

"But you know nothing of me other than what he told you. Why would you trust him in this?"

"Because I've spoken with you. I can see your heart just there, on your sleeve where you wear it so proudly, unapologetically. I have no qualms with you. I don't understand what it is you see in my cousin, especially knowing what you do—"

"I'd like to add one small detail, if you'll allow it?" Calder nodded his assent. "I didn't know these things before I—before we met. He was a complete stranger to me. He wouldn't even give me his name. In fact, he tried to get rid of me on at least two occasions; he professed daily how badly his family would react to finding me in his home. His concern lay entirely on the fact that he didn't want to insult you or cause further harm or distress to you or his brother by any of his actions."

"That is quite decent of him, yet I'm still not—"

"No, no, of course. I'm not trying to change your mind..." His eyes narrowed as he gazed at her. "Okay, perhaps I'd like to. But I do believe that if you have all the information, you may be willing to give him a chance to atone for what he's done. I can't imagine being in your position. It's an untenable place to be."

He laughed then, just a short burst of humor. "And your position is simple by comparison, is it?"

"God yes. You have to deal with a known past, and me? I just have to find a new life to squeeze my existence into. Somehow."

They sat quiet for a moment. She was surprised at how comfortable it was to be with him. He leaned back, resting his chin on his hand, his elbow on the arm of the chair. He rubbed his lip as he considered something, and she relaxed into her chair, letting go of some of the emotional exhaustion she'd pent up.

"I hope—" He shook his head. "I don't know what I hope. I still don't ever wish to be around him, but that isn't a choice I have."

She nodded. "I'm sorry. I know that's inappropriate in so many ways, but I am. For everything that's happened to you. I wish it could have been different. I wish I could have met you under different circumstances, I feel like we could have been friends."

He cut a glance to her as he considered the words. "Perhaps we will be. I appreciate the thought, at any rate, but you must understand that—for you and I—it won't be so simple. I can't know if you're genuine, or playing me the fool on his behalf. It would be nice to be able to say differently, but lies are never nice."

He stood, and Willow followed him to the door, where he turned, leaning against the doorjamb, his arms crossed against his chest. He really was lovely, and it broke her heart that he'd been so terribly treated. She knew she'd compartmentalized these pieces of Mads, because how else could she reconcile the truth of this man before her with the truth of the man she loved?

"Until we meet again, Willow, it was an enlightening conversation, to say the least," he said with a smile. She returned it.

"The feeling is mutual. Are you sure you can't take me with you? This waiting-to-be-married-to-a-stranger business is really getting on my nerves."

"Oh, come now, what's better than an arranged marriage in which you've never even met the groom? It's the perfect adventure. You may have to get to know each other a little upside-down and backward...but upside-down and backward can be quite entertaining." He winked and grinned and Willow laughed and it felt *so good* to laugh. He took her hands, and she was shocked to silence. She looked down, watching as his big hands covered hers, squeezing gently. "May I visit again?"

"Really? I mean, I would appreciate it. I'd like the opportunity to get to know you."

"Well, we'll see about that. We can't be too familiar, you and I. Small steps."

"Thank you," she whispered. "For everything."

"Oh, I haven't done anything. Yet." Calder bussed her cheeks and left her standing there in the doorway to her room. She watched him walk down the long drafty hall until her guard loomed, forcing her to retreat into the room so he could shut the door.

Upside-down and backward. Adventure didn't quite cover it.

Calder visited every day over the next week. Tea with him had become the highlight of her captivity. He brought letters from Lulu and Francine and Celeste, and she wrote back. Apparently, the women of the Trumbull clan weren't allowed visits with her yet, but Calder had a way with convincing the Queen.

She didn't know what would come of their tenuous friendship, but she was grateful for it. Not only for passing the time but for the opportunity to get to know Madoc's family a bit. That, and that it kept her from spinning on the anxiety of her contracted marriage, which approached rather quickly.

Marriage.

To a complete stranger.

Truth be told, his accommodations were quite a bit better than The Tower. He'd no freedom, but that was the least of his worries at the moment. He'd no idea where Willow was, if she was well, if his family had her, if the Queen was still mad, nothing. He didn't know anything but the length of days in this well-appointed prison. He was being held in one of the smaller guest rooms at Buckingham. Clothes had been brought for him. Books to pass the time. Meals. Nothing else. Certainly no information.

He stood at the windows overlooking the private square behind the palace and wondered where she was and how he would find her. He'd promised—but he'd also made a promise to his family and to the Crown. He understood the hierarchy of these promises, so he would bide his time for another day. He could not damage his family by his action. He could not make a further enemy of the Crown by his action. He couldn't hurt her by his inaction if delayed, so he would delay.

A knock came at the door, about the same time the bells at Westminster Abbey began to ring. He looked to the clock on his mantelpiece and saw they were not ringing the half hour. There was a ceremony of some sort happening. He waited for the door to open, listening to a key scraping the faceplate as they searched for the hole. Then it swung wide.

"Gray." The relief that flooded his body forced the air from his lungs, but his heart stalled when he looked into his face. "What is it? What's happened."

Gray shook his head. "I've brought your clothes for the ceremony."

"Ceremony?"

"Yes. Ceremony. The Queen requires all peers in London to be in attendance. As nobody knows you're currently under lock and key, she decided that would include you as well."

"Ceremony."

"Madoc..."

"Why can't you look me in the eyes?"

"Madoc I—" Gray closed his eyes and shook his head.

"Who is to be married?"

"The princess is to be married today."

"The princess... You mean Willow. She is to be married?" Madoc turned away, casting his gaze out the window into the bright of the sun to counter the sting. Gray's hand came down on his shoulder. Squeezed. A month ago he would have fought his brother outright for deigning to touch him, and his brother would have happily complied. But today, he turned. "I cannot lose her." He'd waited one day too long to act.

Gray took both of his shoulders and held him tight as though he couldn't decide what he should do. Then he pulled him into an embrace. Madoc fisted the back of his coat. Both hands twisted in the fabric. If he could hold on to this one tangible thing, perhaps the rest of his world wouldn't crumble as it seemed to be doing. Gray leaned back, and Madoc stared at the space between them.

"We have to go. It wasn't a suggestion," he said quietly.

Madoc released his coat. Turned for the clothes Gray had brought for him. He dressed, the donning of his formals perfunctory after all these years. His brother helped with the jacket, which had been cut so close he couldn't have put it on himself if he'd tried. Then his brother reached for the riband. He started to shake his head, but Gray gave him a simple look that said he would allow this.

Mads closed his eyes and ducked his head, and Gray lifted the riband over his head, securing the garter pins and other shields so they wouldn't slip. Then Gray looked down to his hand, removed the Duke's ring from his finger and placed it on Mads. "I forgot this. I should have given it to you long before now. I apologize."

Mads stared down his bejeweled chest to his hand, the ring with the seal of the title on his finger. "I don't want this."

"That makes two of us, yet it is yours by rights. And you will respect Her Imperial Highness and your position today. Tomorrow we will figure out what happens next."

"These women, Gray, I don't understand any of it. Cecilia...she isn't Cecilia at all, is she?"

Gray tensed, and Mads wasn't sure he'd get an answer, that he'd perhaps gone too familiar. "She's not," he said finally. Mads knew there was a possibility for him in the future, maybe not right now, maybe not soon, but someday he may be allowed a relationship of sorts with his brother. It was something. The smallest bit of hope in an otherwise terrifying moment.

He'd never been in this place before, at the mercy of Her Imperial Highness. Yes, absolutely, at the mercy of whatever decision she'd made with regards to someone he cared about. Was this what love was supposed to feel like? This hopeless, lost, lack of control?

"It's time to go," Gray said.

"Thank you," he said and Gray nodded once. "No, Gray... you've given me—you've shown me a kindness that is beyond what I expected or deserve. Thank you."

Gray tilted his chin up as he considered this, then looked down at his boots, then back up to catch Mads' gaze. "You're welcome."

Gray turned for the door, putting one hand on Mads' shoulder and pushing him forward.

TWENTY-SIX

"If nothing else, take strength in the fact that I will be there, at The Abbey, and when you're married, I will not abandon you," Calder said as he stood at the entry to her room. "And you do look beautiful in this dress."

"You are so sweet," she said, her voice breaking on the words as she stifled her frustration and sadness. Willow still believed Mads would save her.

It was all she had, really, this belief. He'd said he would, and so she believed because what else was she to do? She was in Victorian England. She had no rights, no life of her own. She had nowhere to go, no one she could trust beyond Madoc's family, and they'd already said there was nothing they could do. Well, Francine had offered money and a swift train. After that though...she was still a woman with no worthwhile skills in Victorian England.

And she wanted Mads. She would do this; she would go where they asked. She would take this carriage and walk this aisle, but if Mads didn't find her by the time she came to the altar, all bets were off. They were going to have one pissed-off, lace-encrusted woman to deal with. She would end up in Bedlam. Better that than marriage to a stranger.

"Calder, fancy meeting you here," Lulu said as she came into Willow's room in Buckingham.

"Yes, actually, I've lost the time and must be on my way. I'm expected," he replied, leaving the rest unsaid because he'd learned while speaking with Willow that every time he mentioned the wedding, she began to cry. "I'll see you at the Abbey." He bussed her cheeks and Lulu's then left them.

Lulu closed the door and led Willow over to the massive cheval mirror by the closet. She quietly checked her dress, her veil, her jewels. There was nothing more to say. The only thing Willow wanted to hear was that Madoc was safe, but that wasn't possible—nobody was allowed contact with him—so Lulu remained blessedly silent. The only thing she knew was that he'd been held somewhere—not the Tower.

So he was alive, he was safe, he was cared for. That was what she knew. What she could feel was that he was close; she knew it in the way she knew the body she was in hadn't always been hers. She stared out the window as carriage after carriage came up to the back entry then pulled away, full of the Queen's family and staff and whomever else would be at this wedding.

Lulu wrapped a warm arm around her middle and squeezed, and Willow nearly sobbed at the feel of it.

"Tell me about your wedding," she begged quietly.

"It was lovely, but...well, not unlike yours today, really. Except I'd met the groom briefly. The day before, granted, but at least I knew I could deal with him. And he wasn't too horrible to look at."

She laughed at that. Grayson was a handsome man, as was his brother. She pinched her eyes, running a finger up the bridge of her nose to stave off the coming headache. "I won't make it."

"I wish there was something—"

"We've been over it...there's nothing. I won't put the lot of you in some sort of danger for my benefit. I'll...figure out something. Or I won't have to, because Madoc will be there. He promised. He—" She couldn't even bring herself to say the words. She closed her eyes and shook her head. "These men, who are they? Why are we here? What does this all mean? I don't understand any of this. How do you manage?"

"Gray," she answered quietly. "Without Gray..."

"Yeah."

A knock came at the door to her suite—it was time to go.

Lulu took her hand, pulled it though the crook of her elbow. "I will stay with you. No matter what I'll be with you. I promise."

Willow nodded and they walked out together, then down the main stair. They didn't go to the back of the Palace as everyone else had, however; they were led to the grand stair, the front entry. A beautiful gilded carriage awaited them with a white team of six, their feathered crowns twitching with their halters. "God—"

"I'm here," Lulu said, and Willow held on tight. She descended the stairs on her arm, a small crowd at the front of the Palace, beyond the open gates. The road lined by guards on horseback. It was a beautiful sight. A man helped Lulu, then her, into the carriage. They sat together, facing forward. The slight crowds cheered as they rolled through the streets of London.

Madoc stared at the circle of men standing in Poets' Corner at Westminster Abbey. Everyone dressed in formal blacks, complete with polished shoes, kidskin gloves and full ribands with shields.

"Perry, Roxleigh, Quinn, Jerrod, Wilder..." He bowed his head at the realization that Calder was not here. The only of his cousins not present today in this family tradition, the men assembling before the wedding in Poets' Corner, even though this was no wedding of theirs. He nodded at each of his cousins as he and Grayson joined the circle. "I don't understand why I'm here."

"Because you're one of us," Calder said as he walked past him into the corner, and Madoc looked up to him, the shock certainly evident. "Well...in name, at any rate. The rest remains to be seen. Though Willow does speak quite highly of you. She casts quite the spell, really."

"Willow?" His knees were suddenly weak and he had to shuffle to catch himself. He hadn't allowed himself to consider her for fear of what it would do to him. Having absolutely no control over her happiness or safety was proving to be beyond him. He'd shut down his thoughts in the carriage for fear of what he might do to try to get to her, alternating between fierce anger that would destroy them all and a sorrow so complete it would destroy only him. He was exhausted. And Willow was to be married. Today. To someone else.

"Your woman, Madoc," Calder said. "she's lovely."

"She is, yes. She…is more than that. I don't know where I'd be without her. She's taught me so much—" He tried to stop speaking, tried to control his emotions, to no avail. "She's everything to me. I cannot continue without knowing she's safe and loved. I cannot live knowing that someone else is responsible for her care and well-being. I don't know how to—" He looked down to his hands, shaking. "Please. Care for her as though she were family. She is family. She should be your family."

"Our family?"

"I would not deign to assume… I cannot say more than I have. You've been more than decent to me. You've done more than any sane human would do, Grayson, Calder. I owe you both such a debt." He took a steadying breath, finding what little strength he had left. "Please do this one last thing for me. Make sure she's happy. I can't live like this. I'll be a hazard to myself and others. Gray will take the title. I'll abdicate and face trial for my actions; that is as it should be. But please see to it that she's cared for, however that must be done. If she must marry…" The bells rang again as a reminder of why they stood at the Abbey. "She must marry…that's a simple fact. I will not stand in the way of what must be done."

"I didn't expect you to give up so soundly."

Madoc swung around to find Queen Victoria standing behind him. "Like a cat, you are," he said, then snapped his mouth closed and bowed before her as his cousins followed.

"It does come in handy on occasion."

"Ma'am, am I to assume you heard everything said, or must I repeat myself?"

"No, it's unnecessary. I heard you. I may not believe you, but I heard you. You think for one moment that you have a say in your life? Or hers for that matter? You have no say; I thought that was made clear."

"Yes, Ma'am, of course it was. I was only…" He didn't know what to say or do next. "I'm not giving up, as you said. I'm doing what is right and good. What must be done. Ma'am, I tried to do as you asked, but this family, my family, they don't deserve the likes of me."

Queen Victoria laughed at that, and Madoc turned, seeing the confused looks on his cousins' faces as well.

"Ma'am?"

"Madoc, if we gave up our family based on how wronged we'd been, none of us would have anyone."

"That seems to trivialize what I've done."

"Perhaps. You were told, you were *all* told, to make amends."

"The fault of this—it's my failure, entirely mine. My family, Your Majesty, is blameless."

She looked past his shoulder at one of his cousins. "What say you?" she asked, and he knew it was asked of Calder. His shoulders fell.

"Ma'am," he said.

"Is the failure his alone?" she asked.

"Not his alone," Calder replied, and Madoc felt defeated.

"And what of the other bit?" she asked.

"Trivialization aside?"

"Yes," she said with a stiff nod. He heard footsteps on the hard stone of the floor, then Calder was next to him.

"He was born into our family, Ma'am, and in our family he shall remain, but not without his bride."

"An ultimatum?" she said, her eyes going wide and a twitch of a grin on her cheek.

"I do as my Queen does," Calder said. "Besides, I'm quite selfish. I've grown quite fond of Willow the last week and wish to keep treasures such as her within our family, regardless the cost." He gave her a leg and swept a deep bow.

"We shall see," she replied then looked at Madoc. "First, I commend you on your behaviour, reactionary as it may be. For your service to the Crown in the matter of the former *former* Duke of Warrick," she said, referencing his father and his ilk, "I see fit to bestow you with a tertiary title. Viscount Basilstoke. It's not a pretty title, and will cause a bit more strain on your capital."

Madoc was shocked, and it took a few very full breaths to recover his wits. "Thank you, Ma'am." He hadn't much capital to work with, considering the state of the Warrick holdings, but at least this meant he'd be returning to society, instead of a cell.

"Yes, and before you refuse for some honorable reason, know that your brother has been bestowed with a title for his exceptional assistance in the matter, as was Calder. Their new titles brought them a bit more capital than yours—I thought it only fitting. I've nearly run out of discretionary titles at this point. So no more noblesse."

Madoc looked to Gray, who nodded, then turned back to Queen Victoria. "Your Majesty, I know not what to say. I am grateful but—"

"One more thing," she said, cutting him off. "This responsibility must be managed properly. The only way I see that happening is for you to make a beneficial match. You'll need a wife."

"A wife? His heart sank for a beat at the idea that he'd been brought here to marry someone at her arrangement for the benefit of the title.

"Yes, a wife with coffers, I might add. Be sure to check the dowry. Perhaps look to those with impeccable lineage. One more thing, Warrick," she said, snapping his title. "You'll need permission."

"Permission?" he asked, and she narrowed her eyes. He went to one knee. "Your Majesty, I implore you and beg upon your mercy to bestow upon me the honor of marriage with..." He stopped, looked to Gray, who nodded to the Queen and leaned in to Madoc's ear to whisper. "Princess Dorothea Feodora Friederike Amalia Beatrice Alice Auguste Charlotte Sophia Wilhelmine Victoria Viktoria Ulrike Elisabetta. Crowned Princess of Prussia."

"My dear boy, My permission for you to marry—" she took an exhausted breath and waved her hand as though to skip saying the full of her name, "—the princess was given months ago. It was why I brought her to London, in fact. The permission you need is not mine." She clapped her hands once as if to brush him aside then walked out, her attendants following her towards the nave, leaving him staring after her in shock.

M

When Lulu and Willow arrived at Westminster Abbey, the crowd was thicker, louder. The stairs were covered with carpet to protect her dress. The door was open, and she was helped out to the ground, Lulu behind her. She took her arm and refused to let go. Even when someone asked Lulu to follow them, she refused and, apparently, in lieu of a scene, they allowed her to remain with Willow.

The doors to the Abbey were wide open, and Willow stepped through to the dim light inside. The seats were empty, no bodies, no faces. "Where is everyone?" Her eyes trained on the altar, waiting for whatever man would meet her there. "Where is he?"

"I don't know," Lulu said.

"Where are the others?" Willow asked, and Lulu shrugged, then a man motioned them through the cavernous empty space. "What is this? Some sort of—"

"Willow?" His voice rent the air, catching and reverberating through every nook and cranny in the massive building.

Willow picked up her skirts and moved toward him. "Madoc?"

"Willow!"

She turned to the right around a massive column and found him, held back by two guards. "Madoc." She ran toward him, and he shrugged the guards off and met her halfway, crashing into him and holding on. "I don't understand," she whispered. "I don't understand."

"Neither do I, but I have an idea." He slid down and hit one knee before her, "Will you be my wife, my duchess, my partner?"

"I will," she said, and he stood, picking her up and with a great yell to the contained heavens, he spun and carried her into yet another room. It was a chapel, small and simple by comparison. His entire family was here.

"Lulu?" She turned to find the woman following her into the small chapel, shaking her head. Gray walked to her and took her hand, leading her to one of the small seats. Madoc walked Willow down the aisle to the altar without hesitation, and not long after they were married.

Mads took Willow's face in his big hands, turning her to him. "Willow…I meant every word said here. You are my wife. You are my life. You've brought me to my knees. You've taught me things I never thought a man like me could learn. I'm not nothing without you, but I'm certainly not myself. I love you."

"Oh, Mads, you've given me a home, you've given me hope, you've given me the world. I wouldn't want to be anywhere but with you in this mad existence. And I love you."

He took her about the waist, and she felt his thumbs push into the soft skin just above her hipbones as he pulled her in tight to him and she gasped, sinking into the gentle twinge of his promised future. Then he kissed her, and kissed her, and kissed her, and she kissed him back.

EPILOGUE

Mads watched from the upper floor as Willow walked across the park to their home. *Home.* He hadn't ever thought it would happen, certainly not here in the house he'd grown up in. Gray and Lulu had insisted the house remain with the title as entailed, since they'd already become quite comfortable in their new house, and Mads reluctantly agreed. He never thought he would feel welcome or comfortable under this roof, but once Willow started taking care of the house and brightening everything with her touch, he couldn't imagine living anywhere else.

He let the curtain fall closed as she started up the front stair, and walked down to meet her. "My wife," he boomed from the top of the grand staircase as she removed her bonnet, handing it to Mr. Crisp.

"My husband," she replied, and the smile she gave warmed him through.

"Have you made the rounds sufficiently? May we have supper now?" he asked as he descended the staircase to her. She was dressed in a pale green confection of a summer dress. Her face and chest flushed from the heat of the sun, making him want for more of her skin.

"Mmmm, I'm starving. I was hoping you could make some stew? It's been awhile."

"It's too hot for stew. I have something else for you."

"A surprise?" she said and lifted on her toes to kiss him. "How were you able to arrange a surprise so quickly? We only just returned from France this morning. I haven't even unpacked."

"You could have unpacked this morning and received your surprise then.'"

"But I haven't seen anyone in months. The baby is crawling now, almost walking! You must go with me next time to see her. She's so adorable."

"Next time, perhaps."

"Are you still nervous?"

"Of course. Nothing's changed, really. We simply went on a honeymoon. Everything here is the same as ever, just as we left it. No better—"

"But no worse," she said with a smile.

"How perfectly optimistic of you."

"Yes. Now. My surprise?"

"We're having dinner in the garden, before the chill sets in. I thought it would be nice, like that bistro in Paris?"

"Yes, yes! I love this idea and I love you."

"Do you?" he asked, letting his voice drag the bottom of his range because it would make her shiver—and he loved it when she shivered.

She leaned into him. "I do."

"Mr. Crisp!" he yelled, and the door to the kitchens opened.

"Your Grace?"

"You may all have the night off. I've made Claridge's aware. They have supper for everyone and a private guest room awaiting you and Mrs. Crisp for the night, so pack an overnight case. Enjoy the evening. Don't rush back on the morrow. We'll be fine."

"Your Grace, thank you," he said. Then he gave a stiff bow and turned to leave.

Madoc took her hand and wrapped it around his arm, leading her to the back of the house. It wasn't quite dark, but it was twilight and by the time they came back inside it would be full night.

As they approached the ball room at the back of the house, he let go of her and covered her eyes with his hand, walking behind her and guiding her through the room to the French doors. "Careful," he whispered in her ear, and she shuddered against him. He reached for the handle and pushed the door wide, guiding her through. Then he let go.

Madoc's hand fell away, and her vision filled with twinkling lights. They'd only been gone a month but the gardens looked like they'd been maintained for years. There were lamp posts along the path, lighting the way. The hedges were trimmed and neat, the green brought back in miraculous order, as though all this garden had needed was someone to care. She supposed that was all it really took with gardens.

"It's beautiful," she said. "I can't believe this happened in a month."

"Well, a bit longer. They've been working on it for a few months while we were here as well, just not when you were paying attention."

"Oh, well, you have had me preoccupied, I suppose."

"Yes."

"This is a lovely surprise."

"This? This is not a surprise. This is me, taking care of our home."

Her breath caught and she tried to swallow past the lump that formed in her throat. "I never… It's just that…"

He swept a tear from her cheek, then kissed her gently. "I know. Believe me, I know."

She nodded. If anyone in this world understood what it meant to her to finally have a home, it was Mads.

She wrapped her arms around him as she stared out into the waning light.

"Let's go," he whispered.

"I want to stay and enjoy this…"

"Have you forgotten your surprise already?"

She perked. He took her hand and led her down the path towards the mews, then off on another path that had taken quite a bit more work than the rest of the garden, she was certain. "You didn't." She pushed past him and pulled up her skirts, hurrying down the path. She remembered her first time here, her only time back here, with him, in the orangery. It had been terrifying, exhilarating, maddening, intense, and the most incredible, absolutely perfect, life-changing experience.

She turned the corner around a large hedgerow and found it, the glittering mass of ironwork and glass. There were lights on inside; they looked to be strung about the interior on wire. The door was closed, and condensation crawled up the bigger panes of glass near the bottom, streaked by heavy drops of gathered water. The inside was heavy with green, bright slashes of color from petals interspersed throughout, and the light inside twinkled and bounced off the glass and moisture, making it feel otherworldly.

"Madoc." She covered her face with her hands. It was too beautiful to look at. His arms wrapped around her, pulling her back into his frame, warming her through. She hadn't realized it was already cooling off. But late summer did tend to fall off faster, especially in London. She spun around in his arms, tucking under his chin and resting there. How could all of this have happened? It was impossible. Her stomach growled, interrupting her thoughts, and he laughed, her cheek bouncing against his chest.

"Come on, let's eat," he said and pulled her toward the greenhouse.

They stepped inside the heat and Willow looked around; the tables and planters had been righted and repaired. The glass was replaced. The ironwork painted. The dirt nearly invisible for all the lush green growth. "A month isn't possible."

"I told you before it was more than a month. Most of the planters were taken out and worked on elsewhere. They filled them with ripe plants and only had to bring them in. The biggest project has been—"

"The tree!"

"I was going to say the glass, but—"

She cut him off, turning and running through the new jungle of growth. The path widened and the green fell away, and there at the center, just where it had been before, was her orange tree. She placed her hands on it, feeling its thready skin. "I'm sorry it took so long. But I hope you enjoy your new home."

"Are you speaking to the tree?"

"Perhaps. Or maybe I'm talking to myself, or perhaps even you. I think it applies to us all really."

He smiled. "It does, yes."

She loved his smile. Working with an apothecary, she'd put together a salve they used on his scars, to soften them. It had been difficult at first, and she'd no idea what would work, but eventually they'd started to see changes in the texture and flexibility of them. They weren't bound to fade, but over time the salve had allowed him to smile, and that was truly something.

Willow walked to him and traced the scar from his forehead to the edge of his mouth. "God, I am blessed to have you."

He shook his head, then leaned in and covered her lips with his own. Kissing her dizzy until she pushed hard enough that he stopped. "Let's eat, shall we?"

She nodded, and he pulled a small chair out for her and held it. She hadn't even noticed the table to the side of the tree when she'd first walked up, but now she couldn't believe it. There were trays of fresh fruit, fresh bread, fresh cheese, and bottles of, well, not technically quite as fresh wine.

He poured a glass and handed it to her then sat across from her. They ate peacefully, feeding each other with their fingers as the sun set and the lights flickered in the humidity of the green house. She heard a sizzle and glanced over to see smoke coming from one of the lights.

"I'm thinking waterproof electricity isn't quite a thing," she said quietly.

"Hmm?" he replied then looked straight at her and smiled his wicked smile. The light bulb popped, then the lights went out, leaving them in darkness.

She screamed and stood, and he was there, his hand over her mouth, his arm around her waist. "Willow, say yes," he said quietly.

It had been too long. Finding ways to frighten and be frightened in glorious French hotels was near impossible. Without drawing a crowd, anyway. They couldn't wait to return home.

"Yes, God, Madoc, please."

He released her and she ran, but she didn't get far. And that was exactly how she wanted it.

THE GREAT ART OF LIFE
IS SENSATION,
TO FEEL THAT WE EXIST,
EVEN IN PAIN

~Lord Byron

Dearest reader,

Thank you for going on this journey with me.

The Lords of Time have been my extended family for the last ten years and I've loved every single moment spent with this family. It means the world to me to hear from readers who have loved them as I have.

I don't know what the future holds for our Lords and Ladies, but I'm enjoying the journey and hope you do as well.

If you like mobile gaming check out the series on the Chapters App from Crazy Maple Studios. It's a fun adaptation of the series and I've enjoyed working with them.

If you want to stay in touch, to learn about future books in the series or other books I write you can join my newsletter here:
JennLeBlanc.com/newsletter

Or come have fun with me on instagram!

@JennLeBlanc

Love and wishes to you all!